BLOOD WILL FOLLOW

SNORRI KRISTJANSSON

Jo Fletcher
BOOKS

First published in Great Britain in 2014 by Jo Fletcher Books
This edition published in Great Britain in 2015 by

Jo Fletcher Books
an imprint of Quercus Editions Ltd.
55 Baker Street
7th Floor, South Block
London
W1U 8EW

A CIP catalogue record for this book is available
from the British Library

ISBN 978 1 78206 338 4 (PB)
ISBN 978 1 78206 337 7 (EBOOK)

This book is a work of fiction. Names, characters,
businesses, organizations, places and events are
either the product of the author's imagination
or are used fictitiously. Any resemblance to
actual persons, living or dead, events or
locales is entirely coincidental.

10 9 8 7 6 5 4 3 2 1

Typeset by Ellipsis Digital Limited, Glasgow

Printed and bound in Great Britain by
Clays Ltd, St Ives plc

To my wife and family.
Seriously. Thank you.

Prologue

Ulfar walked, and the world changed around him. With every step the colours shifted from green to yellow, from yellow to red, from red to brown. Around him, nature was dying. Every morning he watched the same pale sun rise over greying trees. He was cold when he woke and wet when he slept. He jumped when he heard a twig snap or a bird take flight. Every shadow threatened to conceal a group of King Olav's men about to burst out of the forest with drawn swords. His ribs still hurt after the fall, but there had been no other way out of Stenvik. They'd hidden themselves among the corpses at the foot of the wall until dark, then made their way in silence to the east, past the bloody remains of Sigmar on the cross and into Stenvik Forest, over the bodies of scores of slaughtered outlaws, after King Olav's army had charged through the ranks of the forest men, killing everything in its path.

Audun marched beside him, hardly saying a word. The blond blacksmith had regained his strength incredibly quickly after the fight on the wall. The only thing that remained was a hole in his shift, front and back, where Harald's sword had skewered him.

Audun had died on that wall. They both knew it.

Yet there he was, marching stony-faced beside Ulfar, hammer tied to his belt. Neither of them spoke of the fey woman on the ship – beautiful, evil and serene in her last moments. Neither of them mentioned her words. Were they truly cursed to walk the earth for ever? Would they never know the peace of death? Audun refused to speak of his experience, as if talking would seal their fate and somehow make it real. Just thinking about it sent chills up and down Ulfar's spine.

On the first night after the wall he'd fallen into an uneasy sleep, only to wake with the breath stuck in his throat and Lilia's falling body in his mind. Audun, standing first watch, had spoken then. He'd known what was wrong, somehow. He told Ulfar she'd be with him for ever and that no matter what he did, he couldn't make her leave and he couldn't make her live, so he should accept it, let her into his head and let her out again. That night Ulfar wondered just how many people visited Audun in his dreams.

The sharp wind tugged at Ulfar's ragged cloak as his feet moved of their own accord, picking a path over stones, tree branches and dead leaves. When they set out they'd gone east, then north, then further east, with the sole aim of putting the most distance possible between themselves and King Olav, ignoring everything else. They were fleeing, like animals from a fire. Like cowards from a fight. At their back was the smell of Stenvik's corpses, burning on King Olav's giant pyre. No doubt Geiri's body was among them.

Ulfar stopped.

He searched for the sun in the sky. He looked north, then south. He looked back to where they'd come from.

Audun shuffled to a halt and glared at him. 'What?'

Ulfar swallowed and blinked. 'I'm going home,' he said. 'There's something I need to do.' Then he turned to the east. He felt Audun's eyes on his back as he walked away.

'Do you accept our Lord Christ as your eternal saviour?' Finn snarled, forearms taut with tension.

Valgard sighed. 'He can't hear you, Finn. Lift his head up.'

The burly warrior snorted, grabbed a handful of hair and pulled the prisoner's head out of the water trough. The bound man tried to cough and suck in air at the same time, thrashing in panic as his lungs seized up.

'Hold him,' Valgard said. Finn strengthened his grip and planted a knee in the small of the prone man's back. The slim, pale healer knelt down on the floor, leaned into the prisoner's field of vision and put a firm hand on his chest. 'You're not dying,' he said. 'You're getting enough air to survive. Breathe,' he added, prodding at the man's sternum with a bony finger. 'In . . . out . . . in . . . out . . . Good.' The man stopped squirming and lay still on the floor. Finn shifted the knee against the prisoner's back but did not let go of the man's hair. 'Now. My friend here asked you a question. Do you believe?' The man spat, coughed and tried to speak, but all that came out was a hoarse wheeze. Valgard's smile flickered for an instant. 'Let me see if I can explain this,' he said. 'King Olav has told us that for a man to accept the faith he needs to be . . . what was it?'

'Christened,' Finn said.

'That's right. Christened. And this involves pouring water over the head. We thought about this and figured that the more heathen you are, the more water you will need. So we have this' – Valgard gestured to the trough – 'and we have you. And we're going to keep christening you until you believe. Do you believe in our Lord Christ?' He expected the tough-looking raider to spit and snap like the others had – either that, or accept his circumstances and lie. Some men had a bit of sense in the face of death, but among the captured raiders that hadn't appeared to be a highly valued trait.

Neither of these things happened. Much to Valgard's surprise, he noticed that the prisoner's lips were quivering. The man was crying silently, mouthing something. 'Put him down. Check the straps.' Finn lowered the prisoner to the floor and quickly did as he was told. When he'd examined the wrist and ankle straps to his satisfaction, he nodded at Valgard. 'Good. Would you bring us something to eat? He's not going anywhere and you could use the rest.'

Finn lurched to his feet, favouring his right leg. 'You staying with him?'

Valgard rose alongside the big soldier and put a hand on his shoulder. 'I don't think we should leave him alone. You go – I'll be fine. You've made sure he's all tied up.' Watching the concern in the eyes of King Olav's captain as he left the house, Valgard had to fight to suppress a smile. It had taken fewer than four days since the fall of Stenvik to bring Finn over to his side. The fact that he'd made the big warrior dependent on the mixture that soothed his aches helped. Mindful of the lessons learned from Harald's descent into madness, he'd gone easy on the shadowroot this time.

Still, Valgard felt the last days deep in his bones. The aftermath had been hectic – much to everyone's surprise, the king had refused to put the captured raiders to the sword. He'd extended the same mercy to the men of Stenvik, explaining to Valgard that he wanted to show all of them the way of the White Christ first. Valgard had nodded, smiled and done his best to patch up those most likely to survive – including his current visitor.

The man on the floor looked to be around forty years old, with thinning hair the colour of an autumn field. Callused rower's hands and a broad chest suggested he'd spent his life sailing; weatherworn and salt-burned skin confirmed it. He'd probably killed a lot of people, Valgard mused. This wolf of the North Sea who now lay trussed up on the floor of Harald's old house had most likely raped, terrorised and tortured with his group of stinking, bearded brothers, like all raiders. Apparently he'd followed someone called Thrainn, who'd been a brave and noble chieftain. But most of the brave and noble people Valgard had ever heard of shared the same trait – they were dead.

He knelt back down beside the man on the floor and waited, listening to his captive's ragged breathing.

'She'll . . . kill me,' the bound man whispered.

Valgard's scalp tingled and the breath caught in his throat. Was this it? He fought hard to keep his composure. 'Who?' he asked.

'She is . . . she is the night . . .'

Working carefully, Valgard eased the bound sailor up into a sitting position. Heart thumping in his chest, he chose his words carefully. 'She was . . . with Skargrim, wasn't she?' The sailor shuddered and nodded. 'And she would kill you.' Again, the sailor nodded and when he tried to look around, Valgard said, 'There's no one here. You are safe. Five thousand of the king's soldiers are camped around Stenvik. No one will attack us.'

This did nothing to ease the sailor's fears. 'She could do anything. We are all in her power.'

Fighting to control another surge of excitement, Valgard asked, 'Who was she? Where did she come from?'

'She raised the dead,' the sailor muttered. 'She was beautiful . . .'

'And she came with you?'

'Not us. Skargrim. Someone told me she murdered Ormar with his own knife. She was the magic of the north. She'll find me. I can't. I can't abandon the gods. She'll find me.' The words tumbled out as silent tears streamed down the raider's cheeks. 'I can't,' he muttered, lapsing into silence.

After a moment's thought, Valgard stood up and moved to his workbench. He came back with a small leather flask. 'Here. Drink this. It's for your throat. To make sure you breathe right.' The prisoner gestured to his tied hands and Valgard snorted. 'Forgive me. I'm thoughtless. Here.' He leaned forward, touched the spout to the bound man's lips and tilted very carefully. 'Sip, but be careful.'

The sailor drank from the flask, sighing when Valgard took it away. 'Thank . . . you,' he managed before drifting off.

'No. Not at all. Thank *you*,' Valgard replied. He watched the sleeping man and listened to his breathing slow down. As it became more laboured, the sailor's eyelids fluttered. The time between breaths increased. Then the man on the floor was still.

Exhaling, Valgard thought back on when he'd first seen someone die. He hadn't been much more than eleven summers. She was an old woman; her hacking cough had irritated him. Passing in and out of sleep, she woke up in the hut where Sven used to teach him about healing. She shouted her husband's name, confused and frightened. Then she fell silent. Valgard had watched as she sank back on her pallet and the life just . . . left. He'd gone out of the hut and vomited. He was easily rattled back then: a sickly, weak boy.

Seventeen years had passed and Valgard had seen more than his share of death since then. Like birth, it tended to involve blood, slime and screaming. Like birth, it was a lot more important to the people it was happening to than the rest of the world. It was a cycle, and it would keep on repeating.

Or so he'd thought.

He replayed the moments again in his head. As much as Valgard had been intent on his own survival when King Olav's army walked into Stenvik, he had not been able to take his eyes off Harald when the raider captain started screaming on the wall, his wife Lilia kicking and squirming in his arms. He'd watched with growing horror as Harald denounced the leaders of Stenvik, mocked King Olav and ripped through Lilia's throat with a jagged piece of wood, sacrificing her to the old gods, throwing her to the ground like a sack of grain. Valgard was on the point of turning away when he saw Ulfar rushing the stairs and charging the sea captain, only to be beaten back by Harald's mad fury. Ulfar stumbled and Audun strode into the fight, throwing himself on Harald's sword to get at the furious raider.

Valgard had seen Audun die in Ulfar's arms after Harald crumpled before him. For all the raiders' jibes, he knew what death looked like. He'd seen the sword come out of the man's broad back, watched the muscles seize up and felt the life leave the blacksmith's body, like it had left countless bodies before him.

And then he'd seen the tiniest bit of movement on the wall. Audun had moved. The shock on Ulfar's face had told the rest of the tale.

Valgard had watched Ulfar jump over the wall, holding Audun – and then the survival instinct kicked in, tore him off the spot and hurtled him along. Blind panic pushed him to his hut just in time to retrieve the cheap cross he'd secretly bought off a travelling merchant when he'd heard the rumours of King Olav's ascendancy. Valgard threw himself to his knees and started praying in Latin, not two breaths before King Olav's soldiers burst through the door.

Since then he'd done his best to please his new master, but he couldn't forget what he'd seen on the wall. Audun had cheated death, and it had to be connected to the attack somehow. That, or something to do with Ulfar.

In his quest for information, Valgard had volunteered to join Finn in christening the captured raiders from the north, but most had either drowned or Finn had snapped their necks when they refused to convert. A handful had come over to King Olav's side, but Valgard did not trust them. This was the first tangible bit of information he'd received about the mysterious presence on Skargrim's ship; there had been a bit of talk about a small, knife-wielding woman who'd been Skargrim's boatman, but after living with raiders his entire life and spending a lot of time with Harald, Valgard discounted that as nonsense. He'd heard the stories after Audun killed Egill Jotun, but anything from the battlefield was to be taken with a pinch of salt too. No women's bodies had been thrown on the pyre.

Well, except for Lilia's.

Now, however, it looked like things were finally moving his way. He'd felt the truth in the sailor's words. The man had been terrified. As sceptical as Valgard was of the old ways, the stories from the far north had always appeared to support the idea of magic, or some kind of connection with the gods. Now it fell to him to determine whether this was true or not. This was what he needed. He needed to go north – but how?

'You must come.' Finn's voice shook Valgard out of his thoughts. The big soldier could move quietly when he wanted to. 'To the longhouse.'

'Why? What's going on?' Valgard said, rising slowly.

'Hakon Jarl has replied, apparently,' Finn said. His face did not give anything away.

Valgard raised his eyebrows. 'Has he? Well then. Let's go.'

Finn did not ask about the body on the floor.

When they entered the longhouse, Jorn was already there, sitting to the right of King Olav. It was very faint, but Valgard still heard Finn's snort of displeasure. The longhouse wasn't anything like as great as it had been in Sigurd's time. War trophies had been ripped off the wall, along with weapons and shields. In their place was a big, broad cross that the king had ordered built out of broken weapons, to signify how faith overcame war, apparently. It caught and broke the rays of the sun. Valgard couldn't help but think that a handful of Harald's men would have turned the components of that cross back into tools of pain and death in an instant.

The king spotted them and gestured to the dais. They walked past an old farmer, sixty if he was a day, clad in muddy rags and clutching a sack that looked heavy. He was flanked by two watchmen as he shivered in the cold air. King Olav paid him no mind; the rough and discoloured woollen sack had all his attention.

'Sit, Finn,' the king commanded, gesturing to his left. Valgard took a seat by the wall. King Olav nodded very briefly to acknowledge his presence. Then he turned to the old man. 'You bring a message from Hakon,' he said.

'Y-yes,' the farmer stuttered.

'In parts?'

'That's what the riders said,' the old farmer mumbled. His voice trembled and he did not dare look the king in the eye. Judging by the sound of King Olav's voice, Valgard thought that was probably a good idea.

'So riders came from the north and brought you this,' Jorn said. Sitting on the king's right, the self-proclaimed Prince of the Dales looked altogether too pleased with himself. A lucky strike against the Viking Thrainn in what was supposed to be the Stenvik raiders' last stand had given him some notoriety among the men; turning on Sigurd had not worked against him as much as Valgard had thought it would. Always well dressed and groomed, Jorn looked at home as the king's right-hand man. He pressed the old farmer. 'Why didn't you tell them to bring the whole message themselves?'

'They . . . they threatened me, my lord,' the old man muttered. 'They told me to take it to . . . the king . . . or I'd be on a spike.'

'Very well,' King Olav interrupted. 'What's in the sack?'

The old farmer shuddered, swallowed twice and drew a deep breath. Then he grabbed the bottom corners of the sack and tipped its contents out onto the floor.

Two rag piles landed with a thud.

'Oh, the—' Finn muttered before he bit his lip.

Jorn stared dumbly at the rags. 'Is that . . . his—?' The messenger's left hand had been cut off, as had his right foot. The farmer shook the sack. Another two bundles tumbled out and clattered onto the floor.

'The men said . . . they said Hakon Jarl says you can come up to Trondheim and collect the rest any time you want.'

Like Jorn and Finn, Valgard held his breath. The tense silence was broken when King Olav smashed a mailed fist on the armrest of the high chair. 'Why won't he *listen*?' he growled. 'I bring *peace*. I bring *prosperity*. I bring *a better life* for him and his stinking herd of miserable sheep!'

'The northern lords haven never been famous for caring much about their flock, my King,' Jorn said. 'Hakon Jarl has always been a hard master. I don't think he would like to be ruled by anyone else.' After a brief pause, he added, 'It is a shame that he doesn't understand what is best for him and his people. We'll show him who rules next summer. Or next spring, even. Before he expects it.'

'I'll make him understand,' King Olav snarled. 'I can't run the country while I wait for him to assemble an army.'

Valgard's face felt hot and his heart hammered in his chest. The chance was here, right now. He cleared his throat. 'Then why wait for spring?'

He barely managed to stand his ground when King Olav turned towards him. 'What do you mean?' Fury was burning in the king's eyes.

'Hakon is a savage, we all know it. He has been ruling the north for longer than I can remember, and he is by all accounts a strong chieftain.'

Jorn frowned. 'Why are you telling us this? We know—'

'But where do you fit into Hakon's world, your Majesty? What are you to him?' Valgard continued, addressing the king and ignoring the dirty look from Jorn. 'An upstart? One of many challengers? Someone to be squashed? Or someone to be feared?'

'More than five thousand men follow me. And the word of Christ,' King Olav said.

'And why do you think he had your messenger killed?' Valgard said. The longhouse was suddenly very silent. 'You knew he wouldn't step aside. He certainly knows it. He also knows that autumn is here and winter is on its way. So he gambles. He decides to send a statement of his strength, to taunt you and eliminate the one man who could have told you what his forces are really like. While you stew down here, he gathers strength. Word will get around that he defied you; when winter clears, his stinking herd of miserable sheep may have grown significantly.'

King Olav watched Valgard intently. 'So—?'

'Take it. Take his challenge – but take it now.'

Jorn nearly jumped out of his seat. 'That's foolish! You could never—'

'Stop.' King Olav's calm voice cut Jorn off. 'Listen. You should listen more.' The Prince of the Dales slumped back in his seat, and the king sat in silence for a little while. When he spoke again, he sounded almost curious. 'Go north in autumn, you say.' His words were directed to Valgard, but he looked to the sky. 'I will . . . think about this. Leave us.'

Valgard followed Finn towards the door. The look on Jorn's face as they left was not lost on him.

'A-a-and then what?' Runar said.

'He just sat there. Didn't say a word. Then he got up and went over to his little prayer table with the Bible, knelt down and started mumbling. He kept looking up at the roof. After a while I just left. I don't think he noticed,' Jorn snapped, whittling at a stick.

'Th-this does not sound good,' Runar said. He paced in the hut they'd been forced to share. Five thousand men were squeezed together in and around Stenvik, growing more hungry and restless by the day. 'But we n-need to th-think about this. There may be opportunities.' Outside, someone saluted as they passed by but got no reply.

'But *when*? When do we do something? Anything?' The knife bit into the stick and sent wood chips flying into a growing pile at Jorn's feet. 'I'm sick and tired of playing nice. Poisoning the food didn't work, and—'

'W-w-wrong,' Runar stammered. 'Poisoning the food worked just f-f-f-fine. Little f-food for them-m, n-n-n—' Runar took several deep breaths to get the words out. 'No b-blame for us,' he added, smiling. 'A-and we m-move when the moment comes. You'll know,' he added. 'Y-you'll know.'

'This doesn't feel very heroic,' Jorn grumbled. 'I'm not doing anything. The men will not think I'm doing—'

'Th-th-that's good, th-th-though. Because right now, K-King Olav is making a m-mistake. Or at least he's thinking about it.'

Jorn sighed and rose. The house they'd been given was wooden, well made but simple, with only a few trophies mounted on the walls. They'd cleared out the dresses and a strange collection of leather bottles and had found a chest under the bed containing an impressive assortment of blades, axes and mean-looking spearheads – killing tools. They had kept these for themselves.

'You forgot that there's also less food for us,' he grumbled.

Runar shrugged. 'That's no problem. You were s-s-starting to get fat anyway.' He grinned. 'Now all w-we need to do is w-wait until he decides how to m-mess this up.'

There was a knock on the door.

'Who's there?' Jorn asked.

'The king requests your presence,' a boy's voice piped up. 'Wall. Now. Both of you,' he added.

Runar smiled again, winked at Jorn and motioned towards the door.

*

They found King Olav standing above the north gate, looking out. In front of him, Stenvik Forest was a wall of red, yellow and brown, with only occasional dabs of green.

'I have sought guidance on the matter. We will send a delegation to Hakon Jarl.'

'A delegation, my lord?' said Jorn. 'But Hakon will—'

King Olav turned and looked at them. His smile was cold. 'Jorn, you are a loyal servant and Christ commends you for your work. But you speak too much and too quickly. Like I said: listen more. We are going north to talk to the jarl. Our *delegation* will number three thousand men.'

Jorn took a few breaths to compose himself and digest the information. 'As you wish, your Majesty. Who do you want with you, and who are you leaving behind?'

'I will take you both with me. Finn will stay behind, command in Stenvik and speak with my authority.' King Olav turned again, and Jorn risked a quick look at Runar. He got a grin and a wink in return.

'Very good,' Jorn hazarded. 'Which men will you take?'

'I want at least eight hundred archers, eight hundred foot, pike and as much experienced horse as we can carry. The rest is at your discretion. You've got a head for this.'

'Thank you, your Majesty,' Jorn replied.

'That is all.'

'Yes. Yes, thank you,' Jorn said. Runar was already moving towards the stairs.

When they reached the ground, Runar turned towards him. His eyes positively sparkled. 'W-we n-n-n-need to talk!' he stuttered.

Jorn simply gestured towards the hut.

Once they'd closed the door, Runar bounded around the cabin. 'Perfect. Perfect!' he exclaimed. 'You've already got the men from the Dales on your side. I've t-talked to some of the boys from the southeast – some of them could be swayed. Skeggi, B-b-botolf and his brother Ingimar might all cross over, and I think that would make up a good four hundred at the least. Now all we n-n-need to do is get them on the right boats. Put K-king Olav in a boat with us, thirty of our men, boat gets lost and the king finally gets to meet his precious m-m-maker.' Runar grinned from ear to ear.

Jorn frowned. 'Keep your voice down. I don't like this. I don't like it at all. It sounds stupid to me, and King Olav isn't stupid.'

'Even s-smart people make mistakes,' Runar said, still grinning. 'Sometimes they don't know they're m-making them until it's too late.'

Valgard shuddered and pressed harder into the chair. It was starting to feel like King Olav's longhouse would never be warm. They'd been in the middle of converting another raider to the good side when the boy had come to summon them. The man had not been . . . cooperative. Yet another soul which would not be joining Christ in heaven. He couldn't help but think that the way this was going, the other side would be having one bastard of a war party.

King Olav gestured for them to approach. 'I have consulted with higher powers. You were right yesterday, Valgard. We should strike, and strike now. Waiting is the wrong thing to do. So we'll take three thousand men up north. Finn, you will stay behind and control this town in my stead. Valgard, you will stay with him to negotiate with the men of Stenvik. You're one of them; they will trust you.'

Valgard had to fight to keep the panic off his face. He hadn't been able to go back to his hut after yesterday's meeting. Instead he'd walked the town, treading paths he'd stopped walking since the battle, allowing his mind to wander and listening to the sounds of the town, the voices in the huts. He'd almost been able to taste it; in his mind he had been on his way to the mysterious north to seek the source of the magic. To find the power. And now it was all being taken away. He had to think of something, fast. 'Erm, your Majesty, I am not sure they'll trust me too much. They will not forgive me for abandoning the old gods.'

'Do you fear them?' The king looked mildly curious.

'I am not a warrior,' Valgard said. 'I have lived in this town all my life, endured their taunts – they hated me because I couldn't fight, they despised me because I knew things they didn't, and now they fear me because I believe in the one true God. I do not doubt that if you were to leave me here, some of them might seize the opportunity to do me harm.'

'Finn will be with you, as my voice. I've known and believed among the savages, and with Finn by my side no harm has yet befallen me. You will be his advisor. He will be acting chieftain of Stenvik.'

Finn coughed, swallowed and coughed again. 'If . . . if that is your wish, your Majesty—'

'It is. I can trust you, Finn, and Valgard can make sure the influence of Sigurd and Sven does not confuse the men. Now go – there is much that needs to be done.'

There is indeed, Valgard thought as he walked out. *There is indeed.*

'What do you want?' The guard posted outside Sigurd and Sven's house was big, ugly and determined. Valgard thought he'd probably been put in front of their cabin because he'd be very hard to move out of the way. A large, hand-made crucifix hung on a cord around the big oaf's neck.

Valgard made the sign of the cross and bowed his head. 'Glory to God, amen.' The guard mumbled something indistinct in return. 'I am here to check on the health of our . . . guests.' The guard stared dully at him and did not move a hair's breadth. 'Finn said I should look them over.' Still no movement. 'If they were to fall ill, King Olav would get very angry.'

The guard inched away from the door.

'Thank you,' Valgard said. The guard ignored him and stared straight ahead. The door was reinforced; the bar across it was at least half Valgard's weight. After struggling with it for a while, Valgard managed to shift the bar just enough to send it crashing to the ground. The guard spared him a contemptuous glance but did not move a finger. Biting back a curse, Valgard sent him a smile instead and opened the door as far as he could.

The inside of the hut was dark and dusty. Sigurd sat with his back against the far wall; Sven was getting to his feet. He had been allowed a pouch of herbs to treat his wounds, but he looked naked without a blade. Valgard stepped towards his foster-father and helped him up. He glanced towards Sigurd; Sven shook his head.

'I'm trying,' Valgard muttered under his breath, 'but there's no reasoning with the king. He's out of his mind. Jesus this, Jesus that.'

'Could you get us some weapons? We'd happily—'

Valgard grabbed the old man's wrist with strength he didn't know he had. 'No,' he hissed. The look of surprise on Sven's face was rewarding. 'You're not cutting your way out of this. There are five thousand men out there.'

'We've seen worse,' Sven said.

Valgard released his grip. 'I know, Father. I've heard the stories. But I think patience is the best way forward now. Just . . . allow things to happen. Give me a couple more days. I've talked to the men. They're behind you. We just need to find the right moment.' He glanced towards the door and the guard outside it. 'I'm not supposed to give you this. King Olav wants to control what you eat so he can keep you weak.' Valgard reached into the folds of his tunic, produced a leather bottle and handed it to Sven. 'For both of you.'

'Thank you, son,' Sven said. His expression was difficult to read.

'You're welcome, Father,' Valgard replied. The breath caught in his throat. 'I must go – I have things to do. His Majesty doesn't like to wait.'

Sven glanced towards Sigurd and for the first time since Valgard stepped through the door he saw a twinkle in the old rogue's eye. 'Tell me about it,' he muttered.

Valgard's smile lasted until he'd turned his back. When he left the hut, the guard was waiting, holding the bar.

King Olav sat down in the high chair, then stood up again. Unable to find a comfortable position, he continued walking around the longhouse and touching the silver cross hanging around his neck. 'How many ships do we have?'

'Sixty,' Jorn said. 'Sixty ready to sail, needing only minimal repairs.'

'Sixty. How many benches?'

'Mostly twenty-seaters, up to thirty-six.'

'And have you decided who we're taking?'

'We've drawn up a list,' Jorn said, gesturing to Runar.

'Very good,' King Olav said. 'What of the grain stores?'

Runar consulted a slate of wood with carved notches. 'W-we have th-thirty sacks of grain left, forty head of s-smoked lamb . . .

Th-they managed to treat what Sigurd had slaughtered and s-save most of it . . . herbs for soup, sixty sacks of turnip—'

'Take what you think you'll need,' King Olav said. 'You've proved valuable, Runar. I do not doubt that you provide a lot of ideas for Jorn. We start the fitting tomorrow morning. We sail as soon as we can.'

'Th-thank you, your M-m-mah—'

A dismissive wave of King Olav's hand stopped Runar in his tracks. 'That's enough. Go. Do what you need to. I have things to do.'

Jorn and Runar rose quietly and left the longhouse. When they'd gone, King Olav walked over to the makeshift altar and knelt.

'Father,' he muttered, 'Father, tell me that this is right. I will risk the deaths of hundreds of my men, Norse warriors who have learned to love you and Jesus Christ. Give me some sign that you value your servant.'

A stillness filled the longhouse. Outside, the autumn light faded as afternoon turned to evening. The door to the longhouse opened slowly and Finn entered with Valgard close behind. After a short while, the big warrior cleared his throat.

King Olav rose without a word. He moved to the dais and motioned for them to approach.

'I'm glad you are here, Finn. We need to talk about your reign as chieftain of Stenvik.' He smiled. 'No need to look so worried, my friend. It will all work very well. Valgard will counsel you and make sure you don't step on any toes.'

Valgard cleared his throat. 'If I may, your Majesty. There is one thing I must mention to you. It is very important. I think that you should be careful—'

One of King Olav's guards burst in. 'My King! My King!'

'You will salute!' Finn shouted. 'What do you want?'

'It's . . . it's Sven and Sigurd! The guard just told me to come and fetch you!'

'What?' the king snapped.

'They're not breathing!'

The morning sunlight filtered through the yellowing canopy. Leaves crisp with night-frost crunched under Audun's feet. He had no idea what this wood was called – it was somewhere south, towards the sea. That was enough.

He needed to get away: away from this country, away from people, away from anyone who knew what happened in Stenvik.

Anywhere would do.

The hill was steep but not impossible to climb. He picked his way over broken branches, minding his step around treacherous mossy stones. The forest was slower going, but it was better than the roads. He hadn't yet seen any of King Olav's men and wanted it to stay that way.

He thought of Stenvik again.

The hot, metallic air in the forge.

The sounds of weapons clashing, men screaming, skulls crushing.

The stench of the blood.

Audun slapped his arm, hard.

'Stop,' he croaked. His throat hurt with the strange effort of speaking. He swallowed and tried again. 'Stop it,' he tried.

Better.

Audun hadn't said anything in a while. Nothing to say, anyway, and no one to say it to. Ulfar had walked off east; he'd decided not to follow – maybe it had been the right thing to do, maybe not. He spat and cleared his throat. 'So where should I go, then?' he asked the trees. 'South?' Nobody answered. 'Why not.' There was something in his voice that sounded strange. An edge. 'Only greybeards and halfwits speak to themselves anyway,' he snarled as he crested the hill.

On the way down, his feet slipped and he had to grab a branch to steady himself. He regained his balance, stopped for a moment to catch his breath and scratched at his chest through the hole in the tunic. 'Oh, for f—' Audun jerked his hand away as if he'd touched fire. Since Stenvik . . . since a couple of days after Stenvik, when he'd recovered fully, he'd tried to stop scratching the spot where—

No. He pushed the memory away.

The ground sloped sharply ahead of him and he could see over the tops of the trees. The forest thinned out at the foot of the hill and gentle waves of farmland stretched as far as he could see. A reedy road meandered over the nearest rise. Far in the distance he thought he could see a thin blue line – the sea.

'South will do,' he muttered.

A twig snapped above and behind him. Much too close.

Audun whirled around.

There were four of them. Somehow they'd sneaked up onto the crest behind him without making any noise. They looked just like he did, filthy, ragged and hungry. The tallest one, all skin and bones and dirty hair, stepped in front of the group and leaned on a long walking stick.

'Give us your food,' he snapped at Audun. Two of his companions started moving off to either side. 'And your shoes. And everything else you've got. Then we'll let you live.'

'Please,' Audun said. 'I don't want trouble. I have nothing to give, and it won't be much of a life if you leave me naked in the woods.' The slope behind him was a tempting option, but turning his back on these men felt like a bad idea.

'Farms round here,' said the tall man, trying to sound reasonable. 'Or you might find someone stupid enough to be walking through the forest alone. Everyone's got to hunt these days.'

Audun looked at the tall man. Stained, pointy teeth. Clumps of dried blood in his beard. Where were the others? The blacksmith's head spun. 'I don't think I will. Thank you,' he mumbled. 'Now go away. Please don't start—'

A tree branch thick as a man's forearm thwacked across his shoulders. He stumbled, nearly lost his footing and grabbed hold of a branch for support. Instinct kicked in and he shifted his weight to the left; another attacker stumbled past.

The tall man strode forward with murder in his eyes. 'Grab him!' he snarled.

Pain exploded in Audun's lower back.

He twisted around to see a wild-eyed man wielding a fallen branch and getting ready to strike again. Backpedalling, Audun slipped and fell. Something hard smashed into his hip and set his leg throbbing. He fumbled around for purchase, dodged a vicious strike from the makeshift club and caught his hand on something sharp.

Fist-sized rock. Jagged edge.

Without thinking, he flexed and hurled it at the next moving target.

There was a dull crunch as the club-wielder's head changed shape. He dropped to the ground. His friends screamed in rage but the noise was almost distant to Audun. The rich, iron-tinged smell of spurting blood stroked him, lured him, called to him.

'Oh no . . .' he muttered.

A feral grin spread on the blond man's face as he rose to his feet.

An attacker charged him, armed with a rock of his own. He swung hard overhead and screamed in pain as his wrist was smashed by a blocking forearm. His cries were cut short when a straight right from the stocky blacksmith drove the man's nose up into his brain.

The tall, gaunt leader approached with caution. He had a stick with a point. The lunge was sudden and surprisingly fast. The blacksmith saw the wood pierce his side, felt it rip into his flesh and didn't care. Wood wasn't metal.

Horrified, the tall man glanced past him a moment too soon.

The blond man grabbed the spear, held on to it and stepped backwards into the path of the third attacker. A hard elbow broke the scrawny sneak's sternum, crushed his ribcage and sent him coughing and wheezing to the forest floor with blood bubbling out of his mouth. Fear blossomed on the tall man's face as he scrabbled to get away, but his feet betrayed him on the slippery surface. As he fell to the ground, an iron grip seized him by the back of the neck. Another grabbed his crotch, squeezed mercilessly and lifted the tall, gaunt and screaming man off the ground, grunting with the effort.

The blacksmith threw the scrawny man down the hill, watched him flailing and screaming as he flew until he bounced off a tree, watched the lifeless body fall and crash into the ground, roll down through the undergrowth and come to a stop at the foot of the hill.

He looked around, but nothing moved. Slowly, almost gently, the thrumming in his temples slowed and the pain returned. Audun's right leg spasmed and collapsed underneath him, sending him to the forest floor. The wooden spear throbbed in his side. The suffocating feeling of bile exploding from his stomach threatened to overwhelm him until he managed to roll over and vomit.

After the first convulsion, Audun reached for the long spear, pulled it out, screamed and lost consciousness.

When he woke, he was wet and cold. His mouth tasted sour and his head throbbed. For the first couple of moments, old dreams confused him. The shivers and the stab of pain from his side cleared his head soon enough, though.

The hill.

The fight.

Audun looked around. The promise of rain still hung in the air. As he moved, an opportunistic fox scampered away from a corpse with a broken skull. He staggered to his feet, shook himself and immediately regretted the decision as lightning flashes of pain erupted in his back. He had to fight for his balance, breathing in shallow gasps.

He coughed, choked and spat. The taste of bile reminded him of other times, other fights. For a brief, tantalising moment, he could remember what he had dreamed about, where he'd just been, but then it was gone.

Biting back the waves of nausea, he started moving again. One step. Then another. He did his best to ignore the three dead men as he picked his way carefully down the slope of the hill. The rain had made the ground even worse for walking. He stumbled, almost lost his balance and had to grab hold of a tree for support. After taking a moment to catch his breath, bite down hard and try his best to ignore the lancing pain in his hip and back, he set out again.

His leg gave way completely and everything tilted. Waves of

heat washed over his back as he crashed to the ground, sliding, moving, rolling. Trees whipped by his head, the horizon pitched and lurched, suddenly he was staring up at the sky, then he was turned around again. His shin smashed into a tree stump; he flailed and grabbed for a bush, a root, anything to slow his fall. When he finally rammed into a big fir tree the breath was knocked out of him and he rolled over, gasping for air. Around him, the red, gold and yellow of the dying forest blurred into the colours of the forge. Tiny stars burst across the blue sky. In a panic, Audun started punching his chest – harder and harder. He could feel the veins in his throat bulging, his face heating up.

Something gave way inside him and sweet, cold life flooded his lungs. He coughed painfully as he tried to swallow all the air in the world. When his heart had stopped thundering, he clambered to his feet. His back screamed at him and he broke out in a cold sweat, but he remained standing.

Then he noticed the tall man, lying like a child's broken toy in the clearing. The side of his head was one open wound.

'I told you to go away,' Audun mumbled. 'I told you.'

He stumbled off, away from death and blood, heading south.

The going was slow.

He'd found a branch that served as a crooked walking staff of sorts but his leg was still giving him a hard time, his back seized up and his throat felt like it had been scraped raw. He coughed and permitted himself a cold smile.

Things had worked out fucking great, hadn't they?

He should never have got involved. And he never should have followed Ulfar off that wall.

The sun was sliding down beyond the horizon. Soon it would be dark. Winter would come. Audun scanned the horizon and found nothing – no shelter, no hills with good caves, nothing. Just acres and acres of fields.

He did not like the idea of sleeping outside again, exposed to everything and anyone, not in this state. Swallowing hard, he turned and walked towards the road he'd seen from the hill.

It was overgrown and underused. Audun shivered and stumbled onwards, gritting his teeth and ignoring his back, legs and aching shoulders. The road led him up onto the small rise. The farmer had not yet done his harvesting, and from the looks of it he'd be too late. Beyond the field, the farmstead appeared about ready to collapse. The road led in a curve alongside the cornfield and into a yard. He could see a ramshackle shed of some sort, a main building and possibly something behind that, but none of it looked very good. The wood was grey with age. About five hundred yards behind it, the forest rose like a green-capped wall.

A sharp wind bit at Audun's back and he felt suddenly sick: sick of it all, the wandering, the fighting, the loneliness. He hunched his shoulders, winced and set off towards the house, tightening his grip on his makeshift quarterstaff. Just in case.

The door to the main house opened when he was about four hundred yards away. He flinched, but kept going. An old man walked out; Audun's heart beat faster when he saw the soft glow of a hearth inside the house.

'Well met, stranger!' the man shouted. His hair was white but his voice was strong.

'Well—' The rest of the greeting was lost in a fit of coughing as his back locked up, his leg buckled and he had to clutch the staff to avoid falling over.

The farmer stood and watched him from his steps.

'Well met,' Audun croaked at last.

'Where are you headed?' the man said.

'South,' Audun replied. 'I seek shelter for the night.'

'I suppose you do,' the old man said. 'I have little, but what's mine is yours.' As Audun approached, the man added, 'It looks like you might need it. Are you badly hurt?'

'No,' Audun lied. 'A fire and some broth should set me right.'

'We can see to that,' the man said.

The house had not looked like much from afar, but it turned out to be well maintained. To Audun's travel-weary eyes it was a palace. Three beds fitted snugly into the corners, two of them unused. Chisels and wood-carving knives were scattered across a small table by the only window, which faced towards the fields. Underneath the chair next to the table, a woven basket stored sticks of various sizes. A small fire gave warmth to the whole room; a bubbling pot sent off smells that made his stomach growl.

'Settle down, stranger. Settle down. Do you have a name?' The man led Audun to one of the unused beds and nudged him to sit. Then he reached into the pouch hanging off his belt and pulled out something wrapped in linen cloth, along with a small paring knife.

'Audun,' he mumbled, settling down with his back to the wall. Looking around, he noted the carvings on the walls. Most appeared to have something to do with battle. He tried to focus, but his head felt fuzzy.

'Audun.' The old man mouthed it, as if it was something he'd never heard before. 'Audun. Welcome to my home, Audun. My name is Fjolnir.' He unravelled the linen cloth, revealing a joint of meat. The weary blacksmith's mouth watered and he swallowed.

Fjolnir saw it and smiled. 'Don't get your hopes up. It's goat, and a tough old one at that. What brings you to Setr Valley?' he asked.

Audun couldn't think of any reason, so he remained silent.

The old man looked at him, smiled, nodded and handed him a slice of meat. 'Help yourself,' he said. Setting the joint down on the table next to Audun along with the paring knife, Fjolnir reached into the folds of his tunic and another, bigger whittling blade appeared in his hand. He reached for a stick from the basket underneath his chair and started gently carving.

They sat like that for a while, listening to the soft crackling of the fire. Audun chewed on the meat, savouring every bite. The steady movement of Fjolnir's hand was mesmerising as it flicked away the bits of wood that weren't supposed to be there, carving out what looked to be a head on broad shoulders. Despite the aches and pains, Audun felt the weight of the last two weeks slowly ease off his chest.

After a while, Fjolnir put down the knife, reached out and stirred the embers with a poker. He glanced at Audun as he said, 'Fire . . . It's a strange thing. It's almost like an animal. If you treat it well it does you good. But feed it too much and it burns down your house; put it out and you're cold and miserable. It's a strange thing, fire.' He looked at Audun again. One of the old man's eyes, the right one, didn't appear to be working properly, but the left eye sparkled and a faint smile played on his lips. He looked about to say something, then he checked himself and went back to the whittling.

Audun frowned, but he was too tired to think. Fire . . . He remembered the flames on the wall, the heat in the forge. A short while later, he fell asleep to the sound of Fjolnir humming parts of an old tune.

He woke to the sound of hammering. Shutters had been opened, admitting the feeble rays of the sun, and Audun could smell the mist on the morning air. Still half-asleep, he got out of bed and stood up, putting all his weight on the bad leg. His brain caught up with him and the shock of impending pain made him draw his breath – but there was none. He pulled the string on his worn, dirty trousers very carefully and checked his hip. All that was left of yesterday's fall was a fading yellow and purple bruise. The injury in his side already looked days old. He reached to scratch the phantom wound in his chest. His thick, callused finger pushed through the hole in the tunic, searching for an itch, but all he found was scar tissue. Somewhere in the back of his mind, the memory of the wall, the wound and the darkness howled and strained against its chains.

Unforgiving pressure from his bladder brought him back and told him in no uncertain terms what needed to be done. 'Fine, fine,' he muttered. There were no things to gather; he'd say goodbye to Fjolnir, thank him and be on his way, then take a piss in the woods when he was clear of the farmstead.

The old man had been busy in the yard. He'd set up a work-bench and was chiselling something that might become a statue of some sort. He looked up, smiled and nodded, then went back to work. After a moment, he looked back up and grinned. 'Want to earn yourself a bowl of broth? There's an axe in the shed. If a man were to need to go to the woods for whatever reason, he could do worse than bring back a bit of lumber. Half again a man's height, about as thick as yourself. Like the piece I have here.'

'That's a tree,' Audun blurted out.

'See? Sharp as a blade, and this early in the morning, too. Pine, if you please.' There was a definite glint in Fjolnir's eye and Audun was sure he saw a smirk as the old man went back to the carving.

Audun stood in the doorway for a moment. Then, cursing inwardly, he went to the shed.

For a farm that looked to be in the winter of its life, old Fjolnir kept some pretty sharp tools. Audun hefted the wood axe. The weight of it was satisfying. The handle was worn smooth.

When he came out again, Fjolnir caught his eye and smiled. He gestured to the east and Audun, following his directions, was soon walking in a sparse forest. Birches stretched their slim branches towards him, but he ignored them. A couple of days ago he might have seen the claws of cold death in the shapes of the soggy trees, but things were easier now. He had work to do.

When he found the tree he was looking for, Audun smiled for the first time in a long while. The bark felt rough under his hand. 'I'll give you a head start,' he said, patting it like a skittish horse. 'Go on.'

The tree didn't move.

'All right, then. Don't say I didn't warn you.' He flexed his muscles, cracked his neck and swung.

The axe vibrated with the force of the blow. He strained to free the blade from the trunk and struck again. His aim was true and a sliver of wood fell out of the wound. The cold, damp air was delicious in his lungs. He could feel his strength flooding back with every vicious swing of the heavy axe. His shirt soon clung to his back, and Audun gave himself up to the work. Before long, the tree trembled with every stroke. A push, a crash and it was down.

Working without thinking, he removed the branches methodically and cut the tree down to the requested size. When he was done, Audun stepped back, put down the axe and scratched his head.

'How—?' There was no horse on Fjolnir's farm, so there could be only one answer. Audun bent down and wrapped his arms around the log. Straining, he managed to shift it up onto the stump of the tree. 'How in Hel's name did he—?' Audun reached around the log again. Frowning, he let go, picked up the axe and cut a handhold on each side. Then he drew back and buried the axe in the wood, well past the midway point.

Audun bent his knees, growled low and hoisted the log onto his shoulder, grabbing the axe for support with his free hand. Turning carefully, he marched back to the farm.

When he got there, Fjolnir was waiting for him next to a big pile of wood-cuttings. 'Very good!' the old man shouted. 'Need any help with that?'

'Not from you, old man,' Audun shot back. Normally he wouldn't have said anything, but something about the greybeard set him at ease.

'Thank you,' Fjolnir said. 'Could you put it over there?' He pointed towards a shed half-hidden behind the house; Audun hadn't noticed it the night before. Fjolnir's farm was definitely in better shape than he'd first thought.

When he came back, the old man had brought out a battered old handcart filled with lumber. He turned to Audun. 'If you're not in a hurry to leave, stranger, I could use some help with these fence-posts.'

Audun shrugged. 'Sure,' he said. To his surprise, he found that he rather liked Fjolnir's company.

The day fell into a steady rhythm: heave rough wood, hammer, nails, move on. Audun had to admit that the old man was an excellent worker. There was no fuss, minimal talking and no stupidity. The old man did what needed to be done and never got in his way. *Thank the gods for every man who isn't an idiot*, Audun thought. Then he grinned. That would be the kind of thing he'd have muttered under his breath crossing the square in Stenvik, before . . .

'What happened?'

The question came out of nowhere and broke the quiet.

'I . . . What?'

'Tell me.'

Audun looked at the old man, who just looked levelly back at him with his one good eye. 'There . . . um . . . there was a siege. Around Stenvik. Someone called Skargrim surrounded the city.' Fjolnir nodded at the mention of the name. 'A lot of good men died.' Audun found he was grasping the handle of the sledge-hammer. His knuckles were white. With great effort, he managed to relax his fingers and put it down.

'And?'

'And . . . we defeated him. Them. There were more.'

'And was that it?'

'No. King Olav came and took over.'

Fjolnir frowned. 'And how did you survive?'

Audun's throat was suddenly dry. His chest itched something fierce, but the words caught in his throat. It felt like Fjolnir was looking through him now. His face flushed and he reached for the sledgehammer.

'I just did,' he growled.

The hammer blow split the fence-post in two.

Fjolnir handed him another without a word and Audun drove it into the ground.

They continued working as their shadows grew longer. Finally, Fjolnir spoke. 'Time for home and food.'

Audun threw the sledgehammer on the cart. He could feel his muscles, but in a pleasant way; it was an ache that said he'd put in a day's work. The pain from his back was gone and the wound in his side had all but disappeared. After he had smashed the fence-post, Fjolnir had not brought up Stenvik again. Audun frowned. Part of his mind sought to understand his current situation, but another part of him remembered all too well. He did not want to think about how the cold steel had pierced his skin, ripped through his muscles and punctured his heart as it tore through his back when Harald had skewered him on the wall.

The thought came like a bucket of cold water. *Injured.* He'd been injured, badly. But it had been all right because Ulfar had jumped and they'd escaped.

Injured. He'd just been injured.

'What do you want to eat?' Fjolnir asked as they headed back home, following the line of the fence they'd erected.

'Food would do,' Audun mumbled.

'Oh. So you can still talk,' the old man said. 'Good. I was beginning to worry that I'd shut you up. So Stenvik was bad, was it?'

'It was,' Audun said.

'You saw things you wish you hadn't seen,' Fjolnir said.

'I did,' Audun muttered.

'And did things you didn't want to,' Fjolnir said. Audun stopped, turned and looked at the old man, who stood his ground and returned the gaze. 'And now it's eating you up and you're afraid that if you talk about it – if you even *think* about it – it'll come back and you'll do it again.' Audun felt his breath quicken, felt his hands clench into fists and still the old man did not move. 'And you're always angry.'

Fjolnir turned and walked towards home. 'I know how it is. Come on, old bull,' he said over his shoulder. 'You'll tell me when we get home.'

Nothing more passed between them until the sun had set and they were back at the farmstead. Fjolnir busied himself getting a fire going, then disappeared for a moment and returned with a basket full of food. Audun saw turnips, roots and a handful of green things, along with meat. 'You've been working hard; you'll need this,' he said as he gestured for Audun to remain seated. 'You're a big lad,' he added.

Soon something was bubbling in the pot and a fat chunk of pork was roasting on the fire. Audun tried to speak up, but he was too tired.

'Right. That's everything. I'll just go and . . .' Fjolnir's voice trailed off and he stepped out again. When he came back, he was carrying a travel chest, which he put down by the door.

'Now,' he said, 'we talk. First I'll tell you of my son. He was like you, a big strong lad. Not too sharp. He meant well, but there was always something in him. Pride, anger, I don't know. I could talk to him, teach him, but only up to a point. The *thing* – the fire in him – it always took over.' The fire in the hearth crackled in agreement and the room twisted and warped with the dancing shadows. 'He left to go and find things – adventure, maybe, or honour, I guess. His place in the world. I used to be . . . I wasn't always a gentle father.' The old man was miles away now. 'So he needed to go away.'

'Do you know where he is now?'

Fjolnir blinked, and for a moment Audun was sure the old man didn't recognise him. Then he smiled. 'Oh yes. I do know. See, I had another son by another woman. Wish I never had. Nasty piece of work, just like his mother. He was smart, too. Had a real knack for letting other people do his dirty work. And he . . . poisoned the mind of my son, turned him against me. He told him I was weak, old and feeble.' The shadows behind Fjolnir were moving more than Audun thought they should. 'I had to . . . I had to discipline them. But they're out there. They're out there waiting to come for me, to claim what's theirs.'

The old man stopped talking and a silence spread in the hut, only occasionally broken by the crackling of the fire.

'Food,' Fjolnir finally said. 'We should eat.' He reached down and produced two mugs of mead from somewhere. 'Drink this,' he said to Audun, who did not need to be told twice.

It was the sweetest, most delicious thing he'd ever tasted.

'Eat,' Fjolnir commanded. He'd carved off a chunk of glistening roast pork. The smell alone was enough to make Audun's stomach lurch with hunger.

They ate and drank.

After a while, Fjolnir said, 'I will guess that you didn't have a good time with your father.'

'You'd guess right,' Audun said.

'What happened?'

'I killed him.'

Fjolnir sat in silence for a little while. 'And was that when it happened?'

The tone – the understanding in the old man's voice – sent a wave of sensation up Audun's arms. 'Yes,' was all he could say.

'Tell me,' Fjolnir said.

'He was . . . I know now what he was. He was a coward and a bully, and he had no interest in a fair fight. I think he might have been good to my mother at the start, but as long as I could remember he'd beaten her. And me, if I made any noise.' The words that had been kept down for so long tumbled out of him. 'And he beat us thoroughly. Mother didn't go out for days on end. Fucking bastard,' Audun snarled. 'He didn't care about anyone but himself, so I started trying to find a place to work. There was a blacksmith in my village; I began doing odd jobs for him, sneaking out when the old man was drunk. For some reason I grew up quick, and was soon doing hammer work. In my twelfth summer, I packed on some muscle, but my father didn't notice. Then once, he came home from drinking and I was standing too close to the door, so he punched me, sent me flying across the room. Then he grabbed Mother. He was rough with her, so I stood up, told him to let her go. 'He laughed at me. I told him again. He said, "Or what?" I said I'd make him.'

Audun took a sip of mead. 'That was one step too far. I got his attention. He went for me with his belt, tanned me, then grabbed me around the neck. He was going to strangle me, and I . . .'

'You felt the fire,' Fjolnir said. 'There was a fire inside you. Something that burned. Some kind of beast that needed to get out.'

'Yes.'

There was a long pause as the two men eyed each other up.

'How did he die?' Fjolnir finally asked.

'I knocked him to the floor and broke his face,' Audun said. 'I smashed it. I couldn't stop hitting him.'

'And then . . . ?'

'My mother – she put a hand on my shoulder. I turned around and the look on her face made . . . It made the fire go away.' Audun took another, deeper, swig of mead. The sweetness was cloying. 'I couldn't stay. His friends would have rounded us up and killed us. My mother pleaded with me, insisted I take all she owned, which turned out to be three pieces of silver. She cried so much that I took them, then I broke into the forge and took a hammer. I left the silver. I have been running since.'

Fjolnir nodded. 'Thank you for telling me your story.' They sat quietly for some time until the old man rose, picked up a poker and moved to the fire. 'Look,' he said, and blew on the embers. Flames danced towards the ceiling, tendrils stretching like flowers to the sun. 'The flame is dangerous. It burns. But you decide how bad it gets.' He looked at Audun. 'It does not own us. It does not decide who we are. We do.' He walked over to the chest by the door, picked it up and placed it in front of Audun. 'I want you to have this,' he said. 'It belonged to my son, but he has no claim to it now.'

'I can't take it,' Audun said. 'Whatever it is.'

'I would ask you to do it for me, as a favour. There will be a lot of trouble on your path before your journey is done, Audun Arngrimsson.'

Grinning, the old man reached into the apparently bottomless food basket. 'Now we eat till we're fat and drink till we're drunk, and I'll tell you a story of what happens if you spend a night in the forest when the moon is full!'

Audun accepted the refilled mug Fjolnir thrust at him and took another deep, long swig. 'Thank you,' he said. 'Thank you for my food. Thank you for—' His words failed him. 'Thank you.'

The old man smiled. 'Shut up and drink. Now, there are many places you can go when the moon is round as a whore's teat, but my forest is not one of them. Let me tell you a story . . .'

The hammer-blows from outside reverberated around the inside of Audun's sore head. His mouth felt like an old sock and his bladder was full to bursting point. He rolled out of bed and banged his knee on the chest. Muttering a curse, he stumbled to his feet and noticed that the hammering had stopped.

Fjolnir's voice rang out across the farmstead. 'Well met, strangers! What brings riders to my end of Setr Valley?'

The air in the barn stank of mouldering hay and horse sweat. Ulfar's stomach turned. His skin was clammy, intermittently cold and hot, and he could feel the sheen of dirty sweat on his forehead under the greasy strands of long, black hair.

She was writhing under him, trying to make a good show of it, whoever she was. 'Come on,' she whispered. 'Come on, stranger. Come on.' There was an odd sort of desperation in her urging, he thought. She groped for him, with little luck. He tried to focus on her face. Sparkling blue eyes, blonde hair, tiny upturned nose. Freckles. She was pretty, in a country sort of way. He reached for her name but got lost in a fog of mead. Nothing was right. All he could feel were his breeches rubbing against the underside of his deflating cock.

He rolled off her. The straw scratched at him. She didn't even say anything; just made a sound in her throat, a mixture of disappointment and disgust. He felt her buck her hips next to him as she struggled to adjust her clothes.

'Fucking wimp,' she spat as she rose and stormed off.

Ulfar didn't care, wouldn't have cared even if he was considerably less drunk. Still, if he hadn't been so busy drinking away his winnings he wouldn't have boned her – or tried to, at any rate.

He snorted, rolled his eyes and mumbled something that might have been a joke as he tugged up his breeches and pulled himself to a position that was almost standing. When he stumbled outside the stables, the cold air hit him like a slap in the face. All the smells of the autumn night were amplified; the manure, the sour reek of horse-piss and wet hay, the rotting leaves in the forest just past the fence. His stomach lurched and he felt the bile rising. He leaned against the wall and fought it back down with great effort.

There was no denying it any longer.

'I fucking stink,' he slurred. 'Fucking *stink*. Need to find clean clothes or something. And a bath.' He grinned, straightened up and looked sternly at the tethering post. 'Where's my bath?' he commanded. 'You there! You're short, but you'll have to do. Fetch me my bath. And a wench to put in it and put it in! Hah!'

'Hey! Limp-dick!' Someone rounded the corner and headed towards him: short, not too skinny. Farmer's build, farmer's clothes, fighter's walk. Behind him came the blonde girl he'd just been with. Ann. Ann something.

'And I'm Ulfar!' Ulfar shouted back. 'Nice to meet you!' He giggled. 'What can I do for you, King Limp-dick? And your fetching wife, Queen Limp-dick?' He bowed unsteadily.

'That's him, Torulf! He tried to rape me!' the girl said.

Ulfar laughed. 'More like the other way around, sweetness,' he said. 'Your wife . . . sister? Both? Tried her best to get me going, only she wasn't very good. If you wait till morning, I might be able to teach her a couple of tricks. Won't charge you much, either.' With great effort, he pushed off from the wall and balanced on his feet.

'He's lying! Hit him, Torulf! Punch him in the face!' The girl's voice was shrill with fury. Torulf was now close enough for Ulfar to get a good look at him and the man turned out to be a boy, and the boy was younger than Ulfar had been expecting. Fourteen, maybe – but country strong. There was murder in his eyes, and somewhere in the back of Ulfar's mind a little bit of common sense appeared.

'Listen . . . Torulf? Torulf. This is a mistake – a misunderstanding. I didn't mean to say those things. Nothing happened. We can talk—' The first blow landed on his shoulder. Torulf did not want to talk. 'Stop. We *oouf*—' The second punch hit a lot harder, just below his ribcage. Ulfar lost the fight against the contents of his stomach and vomited all over his attacker, who squealed very unheroically. His lady unleashed a string of expletives at Ulfar.

'You should watch that language,' Ulfar slurred, drool dripping from his mouth. 'You could shrivel a man's cock with that mouth. Oh, wait. You already did.' The girl shrieked, pushed Torulf out of her way and picked up a stone to throw at him. The fury in her eyes awoke Ulfar's survival instinct and he stumbled away. She did not let up until she'd chased him out into the woods and the last missile had whizzed past his head, thwacking into a tree.

Ulfar collapsed in a huffing, sweaty, drunken heap. His limbs felt soft and squishy; his head was starting to pound. 'Fucking bitch,' he muttered. 'Fucking bitch fuck it all.' He hawked, spat and lay down on his back. The ground was cold, wet and solid. Above him, stars dusted the night sky. The night air was sobering him up some, and through the thumping in his head he could hear running water somewhere.

He vaguely remembered crossing a stream earlier in the day, just before he'd walked into town. If you could call it a town – longhouse, a few huts. Farmers nearby, fifty people at a push. He'd heard a few mutterings about King Olav taking some of the best farmhands but thought it prudent not to ask questions. They didn't care much for their new king – that was good. They had ale and they had a worn old Tafl board and so he'd quickly found himself hustling for coin. Now he wished he hadn't spent it all on drink in the hope that it would help.

It hadn't helped. However much he drank, she never went away.

It hadn't helped to crawl on top of that village girl, either, and somewhere inside he'd known it wouldn't. Now he just felt dirty. No matter what he did, his mind still went to Lilia every night, and the time they'd stolen in Stenvik. Little flashes of her were burned into his eyes: her crown of red hair made of fire in sunlight; the necklace of blood that dragged her down to the ground like a stone in the ocean. And she would come back to him tonight, before he slept.

'So I might as well enjoy life until then,' he muttered. Grabbing hold of a low-hanging willow branch, he levered himself up and went in search of more ale.

'He was horrible. Really drunk. And he *stank*.' Anneli sniffed, wiped her face with her sleeve and moved closer to where Jaki was sitting on the edge of his bed. 'He held me down and . . . and . . .' She whimpered. 'And he would have taken me, too, if your brother hadn't dragged him off and punched him.' She pushed her chest against Jaki's arm. 'But then, instead of fighting like a man, he threw up on poor Torulf!'

Jaki's laugh was harsh and mirthless. 'Pussy Swede,' he sneered.

'Yes,' Anneli said, 'not a real man, like you.' She leaned in and her hand landed on Jaki's thigh. 'My boys. You and your brothers have always protected me from everyone, Jaki. Everyone. And now this . . . stranger comes into our village—'

'What'd he look like?'

'Tall. Maybe taller than you. But skinny, and long black hair. Like a girl,' Anneli spat. 'Disgusting.' She sniffed again. 'I don't know what he was wearing – maybe a blue cloak over a grey tunic, with a silvery dragon brooch and a brown leather hairband? I didn't really look. I'm so scared, Jaki. So, so scared. He might wait for me and try to do it again and maybe you won't be there to protect me and—'

Jaki stood up and puffed out his chest. 'That's enough. No more talk now. I'm getting Jarli and we're gonna sort this out. Stay there.' He grabbed a shift and struggled into it.

'Of course. Just . . .' Anneli started, then, 'Jaki – be careful . . . please?'

The young man set his broad, powerful shoulders and scowled. 'I'm not the one who should be careful,' he said.

Anneli watched him leave. The moment the door closed, she stood up and followed, a glint in her eyes.

'Jarli!' Jaki banged on the door-frame of his brother's hut. 'Come on! Now! Hurry!'

The planks that formed a makeshift door moved and a large, stocky young man peered out, rubbing the sleep from his eyes. His blue eyes matched Jaki's, as did the turn of his mouth. 'Whadye want?' he slurred.

'Get your clothes on. Stranger tried to rape Anneli,' Jaki snapped.

The sleep vanished from Jarli's face. 'Coming,' he said. The door shut; moments later he stepped out, holding two inch-thick axe handles, one for him, one for his brother. 'Where is he?'

'Torulf tried to fight – the bastard threw up on him and staggered into the bushes,' Jaki said. 'Can't have gone far.'

Jarli looked at him. 'Threw up? Really?'

'Yes. Anneli says he was very drunk.'

'Right.' Jarli's lip curled. 'Let's go. Wanna get more?'

'No. This is for us.'

Jarli nodded and the two brothers strode off into the night.

The longhouse was almost quiet now, save for a few greybeards. Ulfar pushed his opponent's king over. 'And that's you done,' he said.

'Bastard,' the old man spat. Behind him, his three friends shook their heads and muttered into their beards.

'Stay away from the corners next time. Might give your opponent a bit of a challenge,' Ulfar offered. 'And pay up.' He raised his mug, drained it and licked the last honeyed drops off the rim. 'Or get me more ale. Your choice.'

The old man slammed two copper coins down on the table. 'Fucking Swedes,' he growled.

'Yeah. Fucking Swedes. Horrible Swedes. It's all our fault,' Ulfar said. 'Always has been. And a good night to you. Who wants to go next?' None of the men standing around the table volunteered and Ulfar cursed himself inwardly. He was too drunk; he'd forgotten a cardinal rule – work the room, make them like you, never turn them on yourself. Sven would have said something about leading a lamb *to* rather than away from the slaughter. With great effort, Ulfar strapped on a smile, which was much harder to do after thinking of the old rogue. 'Come now, lads. Anyone fancy their luck? I'll put two down to your one.' He grabbed his empty mug. 'Or three if someone fills this up.'

The door to the longhouse flew open and two burly young men stepped in, scanning the room. Ulfar was up before he knew fully what he was reacting to.

'You,' the shorter one said, pointing at him.

'Yes?' Ulfar replied. The men around him shuffled quickly towards the walls. He could feel the warmth of the liquor draining away, replaced by the sinking feeling in his stomach. The headache started about then too. This did not look good.

'Out,' the short man said.

'I'm fine here,' Ulfar replied. 'Would you like a game? We were having such a nice time.'

'Jarli,' the shorter one said. The big guy stepped towards him and levelled what looked like the haft of an axe at his chest. 'Out,' he rumbled.

'Why?' Ulfar said, retreating. He felt for the sword at his hip. 'I don't have a quarrel with you.'

'*Shut up!*' the smaller one screamed. 'Shut the fuck up, you fucking piece-of-shit Swede! You know what you did and you're not fucking walking away from my town! He tried to rape Anneli!' he exclaimed to the greybeards in the longhouse. His big companion advanced, careful brawler-style.

Still holding the mug, Ulfar jumped up on the table and kicked a soup bowl at the larger one's head. He swatted it away and took two more steps. He'd be within striking range in moments. 'I didn't – *do* – anything!' he shouted. 'The girl wanted to go with me. I was drunk. I was too drunk, in fact, and then she stormed off! Just leave me alone!'

'Liar,' the big one growled and swung for Ulfar, hard enough to break both his legs.

Screaming with rage, Ulfar leapt over the axe handle, landed and smashed the mug on the big man's forehead. The big man bellowed and staggered, clutching his bleeding head and tilting it backwards to get the blood out of his eyes. His smaller companion screamed and rushed towards them, but at that moment Ulfar jumped off the table, planted his foot on the big man's chest and pushed hard, sending the two men crashing back towards the door. He landed softly and was up in an instant with his sword drawn. He took two steps towards the young men getting up off the floor, who suddenly looked a lot less confident.

'I said – leave me – the *fuck* – alone!'

'You raped—' the smaller one started, squirming away from the point of the sword.

'You say that one more time and I will spit you like a pig. I didn't rape anyone. Your little slut friend was begging for it and she's pulling you along by the cock to make things happen in this shithole so she can have a thrill,' Ulfar said. 'Now get the fuck out of my way so I can leave you sheep-fuckers to it.' The larger one shot him a baleful look as he stood up, but he stepped out of the way. 'And drop the stick,' he added. 'You too,' Ulfar snapped at the shorter one, who looked reluctant to let it go. 'Get some sense, boys.' Exhaustion hovered at the edge of his fury. 'Just . . . get some sense.'

The big man grabbed his brother by the shoulder and pulled him aside and Ulfar walked out of the longhouse with his sword drawn.

Something moved quickly in the shadows to his side, just at the edge of his vision. Still tingling from the fight, Ulfar spun around, seized the hand holding the rock and pulled the arm down hard across his knee, dragging his surprisingly light attacker off balance. He felt the snap and heard the rock tumble to the ground. The piercing scream was loud enough to save Anneli's life – Ulfar's sword stopped a finger's-breadth from her neck.

'You bastard,' she sobbed in the darkness. 'You fucking bastard. You broke my arm.'

'Oh, you poor thing,' Ulfar snarled. 'Want me to kiss it better?' He sheathed his sword and kicked the prone figure once for good measure. 'Fucking bitch,' he muttered as he walked away from the form sobbing in the shadows. Behind him he heard the commotion as the doors opened. Somebody shouted something after him; he didn't care. He hawked, spat and walked on.

The faint moonlight quickly turned the nameless town into just another shade of darkness and he covered the first few miles quickly, cooling his blood. It took him a good couple of miles more to realise that he was slowing down.

He was hungry, hung-over and angry at everything.

And he still stank.

Veering off the road, he found a thick-leaved bush and crawled under it. Mangled visions floated before his eyes; he imagined spearing Anneli, ripping open her throat and throwing her off a wall somewhere in front of a thousand helpless brothers. Sleep caught him and gave him dreams of Lilia.

EAST OF VALLE, WEST NORWAY
OCTOBER, AD 996

Sunrise brought another headache and a woolly mouth, an aching bladder and a back all knotted from the hard ground. *I'll never speak ill of any bed ever again*, Ulfar thought as he crawled out from underneath the bush. It was the kind of thing Geiri would love to tease him about. Retracing his steps, he found the road again. It led to the east, which suited him just fine. He started walking.

Rubbing the sleep out of his eyes, Ulfar opened his mouth to speak.

Then he blinked.

Geiri wasn't there.

He would never be there again.

Ulfar looked around and took a deep breath. Then another. He touched the rune that hung from a string around his neck and his lips trembled for a moment. 'How . . .' he started, but there was no one there to talk to. He hadn't asked Audun to follow him. Nobody could tell him what to do. His chest tightened and the pain behind his eyes settled into a dull, steady throb.

There was nothing for it but to start walking.

There was a world around him, but he didn't notice, didn't care. Right foot, then left. Simple. Right foot, then left. The rhythm of it lulled him, sang him into a daze. He didn't need to think – he just needed to walk. Right foot, then left. Right, then left. He tried not to think about what would happen when he reached his destination, or what he was walking away from.

'Hail, traveller!'

The shout made Ulfar stumble and blink. Then he swore and turned around. He'd been walking half-asleep, oblivious to his surroundings.

Luckily the man behind the voice was a good hundred yards away. He was tall, dressed in rough wool, but he carried himself like a soldier; he looked like the kind of man you'd put by something to guard it. He was leaning on a big walking staff. A huge mastiff sat next to him, long pink tongue lolling out in stark contrast to its white coat.

'Hail,' Ulfar shouted back.

'I thought I'd let you know of us,' the old man said. His voice carried surprisingly well. 'You've not looked back for quite a while.'

Ulfar shrugged.

'Where are you going?' the old man ventured.

'East,' Ulfar answered.

'Would you care for company?' the old man said.

What could it hurt? Numbers weren't a bad thing on the road. 'Sure,' Ulfar said, working hard to muster up some enthusiasm. The man caught up with him quickly, long legs covering the distance with ease. The big dog trotted at his side, glanced at

Ulfar once and deemed him uninteresting. 'Well met. My name is Gestumblindi,' the man said.

'Well met. I am Ulfar,' Ulfar replied. 'I've recently come from—'

'I know,' the man said. Ulfar tensed up, but Gestumblindi didn't appear to notice. 'You just came through Valle. I gather you made quite an impression.'

Tension flooded out of him as quickly as it had come and Ulfar couldn't help rolling his eyes. The man shot him a conspiratorial wink. 'The . . . salt of the earth are sometimes, what can we say, overly protective of their womenfolk,' Gestumblindi added. 'And quite ready to believe young, hot-blooded ladies who complain about exciting strangers in small towns. Often a little after the alleged crime.'

Ulfar couldn't help but smirk.

Gestumblindi gestured towards the road, and they started walking.

'I take it you didn't believe them, then?' Ulfar said.

Gestumblindi smiled. There was an easy air about the tall man; something that suggested command. 'I had the measure of the two boys who were talking about you, and I've seen my share of small towns. So, no. Still – I thought you'd be bigger.'

'Fuckers,' Ulfar said. 'Mind you, I've just about been there myself. Gets your blood right up if you think the womenfolk have been wronged.'

'Sure does,' said Gestumblindi. 'If you're a decent sort.'

'Yeah,' Ulfar said. 'And I suppose they were decent boys . . . in their own way.'

'The boys, yes.'

'The girl was a piece of work, though. Bet you all the coin I spent on ale last night that she'll be making some poor man's life miserable in a couple of years.'

'The way those boys looked, I'd say she's already ahead of you on that one,' Gestumblindi said, and they both grinned. Above them, thick grey clouds had melted into nothing. The sun caressed the curves of the landscape and fields of wheat stretched away in front of them. Dark blue mountains with white caps rose from the horizon in the north. The world was but a faint line of autumn in a sea of blue.

The two tall men fell into an easy, mile-eating stride, the dog trotting alongside them, until he suddenly caught wind of something. There was a whimper, a soft-spoken command and he was off like a bolt into the fields.

Ulfar watched the big animal go and whistled appreciatively. 'He's quite a beast, that one,' he said.

'Name's Geraz. Had him since he fitted in the palm of my hand,' Gestumblindi said. 'Love him like my sons – more than my sons, in fact. I have two – the other one, Frec, doesn't care much for company, so I let him range. He'll be back tonight. They're good to have on the road.'

'I can imagine. But what brings you to this corner of nowhere?' Ulfar eventually ventured.

'Hm,' the old man said. 'What brings me here?' He looked Ulfar up and down. 'I'm . . . how shall we say? I am on a mission.'

'What kind of mission?'

'I'm searching for something. Or someone, rather. I used to travel quite a lot, seen a lot of places – all of them, pretty much. I had some friends in Jomsborg,' he added, winking at Ulfar. 'Still have, in fact.'

Ulfar swallowed and fought hard to not feel for his sword. His breath caught in his throat. Suddenly the old man's military bearing made sense. 'That's . . . good,' he said. 'So—'

'Hold on.' The old man turned away from Ulfar and appeared

to be listening to something. 'Good boy,' he muttered. 'Good boy.' Moments later, Ulfar spotted a white speck in the distance. The dog was coming towards them at full speed. Gestumblindi stopped walking and focused intently on the dog, Ulfar forgotten.

As the big animal drew closer, Ulfar noted a brown stain near its jaws. A bit nearer, and he could see the stain was moving, bouncing in time with the bounding dog.

Closer yet, and now Ulfar could see that its jaws were wrapped around the neck of a hare.

It was only when the dog was skidding to a halt in front of them, the joy of speed and power shining in its eyes, that Ulfar saw the captured hare blink and continue to struggle. It was still alive.

'Oh, good boy, Geraz!' Gestumblindi said and scratched the big dog behind the ears. It thumped its tail in response, beaming with pride and gazing at its master.

Something in the tall man changed. 'Now – kill.'

A wet crunch. The hare stopped moving.

A heartbeat, and Ulfar remembered to breathe again.

The hare fell from Geraz' jaws to the old man's feet with a thud. 'That's food for tonight, I think,' Gestumblindi said with all the pride of a new parent. He scratched the big dog's head, picked up the hare and started walking again. Ulfar had to shake himself – the sharp stench of the hare's blood, shit and fear stung his nostrils and lingered where it had died.

'Where was I? The Jomsvikings,' Gestumblindi continued when Ulfar caught up. 'That was an age ago, though,' he added. 'I'm long done with that life. I was a pup, like you.' The dog at his side barked once and the tall man reached down to scratch its head. 'Yes, yes. You were a pup, too, once. Way too long ago, you bucket of lard.' Geraz appeared to be quite happy with the attention and the tone of his master's voice, and less worried about the insults.

'How did you manage to leave the Jomsvikings?' Ulfar asked.

The tall man winked. 'I had more important things to do.'

Ulfar's mind raced. 'How—?'

Gestumblindi smiled and took his time before replying. 'It does sound improbable, doesn't it?'

'Yes,' Ulfar said. 'I mean, the Jomsvikings never lose.'

'We're never on the losing side,' the old man replied, grinning. 'There is a subtle difference, but as the winning side tends to tell the tale, it's one that is rarely thought about.'

Despite his concerns, Ulfar smirked. The old soldier had an instinct for putting people at ease. *Much like Sven*, Ulfar thought, and his smile faded. The greybeard from Stenvik had made him feel at home, for a while at least.

'However, there is a need to . . . to find new blood. From what I heard about last night,' Gestumblindi continued, 'in the longhouse, I'd say you can handle yourself.'

Ulfar frowned. 'Not like one of the Jomsvikings.'

Gestumblindi turned towards him. 'Don't sell yourself short, Thormodsson. You have . . . you have something, I think.'

The day was mild, but Ulfar still felt as though the air around him had grown colder. The compliment left a bitter taste in his mouth.

'I don't—'

'So I would like to extend you an offer. Join my side and you will get the fight of your life, with spoils unimaginable and—'

'No.'

Gestumblindi stopped and turned to face him. Sensing a change in his master's stance, Geraz growled low in his throat.

Ulfar took a measured step back.

'No?' The old man eyed him with something . . . intrigue? Anger?

'I cannot,' Ulfar said. He felt light-headed. The ground tilted around him.

'Why not?' Gestumblindi said. His grip on the staff tightened.

'There is something I must do.'

'What?' the old man said.

A sudden flare of determination made Ulfar look the old man straight in the eyes. 'I have to go to Uppsala. I have to find a man called Alfgeir Bjorne. And I have to tell him that his son is dead. I also have to tell him that it is my fault.'

The space between them appeared to stretch in all directions at once. Behind Gestumblindi the horizon warped, twisted in on itself and became its own mirror; above them the sky stretched so far as to become the ground they stood on. Suddenly Gestumblindi looked impossibly tall and Ulfar's chest tightened; his breath came in ragged gulps. He staggered to keep his balance but it was too late – his head felt ever lighter, his eyes rolled up into his head and he crumpled to the ground.

He dreamed of spaces, of stars and cold black, and a big hall somewhere in a forest. He didn't go in. The world spun around him, and he had to fight against the memories of Stenvik, the woman on the boat, the curse – the shock when Audun came back.

Later, Ulfar opened his eyes. There was nothing wrong with the sky above him. He moved his elbow to roll over – and something growled; something big and close. A base fear coursed through him and Ulfar shuddered. He shifted his elbow again; another growl, this time more insistent. Curled lips over sharp teeth. A warning.

Ulfar eased onto his back and lay absolutely still. Glancing to both sides without moving his head, he thought he saw the shadow of something, but it was too big to comprehend. His heart thumped in his chest and for a moment he thought he felt the fangs, the hot breath, the wet jaws clamped over his throat and shoulder.

But nothing happened, and Ulfar's mind decided he was safer somewhere else.

When he opened his eyes again, the sun had travelled almost all the way across the sky and the smell of roasted hare made his stomach growl. The evening chill was just beginning to bite, but the soft warmth of a distant fire was creeping slowly from his feet towards his knees.

'Welcome back,' Gestumblindi said, somewhere out of sight. Ulfar's reply was not much more than a mumble. 'Shut up and lie still,' the old man continued, not unkindly. 'Have you been feeding yourself recently, brave wanderer?'

'Not much,' Ulfar managed.

'You smell like you've watered yourself, though. Regularly,' the old man added.

Ulfar did his best to shrug while lying down.

'Here,' the old man said as he entered Ulfar's field of vision. He had a knife; speared on its point was a bit of lean hare meat. It was burned crisp on one side; the other was rosy pink. Ulfar's mouth watered and he propped himself up. 'Gently,' the old man said. 'You've been pushing hard, you've been drinking on a mostly empty stomach and you've not been eating right. You just fainted.'

'Er . . . yeah,' Ulfar mumbled. He took the proffered knife and pinched the piece of meat with his thumb and forefinger. 'Been . . . been walking a while, I suppose.'

Gestumblindi had gone back to the fire and was busying

himself turning two hares on a spit. Geraz, sitting close to the warmth, followed his master's moves intently. Something in the dog's shadow caught Ulfar's eye, but it disappeared again almost immediately.

'Here,' Gestumblindi said, passing Ulfar a distinctive silver flask etched with a picture of a well. 'Drink this. It'll make you better.'

'Thank—' The words got stuck in his throat and he tasted bile. Swallowing it down, he raised the flask to his lips.

He could feel the water flowing through his body, tingling out into what felt like his fingertips, washing before it the dirt that was inside him. There were only a few drops in the flask, but it felt like a full flagon. Ulfar exhaled. His head cleared. The stars winked at him and told him exactly how to get to Uppsala. A weight lifted off his chest and he felt for the first time since the decision that he would be able to do it, be able to face Alfgeir Bjorne.

'It's what I keep telling them,' Gestumblindi said. His hands appeared to function with a will of their own. He turned the spit, sliced off meat onto a bit of cloth next to Geraz and went back to the hares, working for every last scrap on the blackening bones. Ulfar noted that the dog didn't consider going for the food, even though it was within reach. 'A man is only as strong as the water he can get. So if you are besieging a town, go straight for their water supply.'

The burned meat suddenly tasted of ash.

They'd walked for four days to get away from the stench of the big pyre outside Stenvik; it had been in their clothes, in their hair, in their noses. Human fat dripping on the flames burned with an acrid, sour smoke; the delicious smell of roast meat sat alongside the knowledge that it was from the bodies of fallen comrades.

Ulfar drank more water but the taste of that bitter smoke was still in his mouth.

A howl broke the silence, the sound of something from the darkest recesses of the human mind, the tearing cry of nightmares. The hairs on Ulfar's arms stood on end, but Gestumblindi and Geraz looked completely unfazed. 'Did you—?'

'That's Frec,' the old man said. 'He likes the moon.' At his feet, the big white hound worried at a bone. It looked almost comically small in his huge jaws.

'Right,' Ulfar said. He leaned back and watched night chase day across the sky. 'Do you want me to take the first watch?'

Gestumblindi chuckled. 'That won't be necessary. Anyone and anything that heard the same thing you just did will have the sense to stay away. Nothing can touch us here. Now sleep, Ulfar Thormodsson.'

The heat of the fire, the meat in his belly and the stars overhead drained Ulfar and he fell into a deep sleep.

Gestumblindi turned slowly towards the sleeping form. Geraz cocked his head and looked at his master, who nodded once. The big white dog stood and sniffed the air.

A grey wolfhound padded into the circle of firelight. It walked straight up to the old man, nudged its head at his thigh and moved over to Geraz. They stood to attention, eyes trained on Gestumblindi.

'You're trouble. Both of you,' the old man muttered. 'But we'll see what's what.' He reached for his satchel, grimaced and clutched his ribs. 'Really didn't need to take that much of a beating,' he grumbled. 'Let's see if this one can do with less convincing.' Rooting around, he found what he was looking for. 'There we are,' he said as his hand came out of the satchel holding a small vial. 'Seems a waste . . . but the belt was always for the smith.' Gestumblindi winced again as he reached for the silver flask, tipped the contents of the vial into it and sealed it again. When he rose, he looked older. 'Right. Let's go.'

The dogs fell in line as the old man walked away, leaning on his staff.

The moon shone on him, but he cast no shadow.

The chime of blacksmiths' hammers on blades rang out across town as weapons were prepared, chain jerkins repaired and shields reinforced; raw voices of chieftains exploded in counterpoint, barking out orders. New Town's square was full of people as Stenvik woke up to its purpose.

Just off the main south road, Jorn stepped closer to Runar. 'Have you spoken to them?' he hissed.

'Y-yes. Botolf and Skeggi are in,' Runar replied. 'I am heading d-down to meet them and tell them who to p-p-put on the boat.'

'Good. We'll make sure . . .' Jorn's voice trailed off.

'W-what?'

Jorn didn't reply but stared at something over Runar's shoulder. The archer turned to look. A group of Finn's men were running away from the square and into the northern part of town. 'Th-that doesn't look—'

'No. It doesn't, does it?' Jorn said. 'Are they running towards—?'

'Yes.'

'Right. We won't learn anything standing here. You head down to Old Town. Keep an eye on things, count the horses, divide stores and make sure we get it right. I'll go and find out what's happened.'

Runar was already moving.

'And you're sure about this?' King Olav said. Since he received the news, he'd been walking aimlessly around the longhouse, as if he couldn't bear the thought of stillness.

'Quite sure, your Majesty,' Valgard replied. Beside him, Finn watched the young king pace. His eyes were sleepy, the smell of the mixture heavy on his breath. Unlike Harald, the burly soldier turned sleepy, even gentle, when the herbs kicked in. The ghost of a smile passed across Valgard's face. He'd still prove useful, if played right.

King Olav stopped in front of the fractured cross, looking at it as if he'd only just noticed it.

'How . . . how will this play?' he finally said.

'With regard to the deaths, there will be anger,' Valgard replied. He'd thought about how to reply to such a question, and the words rolled off his tongue with ease. 'There will be men of the Westerdrake who'll assume that you had them killed—'

'Which I did not.'

'Which you certainly did not. You gave no such order.'

'Exactly.'

The chance was there. 'Regardless of how convenient it is for you.' He watched the king stiffen in front of the cross, but he said nothing. If anything, King Olav appeared to slump a little. 'However, I have been taking care of them. So if it is to your Majesty's taste—'

'Nothing here is to my taste.' The king's voice was cold.

'I could . . . I could tell the men about the wounds Sven and

Sigurd suffered earlier, fighting the raiders. And how they got battle fever and there was nothing I could do for them.'

Silence. King Olav was still staring at the cross, craning his neck to take it all in. *Like a boy seeking his father's eyes*, Valgard thought.

'Do that,' the king said. He did not look at them. 'We still sail tomorrow.'

'The men will expect full chieftain's treatment, your Majesty: a burial to befit Sigurd's standing. They'll want a ship,' Valgard offered.

'Sigurd Aegisson does *not* get a fucking ship!' The king spun around and glared at them. His face was flushed with anger. 'They had the . . . the *insolence* to die now when they were not supposed to and they do not get a ship. No ship. You can have what you asked for with that other thing, but I will not give those two a heathen burial. No chance. Then they win.'

Valgard said, 'It would be wrong.'

'Heathen,' Finn added. 'Against the word of the Lord. No matter what the men may think.'

Taking his time to make it look like he was thinking, eventually Valgard said, 'Might I suggest . . . ?'

The cordon around Sigurd and Sven's hut was three men deep. They all looked the same – big, broad, and dully determined. None of them appeared inclined to move for or even acknowledge Jorn. He'd suggested bargaining, he'd tried veiled warnings and was about to escalate to very direct threats when the men suddenly stepped aside.

'Thank you,' Jorn muttered and reached for the bar.

'Hold it,' Finn's voice barked. 'You wait for your king.'

Jorn rolled his eyes before he turned and stepped away from the door. 'Of course. Your Majesty,' he said as he bowed his head. The three of them – Olav, Finn and that slimy healer – looked oddly worried, which made little sense – they should have been at least content, if not singing in the street. This solved a lot of problems for the king and should strengthen his hold on Stenvik, but they still looked like they had a lot on their minds. Before Jorn could put a finger on what was bothering him about the scene, Finn barged past him and wrenched open the door. Valgard entered second and immediately went to the two bodies lying inside the hut, kneeling down to feel their throats.

Behind him, King Olav entered the hut.

'Dead. Cold, no pulse, no breath,' Valgard said.

'Fine. Bring them to your hut, Valgard. Take Finn – prepare them for sea and fire. Quickly. They will meet their gods tonight.' King Olav turned to face him. 'Is my army prepared, Jorn?'

'Almost, my Lord.'

'Get to it,' the king snapped. 'We sail tomorrow morning.'

He only just managed to step out of King Olav's way as the king stormed from the hut. The king's fury was a tangible thing.

Runar weaved his way between skeletal huts and burned-down houses towards the harbour. The biggest ships had been moored at the docks, but to each side of the wooden structures beached boats were being inspected, repaired and even loaded. Experienced men helped the less proficient, barked on by veterans who in turn answered to their chieftains.

He found a vantage point just at the edge of the half-moon that had served as quayside and town square in the Old Town. A constant line of men carried supplies to the square in preparation for tomorrow morning. There were sacks of dried beef and barrels of drinking water – and large bundles of throwing spears, lest he forget the purpose of King Olav's 'delegation'. A group of men carrying firewood and kindling moved to the edge on the other side of the square and started stacking it haphazardly. In the oddly coordinated chaos of the harbour, the impossibility of mobilising an army struck Runar. How did it ever work? So many men working towards a common goal. The fact that there had been only four fights so far among the thousand men at work was nothing short of remarkable.

A slim, scarred man sidled up to him, apparently out of nowhere. 'Tomorrow,' he said.

'Botolf.' Runar said. 'Well met. Are you r-ready for tomorrow?'

'We are.'

'On the boat, we want—'

'I know what you want. But we haven't talked about—'

'R-r-reward?' Runar said.

'Correct,' the slim man replied. There was a glint of greed in his eyes as he brushed thin strands of black hair from his face. 'And the Prince of the Dales is ready to promise, is he?'

He might be the ruling lord of large parts of the southern coast and a powerful ally, but Botolf Ornsson thoroughly repulsed Runar. 'Y-you will b-b—' He fought back the fury, drew a deep breath and looked Botolf straight in the eye. 'You will be rewarded.'

The chieftain smiled and nodded. 'I just wanted to make sure we're clear on this. I know the Dalefolk well, cousins on my mother's side, but I know my men better. And I've never seen anyone block a dagger with a favour.'

Runar smiled back. 'Acts of faith are rewarded, Botolf.'

Botolf's scars danced on his face as he smiled. For a moment, Runar thought he saw something in them, some kind of emotion, but it was gone in an instant. 'Let's hope so, Runar,' he said.

'B-b-battle nerves,' Runar muttered to himself as Botolf sauntered away without a care in the world. 'Of c-course he's concerned. After all, what we're going to do . . .' Thinking about the moment made him smile. The moment when King Olav would realise that he was not among his imagined true believers after all. The moment when the king's men would become Jorn's men, take up pikes and swords, spear the king like a pig, slit his throat and throw him overboard. The look on his face—

In the distance, he noted that Botolf had stopped by a house and appeared to be addressing someone out of sight within. Moments later Skeggi emerged, clasped Botolf's arm in a warrior's grip and turned towards Runar's vantage point.

Runar watched him approach. Where Botolf was all slinking menace and fox-like grace, Skeggi was the bull in the field. The likes of him were precisely why King Olav had done what he did – small kings who ruled with an iron fist and a generous helping of dim-witted cruelty. It was only animal cunning that had landed Skeggi on King Olav's side. He'd been quicker than the others to see which way the wind was turning. Runar raised a hand to the warrior.

'Botolf tells me you've promised a reward,' he said the moment he was in earshot.

Runar bit back a response and forced a nodding smile. 'Th-th-that is t-true,' he countered. 'B-but we cannot go into detail right now.'

'Right,' Skeggi said. 'Never know who's listening, eh?'

'Right. Well observed,' Runar said and gave the big lump of a man a conspiratorial wink he suspected would largely go to waste. 'W-we d-d-don't need to say to Botolf, for example, that whoever takes c-care of getting one king out of the way can expect r-rewards from the n-next.'

Skeggi's thick brow furrowed even further as he puzzled out the meaning of the words. When he finally arrived at the destination he wished to reach, his face lit up. 'Right,' he rumbled and tapped his thrice-broken nose. 'Tomorrow morning. What happens?'

'We will try to get lines going from the south gate,' Runar said, pointing, 'and divide the men down to the east and west. You and Botolf will provide us with ten men each; they'll board the king's ship. It's the one over there with the dragon's head.'

'Mighty fine boat,' Skeggi said. 'I'll be on that one, too. Just to make sure everything goes right.'

Runar's mind raced. 'Is . . . are you sure? It would p-possibly be b-better if, um—'

The big man fixed him with a stare that was neither dull nor slow. Thick bands of muscle flexed under his shift. 'I'm going on that boat. As is Botolf. You can't ask us just for our men. I want to be there when it goes down – to see the look on his face.'

'Yes. Of course.'

'And you want to be up close for that sort of thing,' Skeggi added, 'otherwise people will think you're a coward.' A bushy eyebrow crept skywards. 'Or an archer.' Runar's cheeks burned. The look on the chieftain's face said he'd noticed. 'So I trust you'll be there with us?'

'Of course,' Runar snapped. In his mind's eye, he imagined putting three arrows through the big bully's throat at a hundred paces, and his heart slowed down somewhat. 'Wouldn't m-miss it.'

Skeggi smiled, and Runar wished he hadn't. 'Very good. I like you, Squeak. You got it all figured out.' With that, the broad-shouldered chieftain turned and stalked away.

Runar exhaled. 'F-fucking sh-sheep-rapist p-pot face,' he spat as he glared at Skeggi's broad back. Next time he'd boot the prince himself into negotiating with his dear subjects-to-be. Turning his mind to the logistics of arming and readying three thousand men, he idly wondered whether they had any chance of making a few more corpses drop overboard tomorrow.

'They're ready,' Finn said.

Valgard looked at his handiwork and allowed himself to feel a little bit of pride. The two bodies on his floor looked just like Sigurd and Sven would have in full armour. Only by taking off the chain-mail jerkins would you see that both of the dead men's necks had been snapped. 'It still feels wrong, though,' the big man muttered.

'I know, Finn. I know. But you understand, just like King Olav did, that it has to be done. We do the Lord's work, though, because we're not giving in to our enemy. We're not giving the old gods two powerful souls for the afterlife. We're just giving them – and all the men – a bit of a . . . a show.'

Finn nodded. With his sloped shoulders and hung head, he looked like a sulky child. He walked over to where Sven and Sigurd lay. 'And what do we do with them?'

'As King Olav said, remember?'

'Uhm,' Finn muttered. 'Yes.'

Scale back further on the shadowroot, Valgard reminded himself. Pliant but useful was the desired result, not sleepwalking idiot bear. He reached inside and found all the command he could muster. 'Get me a cart, four blankets and three horses. Now,' he snapped.

Finn appeared to come alive. His chest puffed out and his back straightened. His eyes were still glazed, but there was more soldier to him.

'Yes,' he said and bowed out of the hut.

Valgard turned to the two greybeards. They looked oddly peaceful on his muddy floor, like they were just in a deep sleep.

'Right, you two,' Valgard said. 'We're nearly ready. I just have to fetch some things first. Don't go anywhere.' He slipped out of the hut, smiling to himself.

Finn was already waiting outside with the cart and three placid horses when Valgard returned. 'What's in there?' the big soldier said, pointing to the large sack Valgard had slung over his back.

'Never you mind. Help me load up,' he snapped. Finn merely nodded and set to work. The two men in armour were soon up on the cart. Ducking into the hut, Valgard signalled for the big man to follow him. When they were out of sight, he fired off instructions to Finn. 'Wrap them in the rugs – like that, good – and tie the ends. Good. Now let's make packhorses out of the remaining two.'

When they were ready, Valgard soothed the two horses, but he didn't need to; Finn had chosen well. The beasts were placid and took calmly to their new role. 'You'll drive the cart; I'll ride out on the North Road when I see people moving south. Once the king has started talking, you make your way north and come find me. Understood?'

Finn nodded. As vacant as he looked at times, Valgard didn't worry for a moment – the big man was good with instructions. Moving slowly but with focus, he soon had the horse before the cart trundling down towards the harbour.

Valgard stroked the two remaining horses and their cargo, wrapped in blankets and slung like sacks over the animals' rumps. 'It's maybe not what you imagined, Father,' he said, 'but it's what you're getting.' He rubbed at his shoulders and tried his best to crack his joints. Now all he could do was wait.

No one called for quiet.

It just spread, like blood on stone, as the orders were given. A rowing crew moved the king's longship out of the way. Another crew manoeuvred a big, stocky boat in; an ice-breaker from the far north. A line of workers formed – some carried logs, others hefted bundles of kindling. As the pyre rose, layer by layer, more and more men drifted to the edges of the half-circle of stone by the harbour. The sense of occasion spread but there were no shouts, no summons – all over Stenvik, men just laid down their tools and moved to the harbour.

Finn watched them. He saw wary eyes, distrust and worry. They could see what was happening and there was tension in them; tension that needed to be directed.

The slow *clop-clop* of metal on stone sounded ponderous, almost unreal in the silence – and then the crowds parted for King Olav Tryggvason.

He walked his horse into the half-circle and surveyed the assembled men, standing crammed in between Stenvik's broken houses, in amongst shattered walkways and burned frames. Finn watched as a charge went through them – now they stared intently at the king, waiting for him to explain.

'Today I have had to make a choice,' King Olav said. His voice was soft but it carried far. 'Two men I respected and hoped would be our allies, Sigurd Aegisson and Sven Kolfinnsson, today lost their fight with battle fever, caught after injuries sustained fighting Skargrim and his raiders. And I did not wish to give them a . . .' The king swallowed, then continued, 'a burial dedicated to the old gods.' The men exchanged glances. 'But,' and the king's voice grew in power, 'I sought counsel!' He looked to the skies and made the sign of the cross. Moving hands caught a soldier's eye, and Finn noted several of the men reflexively signing themselves. 'And the Lord told me that we could give back to the old gods what was always theirs.'

Finn didn't need a signal. He led the wagon towards the funeral ship and motioned for two of his own men to follow. He could hear King Olav continuing behind him, '. . . has rejected them! Because the Lord does not accept just anyone! You have to be *chosen* to enter Jesus the White Christ's halls! And the Lord chose *you*!' A cheer went up from the crowd as Finn's men clambered aboard, carrying the bodies. 'The Lord chose you to fight for his realm on earth!' Another cheer. 'Hurry up!' Finn hissed under his breath as one of the bodies was unceremoniously thrown on top of the pyre. The other soon followed and Finn's men retreated, grabbing oars as they went. Behind them, King Olav's voice was rising to a crescendo. Finn reached for his fire-steel.

'The *Lord* will send you—'

Sparks flew and caught on broken twigs, crisp leaves, dried grass.

'To do his bidding—'

Finn knelt and blew on the embers, gentle as a lover. A tiny flame rose to meet him.

'He will send you across the sea—'

Finn moved away. Rejected, the flame sought food for its hunger.

'With *steel*' – a cheer – 'and *faith*—'

Crackling and hissing, the yellow-white tendrils gusted through the grass, bit into the wood.

'Push!' Finn hissed. His helpers used the oars to push at the solid hulk of the ship; gradually it started inching along, picking up speed.

'And he will *send you to watch Trondheim burn*!'

The old ship picked up momentum and floated clear of the harbour just as the first flame breached the barrier of wood, licked the cold, dead bodies and reached for the sky. An animal roar went up from the mass of men; the flame fed on it. Rising like dragon's teeth, it fed on the air, on the wood, on itself, on the world. Finn and his helpers disappeared into the darkness created by the spectacle of moving flame; the men on the quayside stood transfixed by the gliding fire. Here and there in the crowd Finn saw men he didn't recognise who stared at the flaming ship as if they were seeing ghosts – tough men, some of them older, one of them shading a single good eye to see better – but the vast majority of the crowd looked energised by the burning, heated by the flame, malleable as a blade in a smithy.

Slipping through the crowds, Finn hurried towards the north road.

The shadows of Stenvik Forest clawed at the North Road. Valgard led the horses at a walk, waiting for Finn to catch up. Convincing King Olav to use the deaths of Sigurd and Sven as a rallying display for the soldiers had been easier than he'd expected. Now he just needed to find the right place . . .

The forbidding barrier of trees appeared to open up to him and a path became visible. Valgard nodded, reached into his sack and withdrew a knife with a curved blade.

'If you only knew what your favourite weapon was being used for, Father,' Valgard muttered as he hacked a wound into a tree next to the trail. The horses followed him readily enough.

It didn't take him long to find the glade. The green-black shadows of the towering pines dropped away in a soft curve around the pond, making a dark sickle on the surface of the water. The rest was dusted by the reflection of stars.

Valgard smiled.

When he'd found the right place, a little square of green just off the water's edge, he tugged gently on the reins and dismounted when the horse stopped. Reaching for the sack, he pulled out a shovel and started marking out the holes.

The air was cold but not unpleasant; the forest enveloped him. Smell of bark, earth and rotting leaves mixed together to form autumn. The stillness was absolute – after the siege, no one had really gone into Stenvik Forest.

His back started aching very soon. He could feel the muscles locking up, feel the joints scraping against each other. His hips seized as well. Valgard leaned on the shovel, gritted his teeth, growled and kept on digging. The square shape started taking form.

He saw Finn before he heard him. Not for the first time, Valgard marvelled at how something so dull and clumsy-looking could still move that softly. The big soldier nodded at him from across the clearing. When he got there, Valgard's tunic was soaked.

'You're late,' Valgard said.

'Hard to get out,' Finn mumbled.

'How did it go?'

'As you thought it would.'

Valgard allowed himself a smile and handed Finn the shovel. 'Well done. Now make yourself useful, big man. We only need about two, three feet – we're not staying out here all night digging. Just enough to get them out of the way of the foxes and the locals, if they'll ever dare to come out here again.' Finn nodded and set to work with the shovel. In half the time it had taken Valgard to mark out and start on the graves, he had the job done. 'Good. Now help me with—' He didn't need to finish the sentence. Working together, they laid Sigurd and Sven each in their separate graves. Finn reached for the shovel.

'Hold on,' Valgard said. He brought up the satchel and spilled its contents onto the forest floor. Finn's eyebrows rose.

'You're gonna—'

'Yes. These are dangerous weapons still. Remember, the men of Stenvik think Sigurd was on that boat. What happens if one of them walks into a storeroom a week after we're gone and finds this?' Moving towards the cold body of Sigurd Aegisson, Valgard laid the heavy, broad-bladed battleaxe on the chieftain's chest. Behind him Finn nodded slowly, as if he was working something out. As Valgard bent to place the knife with the curved blade in Sven's hand, something caught in his throat. His knuckles grew pale around the handle and his muscles seized up. Behind him ripples formed in the middle of the pond. Breathing rapidly, he bit down as hard as he could, forced the cramps back and laid the knife stiffly on the old man's chest.

'Cover them,' he whispered and turned towards the forest.

He didn't see the earth fall on Sven's chest, on his legs, didn't see it cover his face.

Instead he tried his very best to look north, focus on what he'd find and imagine life from above, rather than below.

When they mounted up and turned back, the pond was still.

The first rays of the morning sun crept over the horizon and glanced off gleaming metal points.

A long line of soldiers had formed at first light, streaming out of the houses of the New Town and down through the south gate. Jorn was everywhere at once, exchanging information with chieftains, running numbers with the supply line and steering men in the right directions. Turning a corner, he almost ran into the bulk of Skeggi.

'How's it going, Prince?' the burly man rumbled.

Jorn nodded. 'A lot to do. Got to get it right,' he mumbled and

made to pass by. Skeggi shifted his weight and blocked Jorn's path.
'Where do you want my boys?'

'Down at the harbour. Find Runar. He'll direct you.'

'And you'll be next to your king, faithful as always?'

'Of course,' Jorn replied.

'Good,' Skeggi said. Although he might look fat, the big man
moved with grace. Jorn's path was clear. 'See you then, Dale.'

'Yes,' Jorn said. 'Amen,' he added and winked at Skeggi.

The big man laughed at that and clapped him hard on the back.
'Yeah. Amen.' Jorn could hear him chuckling as he walked away.

Down at the harbour, Runar counted heads, muttering to himself
and carving lines on a wooden slate. He didn't notice Botolf
approaching.

'Runar,' the skinny chieftain said.

'Y-yes?' Runar replied, his voice unsteady. The thumping heartbeats slowed quickly.

'Here they are.'

Behind Botolf, a group of men stepped out from the shadows,
all of them focusing intently on Runar.

Lost for words, Runar just nodded. It was really happening. They
were going to do it. He was going to put Jorn, his brother in play
for the last twenty years, on the throne. A wave of feeling washed
over him and he found himself fighting to suppress a smile.

'G-good. We knew we could rely on you.' Botolf smiled and
nodded back. 'I suppose you can send them to prepare the *Njordur's
Mercy*.'

'Thank you,' Botolf said. 'I will go with them, if you don't mind.'

'Go a-ahead.'

Around them, the stream of warriors was continuous. Two
horsemen for each ship, three for the larger ones. An even mix

of archers and foot, with a smattering of pike for good measure. They had decided to divide evenly on all boats, minimising the risk of losing all the archers, for example. It worked because Jorn had succeeded in breaking up old alliances; there were no old feuds to settle any more. They were all part of King Olav's army.

For a little while longer, at least.

Runar had no problem spotting Skeggi's approach. A shout of protest was soon followed by a growling argument and the men in front of him were shoved out of the way.

'You pussies can all rest easy. We're here now,' he said. No one around him spoke. He turned to Runar. 'We're here – my ten.' None of the men in his retinue had Skeggi's finesse, but from the looks of them they could be counted on for a healthy dose of violence. With cold, fear-borne clarity, Runar considered that he might be closer to death now than ever before.

'Go aboard the *Njordur's Mercy*,' he said. 'And welcome.'

'Hah! Welcome, he says!' Skeggi guffawed. A rumble of laughter travelled through his collection of companions. 'You say that but you're going on my boat, remember?'

'The *king's* boat,' Runar reminded him.

'The king's boat!' Skeggi roared. This time all the men laughed with him. 'Come on, boys! Let's go and serve the king!' the big chieftain shouted and pushed Runar aside. His men followed, shouting vaguely comprehensible insults to no one in particular.

Runar clenched his wooden tablet until his knuckles turned white.

'A bit of a handful, isn't he?' a familiar voice said by his shoulder.

Runar turned around and stood face to face with Valgard. 'H-he-he is,' he managed. 'A-and . . . he may be a b-b-bastard—'

'But he's our bastard,' Valgard finished for him, smiling.

'Yeah,' Runar replied.

'He's the kind of man you want on your side when things go wrong,' the skinny healer said.

'Ah-ah-absolutely.'

Valgard smiled again and bowed with mock courtesy. 'With your permission, my good man, I would like to go aboard the *Njordur's Mercy* and oversee the "preparations" of our highly capable travelling companions.'

Runar smirked. 'G-go ahead. J-j-just try and ah-avoid t-t-t-too much conversation,' he said.

Valgard winked at him. 'I'll do my best.'

As he moved towards the biggest ship in the harbour, Runar watched the healer. Maybe he'd been wrong about him. Maybe he'd tell Jorn to spare the scrawny bastard's life later today.

And maybe not.

Runar's mouth twitched towards a smile. Power felt good.

The wind snapped and bit at the sails. The clouds were few and far between, and the waves sat at their back, pushing them on.

From his place midway between the mast and the aft of the ship, Jorn looked back. The view took his breath away.

Sixty ships spread out behind them, a wake of wood and wind and blades.

Stenvik was somewhere behind them, a shell of a town.

While he'd questioned the wisdom of setting off with winter so close, he had to say that it felt good to be on the move. Runar had suggested that when they beached after King Olav had been taken care of, he should pin the murder on Botolf and Skeggi and let the fanatics do what they wanted. Like all of Runar's ideas, it was solid.

They were a good team. A good team that was going to run the country a whole lot better than King Olav would, standing at the bow with Finn and his slimy advisor. Praising the White Christ for his benevolence, no doubt.

They were flying before the wind. The oars were up. It was time.

Jorn caught Runar's eye and nodded. The archer shifted to his left, nodded at Botolf and signalled to Skeggi. All three of them turned and nodded to him.

Jorn cleared his throat and shouted. 'Olav!'

The men sitting on the rowing benches shifted, their eyes on the king. Jorn could see some of them reach for weapons. The king didn't turn.

'Olav Tryggvason!'

Finn appeared to hear him, but he did not move. A couple of Skeggi's men were on their feet.

'*King Olav!*'

The man at the front of the ship turned slowly. He set his feet and looked at Jorn as if he'd never seen him before – as if he'd woken up and found a stranger in his bedchamber.

'Your mission is mindless! And now your reign ends! You are not fit to be a king!'

At this, King Olav smiled. 'And I suppose you are, Jorn, Prince of the Dales?' Even against the wind, the king's voice carried well.

'I am!' Jorn shouted. His voice broke, and it came out as a pathetic squeak. 'Skeggi! Botolf!'

Botolf's arm moved almost too fast to see. Blood burst out of Runar's throat and he went down, coughing, kicking and clutching a throwing knife. Jorn's stomach dropped, his jaw dropped and he only just felt the touch of the spear-tips as they nudged his ribcage, his spine, his stomach.

Glancing down, he saw the thuggish, grinning faces of Skeggi's men. Their spears were angled upwards. Spear-points tickled the backs of his knees. If he moved in any direction he'd be dead.

King Olav looked at him and smiled. Then he leaned over towards Finn, whispered something in his ear, turned around and took up his place at the stern.

'Wait!' Jorn shouted. 'Listen! I can— I was just testing them! This is a misunderstanding! It was all Botolf's plan!' A spear-point pressed uncomfortably hard in between his ribs.

The king did not move.

Finn and Valgard walked towards him. Behind them, daggers flashed as Botolf's men made sure Runar was dead before they threw him overboard. Jorn watched the corpse of his childhood friend disappear in an instant beneath the waves.

Valgard ducked under the boom and looked at him with something resembling pity. 'Your instinct was right,' he said. 'You should always keep your voice down. You never know who might happen to be walking past your house. I heard everything you said.'

'You . . . you . . .' Words escaped Jorn. All he could feel was the horrible plunging sensation in his stomach, behind his ribs. He wanted to throw himself on a spear but the urge to live burned him, screamed at him. With tears in his eyes, he looked at the healer. 'Please,' he whispered. 'Show mercy.'

He saw the creases form in the sallow skin before the laugh burst out of the skinny man's mouth. Valgard smiled the gentlest smile, nodded and tapped Finn on the elbow. The big man turned reluctantly and made his way forward. He shot Jorn one last hateful glance before he was obscured by the mast.

Skeggi looked up from polishing a set of long metal pins with sharp points. Some were smooth, others were barbed, yet others square. One of them had a hook. 'Right, *Prince*,' he said. 'I have no quarrel with you. Not really. Except for thinking I could be bought and that I was disloyal to the king, which is a bit . . . you know.' He turned to a small metal dish mounted on three legs, filled with coals, twigs and grass. He lit it casually with a fire-steel. 'Neither does my father with your father. But your grandfather . . . he once stole three pigs and blamed it on my grandfather. So I figure I am owed an excuse.'

'I'm sorry! I'm sorry! I beg your forgiveness!' Jorn blabbered.

'Oh no,' Skeggi said, placing the tips of the pins gently on the brazier. 'You're going to have to be a lot louder than that, Prince.'

Jorn's screams carried across the waves for quite some time.

NEAR BYGLAND, WEST NORWAY
OCTOBER, AD 996

'We come here for the king!'

Audun swallowed and blinked. They sounded far away, maybe two or three hundred yards. Hoof-beats echoed off the walls. The door was his only exit – straight into the face of whatever was out there. A cold fear gripped him. They knew. He'd said too much and they knew. They had found him somehow. They were here for him. Audun tried to move but his feet did not obey. He only just remembered to breathe.

'Well met, strangers,' Fjolnir shouted. 'I'm afraid I can't help you. The king isn't here.' He sounded like he was smirking.

'Funny,' the other voice said after a while, sounding closer. In the yard. 'Well met, old man. We come on behalf of King Olav.'

'And welcome you'll be,' the old man said. 'I am Fjolnir, and as you can see, mine is a humble home. What can I do for you?'

Dreamlike, Audun noticed the feeble autumn light leaking around the shutters covering the window, seeping in between wall boards, dancing around the dust motes. *Should fix that before winter*, he thought in a daze. Hooves on hard earth shook him out of it. Sharper now. Closer. Two horses? Four? The way the sound bounced off the buildings made it hard to determine. There were many of them, though. Too many. Audun's chest felt tight and his heart swelled. The horses were slowing down outside.

'You can give up whatever farmhands you have to the fight for the kingdom in the name of Our Saviour Jesus the White Christ,' the voice snapped.

A brief pause. 'I wish I could,' Fjolnir said. 'But as you see, the time of young men has long passed in this corner of Setr Valley, I'm afraid.' There was a note of regret in his voice.

Men dismounted outside. 'That's a shame,' the voice said. 'So you're the only one here.' It snapped out orders. 'Look in the barn, search the house as well,'

'Do you seek shelter?' There was a cold formality to Fjolnir's tone now. It was part question, part command, followed by a thump and a groan.

'Fuck your shelter, old man,' the voice snarled. 'See if there is anything of use here.' The sound of wood breaking; doors smashed in.

'Over here,' someone else shouted.

Movement outside the walls. Indistinct voices, shouting. Sounds of anger and violence washed over Audun and finally the memory caught hold of him, squeezed him until he almost couldn't breathe. Stenvik came back in rushes of sound, smell, sight; how he'd felt his body go cold, blacken from the fingertips, how he'd faded away until he was almost gone. How the centre of him had felt blue and cold and hard like a fist-sized diamond, and the words:

> *Strong, the living*
> *Drawn to struggle*
> *Weak men's champions*
> *Live in dying*

Ever losing
Soul and spirit
Changers, movers
Starkad's brothers.

He remembered being dragged back in agony from death, screaming into the disappearing blackness. Tears rolled down his face, caught in his stubble. His breath came in gasps. Snarling, he pummelled his thighs.

'Move!' he spat. 'You bastard! Move!'

'Tools!' someone shouted from the yard. 'Find some fucking tools!' The voice came closer. 'You fucking—' A thump and a groan. And another. 'Come on. Get up.' Pause. 'Pull him up.' Pause. 'You're lucky that the king says thou shalt not kill—' Thump. '—unless necessary. Fucking—' Thump. Thump. Cough. Spit. '—lucky.' The voice was out of breath. 'But it looks like you've spent some time making those, so you're going to watch.'

Something scraped along the earth. Sounds of logs thrown down.

They'd found the statues.

Audun stared at the door. It looked infinitely far away. The walls warped and twisted before his eyes, lengthening in all directions.

'Check the house.'

Time slowed down. Audun watched himself dive to the floor, squeeze his bulk under the bunk in the corner furthest from the door, reach and haul Fjolnir's travelling case in front of the bed just before there was a wall-shaking crash. Footsteps, then nothing. The case in front of him disappeared up and out of sight with the sound of a man straining; tough leather boots not five inches away from his nose. The smell of horse-sweat and wet earth washed over him.

'This better be good,' someone mumbled. The boots turned and the man walked away, over the smashed door, out into the dusky morning light. 'Look at this!' the man shouted.

Audun tried to move but he couldn't. His body no longer felt like his own.

'What's that?'

A crash as the box hit the ground.

'What's this, old man? Leave the belt. Arngrim, take that hammer. Looks all right. See if you can improve on the looks of those statues.'

The first stroke of metal on wood blended into the second and the third, until all he could hear was one sound of destruction and pain.

Words came later. Shouted words. More pain.

After the horses left, there was silence.

A long while later, the steps creaked.

'You can come out now,' Fjolnir said. 'They're—' He coughed. 'They're gone.'

The rough wooden floor scraped Audun's elbows as he inched from under the bunk, rose to his feet and looked at the man in the doorway.

Fjolnir's right eye was swollen shut and turning a dark shade of purple. His lips were cracked and pink, spit-mixed blood seeping from his gums. He stood in the doorway wheezing, bent at the hip, clutching something in his hand. Audun swallowed and started to speak, but fell silent as another series of coughs wracked the old man's body.

As Audun went to help, the old man shook his head without looking at him, raised his hand and straightened up as much as he could.

'I was going to give you a good hammer, blacksmith,' he said.

'They did not – do not – know what they're doing, and that will be the end of them.' His face was a grimace of pain, but the left eye was hard and cold. 'They did leave you this.' In his outstretched hand was a belt.

Burning with shame, Audun swallowed again. He tried to speak but the old man looked at him, almost kindly, and shook his head. 'Take it,' he said.

He touched the belt. It was wide – nearly two inches – and felt supple under his fingers. The leather was thick, but the buckle made him pause. It was woven with what looked to be strings of steel, and the clasp was made of two interlocked hands that were somehow both delicate and oversized. It was a piece of singular craftsmanship. Out of habit, Audun turned it around to look at the back; familiar runes were etched on the flat side. *Control* and *force*.

'What is this made of?' he asked.

'You wouldn't believe me if I told you,' Fjolnir said. A shadow of a grin ghosted into his one good eye. 'Put it on.' He motioned for him to put the belt on. The movement made him wince and clutch his ribs, but the old man still fixed him with a firm look. 'This belt will give you strength, Audun Arngrimsson. It will help you keep the flames at bay. I wish I could say otherwise, but the words she spoke will give you trouble wherever you go. The quicker you embrace it, the better. Stay alive and stay strong.'

The belt fitted perfectly. When the hands clasped with a soft *clink*, something unlocked inside him. A sudden plunging feeling took his breath away, and he felt . . . *alive*. In control. Something swelled in his chest, and for a moment he felt like he belonged up among the stars.

The old man looked intently at him. When he saw Audun's eyes open again, he grimaced. 'It fits you well enough. You need to go now, though.' Fjolnir shuffled to one of the beds, still talking. 'Those bastards are like to come back at any moment. If you stay here there'll be more trouble – it'll seek you out. Keep moving.' He rummaged under the bedding until he found what he was looking for. 'Here – take these as well,' he said, handing Audun a bundle of clothes. 'Your trousers smell like horse shit and your tunic has a hole in it.'

In a daze, Audun accepted. The old man shuffled back and almost pushed him out of the house. 'Now go, blacksmith,' he said. 'Go and find whatever you need to find. And remember – you know fire. You've run a forge. Go.'

'But . . . you're hurt,' Audun said.

'Yes, I am. But I'll heal,' Fjolnir said. 'I'll heal faster if you're not here to cause trouble and eat all my food,' he added with a grin. 'Swear you will go.'

'I swear. Thank you,' Audun muttered, but Fjolnir waved him off. He walked backwards over the smashed door and out of the house. Turning around, his breath caught.

The doors to the barn and both of the sheds had been broken. Six of the statues, half again the height of a man, had been dragged out into the yard and thoroughly destroyed. Audun bent down and picked up a piece. The detail in the carving showed a full-figured woman with flowing hair. Her fractured face looked back in sadness.

The scraping of wood on wood made him turn his head, just in time to see the remains of the door to the old grey house slot back into place.

A heavy loneliness settled on his shoulders like the yoke on an ox. Without a word, Audun got his bearings and walked towards the south.

When he had been gone for a good while, the door to the house toppled outwards and Fjolnir stepped into the yard, leaning on a sturdy walking staff. He put his thumb and forefinger in his mouth and whistled loudly. Two large dogs came bounding from the forest. The smaller one, a white mastiff, sat down at the old man's side. The larger, a grey wolfhound, stalked around him. Sniffing at his wounds, the beast growled.

'Shh, Frec. None of that. There is no need to chase. Where they're going there are plenty of wolves in the woods.' The old man smiled and straightened up, looking an inch or two taller and a decade younger. There was a military air about him now. 'No, they'll get what they deserve,' he said. 'Come on. We have work to do.'

He snapped his fingers and strode off into the forest, towards the east. The dogs fell in line behind him.

Alone on a long, winding road heading south along Setr Valley, Audun tried his best not to let his mind wander. The sky above him was clear and blue, with only the occasional wisp of a cloud spread across it. After putting on Fjolnir's old clothes he looked more like a migrant worker and less like a roving wild man, but he still dreaded meeting the next traveller. So he walked.

Left, right, left, right.

Why had he not been able to charge into the fray and save Fjolnir from the beating?

Left, right, left, right.

Had he . . . died on the wall?

Left, right, left.

What was that thing he could feel? The blackness in his chest?

Right, left.

His heart beat faster. Filled with an urge, a longing to move,

Audun started running, away from the farm, away from the shame, away from the questions in his mind.

The sun was past half-set and darkness crept across the fields in its wake. The shadows had lengthened around him as he ran, and he was already winded and sore when he saw the fire. It was still just a dot but it was clearly on his path. Breathing hard, Audun realised he could see white vapour coming from his nose and mouth.

It would not be a good night for sleeping rough.

His feet hurt from the running, as did his legs and back. He'd really given himself to it, enjoyed the raw feeling of cold air scraping his lungs, the soft ache in his legs. When he found his stride he'd decided that he was not allowed to stop; then he had started counting things as he went, anything to keep from thinking about everything. Slowing down now, Audun tried to gather his swirling, scattered thoughts. He waited for them to sweep him away, but they didn't. Instead they were just . . . there, like a fire in a forge: a fire that could be stoked and controlled. Without thinking, his fingers brushed the girdle of his belt. It felt slightly warm to the touch. He pushed the thoughts away and tried to remember how to speak to people.

It was almost dusk when he neared the camp. There was a handful of travellers, men and women. He took this for a good sign and approached, making sure to show himself.

'Well met!' he shouted. His voice felt rusty.

Two of the men rose from the crackling fire and peered out into the darkness. 'Well met, stranger,' the shorter one said.

'I seek shelter and a bit of warmth from your fire,' Audun said. 'It's getting cold out there,' he added lamely.

'Step closer and give us a look at you,' the shorter one said.

Moving into the outer circle of flickering firelight, he showed his empty palms to the two men.

A brief glance passed between them, and then the shorter one nodded. 'Enjoy our fire, stranger. Do you have a name?'

'Audun . . . Fjolnisson,'

'Well met, Audun, son of Fjolnir. I am Breki and this is my brother, Bjorn.'

'Well met, brothers,' Audun said. He could feel the soft touch of the fire on his skin as he came closer.

'Bjorn will sit the first watch. You'll sit with him and make sure the fire does not go out.'

Audun nodded. Twelve men and women sat around the fire; some acknowledged him with a look, others muttered a greeting, yet others did not seem to care. At the far edge of the light he could see four horses grazing and behind them he could just make out the shape of two carts.

'Where are you headed?' he asked Bjorn, who turned out to be younger than Audun had thought.

The tall man stroked his chin, plucking at his poor excuse for a beard. 'South, I reckon. You?'

'Same.'

The camp lapsed into silence. Breki, older than Bjorn by a good ten years, looked at Audun, then handed him a bite of meat. Audun accepted, wincing in the dark. It felt like a while since he'd last paid his way in the world.

Slowly but surely, the other campers fell asleep. Bjorn caught Audun's eye and conveyed with hand gestures that he'd be doing the rounds. His lanky frame became almost invisible once he'd moved from his place near the fire. Audun's thoughts went unbidden to the start of the journey. Where would Ulfar be now? Doing better than him, that was pretty certain. He wondered whether he'd see the mouthy Swede again. A soft whinny brought him back to the fireside. Bjorn's outline was just visible as a black form against the dark purple sky and its dusting of white dots. The young man was stroking one of the horses and murmuring in its ear.

Audun moved his legs and winced. They'd need stretching. As he rose, the horse's head snapped to attention. It snorted and took two steps backwards.

A sharp, toothy howl cut across the night sky. The horses snorted and stamped. Swearing, Bjorn grabbed the reins of three but the fourth reared and neighed loudly and took off – but Audun was there in a couple of steps. He grabbed the rough reins and held tight, but the wide-eyed horse was terrified. It reared, bucked and pulled back – and nothing happened. It was hard to tell who was more surprised, Audun or the horse. He'd braced himself for a struggle to subdue the beast like he'd seen tamers do several times, wearing out panic-stricken horses by hanging on to the reins as if their lives depended on it. This time the tugging of the strong draft horse was no stronger than that of a kitten. Underneath his tunic, Audun could feel the heat emanating from his belt buckle. The horse reared again, but with less conviction. After a couple more tries it gave up and resigned itself to its fate. Meanwhile, Bjorn had steadied the others and was muttering to them gently to calm them, flitting between them like a shadow.

Audun led his runaway over to Bjorn. 'Sounded like a wolf, that did,' he muttered to Bjorn.

'Yeah, though 'tis a bit far south if you ask me,' he replied.

'They have to eat, too, I suppose. Maybe the winter is lean up north.'

'Well,' Bjorn said, 'we'll see if they can chase us across the strait.'

Overhead a thin green line curved across the sky and grew into a river of light flowing silently across the vast black expanse.

Audun and Bjorn stayed with the horses, waiting for a second howl that never came. Whatever it had been was gone, hunting elsewhere.

The road under their feet changed from well-travelled highway to trodden path and back as it snaked across fields and over hills. Audun walked at the rear of their modest caravan, beside one of the carts. In front of him, Bjorn shuffled alongside the other cart with the economy of a born traveller. Occasionally they passed under the wooden kings of autumn with their golden crowns and torches frozen in mid-flame. Mostly, though, they walked,face forward, one foot in front of the other, existing in a constant state of slow movement. Bjorn and Breki proved pleasant enough but the rest of the party kept communication down to grunts and nods. From the glances they shot him, Audun could tell that the decision to invite him along might not have been approved by everyone.

He couldn't care less.

After the first night, he woke up feeling ill, but he'd ignored it and volunteered to look after the horses. In the past he'd taken the animals for granted; they were just there, they served a purpose and someone else made sure they didn't die. He'd shoed a few, but never gone out of his way after that kind of trade.

Now they were his best bet for silent company.

It was also quite reassuring to watch someone who knew what he was doing, and Audun found himself trailing Bjorn, observing him work around the animals. During the first couple of days, he had started learning the order in which to groom them, when to brush or dust them down, how hard to apply the comb, how to pitch his voice when they were skittish. It was something to do, and it kept him from thinking too much.

The cart ahead of him slowed. 'Look there,' Bjorn said.

'What?' Audun said.

'The Otra.'

Audun pulled gently on the reins and the horses stopped. He walked past them and to Bjorn's side. 'What do you—? Oh.'

They stood on a small rise. Below them, the road wound down to a ferryman's shack next to a small pier. The river itself was at least sixty yards wide. The other bank was a good six feet above water level, with a forbidding wall of pine trees all the way to the edge of the water.

Audun whistled softly.

'Yep,' Bjorn replied. 'Can you swim?'

'I suppose,' Audun said. 'Didn't know I'd need to.'

'You might not, but it means I can stand you next to the edge, if need be.'

'The edge of what?'

A big, ungainly raft bobbled into view around the river bend, apparently floating upstream. Four bargemen stood on it, one in each corner, poling the craft towards the pier.

'The edge of that,' Bjorn replied. 'That's our passage down to the Sands. You're going to learn a lot more about tending horses real fast, Fjolnisson,' the tall man added. Audun wasn't sure, but it almost looked like he was amused.

'I'm never, ever going on one of these again,' Audun muttered.

'What's the matter, big man?' Breki said, slapping him on the back and grinning. Audun scowled but he did not notice. Bjorn's older brother did not appear to worry overly about other people. 'No stomach for the waves?'

'You can say that,' Audun replied, wiping his mouth with the back of his hand. 'Too much movement.' The river churned beneath them.

'That's what your mother told me!' Breki said. He laughed heartily at his own joke. Audun saw another couple of smirking faces. 'Whoa!'

The barge heaved under them. It was only just big enough to fit the two carts side by side. The rest of the party had squeezed in behind them at the back. The bargeman and his three flat-faced, thick-necked cousins had posted themselves one on each corner and were barking orders to each other in some kind of strange river language; only the occasional word was intelligible. Audun glanced at the one closest to him. The man stood braced against the two raised edges with his white-knuckled hands around a big, thick bargepole. The four men guided the vessel downstream with a carefully choreographed series of pushes – Audun suspected they knew the precise location of every sandbank and mud hole in the whole river.

'How much longer?' he shouted to Bjorn.

'We'll be there before nightfall,' the tall man called over the backs of the horses.

'Left!' the thick-neck next to him shouted, his eyes suddenly going wide. 'Rocks! *Left!*'

Apparently they didn't.

Time turned into dripping candle wax as the barge began to rotate, slowly at first, under the power of its own momentum. Panicked shouts from the other corners blended into the growing roar of the river. The bargeman next to Audun strained against his pole, tugged and shoved, but something had caught it at the bottom and it didn't budge. The veins on the man's wrists bulged and Audun watched him roar as he pulled for all he was worth, but it was all for nothing – he was slowly being lifted up into the air as the barge shifted under him.

As if in a dream, Audun reached for the pole.

His hands closed on the rough wood.

He pulled.

Every thread of every muscle in his body leapt to life and filled him to brimming with power, so much power, so much strength. He could feel the life in the wood, the pummelling force of the water, he could feel where the point was jammed between the rocks. Heat spread from his steel-woven belt buckle.

The wood creaked in his hands.

Something heavy shifted at the bottom of the river and the pole came loose.

The bargeman stumbled back down to the deck, found his feet and shouted a quick series of commands to the other corners.

A wave of nausea washed over Audun. Cramps stabbed his gut and he vomited over the edge, spitting bile.

'Oho! We'll have a ways to go with him yet before he's a proper traveller!' Breki shouted. 'Come on, Audun! It's just like being with a woman! Or in your case – good training for the first time!' The panic on the barge dissolved into laughter.

'Don't be an idiot, Breki,' Bjorn said. 'Audun – are you ill?'

With supreme effort, Audun straightened up. 'I'm fine,' he said between gritted teeth. 'Just don't like this river much.' His insides felt as if they were being squeezed out through his throat and a hot ache coursed along his spine, setting his teeth on edge. The buckle was hot against his skin.

'It gets better,' Bjorn said. 'We're nearly around the worst of it.'

'I hope so,' Audun said. The packhorse leaned over, nudged his chest with its head and snorted gently. He reached out and patted the animal's neck. 'Easy,' he mumbled. 'Easy.' The horse repeated the gesture, and as the raft glided onwards, Audun wasn't sure who was comforting whom.

THE SANDS, SOUTH NORWAY
LATE OCTOBER, AD 996

The Sands were not a patch on Stenvik, Audun thought.

After the rapids, the river had slunk through a forest, under intimidating cliffs and at last opened up into a narrow mouth that eventually became a bay. The light was fading as they arrived and torches flared on poles above a smattering of large houses, but there was no longhouse to be seen and no town walls.

Behind that was the sea. After the trees and the cliffs, the immensity of the sky and the width of the horizon briefly took his breath away. The deep hiss of waves had crept into the background; it was always present, like a pulse.

When they got closer, he spotted a low pier. A short, fat man stood there waiting for them, hands on hips. 'Well met!' he shouted.

The leader of the bargemen exchanged quick words with Breki, who was not very happy when he turned away. 'Well met!' he called back. 'Coming in for the night. Seeking shelter.'

'You and everyone else, friend,' the fat man replied cheerfully as the bargemen steered them towards him. As the vessel docked, the fat man shifted so that he was sure to be awkwardly in the way. 'And it does appear that folk out there have discovered that it's mighty hard to shelter behind a coin.'

Audun saw Bjorn reach out and lay a hand on his brother's forearm. The words died on Breki's tongue and were replaced with a forced smile. 'Wise words from a good man. Wise words. So what say you we trade? A couple of our coins for a little of your shelter?'

The fat man smiled and stepped out of the way. An elbow from Bjorn jostled Audun back into action, and he whispered soothing words to his horses as the first cart rumbled ashore.

It happened on the third night.

They'd set down at the Sands, camped by their wagons and spent two days eating, drinking and dicing with the locals. Audun had earned a couple of silvers mending carts, but there was nowhere near enough trade for him to set up shop, even if he'd wanted to. He looked west, towards the retreating sun, and envied it. At least the sun got to leave this dump once a day.

Breki, Bjorn and a couple of their travelling companions had started a fire. A handful of locals drifted along; Audun just sat and listened. There was campfire chatter about King Olav – apparently trouble was brewing. Someone said he'd sailed north with six thousand men; someone else said that'd be suicide this late in autumn. Some of the Sands men had met a caravan further up the valley that was headed for Stenvik with supplies and men, both of which were apparently in short supply. The consensus was that the king was probably mad as a hovel of foxes, but none of the present company volunteered to go and tell him.

Near midnight, a bull-necked sailor turned to Breki, who was in the middle of a story about a milkmaid and three farmhands that was not headed anywhere nice. 'Oi, big mouth. Why are you still here?' he asked. Audun took one look at the man and felt a familiar tingle at the back of his neck.

'Waiting on a ship,' Breki said.

'You'll be waiting a while, then,' said the sailor. 'The strait is chock full of sea-wolves. We've had one in the last four due come in, and them badly wounded. Looks like you're going to be stuck here losing your money at dice,' he crowed and showed a gap-toothed grin.

'And why the fuck would anyone want to sit outside or inside a shithole like this?' Breki snapped.

And that was that.

The sailor shoved Breki hard and dived after him as he hit the ground. Two of his friends jumped up and ran across the fire to help. A moment slow to realise what was going on, Bjorn was almost up on his feet when Audun pulled him down and shook his head. 'If you go in there they'll smack you as well,' he said.

The fury in Bjorn's eyes was worse than a slap. 'He's my brother,' the tall man hissed. With that he was up and gone, wading into the darkness and the pile of bodies.

Blinded by the sparks, it took Audun a couple of breaths to come to his senses.

'Fenrir take your bones,' he snarled. 'All of you.' He rose and strode into the fray.

Bjorn did not speak to him for two days. Breki's jaw was bruised and both his eyes were swollen; he still managed to glare. The townsfolk gave them all a wide berth.

Audun sighed. He really didn't have a knack with people.

He'd tended the horses; there was nothing else to do. He couldn't walk any further south without getting wet fast. The ocean seemed to surround him, fill out his field of vision, mock him with its serene infinity. All straight lines . . .

And one sail.

A ship was heading for the Sands.

Without thinking, Audun hurried towards the makeshift harbour. When he approached, he saw that others had indeed noticed. A group of hard sailors had taken up positions to meet the newcomers. Some held clubs, some leaned on spears, some wore swords or axes in their belts.

It felt as if the ship was taking for ever to get there. Around Audun, hands tightened on weapon grips.

The fat man who had met them at the pier elbowed his way to the front. 'Who goes there?' he bellowed.

'Oh, shut up, Ivar,' someone shouted from the stern. 'And tell your boys to calm down.'

Ivar turned around with a big smile on his face. 'It's all fine. It's Hrutur.'

A ripple of relief spread through the assembled men. Loud, nervous chatter replaced muttered curses and some of them called out well-meaning insults to the approaching captain. Shouted commands guided the ship into the dock. She was a stout knarr with five cross-benches for rowers. Audun noted that not all of them were manned.

'Come on, you old bastard!' Ivar shouted. The captain barked a string of orders and the ship docked smoothly. A wiry man leapt ashore and embraced the fat chieftain, who punched his arm.

'Welcome back, brother.'

'Thank you,' the leathery-skinned captain replied. 'Can't stop, though. It's worse out there every day and we'll need all we can get. Men, supplies, anything.'

'Right,' Ivar said. 'You!' he snapped, pointing at Audun. 'Get your big-mouth friend down here – right now if he wants to do any trade.'

When Audun brought Breki and the carts, the men on the docks were nearly done unloading the ship. Piles of furs, sacks of flour and barrels of fish stood on the harbour. Townsmen were ferrying barrels, boxes and sacks towards the harbour – wood-carvings, amber jewellery, bars of marsh iron. Ivar and Hrutur stood to the side, locked in heated discussion.

'That the captain?' Breki said.

Audun nodded.

Breki strode towards Hrutur. The swelling was down, but the short man's face was all the more colourful for it. 'Well met, Captain,' he said.

'Well met. Is this Breki?' he asked Ivar, who nodded. 'My brother says you have trade.'

'Amber, cloth, wool and furs.'

'On the carts?'

'Yes.'

'Sounds good. How much?'

'Fifty silvers for the lot.'

'Hm. Forty.'

'Done. And I'll need passage for six people.'

Hrutur's laugh was short and sharp. 'I'm not a ferryman. Can't help you.'

What was still white in Breki's face turned beetroot red. 'But – but—'

'I need the speed and the Danes don't want more people. Still forty?'

Suddenly Breki looked completely deflated. 'Forty-five,' he muttered.

'Done.' The sea captain spat in his hand and extended it. Breki reached out, squeezed it and walked off without a second look at Audun.

'Poor man,' Ivar said.

'Seen worse,' Hrutur said. 'Don't need passengers. I just need a couple of oarsmen.'

Audun cleared his throat.

The ship had been filled with supplies, the men rested and fed. Audun had found his place on the empty rowing berth and got to grips with his oar.

'Off you go and may Njordur's blessing see you safely across,' Ivar intoned.

'And may Freyr keep you out of too many wives' beds while I'm gone,' the captain shouted back.

A small crowd had gathered to wave them off. The caravan brothers were nowhere to be seen.

Audun sighed and tried to quell the rising anxiety in his stomach. But if King Olav was on his trail, at least he'd make the bastard chase him across the sea.

'A lot of them out today,' a burly sailor behind him said.

'We're the first in two weeks,' another said.

'Two weeks?'

'Hel's tits.'

'Yes, boys, and don't you forget who you have to thank for that,' Hrutur snarled. 'Don't think too hard about it, otherwise you'll shit yourselves. Just get going!'

Audun leaned into the oar and pulled, flexing his muscle against the endless sea. The man behind him grunted once, appreciatively. He settled into the rhythm and the knarr started its slow crawl towards the horizon.

A while later, Hrutur shouted for oars up and sails down. The crew stirred into action without a single wasted movement. They were well clear of the Sands, now just a thick, black line on the horizon behind them. Audun tried his best to stay out of the way when they didn't need extra hands to pull against the wind.

The boat rocked and sped across the gently tipped waves. The sea air filled his nose and lungs, teased salt water out of his eyes and cleared his head. The sickness from the barge was gone – as were the encroaching cliffs and forbidding wall of pines. *This is life*, he thought. This was freedom.

He permitted himself a smile.

'*Sail! Oars!* You're going to row, you fuckers, unless you want to be skinned!' Hrutur screamed as he yanked at the rudder.

The sailors scrambled to their benches and grabbed oars.

Audun stole a backwards look. Two longships were approaching at terrifying speed.

VALLE, WEST NORWAY
LATE OCTOBER, AD 996

The world re-formed around Ulfar's head. The breeze that woke him was chilly and crisp, but it didn't bite, not yet. He propped himself up on one elbow and looked around. There was no sign of Gestumblindi, nor Geraz or the phantom Frec, but the sun was shining and last night's clouds had departed. The fire-pit was almost invisible; all that remained was the hint of a burned circle in the grass.

He knelt by it, ran his hands over the green blades, felt the lines the points traced on his palm. He was . . . lighter, somehow. His body felt better than it had in weeks.

But the taste of ash still lingered in his mouth.

Sunlight caught on silver. A small flask lay in the grass a couple of steps over. Ulfar bent down to examine it and caught his breath. It was small, delicate and exquisitely crafted – the side had a scene of some sort etched into it, depicting two men by a well. Slowly a handful of last night's events came back in a confusion of images. He picked it up and shook it gently. Something sloshed around inside. He touched the stopper, then reconsidered and tucked it in the small bag hanging off his belt.

Without a word, he rose and walked towards the rising sun.

TELEMARK,
EARLY NOVEMBER, AD 996

Fields gave way to forests, forests to fields, fields to hills, and still Ulfar walked. His pace was relaxed; through some means he couldn't quite fathom he knew exactly where he was going. It was something to do with the stars. The world's travellers must have been heading somewhere else that morning because he had the pleasure of solitude on the road for the best part of the day. The touch of autumn was heavier now; behind and below him, blushing red trees, golden branches and multicoloured leaves turned the slates of forest green into a picture of vibrant death. The fields were pregnant with wheat, barley and corn, waiting for the harvester who never came.

Not for the first time, Ulfar wondered whether King Olav realised the damage he'd wrought on the nation he was seeking to unite.

The path levelled out under his feet and started sloping downwards again. On this side of the hill the forest was thicker; pines stood shoulder to shoulder, creating a green-brown roof over their thick trunks and obscuring his view of the valley below. Ulfar tried to picture himself as an eagle, soaring above the treetops, drifting up towards . . . *something*, but in his mind the gentle curves of green below turned into sea, and then he was on that boat again facing the woman in white, living the nightmare.

Raised voices up ahead broke the spell and pulled his mind back to earth. They were coming from somewhere down the hill, around a bend, and were clearly in some disagreement. As he drew closer, the strings of noise broke apart into words.

'. . . and if you hadn't tied the straps like an old woman—'

'An old woman? You're one to talk! If you hadn't filled the bag—'

'You told me to fill the bag! You *told* me!'

The voices grew louder with every step Ulfar took.

'You are an idiot! Mother always said so! She said you were an idiot and that you'd fallen on your head when you were little and that I should never trust you with anything!'

'No! She loved me best! You are a horse-faced bear-arse and I hate you!'

'You shut up, you disease-ridden scumbag milkmaid-botherer! I hate you more! Your father was a useless wimp! You always mess up everything I do! If only Erik was here! I'm so tired of you I could—'

The first thing Ulfar saw as he rounded the bend was a sack of turnips lying on the road. It had opened and spilled some of its bounty on the ground.

The next thing was a horse standing by the side of the road, stoically munching on whatever it could find.

And lastly, two men well past their prime who stood in the middle of the road and stared at him with open mouths. They were both clad in ill-fitting clothes; one had a shock of greying red hair that pointed in all directions at once, the other tufts of blond that made him look like a badly sheared sheep.

'Efh . . .' one of them stammered.

And just like that, Ulfar saw what needed to happen. He smiled, walked over to the sack of turnips, gathered up the few strays and put them back inside, retied the sack and hefted it up onto the horse, which protested only nominally.

'Fhn . . .' the other muttered.

'Well met, strangers,' Ulfar said, and the spell was broken.

'Well met!' the blond one replied, far too loudly.

'Yes! Well met!' Red-hair added, louder than the first. 'I am Gisli, and this is my sworn brother—'

'I am Helgi!' the blond man shouted. 'We're cousins!'

'Half-brothers, you moron,' Gisli snapped.

'Really?' Ulfar said. 'I would never have guessed.'

The men laughed loudly. 'No one does. We're nothing alike,' Helgi said. Gisli looked on the verge of saying something but bit his tongue. 'Where are you going?' Helgi continued. 'We're headed south when we come down off this hill.'

'That's lucky – so am I,' Ulfar said.

'Would you like to join us?' Gisli said.

'So that's *your* offer to make now?' Helgi said.

Gisli puffed himself up. 'And why shouldn't it be?'

'I'm older!'

'Oh, don't start that again. We both know Mother loved me best. I'd bet you're a changeling! The trolls brought you! I—'

Ulfar cleared his throat loudly. 'Helgi: would you be happy for me to join you on the road?'

'Of course,' Helgi snapped. 'Anything else would be rude. Just like you,' he said as he turned towards his half-brother, voice rising. 'You're a fool and a lackwit and I can't believe that we share the same mother. I think if I left you to your own—'

'Where is he going with the horse? This is all your fault!' Gisli shook his head frantically, sending his wild red hair flying. They set off after Ulfar, who had taken the reins of the horse and started walking down the road.

'Wait! Wait!' Helgi puffed. 'We're coming!'

At the head of the strange procession, Ulfar sighed.

'Camp! We need to camp!' Helgi said.

'What would you know about camps?' Gisli snapped. 'Last time I let you choose, a bear nearly ate us!'

'That – was – a – *moose*! You saw the tracks the next morning!'

'Well, it was big,' Gisli muttered. 'And moose are dangerous.'

'Only if you're an idiot,' Helgi shot back. 'So in your case that's true. Sorry I nearly got you killed.' Gisli harrumphed and Helgi replied with a smirk. 'Ulfar – any opinions now that we're off the mountain?'

Ulfar pointed towards a glade only just visible in the twilight.

'Very good choice,' said Helgi. 'It is refreshing to travel with someone who knows things for a change.'

Gisli sulked in the background.

Ulfar led the horse to the glade where they staked out their camp. Gisli went to start a fire; Helgi followed and criticised everything he did. Their bickering had long since stopped meaning anything to Ulfar – it was closer to the sound of the sea than any kind of conversation.

Eventually, though, even the brothers settled down and as night fell they bid each other goodnight.

Ulfar, knowing what awaited him, slept very little.

Around midday, Ulfar finally relaxed. It had been a while – a long while – since he'd been on horseback and he was thankful the animal was so placid. He'd woken up, eased past the brothers' sleeping forms and led the horse to the road. They'd been off the hill by mid-morning and far away from Gisli and Helgi by noon. The land was flat and tree cover scarce, but still, he knew where he was going. He patted the horse's neck and mumbled, 'Good boy.' A mild protesting whinny was all he got back, but it shuffled onwards. He found he did not care one way or the other about stealing the horse. They'd manage the bag of turnips between them, and now they'd have something new to argue about.

Something rustled in the bushes off to his left and a bird cried out. The horse snorted once, shook its head and kept walking.

Maybe that was just what he needed to do in life, he mused. Shrug and move on. Whatever was in that bush was being hurt quite badly, though. The cries were getting louder and more piercing. The horse quickened its step, eager to be away from the tortured sounds. A sudden wave of irritation washed over Ulfar. 'Die already!' he shouted and leapt out of the saddle. The horse shot him a reproachful look, trundled to a halt and promptly turned its attention to the roadside grass as Ulfar drew his sword and waded into the underbrush, unleashing a string of profanities. Branches scraped his face but he didn't care. He just had to make that noise stop. The squawking grew louder until something clamped down on its victim's throat.

Ulfar arrived just in time to see a sizeable fox scamper away with a pheasant in his jaws.

Blood rushed to his head and his knee buckled. Struggling to remain upright, he staggered over to the nearest tree. Bile rose in his throat and his heart thumped in his chest.

He looked at the trees. Then he looked at his own drawn blade, raised the point up at the nearest trunk and shouted, 'Defend yourself! I am Ulfar the Pheasant-Saver!'

His legs gave way and tears streamed from his eyes as he sat alone on the leafy forest floor, laughing until his stomach ached.

The smell of the sea reached him long before they saw the blue scar on the horizon; warm salt in the sun, wet weeds on rocks. Up ahead seagulls circled, complaining to each other. Ulfar urged the horse into a reluctant trot. 'Come on, boy,' he whispered. 'Help me home.'

When they cleared the treeline, he counted the houses. It didn't take very long. There were twenty of them, some sizeable. Thin wisps of smoke drifted up from roofs to be caught by the brisk sea wind. 'That will do,' Ulfar muttered. 'That will have to do.'

As he rode in, a dog came running at them at full tilt, baying and snarling. Ulfar redoubled his grip on the reins but the horse had seen enough country dogs and kicked out once, close enough to the animal's snout to send it scampering away. Ulfar stroked and scratched the scraggly mane; it dipped its head once, snorted and ambled along.

He could feel eyes on him: watchers in darkened doorways and shadowed corners, but he was beyond caring. Let them watch. Let them watch the newcomer, calculate how much they could take him for. Let them fucking try. He had to concede, though, that by the look of him that probably wasn't so much any more. His clothes were thoroughly travel-worn by now and he didn't have a silver piece to his name. All he had was the sword . . . Ulfar thought of Audun and wondered what the mad blacksmith might be doing. Probably not riding into a strange town on a stolen horse.

He bit down hard to suppress the laughter and rode on.

The harbour smelled of fish guts and cold air. A large man sat on a rock in the fading light, hunched over whatever he was doing with his hands. Ulfar dismounted and walked towards him.

'Evening,' he said.

'Evening yourself,' the man said. He was weathered, somewhere between thirty-five and fifty summers, tatty beard with streaks of white and a downturned mouth. In his hands he had a line with small hooks attached which he was twisting, turning and coiling down into a basket.

'Good catch today?'

'Same as always.' The man spat and looked at Ulfar for the first time. 'Who are you?'

'My name is Geiri,' Ulfar said, the lie only just catching on his tongue. 'I'm looking to get across to the Svear.'

'Well, Geiri,' the fisherman said and spat over his shoulder, 'a trader sails tomorrow morning. Might know him. What are you paying?'

Ulfar flashed a condescending smile and waved the question away. 'Do not let my garb fool you. I am a man of means.'

'As long as you're not a man who means to pay but never does,' the fisherman said.

'Well, we're in trouble if a man's word means nothing.'

'Have you looked around lately, man of means?' The fisherman struggled to his feet and limped towards him. 'We are in a whole lot of trouble. Trouble all over. I'll talk to Hedin for you.'

'Thank you,' Ulfar said. 'Thank you very much.'

The fisherman shrugged. 'Can't promise. We'll see what goes.' With that, he limped away.

Ulfar watched him leave, and then he was all alone on the pier. Alone and useless.

What was he good for, anyway? Wenching, gaming and killing. The occasional joke. A deep pressure built inside him and he felt like he would burst. He tried to swallow, but nothing happened. Panic flared, but as soon as it had come it was gone again.

Ulfar had to strain to unlock his jaws and open his mouth. Looking around, his eye came to rest on the bucket. The fisherman's line was tangled up. He thought back on the old men he'd seen threading hooks in Uppsala: they'd been proper, *useful* men. He sat down on the stone and reached for the line.

'Ow! Bastard,' he exclaimed as a hook buried itself in his index finger.

'Get away from my line,' the fisherman snapped from across the pier. 'Took me long enough to sort it.' A portly man waddled up behind him as Ulfar struggled to nudge the hook out of his finger. As it came free, the cold air nipped at the blood. 'This is Hedin,' the fisherman said curtly. The two of them made their way slowly towards Ulfar, the old horse and the fisherman's seat.

'Well met, Hedin,' Ulfar said as he rose, finger and cheeks throbbing.

Hedin fixed him with dull, sunken eyes. 'What do you want?'

'Passage,' Ulfar said.

'You can't afford it,' Hedin snapped as he looked him over with a practised eye.

Ulfar offered his most winsome smile. This was a game he knew. 'Not only can I afford it, but my father, Alfgeir Bjorne, would probably be very grateful to anyone who ferried me across.' Behind him, the sailor lowered himself back down onto his rock and muttered a curse, but Hedin's expression changed immediately as the merchant put on what Ulfar assumed must be his charming face. The effect was not pleasant.

'Of course. And we'll settle the fare—'

'When I am across. My father didn't raise a fool.'

'Of course. Of course.' Hedin wrung his hands and squeezed out a sickly smile, and Ulfar's insides lurched. For a moment he was swimming in sludge, sitting outside himself and watching as he stepped in, grabbed the merchant by the hair, kicked his legs from under him, smashed the man's nose on the pier and hammered his head down onto the planks again and again until he stopped screaming, stopped moving, kept bleeding silently. The sensation was so powerful that he had to swallow the vomit rising from the centre of him. It felt like something was scraping his insides – something hard and cold.

'—but we can see to that. Maybe a rug or something to keep

you warm. Not free, of course. Nothing is, these days. And when would you like to leave?'

Ulfar blinked. 'What?'

'When would you like to leave?' Hedin gazed up at him, greed and grease lining his features.

'Early tomorrow morning,' he stammered.

'Of course. Very good. We will meet here,' Hedin said. 'That's my knarr over there,' he added, and pointed to a well-worn trading bucket. Memories of cold, wet journeys washed over Ulfar and he forced a smile.

'Tomorrow morning. Farewell, Hedin.'

'Of course. Yes.' Hedin saluted and left.

A couple of moments passed.

'Want me to look after the royal mount?' the fisherman said. Ulfar turned to stare at him, but the weathered face remained studiously neutral. 'For when you come back this way?'

'Yes . . . Yes, do that. He's good for decent work,' Ulfar said.

The fisherman's attention was back on his line. 'Tie him up by the shed; I'll feed him tomorrow morning.'

The road caught up to him. Without a word, Ulfar tethered the horse, patted him down and wandered off in search of somewhere to sleep.

WEST COAST OF SWEDEN
LATE OCTOBER, AD 996

'So where is my silver?' Hedin snapped. They'd beached easily enough after an uneventful day's sailing and Ulfar's heart jumped at the subtle things – the trees were thicker and shorter, the soil richer. They were definitely in Svealand. Home, but he still had a long way to go. The sun was halfway across the sky but the chill in the air spoke of a hard winter to come. 'You said you had the means, and what about your father's reach?'

This was his land, and now, his rules. 'Ah, but you see—' Ulfar smiled. 'My father, I am afraid, may not be as fatherly as he once was. He might not actually be my father, come to think of it. And my fortune is all on the side we sailed from.' The merchant's face turned scarlet and he sputtered, struggling to choose the right curse-words. 'The horse I left with the fisherman should be payment enough.'

'Th-that old nag is not worth even a day's rations!'

'That's no way to speak of your wife, brother Hedin,' Ulfar admonished as he leapt over the side of the boat and set down on the beach. The fat merchant appeared to consider going after him, but Ulfar put his hand on the hilt of his sword and shook his head just a fraction.

Hedin deflated. 'You're a shit,' he spat.

Ulfar just shrugged, turned his back on the merchant and walked inland, followed by fading curses.

The sun set and somewhere up above, the stars told him where to go.

Soon Hedin's angry face was nothing but a memory. He found what could charitably be called a road or track of some sort that appeared to go in the right direction, so he followed it. His stomach rumbled but he paid it no heed; when it started cramping, he chewed on leaves. A brook on the way provided fresh water. Ulfar let his feet lead him and tried not to think about anything.

Some time later, when he saw the lights on the road ahead, he thought long and hard about whether he should avoid people altogether, considering how it had gone so far. Eventually, however, his rumbling stomach settled the matter. He drew a deep breath and walked towards the settlement.

EKARSTAD, WEST SWEDEN

LATE OCTOBER, AD 996

Make them like you. The thought echoed in Ulfar's head along with the coarse laughter, bad singing and assorted other noises of the hall. *Make the bastards like you. Lead the lamb to the slaughter.* Something lurched inside but he pushed it down, held it together and didn't let it out. Instead he focused his efforts on looking like his opponent had stunned him with his last move.

It worked, too. Out of the corner of his eye he saw the trader's friends winking at him. One went so far as to pat the stocky man on the back. Playing along, Ulfar tutted, frowned and shook his head. 'Serves me right,' he mumbled. 'I should never have offered you double or nothing. I knew I was lucky in the first game.'

The man, a root-faced Swede from the north, nodded and grinned, revealing rotting teeth. 'Maybe you did get lucky,' he said. 'Or maybe I was just stringing you along.'

It was all Ulfar could do to keep the smirk off his face. *If that's the truth, you're twice as smart as you're ugly*, he thought. Discarding the easy win, he picked the second-best move. Root-face was still on his way to a slow and painful death on the board, but it would not be as obvious. Ulfar sighed as he pushed his piece away from the other man's king. 'I guess this is the best I can do,' he added.

With barely a moment's thought, his opponent walked into the trap, smiling while he did so. 'That should teach you soft southerners never to play a Northland man in games of smarts,' he crowed.

Ulfar nodded apologetically. The next couple of moves were

obvious, but they needed to be played right. He'd purposefully taken small sips of his mead to keep a clear head.

'I know, I know,' he said. 'The men of Uppsala always brag about how they're smarter than the thick moose-fuckers from up north, but we all know that's just bluster.'

Root-face hawked and spat on the floor. 'Only too right, whelp,' he snarled as he pushed his king exactly where Ulfar wanted it. 'We see you when we come south with furs, smirking at us when you think we're not looking.'

'Oh, but I never did,' Ulfar protested meekly as he made his move. 'I was always afraid of Northlanders, to be honest. They all looked like they could wrestle a bear.'

'You mean Northlander women,' an onlooker quipped to roars of laughter. Even Root-face seemed happy about this, and moved quickly. Mugs of mead clinked around him. 'Now come on, boy. Give up and hand over the silver.'

Careful, Ulfar thought. *Scratch the animal behind the ears before the knife comes out.* 'Is it okay if we play a couple more moves . . . ?' he ventured cautiously. 'I want to learn as much as I can.'

The Northlander rolled his eyes. 'I don't know what I can teach you, Southerner. You're only' – Ulfar made his move – 'putting off the' – Root-face's voice trailed off, and the last word was just a whisper – 'inevitable . . .'

A silence settled around the table as the onlookers comprehended the Northlander's predicament. Ulfar's pitifully retreating forces had simply been stepping back to plug all possible escape routes for Root-face's king. The game was all but over. 'You—'

'Oh! Oh, that's lucky! Loki is smiling on me today. I was absolutely sure I was good and beaten.' Ulfar stifled any hint of smug grin and the urge to reach for the silver. Instead he strained to appear surprised.

Root-face stared at him with murder in his eyes. 'You . . . You cheated!' He slammed his grubby hand over the silver on the table.

Ulfar saw his food and drink money disappear, felt the cold, biting touch of hungry sleep outdoors and within him something snapped. The edge of his mug smashed down on the man's wrist and everything went blurry inside his head. He spat words about honour and death, grabbed a handful of silver and dodged Root-face's clumsy swing. Pulling back, his foot went under the table and he *pushed*. The table lifted, Root-face disappeared behind it. Frightened faces retreated, but Ulfar didn't care. This was too much. He was already out of his seat and on top of the frightened fur trader, swinging with the heavy fistful of silver. There was a crack, a scrape and a sickening squelch as the man's face opened up, and then there was blood, and more screams, some from him. He kicked out, connected once. Root-face flailed but didn't come close. Ulfar's throat felt thick, almost closing; his cheeks were pulsing.

He reached for the sword and saw how he felt inside reflected in the eyes of the man he was about to kill.

With his hand on the hilt, Ulfar looked around the hall.

Everyone was staring at him, their faces etched with fear and disgust.

'I will . . . I will not have my honour questioned,' he croaked and let go of the hilt, heat rising in his face. 'Not by you' – he pointed at the quivering Northman – 'or by anyone else.' He looked around the room. 'Understood?'

Root-face nodded and inched slowly backwards, as if he was retreating from a rabid dog. 'Understood. I was wrong.'

'Y-you . . . I'd—' The words would not form. Ulfar scowled and stormed out.

*

The tears didn't come until later. He'd veered off the road into the forest and wandered without purpose for a while; now he just sat slumped against a big pine. He was well clear of the town, and he was still hungry, still angry. His fist throbbed inside and out, knuckles aching from the punch, palm sore from squeezing down on the silver.

It took him slowly: a soft touch of the wind on his lips, the smell of cold on the air. With his back against the tree, he remembered Stenvik and the moment they'd had after Geiri's death. A lump formed in his throat. He tried to clear it away but it grew despite everything he did until his lips started trembling . . . he blinked rapidly and finally the grief surfaced. With shaking shoulders he gulped mouthfuls of air at a time, then he bent over double to shield his heart from the world. He coughed through the crying, raw repeated coughs, trying to dislodge and squeeze out the hurt, the pain, everything that had happened since that day by the harbour.

Her name formed on his lips but nothing came out; instead a fresh wave of grief swept him away, bigger, harder, faster as he wept for his father, for Geiri and for everything he thought he'd known.

His body was no longer his own. He convulsed on the forest floor, twisting this way and that. He screamed at the world, opened his mouth and let everything go for the first time. The heart-rending noise lifted a flock of rooks out of the nearby trees but it didn't last; a bout of coughing shook him, smashed his insides together, knotted up his stomach, squeezed his neck and the back of his head.

When he had no more to give to grief, sleep took him.

*

He woke up and the sky was wrong. He was wrong. Everything was wrong. He tried to remember what he was doing, but it was hard.

He'd fallen asleep in the night and now it was morning. His throat was dry and he swayed when he stood. His back ached. Something touched his ribs and he felt for it: a silver bottle in his tunic. He unstopped it and swallowed its contents in greedy gulps.

Like falling into the freezing sea, suddenly Ulfar knew everything.

The forest rushed at him, into him, he *was* the forest. He was cold and warmth and the grass in the ground. He knew it; he knew everyone. His chest swelled and he felt like he would burst. He knew the worlds. He rose from his throne and through one eye saw the warriors, his warriors. He walked through the hall under the light of burnished shields – his hall, his shields – and thrust open the doors, stepping into battle. He fought the Jotuns, he grappled with Hel but all for naught, because wherever he went, Loki's cape vanished into the shadows before him. He walked the bridge of colours and—

He saw Stenvik.

He saw Lilia.

What little there was left of Ulfar dug its heels in. Geiri's face flickered into view, and a dark cape swished around a corner.

He saw Lilia in Harald's arms, saw – *felt* the wooden shard rip and tear into her flesh, was the blood that pumped out of her body, was the ground that caught her when she fell.

Ulfar screamed, drew the sword and drove it forcefully through his own heart. The vision of Stenvik shattered, exploded into shards that dissolved, revealing the stars around him, the stars in his eyes. Streaks of pain clawed at the black sky, stripping it away, revealing blue behind it, edged with treetops. The world *lurched* and Ulfar coughed again, once, blood bubbling up out of his mouth, bursting with a wet *plop*. Now the stars were just dots of bright light in his eyes, pinholes in a picture that was fading around the edges.

He looked down at his chest.

Blood was flowing freely around the remaining inches of the blade, pumping out in ever-weaker spurts. A chill rippled through him like a winter wind; his hands felt numb. After the shuddering came a cloying warmth, a feeling of being wrapped up in woollen blankets, and Ulfar smiled a vacant, tired smile. He could drift to sleep now; just lie down and sleep for a while.

He fell to the ground, face-first.

The sword hit the ground and pushed through him. The pain was impossible; it was bigger than him, bigger than the world. It overwhelmed him, and finally he knew: this was it. This was death. Spasms wracked his body. He would be levelled by this great shield of pain, crushed flat, obliterated. He felt himself fade, felt the life leave him.

Ulfar's eyes closed for the final time – and then they flew open again.

His very core was cold. It was hard, it was wrong and it would not die.

He screamed.

ON THE ROAD, NORTH OF LAKE VANERN,
CENTRAL SWEDEN
LATE OCTOBER, AD 996

Goran yawned, scratched his grey stubble and wondered, not for the first time, if he should have stayed at home in the valley all those years ago. As the middle brother he wouldn't have inherited the farm, but he could maybe have become a blacksmith. Or a wood-carver, perhaps. But no, he'd thought the life of a Viking would be full of riches and excitement.

No one had bothered to tell him about sea-stomach.

After three miserable attempts, each more bile-filled than the next, he gave up. He'd had a knack with the fighting, but getting there and back was too much for him. That left just caravan duty, but it was all right. He didn't need to think, could just stand and look hard. Or walk, in this case. That was fine, though – he'd grown used to walking with a staff and took the jibes from the younger guards in stride. Let them mock his age and call it a walking stick. You never knew when a good, thick staff would come in handy.

Their little party consisted of four wagons, six merchants and four guards. They were making good time and the merchants paid well; considering what they were carrying and where to, they could afford it. With any luck they'd be there in ten days or so. The boys were talking up the wenching and drinking they'd do, but Goran had seen them give it a shot and thought their chances modest at best.

He was about to join in and shoot down Heidrek again when he felt something . . . wrong. He spun around just in time to see the blood-covered apparition crash through the bush and emerge onto the road, screaming and waving a sword not three steps away from the merchants. Even the placid draft horses reared and whinnied.

Without thinking, Goran swung his walking staff and connected with the man's temple. He crumpled to the ground.

In a blink the situation went from lethal back to harmless. Swords were sheathed, horses calmed; even the nervous chatter died down eventually. Ingimar, who looked more of a fool than usual in his expensive but ill-fitting robes, jabbed a stubby finger at him and squeaked, 'Who is that? What is the meaning of this? Why did he get so close? Who is he? Why didn't you stop him?'

'He looks stopped to me,' Heidrek chipped in.

Goran suppressed a smirk.

'Yes . . . Who is he?'

'I don't know,' Goran said. 'He looks wounded, though.' He bent down to examine the prone figure.

'Careful!' Ingimar squealed, but Goran ignored him.

'Ooh. Nasty,' Heidrek said, peering over his shoulder. The wound was clean, fresh, and incredibly close to mortal. 'He is one lucky bastard.'

'I'll say,' Goran said. He turned to Ingimar. 'What do you want to do?'

The merchant looked at the man on the ground. 'Show me his sword,' he said, visibly calmer now that the man was proven to be out cold. 'Good. And now loosen his tunic. What is that around his neck?'

'It's a rune of some sort, on a string.'

'Is he definitely out?'

'Flat on the ground, like Regin's mother,' Goran said.

'Nah, his legs ain't spread enough,' Heidrek chimed in.

'Shut up,' Regin muttered behind them. 'I'll slap every one of you.'

Ingimar clambered off the wagon and bent down beside Goran. 'Ah,' he said, appraising the stranger. 'Tie him up.'

'Why?' Heidrek said.

'Just do it,' Ingimar snapped. 'Tie him up and throw him on the fur-cart. And keep him alive.'

'What?'

'We're taking him to Uppsala.'

'In the old days, you'd say a sailor this late in the year had Hel in his wake,' Skeggi rumbled. 'On this one, I'd say the bitch is sitting comfortably in the back and inching forward.'

'Hard to argue,' Finn muttered and crossed himself.

As if in agreement, a sharp crack of wind from the north snapped at their sails. The king had taken to having men row just to keep warm; Valgard was huddled under three furs by the mast, shivering even so. They'd lost two men to cold already – their muscles had seized up and they'd toppled overboard: the sea had taken what was owed. King Olav had said a prayer.

Botolf sidled up to them, quiet as usual. He raised an eyebrow and looked to the coast. 'Interesting . . .'

Finn tried to follow his gaze. The mass of blue-grey and dark green on their right had long since blended and blurred into one big slab of country; the islets and holms on his left had given way to endless open sea. When he finally saw what the slender man was looking at, his breath caught in his throat. 'Signal fires! A chain! We must—'

'All to plan, Finn. All to plan.' King Olav stood in the bow, unmovable. His voice carried on the headwind; the king did not turn. 'The Lord sails with us and we will not come to harm. Hakon does not have the strength. All we know will work in our favour. The signal fires just mean that a small number of men will have the time to wonder what it will be like when an undefeatable force arrives.'

'If Valgard is right,' Botolf muttered under his breath.

Finn crossed himself again and looked down at the white-tipped waves. Turning, he noticed that Valgard had managed to rise. The skinny healer leaned against the mast, grey-faced and shivering.

'Are you well?' Finn muttered.

Valgard glared at him. 'I hate ships. How many fires have you seen?'

'Three . . . ?'

'Seven,' Botolf said, just by his ear and Finn almost jumped. The dark-haired southerner made his skin crawl. On their right-hand side peaked hills rolled past, dotted with fire and smoke; on their left the sea stretched as far as the eye could see.

'Thank you,' Valgard said. 'That should mean we have no more than half a day's sailing left.'

'About right,' Botolf replied. 'Are you aiming for Thorgrimsstrand?' Finn could hear the smirk in his voice and suddenly wanted to plant a fist in it. He turned so he could see the southern chieftain's face. It was skinny, stretched and shaded. It was not an honest Christian's face.

Valgard smiled and shook his head. 'Bjornevik. And Loki's Tooth.'

'Very good. That'll keep—'

'And Trondheim pier.'

Finn had never heard Botolf laugh before. It was the sound of a wolf growling before its kill. 'If I ever fight you, Grass Man, I'd like to do it at sea. At sea, and man to man,' he said, smiling.

'Let's try to make sure that doesn't happen, then. Talent like yours is hard to find. And while we're on the subject – those men you said you could spare?'

'I've talked to them. They're yours.'

'Thank you. Now if you want to take a seat – we're about to start the dance.'

'As you command,' Botolf replied, still smirking as the man appeared to float along the deck to his post at the back next to Skeggi.

A whole host of questions thundered through Finn's head. 'What—? How are we—? But—' he stuttered.

Valgard silenced him with a hand movement and muttered, 'Just watch. We should be rounding soon now.'

'When was this—?'

'You were busy making sure everything was going to plan with the two rats. I was talking to our friends at the back. The king' – Valgard crossed himself and inclined his head towards the bow – 'the king went to a couple of chieftains we knew he could trust and divulged the plan. Listen—'

Valgard cocked his head. The ghost of a smile played on his lips as shouted commands began to drift across the water. Their own rowers lifted their oars, tucked them to the side and just sat, allowing the rest of the fleet to catch up.

'That's where we turn,' Valgard said, pointing to a large mountain jutting out into the water maybe three miles ahead of them. 'After that it's straight sailing into Hakon's hole.' He looked both worse for wear and more alive than Finn could remember.

Around and now in front of them, ships were moving into groups. The first ships were powering ahead, foaming sea around their oars; the group behind them kept pace but stayed back. Soon both groups of ships disappeared around the horn.

King Olav raised his hand, palm flat.

Silent expectation spread like rings in a pond.

The moment seemed to stretch out for ever – but then the king's hand turned into a fist. Lowering his arm, he pointed forward.

As one, the oars hit the water and the men pulled with renewed vigour. The *Njordur's Mercy* leapt forward, the sail billowed and behind them, another twenty ships fell in line.

When they rounded the horn, Finn watched a rare smile light up Valgard's face. At the first available landing beach, a very handy stretch of soft sand, hastily erected fortifications had been equally hastily abandoned. About four miles further along, a third of their ships had beached with ease and overwhelmed a token force; the bulk of the defenders were rushing back to meet the enemy. Sparse reinforcements from Trondheim were stuck battling the men from the second wave, who had cut them off just outside the city by running their ships aground and wading ashore on the rocky promontory of Loki's Tooth. Sounds of battle were turning into sounds of murder.

Finn caught Botolf and Skeggi exchanging approving glances.

King Olav's chosen warriors sailed on, straight into the heart of Trondheim.

TRONDHEIM, NORTH NORWAY
EARLY NOVEMBER, AD 996

Hakon had sent his strongest fighters out to meet the invaders; greybeards and fuzzcheeks remained and it did not take Skeggi and Botolf's men long to clear the pier. They flowed ashore like murderous waves before King Olav, who walked into Trondheim slaying anyone and anything in his path. Drifting in his wake, Finn looked around. The smell of blood was rising in the air and he could see it in the eyes of the fighters. Around him boys and old men were being hacked to death – quickly by Botolf, brutally by Skeggi.

At the very moment when the spirit of Trondheim broke, King Olav bellowed for his men to stop in the name of the White Christ. The order spread quickly and within a couple of breaths, swords had been stilled. The fighters took up their positions behind King Olav. The sounds of battle died down, to be replaced by the fading moans and cries of the wounded.

On instinct, Finn commanded four of his warriors to clear a space in front of the king, who turned around and shouted, 'Hakon!' over the assembled mix of houses as the warriors dragged badly mangled bodies from beneath his feet.

There was no answer.

'*Hakon!*'

The people of Trondheim formed a shapeless, dull-eyed wall that stared at them, hostile and silent.

'Hakon Jarl – come out or I shall proclaim you a coward and put your kin to the sword!' King Olav bellowed.

Heads turned, bodies shifted and a path opened up. A large man with thick grey hair and a greying beard walked slowly through the crowd and stepped into the square. He wore a mail shirt covered with a long, flowing white bear pelt and carried a sturdy-looking helmet under his arm; a long axe hung from his belt. The blade had not been bloodied yet, but Finn reached for his sword all the same.

There was a cruel twist to the man's mouth as he sneered at King Olav and gestured towards the bodies of the dead and dying. 'Is this what your so-called God commands you to do? Slaughter boys and old hands?' he growled.

'I will deal with them according to your conduct, and by your own standard will I judge them,' King Olav replied. His voice bounced off the mud-padded and wood-clad walls.

'I don't care about your words,' Hakon said. 'But you've made your point. Now what happens?'

'You bend the knee,' King Olav said.

Hakon swallowed, hawked and spat. He reached for his axe and metal rippled behind King Olav as four hundred seasoned warriors showed steel. With great effort, the old chieftain stayed his hand and stepped into the cleared square. King Olav did the same.

Finn thought he saw flashes of disgust in the faces of the northerners when their chieftain chose life over death and knelt before his king – their king.

Valgard found the healers in the town without too much trouble. One was a green-faced apprentice boy who would be useful for nothing but clearing shit; the other was an old crone who knew her work but was painfully slow at even the simplest jobs. It was clear that it had been a while since Trondheim had seen any kind of scrap. He'd asked for the town's master healer, but apparently the man had been unable to put his own head back on his shoulders. Valgard sighed, ordered them both to work making poultices and supplying water and then set about healing the wounded.

He worked without pause until sundown, then had someone fetch a light. The stink of the big seal-fat candle was rank at first, but it did help mask the blood. Valgard kept his mind on the work, bandaging the wounds of friend and foe alike, sending them away better than they came. He couldn't help but note that there were significantly more foes to bandage. Some of them were mean-spirited and required special attention – if he disliked them enough, he asked Skeggi's men to look after them for a little while. Most of the fighting men accepted their fate wearily – they'd been in scraps before, on both sides. Some were even grateful for his skill, and Valgard made a point of noting their faces.

King Olav had forbidden the taking of spoils and for the most part the men adhered to this command. After dark, however, a few women showed up with familiar wounds, and Valgard could not help but think of Harald. He would have been worth any five of these men but he would also be out now, delighting in causing pain and fear, sowing the seeds of hate and leaving before they sprouted. That was the old way.

The boy drifted nervously into his field of vision and Valgard squeezed out a smile. 'What is it?'

'It's . . . it's . . .' The boy turned beetroot-red.

'Bring her,' Valgard said.

The boy darted out and returned with a slim young girl hanging off his shoulder, only barely supporting her own weight. Her clothes were in tatters and lank, dark hair hung in front of her face. Valgard didn't need to look in her eyes to tell how much she was hurting – her legs shook, she twisted her upper body as if trying to relieve something in her shoulders and blood dripped on the floor where she stood. Two of her fingers on each hand were pointing in the wrong directions.

'Get hot water,' Valgard snapped. The boy looked at the girl, then him, then sprinted off. The girl almost fell and Valgard took three quick steps towards her. His back flared, but he didn't care. Gently brushing her hair away from her face, he tilted her head up.

Both her eyes were blackened and a tooth had been knocked out. Her hair had been pulled so hard that her scalp had torn, and thin, pinkish blood seeped out past a crusting scab.

Her eyes were open but vacant.

Valgard frowned. He'd never understood why big, strong men

needed to hit girls to get their cocks hard. He'd seen quite enough to know what had happened here: the screaming might start at some point but not just yet, so it would be good to get the work done first. Putting his hand on the girl's good shoulder, he guided her gently to a table, laid her down and started tending her wounds.

As he worked, an idea came to him and he smiled even as his hands continued working gently to ease the girl's pains. Maybe there was some light in the darkness, even this far north.

Hakon Jarl's hall was as big as the hovels in his town were pitiful. Rich furs covered every inch of the benches and polished silver overlapped copper and gold on the walls. A tapestry from Ireland depicting a thin man being attacked by flying beasts held pride of place on one long wall; the other had a picture of an impossibly long raiding ship; at the bow end was a broad-chested figure wearing a white bear cape.

The dais at the end of the room was easily the height of a man. Steps were set into one side and there was a chamber off to the back. In front of it stood three chairs, positioned to be at the chieftain's feet. King Olav sat in the high seat and looked down on the hall with disdain. 'Savages,' he muttered. 'Magpies and savages, stealing and murdering. Treasures gained by wickedness are worth nothing.' He made the sign of the cross as he cast a lingering glance towards the tapestry of the ship.

Finn entered at the far end. The size of the hall and its furnishings made the warrior look almost small. He saluted from the doorway and bowed his head.

'Come, Finn,' King Olav called. 'Bring a chair.' He gestured to the space beside him.

Finn approached the dais and looked up. 'Are you sure, my King?'

'It is clear to me that Hakon wanted to place himself above all others and closer to his . . .' The king's face curled in distaste. 'Closer to his gods. But I shall not be found guilty of such vanity.' He rose from the high seat and looked down on Finn. 'If we had the time I'd level it all. Pass it here.' Finn lifted the chair up and the king grabbed it without any visible effort. 'Good. Now come up and have a seat.' As the big man made his way around to the stairs, King Olav sat down again. 'You are my right hand in war and peace, and I need you to tell me what you've seen and heard. How many dead?'

Finn manoeuvred his large frame into the chair. 'As far as I can gather we lost six men. Hargrim's men on Loki's Tooth lost twelve and seventeen of Orlygr's at Bjornevik.'

'Hm,' King Olav said. 'It pains me, but they shall walk with Christ. What of Hakon's men?'

'Somewhere around three to four hundred dead.'

The king's eyebrow rose. 'Which leaves him with—?'

'About six hundred able-bodied men.'

'And we have?'

'Two thousand eight hundred.'

'Hah!' King Olav leaned back. 'That sly healer of ours, he got this one right. But there is more we can do.'

'More, my Lord?'

'Yes, there is. Christ's will must be done.'

Valgard stared at Finn and pulled back. 'He wants to do *what*?'

'Round them up and kill them all,' Finn replied. 'By the morning. Says we need to make sure.'

'Make sure,' Valgard repeated. His shoulders slumped. 'But Hakon has already bent the knee, hasn't he? Well . . . thank you for telling me, Finn. You are right – it will be difficult. Do you think I could maybe come with you?'

'That would be good,' Finn said.

Valgard looked over his shoulder at the far end of the tent, where the crone and the boy were faffing around looking equally inept. He rolled his eyes, sighed and approached them. 'You two. I need to go off now. You're in charge,' he said, pointing at the crone. 'You—' He pointed at the boy, who just gazed at him. 'Never mind. Do your best. Oh – and no one touches the girl but me,' he added, glaring at the boy. 'No one. Understood?' They both nodded, wide-eyed.

As he walked away, he braced himself against the cold. 'Try not to kill anyone,' he muttered.

Over in the east a milky-grey stripe of dawn could be seen. With Botolf and Skeggi's help, they'd rounded up Hakon's soldiers and tied them up in groups of ten or so, and set a handful of armed guards to watch over them.

Finn and Valgard found the king lying on a pile of furs in the chamber behind the dais, fast asleep. Finn cleared his throat.

'Your Majesty . . .' he mumbled and cleared his throat again.

Valgard stepped forward and put a hand on the king's shoulder. 'Your Maj—'

King Olav's left hand shot out and closed around Valgard's throat. Eyes flashing, the king twisted off the piles and rose, bent Valgard to the ground and raised a mailed fist, ready to smash his attacker's face.

'My Lord!' Finn shouted and grabbed King Olav's right arm.

Through the fog of suffocation, Valgard thought he saw the king blink, blink again and shake the confusion out of his face.

Then when Olav looked down and saw his own left hand crushing his healer's windpipe, he recoiled and stepped backwards.

'Valgard! I – I—'

Racked by coughing, Valgard raised a hand to stop the king from saying any more. When he'd regained his voice, he croaked, 'Don't worry, my King. Anyone would be happy to follow a man who is twice the warrior asleep than I am even fully awake.' He added what he hoped would be read as a smile.

The king was visibly shaken, but recovered quickly. 'You are most kind. What brings you here?'

'Well,' Valgard said, rubbing his neck. 'I wanted to tell you something. It's about a girl.'

King Olav's men walked around Trondheim in the morning, banging their shields and forcing every man, woman and child out onto the walkways, roads and streets. Slowly the crowd gathered in the largest field outside the town in front of a hastily erected platform, surrounded by a ring of the king's soldiers.

There were mutters of unease when Botolf and Skeggi led in the remaining six hundred of Hakon's soldiers, bound and disarmed, and positioned them in rows below the platform, then surrounded them with a shield wall.

The mass of people didn't notice Hakon Jarl until he was halfway up the steep steps to the platform. A smattering of cheers was heard, but died quickly. King Olav followed in his footsteps. No one celebrated.

Standing some distance away in the shadow of an old barn, Finn leaned over to Valgard. 'I really hope this works,' he muttered.

'It'll work,' Valgard said. 'It'll definitely work.'

Finn drew a deep breath, turned around and signalled to his chosen men.

On the platform, King Olav raised his arms. Below him, the crowd fell silent. There were about two and a half thousand townspeople in there, Valgard estimated. Maybe not enough to overwhelm the invaders, but if it went wrong . . . This was a good time to find out whether King Olav deserved all the admiration Finn appeared to give him. If the king didn't sweep them along this could turn very ugly indeed. They'd only be able to withstand a—

'People of Trondheim!' King Olav exclaimed, and Valgard could not help but be drawn to him. 'Hakon Jarl' – he gestured – 'has made a very difficult but important decision. He has looked into your future and done what is best for Trondheim – and for all of you.' Hakon Jarl looked even angrier than usual.

Behind the platform, six burly sailors walked towards the steps carrying carven idols of the old gods.

As the men ascended, dragging the statues behind him, King Olav continued, 'These are the gods from Hakon's own godhouse. He has given them to us to help me show you what the old gods are capable of. These are the same gods you've placated with sacrifices and blood offerings.' The king paced along the very edge of the platform. The burly sailors had by now raised four idols and placed them near the front, just behind King Olav, with a man taking up position behind each of them and holding on to them by the head. Even from a hundred yards away, Valgard could tell that these were exquisitely carved, their beauty tarnished only by the lids nailed over the open mouths, where normally they'd put in food during ceremonies. But he'd expected that, because he was the one who'd ordered those lids nailed in just before daybreak.

The sixth god was in place now. King Olav stood next to Freyr, Freyja, Loki, Thor, Njordur and Odin. 'Your axe, Hakon,' the king said, and the Jarl obliged and handed the king his weapon.

'I am a warrior of the White Christ. He will stand in my defence as your old gods move to smite me. And they will try' – the king set his feet – 'because now we'll see what your old gods are really' – King Olav swung – '*made of*!'

The axe met the wood with a dull *thwack*, the lid flew off Freyja's mouth and a big crack opened in the hollow statue. Moving with the swing, King Olav sidestepped and was on to the next one even as the sailor behind the statue tipped it out over the edge of the platform. The crack of the axe mixed with screams of horror from the crowd as rotting fruits, putrid meats, rats and mice and crawling insects of every kind tumbled out of the broken statue and fell down onto the heads of the six hundred bound men. The statues emptied one by one onto the crowd below as Hakon Jarl's men tried to dodge the disgusting missiles, but they could do little with their hands bound and ended up pulling against each other as the vermin clawed, bit and scurried away; some met their end under stamping heels. Several of Hakon's warriors ran head-first into King Olav's men, but they'd been told what to expect and the shield wall held.

Up on the platform, the broken statues had been removed. King Olav stood at the edge, regarding the spectacle. When the turmoil finally subsided, he spread out his hands again, as if pleading for calm. Slowly the crowd fell quiet.

'Did you see that?' he shouted. 'Did you?' The silence did not deter him. 'Your so-called gods are old, hollow and full of decay. Should they not have struck me down?' He turned to Hakon. 'Did you see them strike me down, Hakon Jarl?'

The old man stood at the back of the platform, immobile. 'No,' he said. Then he repeated, louder, 'No, I did not.'

'The White Christ protects me!' King Olav shouted, 'as he protected you from the wrath of the old gods! The White Christ stands by his people.' On cue, one of the sailors carried a slim girl to the stairs and helped her up onto the platform. Standing behind the crowd, Valgard nodded. Dressing her in white had been a nice touch.

Two of Finn's men moved towards the stairs with a bound and hooded fighter who was kicking and screaming, though to no avail. They half-pushed, half-dragged him up onto the platform.

'This creature of the Lord,' King Olav intoned, gesturing at the girl, 'this creature was attacked tonight. She is one of yours, people of Trondheim. She is someone's daughter, someone's granddaughter. And the White Christ believes that the daughters of Norsemen deserve to live safely! He does not believe in the old ways. I told my soldiers that they could not claim their spoils here because the people of Trondheim are brave, they are our kin; they are Norsemen, just like I am. But she was attacked, three times, brutally, and the rule of our Lord is very specific.'

The bound man on the platform was unmasked. It was one of Orlygr's men. Valgard hadn't met him before; he'd asked around. Maybe he'd done it and maybe he hadn't but it didn't matter so much. What mattered was that the people of Trondheim were hanging on King Olav's every word.

'The rule says,' King Olav continued, 'that you should do unto others as you would have others do unto you.' The other sailors moved up onto the platform. The last one held a foot-long belaying pin. 'Do unto others as you would have others do unto you. And so I say to you, even though the White Christ is new and different, he is no more merciful or forgiving than Odin himself.' Behind him, the bound man was thrown onto the platform, face-first. Two large men pinned down his upper body. 'Like me, the White Christ is generous to his friends.' A knife flashed. The bound man's sliced breeches were thrown off the platform, fluttering in the morning breeze before they landed in the mud. His pale flesh almost shone in the morning light. The audience was very silent. 'But to those who disobey, he gives no quarter.' The thrashing man's legs were spread and pinned down. Grim-faced, the sailor with the belaying pin knelt behind the fighter who was now obscured by bodies.

'So I say to you, people of Trondheim!' King Olav's voice boomed out, strong and clear. 'Follow me! Follow Hakon Jarl! Or—'

The scream was human, but only at first. It changed into something else, something animal and tortured, a wailing wave of pain that faded into crying whimpers. King Olav glanced at the sailor, who clenched his jaw and *twisted*.

Valgard could hear the man's vocal cords breaking. It didn't stop him from screaming: a garbled and teary string of invective, excuses and begging for forgiveness followed, but none of the big sailors moved an inch. The words drifted apart on the morning breeze. A faint smell of dying reached Valgard. It didn't bother him any more; it hadn't done for a long time.

The sailor twisted and pushed.

The warrior choked on his own spit. He tried to smash his head into the wood on the platform but the sailor sitting on his left arm grabbed him by the hair before he could knock himself out.

'Thrice you attacked, thrice you've been attacked,' King Olav intoned. 'Stand him up!' As one, the sailors rose and hauled the man to his feet. He could hardly support his own body weight. His face was ashen and blood flowed freely between his legs.

Valgard's eyes were cold. That looked about right. Beside him, Finn had grown ghostly pale.

'You have reaped what you have sown!' King Olav shouted. 'If you do unto others, others will do unto you.' Some unspoken communication passed between the king and the sailors, who let go of the man. He dropped to his knees. 'But you also betrayed me. You disobeyed me and therefore you cannot be trusted,' King Olav said. Stepping behind the man, he moved fluently, took jaw in one hand, a fistful of hair in the other.

Twisted.

Snap.

The man's lifeless body collapsed onto the platform.

King Olav looked up at the gathered mass of people. Calmly, he said, 'Now that Hakon Jarl has bent the knee – this is what happens to the enemies of Trondheim.'

Cheers spread through the gathering and grew in volume as they bounced back across the cold, dirty bodies of the bound men. They grew louder still as King Olav gave commands and the shield wall dissolved. Soldiers moved among the captives, cutting bonds. The people of Trondheim turned around and gazed at the entrance to their town.

Some of Hargrim's men, sent to raid local farms, appeared with freshly slaughtered sheep and cows. Fires were up and running, lining the road; cuts of prime, half-roasted, half-raw meat were offered around. From Hakon's basement, Skeggi had conjured up several barrels of mead and King Olav's men led the people of Trondheim back to their houses, making sure everyone got at least a bite to eat, a mouthful to drink. King Olav stood next to Hakon Jarl, watching them leave. Their faces were coloured as much with relief as with meat juices and mead.

From their vantage point, Valgard leaned over to Finn. 'I'd say that worked, wouldn't you?'

Valgard's chance came three days later. The town had gone back to normal, more or less. In the end it didn't matter much who waved the swords; fish still needed to be caught and crops had to be harvested. King Olav installed himself in Hakon's hall but kept the Jarl close. Then news came to them of three families banding together up in the valleys and muscling in on their neighbours. King Olav sent Hakon Jarl to bring the farmers back in line.

Valgard watched the party as they left the town: Hakon, a smattering of the men from the *Njordur's Mercy* and Botolf himself, seasoned fighters all, and used to wet-work.

The morning air was heavy with the promise of rain as he levered open the door to the hall. Much like Hakon, the wood was warped by north winds and sea-salt but gave way eventually.

'Well met,' the king said. Sitting on the dais, in that ridiculous high seat, King Olav looked small, inconsequential, almost mortal.

'Your Majesty,' Valgard said, bowing down.

'Come on, Valgard,' King Olav said. 'You brought me here, you saved the lives of countless of my men with your advice and you delivered me Trondheim on a platter. I am in your debt.'

Valgard approached the dais. 'Your Majesty is too kind.'

'I am not,' King Olav said. 'Plenty of villagers in our wake can tell you that.'

'True,' Valgard said. 'How is Hakon acting?'

'Exactly as you said he would,' King Olav said. 'He has taken no better to giving up his place than anyone would, but treating him as a man of note and allowing him as much control as possible meant I could send him to the Dales, which shows that I trust him. Of course, Botolf goes with him.'

'For his protection.'

'Of course,' King Olav agreed. Both men smirked. 'Now. Why are you here, Valgard?'

'I—' The words caught in his throat at first. 'Do you remember, my King, our time in Stenvik?' King Olav raised an eyebrow. 'Yes. Well . . . when I overheard Jorn and Runar talking and came to you, I asked . . . I asked for—'

'You asked for men.'

'Well – yes – cast-offs. Those you can spare.'

'I know. I gave you the girl and the bastards. Why?'

'I need more.'

The walls of Hakon's hall appeared to be moving in, all of a sudden. Valgard became uncomfortably aware that the king was carrying his sword.

'Why?' The king's voice was cold.

'Because a small group of well-trained people working alone and reporting only to me can see and hear things that your men cannot, go where your men cannot and bring back information your men could never get close to. And that information saves lives – yours included.'

'So you want me to spare you fighters?'

'Not necessarily, no.'

King Olav's eyebrow rose again.

'They must be able to take care of themselves, but I don't need all of them to be like Finn.'

'Good,' King Olav said.

Something in the finality of the king's tone worried Valgard, but he ploughed on. 'I have some people in mind; I have suggested something of the sort to a few of them. I thought we could go around saying we're collecting taxes.'

King Olav looked at him for a long time. The silence was turning quite uncomfortable when the king finally spoke up. 'Well. You have proven that you can be trusted. Take your people. Do what you think best. But you can't have Finn.'

'I understand,' Valgard said quickly. 'You will not live to regret this.'

'Make sure I won't. Now go and find Finn and tell him to come and see me.' The king waved him away and Valgard walked to the door, heart hammering in his chest.

He'd got them. He'd really got them.

Now he just needed to decide on the best way to use them.

Most of the fighters who would walk again had already walked out of Valgard's tent by now, so there was little to do. The girl had come to a day ago and cried since; the boy fussed over her, brought her broth and held her when she needed to be held. The old woman had just shrugged; like Valgard, she'd seen worse.

Finn came striding down the street from Hakon's hall. When he reached the tent, he had to pause to get his breath back.

'He's – he's— I'm going back.'

'What?' Valgard said.

'Stenvik. I'm going back to Stenvik. Me and a third of the men. Not enough provisions here; not enough men there.'

Valgard frowned. On the surface it was a moderately sensible decision – but it wasn't his decision, and it wasn't convenient for him. 'Hm. Well, you'll be a fine chieftain,' he said.

'Don't make fun of me,' Finn said. The burly warrior looked almost frightened. 'How am I to order men about? I am not a leader.'

'Oh, but you are, Finn. Just imagine . . .' Valgard drew a deep breath to still the laughter in his throat. When he'd found his serious voice, he tried again. 'Just imagine that King Olav speaks to you: decide what needs to be done, say it to yourself in his voice and then tell others.'

Finn stared mutely at him, but then like clouds from the sun, confusion lifted and he understood. 'Thank you!' A bear-paw hand slammed down on Valgard's shoulder, squeezing it. The large warrior beamed at him. 'Thank you. You are a true friend. I will miss you.'

Valgard winced, expecting the snap of dry bone at any moment, but Finn eased off on the grip and started pacing. 'I'll have to make sure there are rotations and rations, put the south coast boys somewhere apart from the Dale boys, and—'

'You'll do fine,' Valgard said between gritted teeth. 'Now go and prepare. Be a leader. Be the best leader you can be – and remember the voice,' he added.

Finn grinned, hailed him and strode off.

Valgard scowled at Finn's back. Then he swivelled and walked into the tent, straight for the girl's corner. 'Up!' he snapped. The boy, who had been lost in thought while combing the girl's hair, almost jumped out of his skin. 'What are you doing?' The boy stammered and tried to start a sentence. 'Shut up. Don't speak unless you know some words, you witless annoyance. Go and fetch me herbs.'

'W-w-which herbs?'

'All of them,' Valgard snarled. 'And don't come back until you've got a bagful.'

'Eb-eb-but—'

'Go. Now.' The backs of Valgard's eyes hurt. He wanted to hit something, bludgeon it, break something. The urge to cause pain was overwhelming him. There was a throbbing pressure in his brain. He just wanted to—

It came from behind. 'Go easy on the boy, will you?' The smirk never left Botolf's voice. 'He's probably been boning the girl when you've not been looking. Best be careful,' the lean man said to the petrified boy, who was frozen halfway between sitting and standing up. 'Make sure she doesn't tell, or King Olav might take his stick and—' The gesture left little to the imagination and the boy's face paled even more.

Valgard got control of his breathing and turned. 'What can I help you with?'

'Nothing,' Botolf said. 'Got something for you, though.'

'And what might that be?'

'You need to come with me. It's in my hut.'

He'd seen his share of captives, but once his eyes had grown used to the dim light in the side room of Botolf's house he wondered if he'd ever seen one treated like this. The scrawny woman was unconscious, her head a matted tangle of hair and dirt.

'You've tied her ankles to her neck?'

'Had to,' Botolf said. 'She took out two of Skeggi's, bit the lip off one of mine and headbutted one of Hargrim's – broke his eye socket. If that bitch moves now, she'll strangle herself.'

'And is that also why she is thrice gagged?'

'Not really; you'll find out soon enough. But she knows something about the north.'

Valgard swallowed. 'What do you mean? I don't know what you mean.' The words tumbled out and he cursed himself.

'Now now, Grass Man. There's something up there and you're planning to go looking for it.'

'How—?'

'Why else would you be in Trondheim? And have gone to such great trouble to get here?' When Valgard didn't reply, he continued, 'I won't tell. I just want to know. I heard the stories about the woman on the ship. My mother was a Finn-witch, and if something is stirring up there I want to know. I want to be in on it. I won't kill you in your sleep either, but you'll need someone on your side who can fight.'

Valgard made a decision. It would be a long trip, with much food to prepare. Problems sometimes solved themselves. 'Fine. Wake her up. Let's hear what she has to say.'

Botolf approached the prone form with a measured caution that filled Valgard with unease. He'd not seen the knife-man scared of anything before, and while he didn't look frightened, he was certainly . . . respectful.

Before he could reach down to touch the woman's face, one of her eyes opened – then the other. She stared at Valgard, but did not move. It occurred to him that she had woken up rather easily.

'Welcome back,' Botolf said. 'I have brought a friend. Now – I'm going to loosen your gags, because we're going to talk. Do you understand?'

The woman nodded, very carefully. Botolf reached behind her head and untied the gags. He moved as carefully as a dog-handler.

When the cloth was out of her mouth, she coughed. 'Water,' she wheezed.

'Of course,' Botolf said, filling a leather cup from a flask in his belt. He knelt beside her and moved the cup towards her lips. Valgard expected her to bite his fingers off, but she didn't. Instead she drank eagerly. When she'd finished the contents of the cup, she closed her eyes and appeared to relax. In the right light she'd have something of a harsh beauty about her, he thought. But then again, so did wolves.

She opened her eyes again.

'Well, aren't you a pair of brave little cockless shit-eating teat-sucklers to have managed all by your twosome to tie up a little girl.' She smiled sweetly at them, and Valgard was again reminded of a wolf.

'Well met. I am Valgard,' he found himself blurting out. 'And that's Botolf.'

'Well, congratu-fucking-lations, Valgard. You know your name.'

'What's yours?'

'I am Thora, and if you get me out of this spunk-dribbling town I can tell you everything you need to know about the north.'

BY THE NORTHWEST COAST OF DENMARK
EARLY NOVEMBER, AD 996

The waves stroked the sides of the boat, slapping against the cutting oars. The sails snapped in the wind. Above and behind them the seagulls cawed, hovering over two longships.

No one spoke.

The men rowed with a will, as if the further away they got the more they would forget, as if staring at the back of the man in front of them would make the images in their heads go away.

Audun sat with his back up against the mast, shivering despite the heat in his veins. He was covered from the chest up with congealed blood, grey skull sludge, vomit. He remembered the fight in frozen moments – strangers with bearded faces twisted in rage, teeth bared, wild eyes. The leap. The surprise on their faces as he landed among them. Screams and breaking bones. The taste of their fear, and the blood. The smell of the blood. He shivered and thought he would throw up again, but there was nothing left in his stomach by now. Audun wrapped the torn shift around himself and tried to huddle into as small a space as possible.

In the stern Hrutur steered, silent but frowning, as the knarr ploughed through the waves, cutting a path straight for the land of the Danes. The men stayed quiet, even when the pale blue line on the horizon became a strip of sand and grass.

A grunt and a nudge, and Hrutur's boatsman took the tiller. The captain turned his back to Audun, knelt and started rummaging in packs by his feet. When he turned and rose he was holding a small travel sack. A hand-axe had somehow found its way to his belt. None of the rowers looked at him as he made his way to Audun's spot by the mast.

The captain crouched by Audun, close enough to be heard over the wind. 'Listen. We thank you for what you . . . did for us. But I think you're trouble, and I won't have any trouble on my boat. We're setting you off just north of Skaer. There's food, some coin and a new tunic in the sack.'

Audun looked up at the weathered captain. 'Thank you,' he mumbled.

A strange expression flitted across Hrutur's face. Shame? Pity? 'It isn't much,' he muttered. 'Just your oarsman's pay. Go south off the beach; the village of Skaer is a day away. Road's a couple of miles inland.' He rose, made his way quickly to the captain's bench and took the tiller from the boatsman. The knarr curved sharply, heading straight towards a sandy beach up ahead.

They landed smoothly and still no one spoke. Audun struggled to stand, then somehow managed to turn and walk towards the bow. As he clambered over the edge he heard muttered voices.

'—beast—'

'—monster—'

'—berserker—'

The freezing water shocked him out of his stupor and he waded onto dry land as fast as he could manage. Behind him feet hit the water and curses rang out, louder than ever, calling for a good push. Mothers were mentioned; insults flew.

Audun staggered away from the boat and up off the beach, sinking into the cold sand with every step. Yellowed tufts on the bank started linking up and soon he was standing on dying autumn grass. Pulling off the bloodied tunic, he allowed the cold wind to bite at his skin for a while. More memories of the fight on the ship trickled back into his head: the pitching deck, the blades that nipped and scratched but somehow never hurt, the crunch of broken faces. He thought about how close he'd been to dying, and the phantom wound in his chest started itching again. He wanted to scratch it, to keep scratching it until he could claw his heart out and throw it away.

The tunic was a serviceable, homespun thing, a sailor's undershirt, woven thin and tight. Audun pulled it on and shivered. The wool clung to his cold skin like a hide and he felt ridiculous. Berserker? Dressing in the fur of the mighty bear to take its powers? Audun snorted. 'Fear the monster! Fear the beast!' he said to no one in particular. Standing on the beach, on his own with the wind cooling his cold, wet skin, he felt decidedly un-beastly. He flexed his shoulders and cracked his neck. Whatever scrapes he'd picked up in the attack were already healing. What he needed now was somewhere to hide from trouble for a while.

The road stretched out before him, weaving across the plains. Far off in the distance, hills rose above the flatlands; to his left, yellow and reddish forests obscured the view.

He sighed and started walking.

JUTLAND, NORTH COAST OF DENMARK
EARLY NOVEMBER, AD 996

The plains ran on almost as far as the eye could see. He'd found the road soon enough, though it was not much to speak of. There was very little out here – he thought he'd seen a faint line of chimney smoke once but it was so far away that he thought no more of it. The good thing about roads was that most of them led somewhere, he thought. There'd be something at the end of this one, too.

Then he saw the hound.

It was a blur of black and white and noise, bounding over the hill ahead of him. Within moments it came to a snarling stop six feet away, head down but eyes up, ears back and hackles raised. Thinking quickly, Audun trained his eyes on the ground, only glancing at the big animal from the corner of his eye: this was the kind they kept to growl at wolves in the night and round up anything on legs in the day, good for snapping his shin in half if it felt like it.

Audun reached slowly into his sack and rooted around for the greasy chunk of meat Hrutur had given him. He teased off a strip and waved it. The dog leapt sideways across the road and barked louder. Audun crouched and held out his hand. 'Come on, boy,' he said in soothing tones. 'Here, boy.' The dog barked furiously at him, but Audun did not make eye contact; instead he kept his gaze on the ground and the hand holding the meat outstretched, but drew it ever-so-slightly closer to his body.

The dog stopped leaping about and approached, still growling.

Audun pulled his hand in further, muttering nonsense all the while in the same calming voice.

Still the dog drew closer, barking once again as if to emphasise that there had been an argument and that it had won.

Audun smiled and threw the chunk of meat over its head.

With improbable speed, the big dog leapt and caught the chunk in midair, but Audun was already up and walking past it. A couple of moments later the dog was on his heels, bounding and barking.

Audun ignored him for a couple of steps, then turned and addressed him. 'Do you want some more?'

The dog barked louder, tongue flapping, tail twitching. Audun raised his hand, made sure it saw and reached for the bag. 'Sit,' he said. The dog paid no notice, so he withdrew his hand. The dog barked. Audun moved his hand towards the bag and tried again. 'Sit!' he said. Now the dog stopped moving. 'Sit,' Audun repeated, as authoritatively as he could. The dog barked once, loudly – and sat down. 'Good boy!' Audun said and quickly tore more meat off the bone in his bag. The dog's tail thumped as the hand came out and it caught the flying chunk again.

Audun started walking in the direction the dog had come from.

Moments later, the dog came bounding after him, still barking at the world. Audun stood still and relaxed his hand by his side. When the big animal nudged him, Audun scratched the dog behind the ears. They fell into an easy stride, the dog loping along around and beside him.

The smoke lines were so thin that he smelled them before he saw them. Cresting a hill, he saw Skaer, thought back to Hrutur's words and couldn't help but wonder what passed for a village these days. This was nothing but a smattering of houses with runty cook-fires and what looked from distance to be a very crude pier set hardly a ship's length into a naturally sheltered harbour.

The dog barked once more and took off at a dead run towards the houses.

'So much for company,' Audun muttered and scratched his arms. Still – they might have work. There was nothing for it but to go and find out.

SKAER, JUTLAND
EARLY NOVEMBER, AD 996

'There is nothing for you here,' the man said, scratching his pock-marked chin. 'I hardly make a living myself, so I don't know what we'd do with another blacksmith.'

Audun looked around his pitiful excuse for a smithy and thought he could probably point out a couple of reasons why the man was struggling for work, but decided against it. 'I see. Do you have any suggestions?'

'Try Helga in Ovregard. She's a widow, our Helga, and will need a hand, although she'll deny it. Mind you, might want to hurry,' the man added with a smirk.

'What do you mean?'

'Oh, nothing,' the man said as his face contorted. Whatever he was trying to dislodge with his tongue popped loose and was swallowed. There was nothing more Audun could get from him on the subject, so he settled for provisions and instructions. The blacksmith took Audun's coins, counted them and gave back a fire-steel, a leg of lamb, a small knife and a hammer that belonged on the scrapheap. They both knew Audun was being fleeced, but that was the way it was. Back in Stenvik he would probably have called it 'traveller's rates'. As a parting gift, the man had told him where to find Ovregard, although 'south' wasn't much to go on.

A good while later, before the sun had completely disappeared across the horizon to his right, Audun had found a copse that offered reasonable shelter from wind, rain and unwanted visitors. He built a fire and sat down to eat his food.

He fell asleep in a new country, but with warm feet and a full belly. His last thought was of the morrow, when he would go and find this Helga and get hired as a farmhand. There was nothing out here for anyone. He'd be hard pressed to find any trouble.

'Will you look at that,' Johan sneered and reined in his horse. 'This whole place is going to shit.' The heavyset farmer dismounted in one swift movement, strode up to the crooked fence-post and gave it a vicious kick before his big, callused hands reached for the sledgehammer that hung off the horse's saddle.

'You will keep your hammer away from my fence-post, Johan Aagard!' The voice cracked like a whip in the cold morning air.

In one swift motion, the hammer swung from over the big man's shoulder and came to rest by his feet. He leaned on it as if that had been exactly what he had always intended to do.

'Helga! The sun who rises in the morning!' he exclaimed. The owner of the voice reined in her horse a good twenty yards away from him and did not appear in the least affected by his charms. Thick, silver-streaked black hair was tied back from high cheek-bones, narrowed eyes with crow's feet and a stubborn mouth. 'Oh, don't be like that, Helga,' Johan said, smi .ng hard. 'I just saw that . . . thing and I thought to give you a hand before it fell over and you lost a cow or something like that.' He was still smiling.

'Hoping that if you fixed my fence-post I might invite you to use your hammer on my bedpost?' the woman shot back.

'And why not? Your land is next to mine; we're doing the same work twice as it is and nobody's warming my bed. What's not to like?'

'You, for a start,' Helga snapped. 'I had no need for you when my husband was alive and I have no need for you now. So with all the neighbourly love that I have to give to you – I'll keep my land as is, I don't mind the work and you can go and fuck your own sheep if you're cold.'

The smile stayed on Johan's lips as he hefted his hammer and mounted his horse, but it had left his eyes a long time ago. 'We'll see, Helga. You're a hard-hearted woman, but I'll win you over yet.'

As he rode off, she exhaled. Her mare whinnied softly in protest, and she found she was squeezing the reins in a white-knuckled grip. She relaxed and the animal snorted under her. 'Forgive me, Streak. He's just . . . he's just such a . . . I don't know what he'll do.' Her features hardened. 'But while his cock is still attached the knife stays under my pillow.' She urged the mare into a gentle trot towards the fence-post and dismounted smoothly.

'Besides, I don't need a man—' She knelt down by the base of the leaning post and fished out a small spike from somewhere in the folds of her tunic. She dug behind it, stabbing hard at the earth and rooting around, grunting with the effort. 'To fix a post.' Satisfied, she stood up, leaned her shoulder on the top of the post, bent her knees, set her feet and pushed. The fence groaned as the rails squeaked back into place. She held the post down and kicked and stamped at the earth around the base until it stood solid and didn't rattle around.

'See? Hammer? What nonsense. Ground's frozen – he'd've split the post. Although he could have hurt himself, so maybe I should have let him.' Helga mounted the horse and patted its neck. 'Now, home with you, lazy old girl,' she cooed. The horse snorted once and turned around, following the fence.

She saw him from a mile away and her stomach lurched. There was no mistaking the man in her yard, standing by her door. Her first instinct was to turn and flee; to head for Skaer or somewhere else. Breathing deeply, she muttered, 'Can't run, Helga. You can't run.'

She assessed the situation. It wasn't Johan. It wasn't any of . . . them. The stranger was – or appeared to be – alone. He did not have a horse so he'd have walked far to get to Ovregard; it was miles inland, which all but ruled out raiders. Nobody from her past knew she was here, and Forkbeard's recruiters had done a good job of rounding up the strays last year – so who was he?

Half-annoyed and half-curious, she set off for home.

Streak thundered down the stretch, enthusiastic to get inside. Helga tugged at the reins, cursing her own reluctance, but eventually the mare slowed down to a canter and finally a walk.

The man had turned when he heard her approach and now he stood in front of her, rocking gently from one foot to the other, keeping more than a polite distance. He was younger than she'd thought he'd be. Or maybe she was just older than she used to be.

'Well met, stranger!' she said as she pulled on Streak's reins and the horse stopped. She cringed inside at her own voice. How did it get so shrill and loud all of a sudden?

The man looked up at her as if he was trying to remember the words. Was he a bit slow? 'Well met,' he finally said in a quiet voice. 'I am Audun. I am handy with tools and a good worker. They said at Skaer that you might need a farmhand.'

Oh, did they, now? 'Was it Skakki?' The man stared at her. 'The blacksmith? Ugly bastard, skin like a cow's arse, always something in his teeth?'

A flicker of a smile was there and then gone. 'Might be, yes.'

'Well, he's about as good with his advice as his smithing.'

The smile turned into a grin, but it was swiftly overtaken by a frown. 'So that means . . . you won't need any help? With anything?'

Helga smirked. There was something about this one that felt right, and she made a decision. 'Not necessarily. How are you with horses?'

Audun shrugged. 'I don't know. Decent? Only recently learned about them . . .' The last sentence faded into nothing.

'Well, let's set you a test, then,' Helga said. She dismounted and did not admit to herself that she was pleased by how gracefully she could still do it. 'This is Streak.' The horse whinnied in response. 'She's a cranky old nag, like myself. Put her away.'

Audun nodded and she watched as his attention switched from her to the horse. Suddenly he looked a lot more sure of himself. He started mumbling and took one step towards Streak. Helga felt herself drawn in – she could hear the odd word here and there, but it was more like a stream of sounds.

Then she looked at Streak, who never let anyone near her and would snap at the Skaer kids if they got too close.

The horse tossed her head and sidestepped. Her ears were pinned back and her head tilted as if she was trying to figure out where she'd heard a tune before.

Audun stepped closer to Streak, and closer still.

He was a lot more substantial seen from the ground. They were of a similar height, and Helga couldn't help but notice the way the material of his tunic strained against his shoulders and chest but not his stomach.

And then Streak stepped towards him, reached her head forward – and nuzzled him.

'Good girl,' Audun muttered. 'Good girl.' Big, rough hands stroked the horse's neck; hypnotic, firm, warm strokes . . .

'Do you have any brushes?'

He was looking at her. The colour in Helga's cheeks rose a lot more than the cold morning required. 'Yes. Stable.' She pointed.

'Thank you,' Audun said. She looked hard at his face for some kind of smirk, a sparkle in the eye, but he was already away with Streak, who was following him like a dog.

Helga remembered to breathe. 'Well . . . maybe I could use a bit of help, just to get ready for the winter,' she mumbled. 'Just for the winter, mind. Nothing permanent.'

She squeezed her eyes shut, shook her head hard, blinked and looked in the direction of the stables.

'Yes. Maybe. Yes.' She took a deep breath. 'Food, board as far as it goes. But just for the winter. And he can sleep in the stables,' she added with unnecessary determination, then spun in a half-circle before she remembered what she was going to do and headed into the main house.

Audun rubbed down Streak, who stood calmly by with her head hung low. He'd struggled to find things to say to Helga for the first couple of days, but it was getting better now. That first time in the yard he'd remembered uncomfortably well how bad he was at talking to women. 'It was lucky you were there,' he said to Streak, who nudged him. 'Saved me from crapping my pants, you did.' The horse snorted in agreement.

It had become easier once they had work to do. She was a competent taskmaster and knew what needed doing. She could tackle most of it herself, too, although her eyes had near popped out of her head when he'd shifted the cracked millstone for her. That had been a heavy bastard and no lies, but he'd found the extra strength somewhere. And that shed had needed to be cleared.

'Audun!'

'Barn!' he shouted back.

A little later, the door creaked. He felt like he could smell her behind him, but that was probably just his imagination. Streak protested at the interruption and he had to drag his mind back to the task at hand.

'So, I thought . . . I—' she stammered from the doorway. The years of living alone had probably made her just as bad at communicating as he was, he thought. 'What do you think we should do when you're finished with Streak?'

'The roof needs fixing,' he said.

'Yes . . . On the shed—'

'Yes. That one.'

'It does. I'll get the ladder and the nails.' With that, she turned and was gone. Audun just caught a glimpse of her raven-black hair swishing around the corner.

Streak reminded him that there was still brushing to be done and Audun resumed, not entirely sure about what had just happened.

'So is tonight going to be the night?' Helga asked, reclining on her furs. The embers glowed in the fire-bowl and the room smelled pleasantly of woodsmoke.

Audun blinked. He'd been half-asleep in his corner of the main house after his stew. 'For what?' Audun asked. When they settled on the terms of his stay, she'd told him that he'd be cooking for her half the time and sharing a meal in the main house. They got on fine now, and he found he really enjoyed listening to her tales. Sometimes it was more difficult than he wanted it to be to go back out to sleep in the stables.

She leaned forward. The soft glow from the fire caught her cheeks and caressed her face; her hair flowed into the shadows. 'For you to yield the mystery of where you came from, Audun Horse-charmer.' Her eyes sparkled.

'Oh, I don't—'

'Come on! Didn't you ever play "you show me yours" when you were a kid?' She smirked altogether too much when he blushed.

'I . . . no.'

'Well – it goes like this. You tell me your mysterious and horrible past – and I'll tell you mine.'

'What do you mean?' No answer. 'What's in . . . how . . . what do you mean?'

'I mean exactly what I say – if you tell me about yourself, I'll tell you about that time when I . . .' Helga's eyebrows arched in recollection. A faraway smile softened her face. Then her eyes trained on him, polished amber across the fire. 'Unless you're scared?'

'No,' Audun said. 'It's not that.'

'Then what?'

'It's just that in my past there are . . .' He looked away and wanted to mumble into his chest, but forced himself to say it out loud. 'There are some bad things in my past.'

Her laughter exploded out of her, short and sweet. 'Oh, boy. You lovely, lovely boy.' He shot her a glance, but she stared straight back at him. 'I am nearly old enough to be your mother.' The way she looked at him suggested otherwise. 'And I am willing to give you one thing for free – unless I've really not been keeping up with the news, you've got nothing on my past when it comes to bad things. So you tell me yours tonight . . . and then I'll tell you mine.'

The swirling chaos within Audun was too much to bear – so he decided to trust his instincts.

He started talking.

They'd rekindled the fire twice. He'd been warm, his stomach full and, fuelled by her rapt attention, he had given her his life's story. Well, almost. His father, life on the road, things he thought he'd forgotten about. Some things had been on the tip of his tongue when he realised that they would just sound like the lies of a madman. And he'd not shared what happened on the wall at Stenvik. But apart from that he'd spoken more this night than he could ever remember doing.

Helga leaned forwards and rested her head on her folded hands. 'Let me see if I got this right. This man, this—'

'Fjolnir.'

'—he knew your name and what had happened where you came from?'

'Yes.'

'And then he took a beating from several men, after which he couldn't see out of one eye? After he'd said wise things to you?'

'Yes.' Audun frowned.

Yawning, she smiled at him. 'Let me guess. Did he give you a gift?' Audun hesitated and she nodded. 'What was it? No, wait.' She reached down and picked up a slate of wood. Then she drew a knife from under her pillow and started scratching on the slate.

Audun watched her, brow furrowed in concentration. When she finished, she put the slate face down on her lap and slid the knife back under her pillow.

'Tell me what he gave you.' The look in her eyes was even more intense.

'It was . . . a belt. Broad, with a big buckle.'

The house was so silent that all he could hear was his heart beating. Helga was no longer smiling. She sat across from him and would not look him in the eye. Instead she handed over the slate. On it were three hastily carved pictures. One looked like a flask. Another was passably close to a hammer.

The third was, unmistakably, a belt with a buckle of hands.

Audun looked at her, dumbstruck. He knew exactly where the belt was: hidden in his pack under his straw pallet. He felt for it every morning and every night. It had not been moved. His stomach turned at the thought of wearing it.

'How—?'

'The belt. Wearing it makes you sick, doesn't it?'

Audun nodded dumbly.

She looked at him with something approaching sadness. 'You still don't know, do you?'

'Know what?'

'The man you spoke to. His name is not Fjolnir.'

Audun looked at her. 'Oh? What is it, then?'

'His name . . .' She took a deep breath. 'His name . . . Well, he has no name. Who he is, is Odin. The all-father. Wotan, Wodin, Valtam, Gestumblindi. A hundred others. He has come to us, and for some reason he has given you Megingjardir, the belt that holds the strength of Thor. But you are not a god, so it will tear your insides apart. You know it will, don't you? I can see it in your eyes. You've felt it. You must choose wisely when you want to use it.'

Audun stood up. His head was spinning. 'I . . . have to go. I'm sorry. I . . . I have to go.' He could feel her eyes on him as he stumbled out into the dark, starry night.

She did not sleep much. When she walked out into the milky grey morning there was no sign of Audun. *He might be out*, she thought, *possibly started early, gone to chop some wood.* She thought back on the previous evening. 'Are you ever going to learn to keep your mouth shut, woman?' she snapped and glanced over at Audun's corner in the stables.

He had not slept there last night.

Streak snorted, swished her tail and moved to nuzzle her. She had been groomed and seen to. Helga relaxed into the familiar movements, saddling and leading the horse into the pale light.

When she returned from her morning rounds he was waiting in the yard. She noticed that he was wearing a fine suit of clothes, cut from very good material, but the wrong fit for a working man.

'Hello, Johan,' she said, biting off every syllable.

'Helga,' the big farmer said. 'I have come to see you.'

'I can tell, because you are in my yard.'

If he understood that she was mocking him, Johan gave no sign. 'I will court you. I have talked about this with the chieftain, and he agrees that we would make a fine pair.'

She wanted to be angry. She thought idly that once upon a time he'd have got a lot more than he bargained for, but now she just wanted him to go. She dismounted and led Streak towards her tethering post. 'Look, Johan,' she said, 'no. I've already said so. No, I do not want to marry you and I am not going to marry you and there is nothing in the law or otherwise that says I have to, regardless of what that pumped-up windbag chieftain says.'

'But you can't live *alone*,' Johan said.

He almost looked hurt, but she was beyond caring. 'I have, I can and I will,' Helga said and continued brushing down Streak. 'If there is nothing else—'

'Don't turn your back on me, woman,' Johan said. An edge had crept into his voice.

Helga spun around. 'Do not presume to tell me what to do or say when you are on my land, Johan Aagard! I would like you to leave!'

She took two steps towards him and wished she hadn't. Johan was a farmer and had been working the land for the best part of forty years. He was a good head and a half taller than her, barrel-chested and solid.

He did not move but looked down at her. 'I have told you: I will court you, and you will be my wife.'

'Loki's balls I will,' she snapped. 'Now leave.'

'No.'

'*Go away!*' she screamed in his face and crumpled as he struck her in the chest. Blinking and gasping for breath, she thought she saw something—

'She told you to leave.'

Audun. Standing by the fence, completely still.

'Oh? So *that's* it, then?' Johan stood over her, impossibly big. 'Someone got there before me?' He chewed this over for a couple of moments. 'It's all right. You're a woman. It was to be expected.' He turned towards Audun. 'Now you, on the other hand, can fuck right off.'

Audun said nothing, but there was a faint . . . change in him. Helga felt her insides go cold.

'I said, you can fuck right off.' Johan took a step towards the blond man by the fence and Helga felt a sharp stab of fear. 'You deaf? Fucking traveller scum. Norse? Probably.'

Two more steps.

'She would like you to leave,' Audun said. He didn't raise his voice, but the statement was loud enough for those who wanted to hear.

Johan was not one of them.

'You fucking—' He stepped in strong, ready to bash, grapple and twist the smaller man to the ground.

Audun broke his arm.

Johan screamed and fell to his knees.

'Audun!' The word escaped her lips and she watched him deflate. He stepped away from the screaming man and took a few deep breaths. Incredibly, Johan staggered to his feet spewing a stream of curse-words, red-faced and drooling. He clambered up onto his horse and rode off, clutching his arm.

Helga clambered to her feet before Audun got to her.

'Are you hurt?' he asked.

She dusted herself off. 'You're going to have to get used to sleeping with a blade,' she said. 'He'll be back.'

Audun sighed and shook his head.

She was about to insist when he walked away.

When he came back out of the tool shed he was carrying a hammer.

Ulfar woke to drops of cold water on his lips. He tried to speak, but all that escaped was a moan.

'Easy. Easy, now,' a man's voice said behind his head.

His eyes adjusted to the light: late evening; sky fading from purple to black. The soft orange glow of a campfire somewhere a bit off. His shoulders were stiff, his back worse. He tried to move his hands, but couldn't. Rope burns tickled and itched. A thick, numb feeling in his stomach slowly dissolved into white-hot pain and his breath caught in his throat.

'You've been badly hurt, friend,' the man said.

Wincing, Ulfar turned to look, but his captor remained out of his field of vision. All he could see was a strong arm holding a water bottle. Now his neck hurt as well.

'Do you remember anything?'

'N-nuh,' Ulfar muttered. He tried to concentrate. *A wagon.* He'd been trussed up and thrown onto a wagon.

'Thought so,' the man rumbled. He moved to stand in front of Ulfar. He was of medium height, greying at the temples. 'I am Goran. I look after a couple of fur-pushers. You are in our caravan.'

'Where—?'

'We're going to Uppsala,' Goran said. 'And you're coming with us.'

The words caught in Ulfar's throat. He leaned back, closed his eyes and waited for sleep.

When he woke again, it was to the merciless bump and jostle of the road. He was still wedged in the back of the wagon; his hands were still bound. The sky was the blue of mid-morning. The chatter of the men washed over him.

'—but where will he go?'

'Forkbeard is heading for the south. We are well north of anything he wants. He'll just take the flat and easy, as usual.'

'Strange choice for a wife, then.'

As the men chuckled Ulfar twisted into a better position for listening. Behind him, someone drew a sharp breath and squealed, 'He's moving! Quick!' The wagon slowed, then stopped and commands were shouted up and down what sounded like a short line.

Someone carrying a staff stepped into view. 'Good morning, friend,' said the man who'd introduced himself as Goran the night before.

'Morning,' Ulfar muttered. His wagon shuddered as the owner of the voice clambered down, out of sight.

'Look! It speaks!' a tall, sleepy-eyed young man said.

'Shut up, Regin,' Goran snapped.

'Calm down, old man. Just saying—'

'Say less.'

Regin huffed and moved away, towards the front end of the caravan, and Goran turned back to Ulfar. 'So. Tell us about your-self,' he said.

Ulfar blinked and stuttered. 'Tell you . . . what? Me? I . . . I was attacked in the forest. Bastard stuck me in the gut and ran away with my gold. I chased him – and next thing I know I'm trussed up on a wagon.'

'Interesting,' said another voice and the owner followed shortly, waddling into view: a squat man with a squashed nose and ill-fitting merchant's clothes. He stared at Ulfar. 'And you want us to believe that? Where are your friends?' He looked comical, but the glint in his eyes suggested he'd be an unpleasant opponent in a game of wits.

Ulfar closed his eyes and thought. Friends? 'One of them went . . . south, I think. The other is dead.'

'Sounds like you're bad company,' Goran said, not unkindly.

'Maybe I am,' Ulfar said. 'But I was making for Uppsala, just like you.'

'Hmpfh,' the short merchant said. 'And who are you going to see there, man of no friends?'

'My uncle. His name is Alfgeir Bjorne.'

Goran glanced at the merchant, who nodded. Ulfar saw the flash of the blade and tried to move, but he was too weak. A strong hand grabbed his arm and with a deft flick his ropes fell away.

'You will forgive the caution,' the merchant said. 'You came stumbling out of a bush, wielding a sword. Heidrek!' He snapped his fingers and another guard, young and bright-faced, stepped into view, holding Ulfar's sword.

'Fancied it myself,' he said as he handed it to Ulfar. The smile on the young man's face was genuine. 'Where'd you get it?'

'A friend made it for me,' Ulfar said.

'I hope he's not the dead one,' Heidrek said.

'I doubt it,' Ulfar said, and he felt a hint of a smile creep onto his face as he stumbled off the wagon and strapped on his sword-belt. 'I seriously doubt it.' It felt good to have the blade back at his side again.

The merchant eyed him. Either he had some serious doubts about Ulfar or he had a naturally suspicious face. Ulfar put on his most winsome smile and hoped for the latter. 'I am Ingimar,' the merchant said, 'and this is my caravan. We'll take you on as a guard – there's no space for passengers. You walk.'

At the front of the line, the first wagon rumbled into motion.

Days passed and as Ulfar fell into the rhythm of the caravan he slowly got the measure of his fellow travellers. The merchants mostly kept to themselves, save for Ingimar, who checked in with Goran three times a day, at morning, noon and camp-time. There were three younger guards: sullen Regin, cheerful Heidrek and Arnar, a quiet, serious man with a big rumbling voice and a big, black beard who'd barely grunted a greeting when Ulfar came to and had not uttered a word since; they answered to Goran, the grey-haired man.

The forest gradually thinned out around them and the land started taking on a curve that looked familiar to Ulfar. There were still a couple of days to go; still a couple of days to make a run for it. The west was behind him and north was nothing but frozen death. He could go south – but that was where Forkbeard was reputed to be. Ulfar pushed the worries out of his mind and concentrated on what he *could* do. At the moment, that meant putting one foot in front of the other.

The sun crept towards the midday mark. Regular as night, Ingimar scrabbled from the seat of his carriage and headed towards Goran. 'Anything?'

'Nothing to worry about,' the guard replied. 'We're fine. Couple of days to go.'

'I know the route as well as you do,' Ingimar snapped, but Goran just nodded and kept walking.

The moment Ingimar returned to his seat, Heidrek started. His favourite pastime was to wind up Regin, and it looked like today's entertainment was just about to begin.

'Regin?' Heidrek said.

'What?' Regin said with a sigh from the other side of a caravan. 'What do you want?'

'You are so much wiser than me,' Heidrek said, and Regin just rolled his eyes and waited. 'If you split a lamb in half, lengthwise, how many legs do you get?'

'Two,' Regin said.

'So if I had a lamb and sold you half, you'd pay me for two legs?'

'Of course not,' Regin snapped.

'But you just said! Two legs! Would you swindle me out of a leg just because you're smarter?' Heidrek asked, a wounded expression on his face. 'I thought you were my friend.'

Ulfar ambled along, listening to the regular plod of the horses and the rattle of the carts.

Regin, smelling a rat, took his time before answering, 'There's no meat on the other leg.'

'But why then does it have the front legs?' Heidrek said.

'If it had big muscles at the front it would run forward and back at the same time,' Ulfar said.

There was a brief silence, and then from the rear of the caravan Arnar roared with laughter so loud it nearly spooked the horses. 'Hah! Forward and back at the same time!' He slapped his thigh. 'If that's not the funniest thing I've ever heard,' he muttered. 'Forward and back.'

Heidrek grinned, and even Regin smirked. When Ulfar turned

to Goran, he found the old man was giving him a calculating look.

'Forward and back,' Arnar mumbled again. 'Well, I never.'

Ulfar knew the road well enough, but it still took his breath away when, after two sharp bends, suddenly the trees thinned out on both sides and the fields opened up before them. In the distance, the hill rose gently and behind it they could see the three barrows. Houses were scattered like toys around the largest building Ulfar had ever seen.

The hof, the biggest temple in the world, was an incredible feat of building: four storeys high and wider than four longhouses set side by side. Behind him he heard Regin mumble a disbelieving half-curse.

'There we are,' Goran muttered. 'Uppsala.'

At that moment the sun broke from the clouds. The light danced across the field ahead of them, slipped between the houses and sought out the top of the hill. When it hit the roof of the gigantic building, the men in Ulfar's caravan had to look away.

'What the—?' Heidrek exclaimed. The roof had turned a bright, shining white, as if it had been struck by lightning.

'It's very impressive,' Goran said. 'They tiled it with gold. They say Thor himself approves.'

'He'd better,' Heidrek said. 'That was something else.'

The nearer they drew to the town, the more the knot in Ulfar's stomach tightened. Soon enough, excited children and yapping dogs were running towards them; the traders largely ignored them, but some of the children gathered around Heidrek. Ulfar was not in the least surprised; the young man looked like precisely the type of man who'd have a knack for entertaining kids.

He tried, but no smile came to Ulfar's lips – and then he saw four men come walking abreast down the winding path around the hill. When the light caught on a cloak of white sable Ulfar ducked behind a wagon.

'Goran?' he hissed. 'I may have to—'

'Count to three, then go to your left,' the tall guard said without so much as a glance in his direction.

One . . . two . . .

A big storage shed loomed up on their left. As Ulfar felt the wagon veering towards it he sent a silent, grateful thought to Goran.

'Watch where you're leading!' Ingimar shrieked.

'Sorry,' Goran mumbled, unseen.

By the time the wagon was straight on the road again, Ulfar was no longer anywhere near the caravan.

UPPSALA, EAST SWEDEN
EARLY NOVEMBER, AD 996

'Welcome to Uppsala, travellers!' The speaker was tall, blond and fair-skinned, dressed all in white so bright that it was almost uncomfortable to look at. He bowed deeply. 'Ingimar!'

Goran watched Ingimar's chin disappear into his chest. 'Prince Karle,' he muttered.

'You're back, you old rogue,' the prince said. 'Worried we'd seen the last of you.'

'You know me,' Ingimar said. 'Like the seasons roll around, old Ingimar will be back in town.'

'That is true,' the prince said. 'Still, hard times. Forkbeard is about, stirring up trouble.'

'He's still in the south, I hear,' Ingimar said. 'We were fine, just me, my fellows and my' – he glanced back – 'guards.'

Goran smiled. Old Ingimar might not be a swordsman, but his mind was sharp enough.

Ulfar's feet found their way without much help. The lambs' path up the side of the hill was still there, leading straight to the longhouse at the top. The door swung open smoothly, but the cavernous space within was empty. Ulfar stepped in, his heart thumping. Something about this felt wrong, like he was thieving.

The familiarity of the place felt worse, somehow, jarring – like a wrong note in a well-loved song. He was halfway to the dais before he realised what was wrong with the place.

He was.

Everything else was the same here, just like he'd left it – a couple of years older, of course, sagging in some places and fresh in others, but essentially the same. The only thing different was him.

'Tell me what happened.' The voice came out of the shadows at the far end of the house and Alfgeir Bjorne stepped into the light from the open shutters. He was still a frightening man at five-and-fifty.

Ulfar swallowed, then blinked in the dim light and glanced around. 'This might take a while,' he said.

Without a word, Alfgeir crossed over to a long bench near the dais and sat down. He looked at Ulfar, then gestured to the next seat.

'Are you telling me the truth, Galti?' Prince Karle smiled, his eyes trained on the young noble.

'I am, my Lord. I'm sure I saw him go up the path to the longhouse just a little while ago. Just when you were welcoming the guests.'

'Longhouse, you say. Hm. So Ulfar's back.' Without thinking, the prince clutched his forearm. 'And he was alone? You're certain of this?'

'Absolutely,' Galti said.

'Well then. Hrodgeir!'

A flushed youth stopped studying his toes and peeked out from behind Galti. 'Uhm . . . yes, your Highness?'

'Is Greta in town?'

'No, her and Ivar are off in the fields, I think. They might have gone home.'

'Find them – find them and make them come here. Tell them I request their company.'

Hrodgeir's eyes opened wide and he glanced at Galti, who snapped, 'Do as you're told!'

'Of course,' the boy said, and scurried away.

When he'd gone, Galti looked at the prince. 'Greta . . . and Ivar. Think it'll work?'

Prince Karle smiled, rolled his shoulders and stretched. 'We'll see.'

Alfgeir Bjorne sat quietly and looked at Ulfar. There was no light in his eyes.

'I'm sorry,' Ulfar muttered.

'Nothing you could do,' the old man mumbled, his voice thick with grief. 'Nothing you could do.'

'But I—'

'Shut up.'

Ulfar did as he was told, and continued to sit uncomfortably in the dusk.

'He liked you. I hope you had a good time.'

'He did you proud, Alfgeir.'

At that, the old man smiled. 'You were always good with words,' he said. 'We both know what he could and couldn't do. He could have been something with a couple of years on him. Now he'll never have them.' He sighed heavily and looked up, as if seeing beyond the ceiling to the skies. 'Not here.'

Ulfar fidgeted, and hated himself for it. What now? In a way, it was like he'd stepped off a cliff; now, floating in midair, he did not know what to do.

'Best stay and wait for Jolawer,' Alfgeir mumbled. 'He needs to hear the news from Stenvik.'

'Jolawer? But . . .' Ulfar's voice trailed away.

Alfgeir looked at him. 'I didn't spend the best part of twenty years raising an idiot nephew. Of course Eric died. That's what old men do. Jolawer has been king for a year and a half. Peacetime.'

'So Sweyn—'

'Yes, Sweyn has had enough of a rest to gather his troops and quite enough time to get sick of that harridan of his, so he's coming, and he's coming soon. I don't know if news of this Olav will worry our young king more or less than the Forkbeard on his doorstep, but whatever they do, it's my job to watch over the boy and so that is what I will do.'

They sat together in silence for a while, until Alfgeir sighed again and said, 'Tell me. Tell me how he lived.'

This was something Ulfar could do. He told him. He told him what had happened from the moment Geiri's boat had set sail from the coast, of their adventures in Rus, tales from Hedeby, the endless roads and endless seas. Ulfar spun and weaved, plucking people from thin air, Goths and Moors, all manner of urchins and locals – and girls. There were a lot of girls. Most of them he gave to Geiri, building a picture of a young man learning life in the best possible way. As he talked, Alfgeir's brow started to lift ever so slowly, and soon enough he was chuckling along, then laughing at the foolishness of his two young pups making every mistake in the book. Midway through a tale of two men with trousers around their ankles escaping by the skin of their teeth from a furious farmer and his inviting daughters, Alfgeir rose, lit the fire set ready in the hearth and poured them ale.

With the setting sun, spirits lifted in the cold longhouse.

With the darkness came King Jolawer.

'My King,' Alfgeir said.

'Alfgeir,' Jolawer said.

Ulfar blinked and shook his head. The boy he'd known as Little Jolawer was now a man of nineteen summers and almost Ulfar's height. He was still scrawny, still looked like a worried bird, but there was something different about him.

And then Ulfar remembered: *King*.

King Jolawer Scot stared at him intently. 'Ulfar?'

'The same, my King,' Ulfar said. He bowed.

'None of that,' Jolawer said. His voice was clear and strong. 'We have history, Ulfar. Although it was inevitable, I was sad to see you go away.' The king scanned the room, then looked at Alfgeir. Something passed between them, and Jolawer looked down at the floor for a moment.

'That is the world,' Alfgeir muttered.

'So it is,' said King Jolawer.

'You need to hear what Ulfar has to say,' Alfgeir said. 'It's a good year for raising armies, apparently.'

Goran had sent Heidrek and Regin to look after the horses. The stable wall was solid enough for leaning on, so he allowed the time to pass and the road to leak from his bones.

Ingimar came out of a house on the left, waved at someone inside and hefted a sizeable sack. Amber, Goran thought, probably. Or something else. He'd never quite understood the men who wanted to take things from one place and put them in the next, only to do it all again at the other place. He could see the idea behind it, but it all just felt a little . . . pointless.

The merchant approached him, wheezing and coughing under the weight of his goods. 'We're nearly done here,' he said. 'Quick sales, good prices. Perfect trip,' he added. *A perfect trip would have been shorter, warmer and better provisioned*, thought Goran, but he kept that to himself. 'Where are the boys?'

'Seeing to the horses.' Goran gestured towards the stable.

'Hmf,' Ingimar snorted. 'Wish I could have taken you out again tonight.'

'You can't do that,' Goran said with a start. 'The horses need to rest and—'

'Yes, yes, I know that.' Ingimar waved his objections away. 'Of course I know. The boys need a bone with some meat and some meat for their bone. Hah!' He laughed and waddled off. 'I'll see you in the big house when it's time for food, old man,' he said over his shoulder. 'We're stuck here for tonight so might as well have some fun!'

As Ingimar left, carrying the sack, Goran looked around, taking in the hardening grasp of autumn, the bare, wet-black trees in the distance, the sheen of dying leaves fading from red to brown. He smelled the cold on the air and watched the rim of the sun setting in the west. The houses of Uppsala were, upon closer inspection, just like the houses in every other settlement. It was cold in the shade of the big temple on the hill and his old bones ached.

Fun?

Didn't seem very likely.

By nightfall the fires in King Jolawer's hall were roaring. The dull, oppressive heat was better than the alternative; the Snow King's fingers were already scratching at the window screens. It was going to be a hard winter and no mistake.

'Goran! Stop being so mis'rable!' Heidrek shouted. 'Have another drink!'

'Y' can't say tha',' Regin slurred behind him. 'Ee 'asn't 'ad one.'

'Outrage!' Heidrek twisted his face into a serious mask. 'Will not do! You bring shame to our home counties!'

Goran rolled his eyes and forced a smile. 'I go thirsty for my good nature, boys,' he said.

'Whaddya mean?' Regin peered at him suspiciously.

'More for the two of you!' Goran shouted.

Heidrek and Regin cheered, clanked their mugs together and swigged the contents. The Svea king's ale smelled passable but Goran had decided tonight would be a good night to have his wits about him. It would make tomorrow's walk better, for a start.

A cold gust of air made him turn his head. One of the welcome committee – the tall one with the nose – had stepped in. The boy dusted off his coat and gazed around the room with a casual air. He repeated the actions three times, and Goran couldn't help but smile. *Why don't you just shout their names?* he wanted to say. *It doesn't look like they're here.*

The newcomer's eyes kept drifting towards the panel at the back of the dais. The three chairs were empty.

A door slammed and a large man who looked only marginally younger than Ingimar walked out from behind the panel. He had the shoulders of someone who enjoyed his work and the belly of someone who enjoyed his wine, and he radiated authority. He calmly sized up the men in the room. The chatter died down very quickly, and Goran couldn't help but think of deer smelling a wolf. Alfgeir Bjorne might be old these days, but he wasn't dead yet.

Favouring his left leg slightly, the large man went and sat in the chair to the right of the high seat.

When Ulfar came out and sat beside him, on the other side of the throne, Heidrek coughed, mid-drink.

''e waschn' kid'n',' Regin mumbled. His head was sinking closer and closer to the table.

A young, slim man made his way out from the back room and sat in the high seat. In between the two other men, King Jolawer Scot looked young, and painfully frail.

'He certainly wasn't,' Goran said, while keeping his eyes trained on the dais. Something was . . . *off* about the three men. Ulfar appeared to be reluctant to look at the other two. The young king's shoulders were stiff, and even from the far end of the hall he looked ill at ease.

'All hail King Jolawer!' Alfgeir shouted, and the men answered with a rousing cheer, but that was it.

'Nothing much to say to their king, it seems,' Ingimar said. 'Gets in the way of drinking time.' The merchant had sidled up next to Goran without him noticing. He was carrying two jugs of mead. In the firelight he looked thinner, somehow. And was that a tinge of grey in his hair? 'Jolawer's found out about Olav in the north. I hear from others that he's taken Trondheim.'

'Hmh,' Goran grunted. The light was just playing tricks with him. 'At least we won't die bored.'

'Hah!' Ingimar laughed and toasted his health. 'Come on, Goran. One for tomorrow and the road.'

The warmth and the food were making him very thirsty. Goran reached for the jug. Just one, this time.

*

King Jolawer ate quickly, taking little pleasure in his food, then he bade goodnight to his guests and ducked through a door in the back wall to the bedchambers beyond.

He caught Alfgeir Bjorne looking at him. The big man had aged visibly today, but at least the spark was back in his eyes. 'What do you see?' he rumbled.

'He's good,' Ulfar muttered. 'He asked all the right questions. I think he'll do well.'

'If he lives,' Alfgeir said. 'If he's around long enough to see things – to see the things you've seen,' he added.

Ulfar didn't answer.

'Boy' – Alfgeir stood up with some difficulty, and Ulfar felt nine years old again – 'get drunk. Talk to someone. Tell jokes. Play games. I've got one dead son and I've no use for a half-dead nephew.'

The lump in Ulfar's throat threatened to choke him, but his mask remained cold and impassive. He favoured Alfgeir with a smile. 'I'm not one to disobey,' he said.

With that promise, the king's right-hand man limped away, climbed down off the dais and moved through the suddenly sparse crowd, heading for the front door. It was odd how crowds always tended to thin out right in front of Alfgeir Bjorne's feet, Ulfar mused. It seemed common sense was still at least a little bit common.

Ulfar let the night wash over him. He met people he knew, though fewer than he had expected, and they talked, but said little. He wandered around the room and found himself at the cook-pots. The mead tasted familiar and the stew was reassuring. He politely declined a third helping and handed his bowl back to the cook, but he did allow a pretty little blonde to refill his mug.

She looked familiar – but then, there was one in every town. He took a sip and winced; it tasted slightly off, but it was sweet enough. Somewhere deep within Ulfar, something felt a little bit right for the first time in a while.

He turned away from the pots and the slap hit him full in the face, leaving his ears ringing.

'You dickless, no-good, oath-breaking shitbag!' The woman in front of him was slight of build but absolutely furious. Her nostrils flared and her eyes were wild.

'G-Greta?' Ulfar stammered, reeling. He could hear cheers and laughter around the king's hall.

'*Greta?* You're *asking*? You don't remember my *name*? You little— *Gaah!*' she screeched and launched herself at him, pummelling his chest, kicking, spitting and flailing wildly.

Ulfar crossed his arms in front of his face. 'Hey! Wait! We can—' Claws swung for him at eye-height and he grabbed the hand on pure reflex. At the back of the room the door flew open.

'Leggo ma sister!' someone shouted. A man strode into the hall. '*You!* Gotta fine face to be showin' round here!'

Greta continued to rain blows on Ulfar with her free hand, all the while twisting in his grip. 'Stay outta this, Ivar!' she screamed. 'I love him!' She was crying now, but her attack on Ulfar showed no sign of slowing down. 'Why'd you leave? You told me we would be together! You told me you *wanted* me!'

She started kicking wildly and her foot connected with his knee. Ulfar cried out and managed to throw her, still screaming, away from him.

Ivar sidestepped his flailing sister and came right for him. 'I'll fucking cut your shit off and stuff your face with it,' he snarled.

Ulfar was dazed, but still found his feet quickly enough to ward off Ivar's clumsy blows. 'Ivar! Stop!' he shouted, but the enraged man chose not to hear him as he snarled curses and imaginative options for Ulfar's genitals.

Backed up against a support beam, Ulfar twisted away from a vicious right hook and face-first into Greta's redoubled efforts. She was snotty and crimson-cheeked with fury and her words made no sense. She wrapped her arms around him in a fierce grip, shouting incoherently into his chest.

'Please, I— *Mph!*' The air exploded out of Ulfar's lungs as one of Ivar's blows finally connected and he staggered, lost his footing and tumbled over on top of Greta.

'Look – they're at it again!' someone shouted drunkenly from the crowd. The laughter was mean.

Ivar roared again, completely incensed, and Ulfar felt pressure on his head, then a sharp pain as he was pulled off Greta by his hair. The woman on the floor didn't move. Ivar shrieked, 'What have you done to her, you bastard?' and twisted Ulfar's hair even more tightly.

A knee smashed into Ulfar's spine, hard, and the tingling sensation in the fingertips of his left hand was made worse when it disappeared and was replaced with nothing. 'She's just knocked out,' Ulfar hissed through gritted teeth. 'And now' – he swung his right hand in a big arc and hit Ivar's wrist with his clenched fist, making him scream and let go of Ulfar's hair – 'I've had just about enough' – Ulfar clambered to his feet and faced off against the man holding his wrist and shooting anguished glances at his sister on the floor – 'of this.' He swung his left arm at Ivar; it didn't feel right yet, still mostly numb, but it worked just fine as a club.

Ivar raised his arms on reflex to ward against the blow and Ulfar used his own momentum to drive his right fist hard into Ivar's stomach.

The blond man doubled over, coughing, and without missing

a beat Ulfar kicked the back of Ivar's knee. As he went down, gasping, Ulfar growled, 'Stay down if you know what's good for you.'

Fucking locals, everywhere the same. He looked around at the red, sweaty faces hoping for more violence. Part of him wanted them to come and have a go – three of them maybe, a handful, enough to keep him busy.

No one came forward.

He looked at them, one by one. 'I didn't ask for this,' he said. 'You saw them. It was years ago.'

A couple of grim nods in the room.

One face registered alarm. The eyes were fixed on Ulfar's knees.

A flash of pain in his leg turned Ulfar's vision bluish-white.

He looked down.

A skinning knife was buried almost to the hilt in his leg. Blood bubbled up out of the wound. Ivar was lying on the floor at his feet, looking up at him, a maniacal grin on his face.

Before he could think, Ulfar let himself fall down. His aim was true: his kneecaps crashed onto Ivar's chest and he felt the ribs crack. After a moment he rolled off, drew a deep breath and screamed. All he could hear was the rattle of Ivar's breathing and the throbbing in his own ears. No one moved to help him, so he dug his fingers into his tunic, clutching the material near the shoulder. The sleeve came off, though not easily, and Ulfar bound his leg tight just above the wound, just like he'd seen Sven and Valgard do.

Breathing quickly, he reached for the knife and pulled it out. The blade slid free smoothly, coated with his own blood.

'Fucking bastard bitch,' he muttered.

The bubbling slowed down to a trickle as he tightened the knot, cut off some extra material from the bindings and stuffed it into the wound. It'd hurt like a bastard to remove, but he wouldn't bleed to death. Not today.

After a while on the floor, he levered himself up.

'Thank you for helping,' he snarled at the nearest man, then caught himself. The faces in the king's hall were all studiously not looking in the direction of the dais.

Ulfar turned around.

'Welcome home, *cousin*,' Prince Karle said. Dressed in his white sable and linen shirt, he looked like a shard of winter. He stood at one end of the room, flanked by three young men Ulfar thought he recognised. The names eluded him. The prince stepped towards him. 'You're causing trouble again,' he said.

'Was him,' Ulfar said. A cold chill went through him. 'Was him started . . .' he tried again, but the words didn't come out right. A spasm racked him and he had to reach for a table to steady himself.

'Of course it was,' Karle said. 'Our very own Ivar tried to kill a *foreigner*' – he spat the word out – 'for no reason. Of course, you're guilty of attacking a man of Uppsala *in the king's hall*,' the prince shouted. 'And of beating a woman! You should be ashamed of yourself,' he added. 'There's only one way this will go.' The prince walked slowly towards Ulfar. 'As the king is not here, nor our beloved friend Alfgeir Bjorne, it is I who will decide your fate.'

Ulfar reached for the words again, but he couldn't speak. There was something wrong.

'What? I don't understand you,' Prince Karle snarled.

Ulfar's stomach turned and pearls of sticky, cold sweat glistened on his forehead.

'Speak up if you want—'

'Guest's rights,' the voice boomed. Arnar stepped forward, placing himself between Ulfar and the prince's men. Up close, he was truly a substantial man. 'We claim the right of guests as spoken of in Havamal, as ordained in the Voluspa, which any good host gives freely. We have shared your food. We have drunk your mead. And fine mead it is, too!' he exclaimed to the gathered men, to scattered but growing cheers. 'We have toasted the health of the men of Uppsala, and we ask nothing in return but to be tried as true and free men.'

Ulfar wanted to shout, to scream and jump at the same time, but his body wouldn't obey him. A strong and bitter taste was the only thing emerging in his mouth.

Poison.

Prince Karle's face soured. 'Take this bag of road-shit with you from the hall and do not plant his shadow on our lands again. The king forbids it!' With that, the prince and his men turned and walked away.

'Don't run forward and back at the same time, Ulfar Thor-modsson,' Arnar rumbled, looking at the grey-faced man currently clutching a table for balance. 'You're going to need some fresh air.'

'Excuse me,' said a woman's soft voice behind them. 'Would you help me bring him to my quarters?' Ulfar tried to turn, but couldn't. A cold claw of fear scraped his bones.

'Are you going to look after him, slip of a thing like yourself?' Arnar said.

'I will,' the woman said.

'Of course I'll help. He's a lucky lad, our boy!' The bearded man stepped in, put his arm around Ulfar's chest and took his weight. Ulfar tried to speak, but his mouth was woolly and dry. The colours of the hall were starting to fade. 'Is he a friend of yours?'

'A bit more than that,' the voice said. There was a note of mirth in it.

'Oh?' Arnar said, walking Ulfar towards the front door.

A woman's face appeared at the edge of Ulfar's vision: blonde, tiny. There was something achingly familiar about it. Something painful.

The woman looked at him, concerned. 'He's my husband.'

Ulfar lost consciousness.

The ships rounded Muninsfjell, and dark clouds crept over Stenvik Forest to meet them. Finn stood in the bow, straight-backed and still, like he'd seen King Olav do. The men had accepted his command, but he kept thinking he heard them speak behind his back. He did not need to turn and check; he knew the other ten ships were trailing in his wake.

A half-hearted cheer went up from the rowers behind him as Stenvik came into view. No one wanted to admit it, but the morning they set out the ground had been covered with a thin glaze of frost and Finn suspected that the men felt they had not so much left as *escaped* the freezing cold of Trondheim. There were no ships in the harbour. Finn gave commands; half of his fleet veered to the left and aimed for the soft beach to the west of the town.

'Sail!'

Behind Finn, ten sails furled in unison. Taking his lead, the following ships slowed down.

'Oars!'

Behind him, wood scraped on wood as the sailors mounted their oars and fell into an easy rhythm with each other.

The greyish-brownish mass on the pier turned into the worn

and much-mended houses of Old Town, but no voices carried out to sea.

'Where is everyone?' the boatsman asked at his shoulder. Finn did not reply but instead looked at the walkways, the shadows and the spaces in between. Sunlight flashed off something above Stenvik's walls and in three oar-strokes he'd made up his mind.

'Weapons!' he shouted.

Mail-clad spearmen emerged from the shadows of Old Town and marched silently to the pier, where they took up defensive positions. Bowmen stepped out from behind the old longhouse and crouched down, ready to fire.

Finn raised his hand and signalled for his fleet to stop. The command spread out behind him.

'We return from Trondheim with tales of King Olav's great victories and demand that you step back from the pier!' he called.

None of the fighters moved, but one or two cast glances behind them.

'In the name of Jesus, our Christ and Saviour! *Step – back!*' Finn shouted.

'Back off,' someone echoed from the beach, and the spearmen on the pier relaxed visibly. The bowmen turned their arrows to the ground and a space cleared around the pier. A heavyset man with grey hair stepped up and stood in front of the assembled men: Gunnar Hovde. He had been a reliable chieftain, but no one of particular note.

As soon as Finn's ship docked he leapt ashore and closed the gap in big strides. 'What is this supposed to mean, Gunnar?' he snarled. 'Do we need to have' – he gripped the hilt of his sword – 'a talk?'

'Calm down,' Gunnar said. 'We just wanted to be safe.'

'Safe?' Finn looked around at the grim faces of King Olav's soldiers. There were hundreds of them. 'Safe from what?'

'You better follow me,' Gunnar said.

'What's going on?' Finn said, but the chieftain had already turned around and was heading towards New Town.

They were soon met with cries of 'Gates! Open the gates!', followed by the rough, grating sounds of heavy wood on stone.

'You closed the gates?' Finn burst out. 'What in Hel's name has been going on here?' But Gunnar did not reply; instead he stopped in the middle of the tunnel, under Stenvik's walls.

'Smell,' he snapped.

And when Finn breathed in, he did indeed smell it: fresh blood.

'We don't know what it is,' Gunnar said, shifting uncomfortably on the bench. 'The day after you lot left, three of the locals went into the north end of the woods, but only one came back. He said he'd lost them others somewhere, and they never returned. The day after, ten men went out to search for them – only two of those came back. I had to stop everyone else from charging out, armed to the teeth. Since then . . . well, strange things have been happening.'

The shadows in the longhouse suddenly looked a little darker.

'Like what?' Finn said.

'Like the tunnel,' Gunnar said. 'That fucking tunnel. Do you remember Hildimar?'

Finn winced. 'Big bastard from the south coast?'

Gunnar's expression was grim. 'The very same. You know how some men enjoy soldiering a little too much?' This time it was his turn to flinch. 'It was a badly kept secret that *accidents* happened around him. Boys' arms would break, girls would get . . . hurt, you know? He was always the picture of innocence, of course, and he was a good man in a fight so King Olav either didn't notice or didn't care.

'But not long after those men disappeared . . .' He paused and took a breath, before continuing, 'We found him in the tunnel one morning, all sliced up. They'd cut off his fucking—'

'How many men did it?'

Gunnar slammed the table and leaned forward, his eyes blazing. 'Listen to what I'm saying, Finn! He was butchered inside – *inside* – the fucking *tunnel*, Finn. Both gates were closed. I think you might want to ask yourself how the actual fuck he got there, who got in there with him and how they got out.'

Finn met Gunnar's anger impassively. 'Did anyone see him enter the passageway?'

'No.'

'Did anyone hear the gates?'

'We're not sure. We've kept them closed since the murder except for those men I know I can trust.'

'And the gates are operated from—?'

'—ropes on the ground, or up top.'

'Watch?'

'Three men on each gate.'

'Bring them.'

Gunnar barked an order; the door behind him opened and closed. Finn ignored the others in the longhouse and focused his mind on the puzzle at hand. How would he approach it?

He looked at the answer, smiled and dumped it in an imaginary barrel of shit. Next he tried to figure out how King Olav would go about such a thing. The solution was fairly obvious and effective.

'Do you know when it happened?' he asked.

'Long after the raven's time,' Gunnar replied curtly. 'A bit before dawn.'

So King Olav's solution was also wrong.

The door swung open and three men entered. Finn vaguely remembered them; they were from somewhere in the Upper Dales. He rose and watched as they stopped, recognised him and bowed their heads. He made the sign of the cross and told them to sit.

'Did you hear anything the night Hildimar was found?' he asked, as gently as he could.

'No,' came the muttered reply, all three answering in concert.

'Did you see anything?'

'No,' they all said.

He looked at the one on the left. 'What was the weather like?'

'Moonlight, mostly. Some clouds.'

He turned to the man on the right and asked, 'Where was your mead barrel?'

'By the wall—' he said and then collapsed as the middle man elbowed him fiercely in the ribs.

Finn allowed the silence to settle. He'd found the third solution.

'And you saw him on that night?' Finn asked.

The man had been dragged off some shrieking wench by Gunnar and now he stood shivering in his undershirt on the walkway. 'Yeah, him and two of the locals,' he muttered. 'Them two who came back from the forest.'

'What did they look like?'

'One of 'em I'd seen before, but I didn't recognise the other. Scrawny bastard, older, looked like he'd had his beard hacked off in a fight or something. Wore a hood.'

Finn smiled and hoped it would hide the sinking feeling of dread. He gestured to Gunnar, who pushed the man roughly back towards the hut he'd been dragged from.

'What's going on?' Gunnar asked. 'What's with all the questions?'

'You'd better follow me,' Finn said and walked towards the steps to the south gate. 'And be quick. The light is going.'

When he was up on the wall, he immediately started looking for the telltale scuffmarks of the mead barrel and sure enough, he found them. 'Idiots,' he muttered. Then he turned to Gunnar. 'Come here,' he snapped. 'Look: barrel.' He pointed to the planks resting against the outer wall. Then he leaned over. 'Handhold.' Tufts of grass had been pulled loose exactly where someone might have hidden up against the edge. 'Powdered nightshade over the edge, straight into the barrel and your guards are out like babies.'

'And then what?' Gunnar snapped.

Finn pointed towards the longhouse. 'Three men come walking out of there. One is drunk, the other two are pretending. One of them says he knows of some pussy in Old Town; she likes it rough, he says. Hildimar is all for it, probably getting hard just at the mention. The gates open on one side, letting them in, then stay closed at the other end, leaving Hildimar stuck in the tunnel. They cut out his tongue first, then they pay back the pain.'

Even in the fading light, Gunnar looked pale. 'But – but – how'd they—?'

Finn walked over to a circular shield set into the walkway on the wall. 'Busted murder-hole from the siege. When you were in the tunnel, you should have looked up,' he said.

'But hold on,' Gunnar said, 'you're saying one man drugged my guards, then the murderers took Hildimar into the tunnel – so who pulled up the gates?'

And Finn knew. He did the old man the courtesy of looking around first and making sure no one was going to overhear before he asked, 'How many of the old Stenvik locals would you want no part of in a fight?'

Gunnar smirked. 'I'd have no part of anyone in this hole – but of the fighters left, the ones who haven't disappeared into the forest? I'd say maybe fifty, give or take.'

'That enough to open the gates?'

The truth hung in the air between them. Neither was smiling any more.

'And where are they now?'

'They were—' As the grey turned to black in the east, the colour drained out of Gunnar's face. 'They all volunteered to come out and meet you.'

The first red-yellow tendrils stretched to the sky from the roof of the old longhouse by the harbour as the fire reached upwards, ever upwards. In the spreading night it was an explosion of light and colour. Within moments the whole roof was aflame, first backlighting and then biting into the huge wooden cross that someone had fastened to the front of the longhouse. Someone had stuck a horse's head on top of it, facing New Town.

Finn and Gunnar watched the conflagration in silence. They saw the shadowy figures move like ghosts in the flickering light, drifting towards the forest.

The last one to leave the pool of fire was nothing more than a streak of moving darkness, but Finn thought he could feel the man's gaze. Something in his bearing had a black promise.

Beside him, Gunnar snapped out of the flame trance and shouted, 'I'll rouse the men! We'll go after them! They're going to—'

'No,' Finn said, his voice flat. 'This is their land, and they will cut you down. You will double the watch at all times and send no one out of the town without armed guards.'

'But—'

'But what?' Finn snapped.

'Why? Where are they going? What – what will they do?'

Finn sighed. 'Just double the guard. Double the guard on the wall at all times. And no one goes into the woods. Ever. Did you get that? No one.' He was pretty sure he'd figured out what had happened in Stenvik while he was away, though he hoped and prayed that he wasn't right.

On Huginshoyde, high up above Stenvik, a tall, white-haired man adjusted his broad-rimmed hat and smiled. Two large dogs lay at his feet. Below him the fields stretched to meet the treeline. 'You're not wrong, Finn Trueheart,' he muttered. 'I really wouldn't go into the woods. You never know what you'll find.'

The scent hit both dogs at once and they scrabbled to their feet, but their throaty growls quickly changed into a high-pitched, keening noise as they backed into the old man's legs, their heads low to the ground.

The old man did not move. 'I thought you might make an appearance,' he said.

'You decided to meddle in my games. I'm surprised you didn't . . . see it coming.' Smugness dripped off every word.

The old man turned and closed his one good eye. The other, milky-white and almost too big for its socket, stared unblinking at the black fox that was perched on a ledge above his head. It looked impossibly sleek, and its posture suggested more shapes than the eye could comprehend. 'Games?' he said, sighing. 'Is that all this is to you? A game?'

'No,' the fox said, 'though it's fun, too.' This time the smile revealed teeth. 'Mostly because I know how the game ends.'

'And how does it end?' the old man said with a sigh.

'More battle. More death. More souls to Valhalla. More belief. More power. More of everything. And then, because no one really believes in you any more, I'll rule. See? Fun.'

Now the old man smiled, too. 'I tend to win at games,' he said. 'And you haven't beaten me yet. I will stop you, Hell-spawn. I will right my wrongs.'

'We'll see,' the fox said. 'Although I admit that the trick you just pulled was quite clever. But those two are not going to be enough. They're old, just like you.'

'We'll see,' the old man said. 'We'll see.'

Without sparing the fox a second glance, he walked away, leaning on his staff. The fox watched him stride down the hill, followed by the two dogs with their tails between their legs. When the old man had left, the fox sprang down from the ledge, stretched in midair, pushed into spaces that weren't there, blurred and *changed*. When he landed, he was a tall young man with silky black shoulder-length hair and smile wrinkles around green eyes that sparkled with mischief. 'And how are you going to get there, old man? By walking? Parents. They're so . . . *boring*.'

Grinning, the green-eyed youth turned and leapt off the cliff edge. Moments later the silence was broken by the beating of newly formed wings and an unnaturally large raven ascended, borne on the wind, heading north.

TRONDHEIM, NORTH NORWAY
EARLY NOVEMBER, AD 996

Valgard exhaled and watched his breath rise in a pale grey cloud towards the rafters of the barn. His chest was tight with worry; it had been ever since he woke up. From his vantage point by the door he watched the men as they loaded horses and packed bags; his chest grew tighter still. This was it. He was setting out to find the source of whatever had nearly brought Stenvik to its knees.

Inside, the men worked in silence. No one asked, no one commanded: they all knew what they needed to do and they were going about it with quiet efficiency. It had taken three days to assemble the group. Some he'd known already, some had come from Botolf and Finn had supplied a few. Whilst there had been those more than ready to leave Trondheim, others had needed a little more convincing.

A shape moved in the shadows on the edge of his vision. 'Good morning to you,' Valgard said.

'Hmph,' Botolf said as he appeared out of the darkness.

'Not a friend of the dawn?'

'Stupid time of day,' Botolf grumbled.

'Depends,' Valgard said.

Botolf spat and stepped forward. 'We'll need more men.'

'These are the ones our Lord gave me. Why do we need more? They look hard enough.'

'We'll lose some,' he muttered.

'Lose some? Why? To what?'

'The cold. The north.' The lanky chieftain looked him up and down then looked away again. 'I forget. You've not done much of this.'

Valgard pursed his lips and swallowed the first three things he wanted to say. At first glance he and Botolf weren't that different in shape, but he'd seen enough murderers in his time to know that size would count for little when the blades came out. 'No, you're right. We need more men. I'll go and see what I can do. Maybe we can ask him,' Valgard said, gesturing through the open door at a scrawny youth with his face pressed up against the wall, peering in through a crack.

Botolf glanced and frowned. 'Skeggi's pot-boy. Hmph.' He cracked his neck and rolled his shoulders. 'If you need to go away and do something, maybe talk to someone for a while, now would be a good time.'

When Valgard looked outside again the pot-boy was gone.

'Why?' King Olav's eyes narrowed. He shifted in the high seat, trying and failing to find a comfortable position.

Valgard cleared his throat. 'I need to extract some information – you know, about the best places to collect taxes.' He teased out a sly, knowing wink and managed to keep his eyes from straying to King Olav's sword, resting in its scabbard by the throne. One step, one word and . . .

'It would be better if I go. He might let something slip.'

'I see. Taxes. Yes.' A flicker of a smile flashed across the king's face.

He looks tired, Valgard thought. *Worn out.*

'You make sure you collect the king's taxes. Not too much – avoid unnecessary killing. Just gather the information.'

'I will, my King. I will. Where is he?'

'He's taken to hiding in the chambers of his old mistress, says it helps him think.'

'If that's where he does his thinking, I can see why he didn't see us coming.'

The king smirked, pointed towards a door at the back of the hall and promptly appeared to forget about him.

Without waiting for further permission, Valgard hurried out of King Olav's sight.

So far, so good.

Beyond the door, steps led to a long earthen corridor that had fallen into disrepair. Chipped struts and skewed slats made it look like an old jawbone. Rubble covered the floor. 'Into the belly of the beast,' Valgard muttered as he picked his way along.

The corridor ended in steps leading up to a thick bearskin covering the entrance to Hakon's rooms. Valgard pushed the fur aside and warm air flowed out to meet him, carrying with it the smell of old sweat and bad blood.

Hakon stood in the middle of the room, one hand on the hilt of a long-hafted axe, watching him. He still struck a formidable figure, but the shoulders sloped, the hands trembled ever so slightly and there was more white than grey in the beard.

'I thought he'd send them in the night – and I thought they'd be bigger. And louder. What do you want?' the old chieftain snapped.

Valgard stopped, one hand on the bear pelt. 'I want nothing,' he said. 'Well, almost nothing.'

Hakon sneered at him. 'You're not offering me anything to eat or drink, *Healer*, that much is certain.'

'Because you're neither a halfwit nor a suckling,' Valgard shot back. His stomach sank as the words left his mouth. There was nothing for it, then. This was how it would have to be played. He watched Hakon's feet for the first signs of the swing.

Nothing happened.

He looked up at Hakon's face; there was a hint of a sparkle in the old man's eye.

'Hm. Maybe you're not all bad.' He shuffled towards a table by the far wall, grabbed two mugs and dunked them in a mead barrel. He turned, smiled and pointedly took a sip from each mug. Then he slammed the mugs on the table and sat down. 'So tell me. What do you want?'

Valgard did not move. 'What do I want?' He smiled. 'I only want what's right—'

'Big breath for bad words. If I was—'

'—for the old gods.'

Hakon Jarl frowned. 'What?' Valgard met his gaze. 'What do you mean?'

'What I say,' Valgard said.

Moments passed like winter nights.

'I am listening,' Hakon said at last.

'King Olav has given me fifty of his best men to go "collecting". He has told me that we are to find anyone who worships the old gods and gut them on the spot for not paying their taxes.' Hakon Jarl's grip on his axe tightened, but he didn't say a word. 'I want another fifty of your trusted men to come with me. I want to have them dispose of Olav's murderers in their sleep, then go around the valleys and the highlands to raise an army for you. I will deliver your message. You are the ruler Trondheim deserves, and I believe you should have all the help I can give you.'

'Hmh,' Hakon Jarl said. 'And what would you do with an army raised in my name?'

Valgard looked straight into the ice-blue eyes of the old chieftain. 'Kill King Olav,' he said.

Botolf watched as the silent workers finished packing bags and preparing the last of the horses. The trek-master, an ugly, fish-faced man named Ormslev, waved a hand in his direction, then headed off with his men.

When Skeggi finally arrived, Botolf was alone.

'So, what's this?' the big raider growled.

'What's what?'

'This.' Skeggi pointed at the horses, laden down with baggage.

'Looks like horses,' Botolf said.

'Fucking cute. Where are you going?' The big man stalked towards the tethered animals.

Botolf stepped to the side. 'Pleasure trip. Thought I'd see the countryside since I'm this far north.'

'Don't lie, you skinny turd.' Skeggi walked around the horses, inspecting packs. 'You don't need this many blades to go and see anything. Unless you intend to kill it.'

'Don't spook the mares, now,' Botolf said.

'Fuck you. I'll spook anything I want. Always have.' Skeggi stepped in between the animals and tugged at a saddle; the horse snorted and tried to step out of the way. The other animals shifted and stamped.

'I know,' Botolf said softly. He moved around towards the horses. When he got to the animals beside Skeggi, he reached for the reins.

'So what's going on?' Skeggi snapped over his shoulder, ripping open a saddlebag and growling at the frightened horse. 'Whatever it is, you're not going without me. I can smell it on you, you little bastard. You're on to something. You've got a plan – a scheming weasel plan. You're going for an easy kill somewhere. What is it? Tell me!'

He didn't see the loops until they fell over his head.

The horses whinnied and reared to get away from the pain in their mouths as Botolf gave both sets of reins a sharp tug. Skeggi's face went red, then purple, as the ropes pulled at his neck from both directions. He kicked, hissed and spat, clawed at the ropes digging into him and tried to loosen them, but that only made the horses back up harder. The tortured wheezes from his crushed windpipe grew fainter. His eyes rolled up into his head and the life left his body.

The horses still tossed their heads and snorted, tugging on the lifeless body until precise strokes from Botolf's sword cut it loose.

As Skeggi's corpse hit the ground, Botolf started muttering soothing noises to the startled animals.

They settled down once he'd dragged the heavy body away, and none of them reacted when he brought out a wooden mallet and a horseshoe from the back of the barn.

NORTH OF TRONDHEIM, NORTH NORWAY
NOVEMBER, AD 996

The lines of smoke were only visible when the greyish-blue sea was behind them. Trondheim was already fading into nothing, just dots of brown and green on a vast white carpet that sparkled with the early rays of morning sun.

'Fucking shithole,' Thora muttered. She staggered and righted herself, swinging her bound hands for balance.

'Where are you from, then?' Valgard asked.

'Another fucking shithole,' she snapped.

The snow hung heavy all around them, piled on the green branches of pine trees, covering rocks and potholes, muffling sound and throwing the feeble light back at them. The party marched in the thick, woollen silence.

The sun climbed higher, and higher still. The cold air burned Valgard's lungs, but he had decided he would put up with anything because this was it. This was his chance. If he could find it – and harness it—

'Here.' The trek-master, an odd-looking man with a fat lower lip and bulging eyes, appeared by his elbow, showing Valgard his fingers. A glob of something sat there, looking like week-old snot.

'Oh. Yes. Thank you.'

'On your face.' The man grabbed his hand, slathered the glob on it, shrugged and walked away.

His stomach turned. It smelled like . . .

'Seal fat. Old seal fat,' Valgard muttered. 'I've really been missing out.'

He took a deep breath through his mouth and started slathering it on his exposed skin. As the grease covered his flesh, he almost thought he could feel the warmth returning. As they crested the hill, the bay spread out before them; the boats were already waiting to take them to the other side.

'So where now?' Botolf asked. The soldiers trudged along behind them, huddled in their thick furs and pushing each other to win the coveted spots between the horses. They'd lost sight of the water early in the day as they headed north, as near as they could, staying out of snowdrifts and out of sight. Old habits died hard.

'Untie me,' Thora said, turning to Botolf. 'Do it and I'll make it worth your while, big man.'

Botolf smiled. 'Nice try, bitch, but you still have teeth. You'll know we're in real trouble when I do untie you. Now tell us.'

'Or what? I'll have an accident like that big fat bastard?'

Botolf fixed her with a level stare. 'I don't know what you mean. Poor Skeggi had his head kicked in by a horse. That's why his face was so badly smashed.'

'Did you bring the mallet?'

'If you keep talking, you'll find out,' Botolf replied.

Valgard watched as a grin slowly formed on Thora's face. 'I like you, Scrawny. I'll kill you last.'

Botolf smiled back. 'Look forward to it. So where are we going, my Queen?'

Thora stopped and peered upwards, looking to the skies. 'I think we're roughly right, but I won't know for sure for a half-march. Ask me again when the stars are out.'

'Fair enough.'

Thora twisted to look at Valgard. He noted that she didn't struggle for balance at all this time. 'So, Slimy. What are you here for?'

Valgard looked at her with all the contempt he could muster. 'Tell us about Skargrim's fleet. And about the other woman.'

'I asked you a question,' Thora snapped. 'You're forgetting—'

Valgard stepped up quickly and jabbed her in the throat with his knuckles, just above the collarbone. He felt oddly calm as he watched her struggle to regain control over her lungs. 'Hard to breathe?' he asked, and jabbed again. Her eyes screamed at him, but her face had started turning red. He shrugged it off. 'Oh, yes. I forgot.' She tried to evade him as he grabbed for her hair, but he was quicker. He yanked her to her knees and forced her face-down into the snow.

'You're getting enough air,' he said calmly, keeping his knee on her back. 'You're not going to die.' He twisted her head around so she could see him. 'Unless you keep flapping your mouth like that, in which case I will slit your throat when I fucking feel like it. Understood?'

'Valgard . . .' Botolf said.

Thora coughed and spat. 'Understood,' she wheezed, blinking away tears.

'Good,' Valgard said, pulling her to her feet.

She coughed again, hawked, turned her head carefully and spat away from him. 'Just wanted to check,' she said when she turned back.

'Check what?' Valgard said.

'That you have a dick.' She grinned. 'I like 'em better that way.' Botolf snorted. 'So if you boys are done playing for now, we should keep moving. We have a ways to go and it gets cold up here at night.'

'Due north?' Botolf asked.

'Due north,' Thora said.

The shadows grew longer around them as they marched, and Valgard winced. Every single part of his body hurt. Walking was painful, but stopping and starting again would be a lot worse. Jagged peaks had risen out of the clouds in the distance, illuminated by the setting sun, and the cliffs were closing in on both sides. They were moving up out of the valleys and into the highlands. He noticed some of the men conferring in hushed tones.

'Time to stop, I reckon,' Botolf muttered through the layer of cloth that covered his face. He gestured towards a shadow below the cliffs on the right-hand side.

Valgard shrugged, and Botolf, taking that for agreement, raised his hand. Ormslev, the bug-eyed trek-master, appeared by his side.

Valgard could not hear their conversation, but he watched none-theless as Bug-Eye nodded crisply and started barking orders. The formation broke up into individual piles of cloth and fur. A group of men brandishing axes went to the perimeter and started shovel-ling snow with the flat of the blades. Within moments, piles had been formed into blocks and blocks into walls.

As the horses were led into the enclosure, Valgard realised what Botolf was doing: the shadow below the cliff was hard ground, sheltered from wind and snow, and the new-built walls would take care of the rest.

The pale sun set on fur-covered fighters huddled around miser-able fires. Sheets of cloth had been strung out over spears set at angles to make a windbreak against the worst of the weather; a light, silent dusting of hard frost had already coloured them white.

'Ah, the life,' Botolf sighed. 'Just us and the wild. It's good, isn't it?'

Valgard accepted the flask Botolf handed to him. The liquid was sour and burned all the way down his throat, but he bit his cheek and kept a straight face as Botolf smirked. Someone shouted something at the other end of the camp; there was laughter. The fiery drink settled quickly in Valgard's stomach.

'You'll be happy to see the rising sun, Grass Man,' Botolf said as he rose, and as Valgard shuddered further into his furs he added, 'Oh, don't be sour now. Come. You need to claim your prize.'

'What do you mean?' Valgard muttered, gritting his teeth to ward off the mounting screams of pain from his spine.

'The stars are out.' Grinning, Botolf offered a hand. When Valgard took it, the tall chieftain yanked him to his feet with a strength belied by his skinny frame. 'Let's go and get our sweet little flower, shall we?'

They found Thora sitting in a circle of Botolf's men, telling filthy jokes. Pinkish liquid had leaked into her eyebrows from a small open cut in her forehead. Someone had stuffed it with snow.

One of the men in the circle sported a recently and very thoroughly broken blood-caked nose.

'Kverulf! What happened to your face?' Botolf asked.

Thora stopped talking. The tough guys assembled around the fire looked determinedly in any direction but at their chieftain. Some of them were smirking; others were trying hard not to laugh.

'I'm sorry, my Lord Scrawny,' Thora said. 'Kverulf here thought he'd take advantage of little old me while my hands were tied. Only he isn't too sharp at the counting bit, is he? There's one of me, but there was only one of him.' Chuckles around the fire; even Kverulf offered a gap-toothed smile. 'And of course I told them of our undying love, how you begged me to marry you and all that. My beloved.'

'Fuck off,' Botolf said. He couldn't quite keep the smile out of his voice. 'You're coming with us.' He yanked Thora to her feet and half-pushed, half-dragged her away.

'Remember to tie her feet and flip her round, chief!' Kverulf shouted after them, and the rest of the men offered their own encouragement. 'And watch the teeth! Hers – and yours!'

Roars of laughter washed off their backs as Thora fell into an easy stride just behind Botolf. 'How far?' he asked her.

'Just away from the fires,' she said.

Valgard hobbled after them, watching closely. There was something in the way they walked . . . Botolf *liked* her.

That might make things a little harder.

On the other hand, if his hunch was right, he'd not need Botolf's muscle – or anyone's.

'Here,' Thora said. 'Hold on.' She turned, scanned the horizon and muttered to herself. 'Yes – there it is. We're going' – she pointed up the slope, towards the highlands – 'that way.'

'Sure?' Botolf asked.

'Get stuffed,' Thora snapped.

Botolf just looked at her and smirked.

Valgard turned and hobbled back towards his lean-to.

Some time later the light changed from dark to a pale milky grey. Valgard dusted the snow off his clothes as he saw Botolf scan the camp; Bug-Eye the trek-master hovered close. Something about the rangy chieftain's stance dragged Valgard swiftly from slumber, through several shades of pain and into the waking world. Try as he might, though, he couldn't catch a word of their whispered conversation. He stumbled to his feet and didn't need to act at all to look feeble and helpless. For a few short moments he thought he might see to his aches, then he counted them and abandoned that notion. Everything hurt, and that was how it would be.

Around him the camp was coming to life. Muttered curses and invocations to anyone or anything promising warmth floated on the air; horses snorted, stamped and shook off blankets of snow. A sudden jolt of panic made Valgard swallow his breath: *the prisoner!* Where was she? He looked all around – and then saw her crawl out of Botolf's shelter, hands still bound.

'We're going,' a familiar voice snapped. Botolf stood behind him.

He fought and defeated the urge to jump out of the way. 'And good morning to you, too,' he said. 'So soon?'

'Fuck off. Piss and shit now, eat on the way. And keep your eyes open.' With that, the tall man strode off.

Valgard watched him leave. Something was wrong, that much was certain.

'Over there,' Bug-Eye whispered and nudged Botolf into position.

The chieftain scanned the horizon to the north and lingered only slightly longer on the treeline that the trek-master had indicated. The forest crept alongside their path, a dense mass of frozen branches and snow. 'Got it,' he muttered. 'Who? And how long?'

'Don't know. I think they watched us last night.'

'How close?'

'Close enough to take a good look, I'd guess, though it's hard to tell how near, what with the morning snow.'

'Anyone else know?'

Bug-Eye looked at Botolf and shrugged. 'Maybe. Maybe not. Haven't asked.'

'Don't,' the tall chieftain snapped. 'Just keep an eye on our prisoner. This – I don't like this. I'll have a look.' Valgard watched him turn, scan the line behind them and pick out his first target, a block of a man with hard eyes. Bug-Eye shrugged and dragged Thora back to her place. He was as imperturbable as ever, but Thora appeared revitalised by her night's activity. She glanced at Botolf's back and grinned as he engaged in rapid, hushed conversation with the fighter. Words exchanged, the two headed on down the line and by the time they reached the end, there were five of them. Botolf led his little group into the woods, where they vanished.

Valgard walked in silence for a long time. Thora and Bug-Eye seemed to communicate naturally in their own secret language of nudges, grunts and nods, which now and again resulted in the trek-master adjusting their course slightly. Around them, the terrain changed as they moved out of the sheltered valleys, past the pine and fir that bounded the farmland and up into the highlands. Now snow-covered hills and heaths stretched out before them, undulating softly. The land was treacherous, the soft white covering concealing cracks, crevices and boulders all fit for twisting ankles, breaking limbs and wrenching backs.

Botolf didn't return to the front of the line until long after the sun had crawled over the horizon. Behind him, two of his four fighters dragged a man bound hand and foot. The other two limped along behind them.

Bug-Eye signalled and the line slowed to a halt. Without needing any further commands, the men split up into groups and started tending horses and doling out rations.

Within moments the stranger was thrown at Valgard's feet. He was a lean thing, and probably younger than he looked. His clothes were old but well mended.

'Who's this?' Valgard asked.

'Couple of his friends had been watching us,' Botolf said. 'Handy little bastards, too.' Valgard noticed the glares from his soldiers at that. 'We lost one, two won't see much any more and I caught this one.' He reached out, grabbed a fistful of hair and hauled the prisoner up onto his knees. 'Didn't I, boy?' The boy hissed in pain but did not speak. *He'd be about fourteen,* Valgard thought. *That's a nasty scar on his neck.*

'Oh my,' Botolf crooned. 'We've got a nice little tough guy here, haven't we? Tell me, boy: you look like someone with a bit of sense in you. So why were you watching men like us?'

Valgard watched the boy's face lock in contempt. His gaze drifted past all of them to some unseen place far away.

'Who sent you?' Botolf yanked the boy's hair again, but all he got for his troubles was a sharp, indrawn breath and blood seeping from the boy's scalp. 'Right.' He reached for his knife.

Hands bound behind her, Thora strode forward. She turned to Botolf. 'Maybe he just needs a woman's touch.' Without missing a beat, she levelled a vicious kick at the prisoner's ribs and the boy crumpled to the ground, coughing. 'Right, you little shit,' she snarled. 'Talk. It's your balls next. Who sent you? Was it—?'

The boy coughed in response and spat blood on the snow.

'Oh, but that won't do, sweetcheeks.' Thora knelt by his side. 'Now you listen to me. Here's what I'm going to do to you.' Her lips almost touched his ear as Valgard watched her whispering something to the boy. Then, quick as a flash, she bit down on his earlobe.

'Stop! Stop!' he squealed. 'It was Hakon! He wanted to – he wanted to make sure you were going where you said! I'm sorry!'

'Hm,' Botolf said. 'Right. Let go of the boy's ear.'

Thora clambered to her feet. 'You can't release him. Give me a knife and I'll gut him for you.'

'With your hands tied?'

She shot him a weary look. 'No. I'll cut myself loose first. And then I'll stab you in the eye, single-handedly kill all your men, eat the horses I won't fuck and ride the last one to Valhalla. Give me the knife.'

Without a word, Botolf handed her his knife and turned to Bug-Eye. 'We're—'

The scream drowned his words and he whirled back around just in time to see Thora stand up again from the boy's body with the bloodstained knife clasped in her bound hands. 'Done,' she said, shuffling towards the head of the line. 'Once you dicks have got your fighting gear on you'll talk a man to death. For proper butchery you need a woman. Now stand up straight, you shit-wipes, and get moving!' With a deft flick of her wrist, she cut her bonds.

The effect was remarkable. The men around her either stood up straight or shuffled to get out of the way. Valgard glanced at Botolf, who was watching Thora.

'We marching?' Bug-Eye ventured.

'Looks like it,' Botolf muttered.

As one they turned and walked away from the boy lying in the snow.

Valgard shuddered and wrapped the skins tighter around him, but it was no use. The cold had grown worse the higher up they got; there was no cover to be had anywhere. The rays of the setting sun shone on a distant peak. The cold sneaked in everywhere; it bit at his ankles and his ears, it slashed at his nose and eyes. Behind him, he knew without looking, was a line of men doing the same thing as him: keeping their heads down, trudging along, following the leader and trying hard to expend as little energy as possible on every step.

The shouts started as faint noise but grew crisper and louder as they travelled on up the line until he could clearly hear them crying, 'Wolf!'

By the time Bug-Eye had signalled for the line to stop, the growling could be heard, along with someone's choked screams. Botolf took off at a run, Thora by his side, and Valgard shuffled after them as fast as he could.

Two of Botolf's men were kneeling over a fallen warrior.

Valgard pushed them out of the way and immediately regretted it. The beasts had gone for the guard's face and all that remained was a bloody mess.

Turning away, Valgard noticed the carcasses. 'Is this all?'

'Was enough,' Botolf muttered.

'There's only three wolves,' Valgard said.

'Ain't right,' he heard someone mutter behind him.

'Why'd they go for us?' another, unfamiliar voice said.

'Maybe there are more,' someone said.

'Shut it, you piss-babies,' Thora said. 'And welcome to the north. If you're not eating, you get eaten.' With that, she walked over to the nearest wolf, dropped to her knees and started skinning it energetically. When no one moved around her, she barked, 'Fine. But you're not getting any of mine in two days' time.'

The men glanced at Botolf, who frowned but nodded.

Bug-Eye joined them. 'Look,' he said, pointing south. A pair of ravens were circling overhead.

'That'll be the boy, then,' Botolf said. He turned and looked down at the dead guard. 'Make sure you bury him properly. I don't care if the ground is frozen. Take enough men to get it done. Put him under rocks.' Bug-Eye nodded and turned towards the line, picking out men as he went.

Botolf looked at Valgard. 'This better be worth it, Grass Man. If you're wrong, I will be happy to tear you apart. For weeks.'

For a moment Valgard wasn't sure whether he felt colder on the inside or the outside. 'It's true,' he said, 'and we're going to find it.'

'And what is *it*, exactly?' Botolf said.

Valgard looked at him and formed the sentences in his head: *It is the source of more power than you can imagine. It is the key to eternal life. It is a direct connection to the gods.*

Out loud, he said, 'It is a treasure unlike any you've ever seen.' Which was true, more or less.

After a while, the line started up again and they marched onwards. It took a long time until Valgard felt he was free of Botolf's suspicious looks.

The sun set and darkness sank over them, strewn with the lights of the gods above. The path had wound alongside a mountain and through a nasty scraping thicket but now they had cleared the forest and were once again forcing their way up an endless hill of some sort, while above and ahead of them, gentle waves of green and purple undulated across the black sky. They'd all been on edge since the wolf attack, but apart from a couple of howls in the distance there'd been no further disruptions. No one was talking – the air was just too cold – and Valgard had long since stopped wanting to think; they just trundled on in silence until Botolf gave the signal and the line stopped. One by one the men broke away and inched towards the edge of the hill.

They were looking down on a valley, sheltered by mountains on three sides and the sea on the fourth. A sturdy jetty had been built, big enough to land two raiding ships. A thick blanket of snow covered everything. Valgard's heart started beating faster. The mounds on the valley floor must be houses.

Thora had been quiet for a long time too. Now she turned to Botolf. 'We're here.'

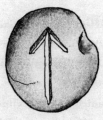

A cold autumn wind whipped the yard in Johan's wake, stirring orange and gold leaves into a whirling dance. Helga stood
silent for a while, her hands on her hips, watching the big farmer
ride over the hill in the distance, hunched over the mane of
his horse.

When she finally spoke to Audun, she did so without looking
at him. 'Go back into the shed,' she said. 'Look under the big box.
If you sweep away the dirt you'll find a couple of blades wrapped
in oilcloth.' She turned towards him. Her jaw was set. 'It'll do you
better than . . . that.' She pointed to the hammer.

Audun shrugged. 'Don't like blades. They break too easy. I know
how to work a hammer.'

Helga frowned. Johan's retreating form was no longer visible,
but the tension lingered in the yard. The cold autumn air nipping
at them smelled of wet leaves and bark.

'Where'd you go? Last night, I mean?'

'Nowhere, I guess,' Audun mumbled. 'Needed a walk.'

'Look – I'm . . . I spoke too quickly. I shouldn't have—'

'No. It's fine,' he said. His eyes met hers. 'I'm just not used to
talking that much. I—'

'Well then,' she said, 'best drag your useless arse to work before you get the hang of chatting.' She winked at him, and received a faint smile in return.

'Guess I'd better,' he said. 'Not gonna earn my keep by telling tales.'

He walked off, still carrying the hammer, and within moments he was hauling timber out into the yard, along with a cutter's axe. Helga noted that he worked facing the path up to the farm and kept the hammer close.

The riders crested the hill just after noon.

Johan rode first, ashen-faced with his arm in a crude sling. Eight of his farmhands rode behind him. They cantered down towards the yard but stopped at a safe distance from Audun. He split a log in two with his axe, put it down and turned to face them.

Helga came out of the tool-shed just as Johan raised his voice.

'You!' Johan shouted and pointed at Audun. 'You're coming with us to Skaer to stand trial for violence! You attacked me unexpectedly, like a coward, and shall be made to pay! You're coming with us!'

From the doorway, Helga shouted back, 'What? You're fucking kidding me! If he hadn't been there . . . I'll—'

Audun raised his arm and Helga's voice caught. 'No,' he said.

Johan looked at him with barely disguised pleasure. 'Then we'll take you in.'

On signal, his companions dismounted and walked towards Audun. To a man they were solidly built, raised on red meat and farm-work. Each of them carried a heavy cudgel.

Audun reached for his hammer, but he was too slow.

Helga was already standing between him and the advancing men, who had stopped in a semicircle around her. She sized them up. 'Every last one of you is closer to death right now than you've ever been before,' she said.

'Step out of the way, woman,' Johan said. 'We're taking your hired hand.'

She ignored him. Instead she spoke to the farmhands. 'How many of you have seen Johan Aagard beat the crap out of big men? Beat them until there's nothing left? Break their spirit? Kick them when they're down and stomp on them until they cry and shit themselves? My hired hand here,' she said, 'snapped your big man's arm like that.' She clicked her fingers. 'My hired hand would have broken his neck if I had asked him to. I didn't, because I thought Johan Aagard would be smart enough not to return. I told my man to get a blade, but he chose a hammer. Do you know why?'

The men exchanged glances. Helga paused, just to make sure they were hanging on her every word. 'Because my *hired hand* said it was more satisfying to feel a man's bones when they break. How the flesh just . . . *gives way*. That is who you are planning on going up against. His name is . . . Audun Blood-smith.' She looked at them for recognition, and when none of them moved, she shook her head sadly. 'You don't even know, do you? Probably haven't seen a traveller in months. Imagine. And you want to take him on, just eight of you. His boat was attacked on the way here by two raiding ships – you've heard the stories; the raiders are all along the coast. Well, these two aren't any more, because my *hired hand* polished them off. He killed every last man.'

'Sure,' one of the bigger men said. 'Sure he did.'

Helga looked him in the eyes. 'Do you want to bet your life on it?' The man stared back at her. 'Do you want to bet the breaking of your jaw? The sound of the smashing of your knees? The shards of bone slicing through your arm? Do you?'

She turned and took them all in, a queen before her court.

The youngest of them shifted uncomfortably. 'Look at yourselves. Look at how . . . *ready* you are. You've got your little sticks, your chests are all puffed up, you're ready to go. And you're big lads; you could do some damage, absolutely. But how many of you have killed a man? I know you've cracked some heads, but how many of you have broken necks? How many of you have stomped a man's life out, and then done it again, just moments later?' She paused for effect, then added, 'Now look at him.'

They all did – and she knew she had won.

Audun stood there beside her, completely relaxed. There was no emotion to him, no flush of fire. He just stood there, hammer in one hand and axe in the other, surrounded by a pile of split logs. He eyed up his opponents like a man ready to do a job – and one by one, Johan's farmhands realised what they were up against. They started inching backwards, like men who have just noticed that the dog is foaming at the mouth.

'Get him!' Johan screamed, his voice breaking with fury. 'There's *eight* of you!' But none of his men took their eyes off Audun as one by one they mounted their horses and rode away. Johan shot her a filthy glance and followed, muttering.

Helga finally allowed herself to exhale.

Behind her she could hear a hammer being carefully placed up against logs.

'Thank you,' Audun said quietly.

Heart thundering in her chest, Helga swallowed. 'I . . . It was nothing.' She didn't dare turn and look at him.

The next thing she heard was the sound of an axe smashing into wood.

They did not speak of Johan again for the remainder of the day. As the sun set, Audun did his customary rounds, checking on shutters and testing latches. His stomach had grown used to regular mealtimes terrifyingly fast and now it was growling at him to hurry up and get back to the house.

It was his turn at the pots. He tasted the stew, added some chopped onion-grass and stirred, checked again. When it tasted right, he glanced at Helga. 'You know him. Do you think he'll come back?'

She winced. 'No. He's been shamed in front of his men; he can't come back now. Even if he were to catch me alone and . . . get what he came for, he'd be condemned. And I've not shown him all my tricks just yet,' she added with a cold smile.

'Good,' Audun said, peering into the pot. He was getting better at cooking, and finding to his surprise that he rather enjoyed it. The room was nicely warm, and Helga was good company. He had told her more about himself than he'd told anyone before, or likely would again, though he could still not bring himself to speak about what had happened on the wall. For some reason, he didn't mind; he didn't think about it so much when he was with her.

It was a strange state of affairs, and one he couldn't remember experiencing before.

For the first time in his life, Audun felt . . . happy.

EAST OF SKAER, JUTLAND.
JOHAN AAGARD'S FARM
NOVEMBER, AD 996

The hooves of a tired horse scraped on freshly frozen ground. The rider's hood was pulled up to ward against the bitter night wind.

'Who's there?' The farmhand's challenge came from the pool of torchlight by the door. Metal clinked as the rider dismounted and pulled back his hood. The farmhand's face went pale. 'I'm – I – I'll go and get him.' He ducked back inside and returned a while later, followed by Johan Aagard.

'Ustain! Well met!' The farmer's face was drawn and grey. He cradled a small leather sack in the crook of his bandaged arm.

'Johan,' the rider replied. The flickering torchlight made the shadows dance on his face. The hint of a smile disappeared quickly. 'You're not that happy to see me. What happened to your arm?'

The farmer ignored him. 'I've had terrible luck with my workers. His Majesty will understand that I simply have none to spare.'

'As usual.' Ustain grinned.

'As usual.' Johan grimaced and threw him the sack.

The thick-necked man caught it effortlessly, rattling the coins within. 'I just hope you make it past spring,' he said. 'Without losing any of your sons.' Johan swallowed and winced. 'Well? Are you going to offer me shelter, like a good host?'

'I am, of course,' Johan said. 'Anything for the king's recruiter. I—' He stopped to think. 'I can maybe even offer you a little more than just shelter.'

Ustain raised an eyebrow. 'Really? Sounds like fun,' he said, ducking ahead of Johan into the welcoming dark of Aagard House.

EAST OF SKAER, JUTLAND. HELGA'S FARM
NOVEMBER, AD 996

Audun liked the rising sun. There was a particular taste to the air during the retreat of cold darkness; the dark blue sky was growing paler as he awaited the inevitable rising of the golden orb. This morning brought a crisp, clear sky and light that bounced off the vibrant leaves in Helga's woods. At least that's what she'd called it when he'd asked: *My woods*, she'd said. *My horse, my land, my hired hand.*

He'd smiled at that. Smiled and nodded.

Audun took a deep breath, filled his lungs with air and held it. As he let it out, slowly, he spotted the rider on the hill and his muscles tensed.

The man just sat there, watching their farm.

'Helga. Rider,' he shouted.

She ran out of the house. 'Oh, for fuck's sake, I was sure he'd— That's not Johan.'

'Anyone you know?' Audun said.

'No . . .' Helga replied, immediately scanning the horizon.

The man had set his horse off at a walk towards them. They watched his approach. Forty yards away, he raised his hand in salute.

'Well met, stranger!' Helga shouted.

'Well met!' the man shouted in return. He dismounted, tied up his horse and walked towards them. He favoured his left leg and stooped slightly, but the soft rustle and clink of his chain mail carried loud enough. His thick traveller's cloak just about covered a longsword and a knife with a long, thick blade. A shield was bound to his back and a hood obscured most of his face. When he was about twenty yards away, he stopped. 'Helga Alfrithsdottir?'

Helga smiled at him, without warmth. 'Do you need to ask, soldier?'

The man straightened at that and pulled back his hood. His skin was red, dry and flaking badly, stretched tight over a bony face. He smiled at her, revealing yellowing teeth. 'No, my lady. I am Ustain, and I have come—'

'I know full well why you've come, and the answer is no,' Helga snapped. 'The answer is no, and that is final.'

Ustain looked at her and cocked his head. 'Really?' he said. 'Are you absolutely sure? Because last time you said you were alone and getting by just fine.'

Helga just glared at him. 'You can't have him. He stays. I don't care what you say.'

'Well, I am sure the king would like to hear what *you* have to say. I will make a point of coming back here in spring so we can talk more about this. How's that? Or – you can help with my noble King Sweyn Forkbeard's efforts and send' – he smiled – 'your *hired hand*.'

Helga went white with fury. 'That – that – *bastard*. He told you, didn't he? He sent you here. I'll gut him – I'll fucking slice his knees open – I'll do him so bad he won't—'

Audun's hand on her shoulder was warm, firm and heavy. 'Helga,' he said, and the words caught in her throat. 'You know . . . you know I cannot stay.' She looked up into his earnest, open face. He smiled sadly at her. 'We both knew this was coming. One way or another.'

'No . . .' she muttered. 'Don't. We'll fight it.' She grabbed his arm. 'Or we'll go together. How's that? We'll travel south together. Find someplace else.'

He embraced her then, held her against him so firmly she could feel his heartbeats, buried his face in her hair.

His whisper was almost too soft to hear. 'I am not taking you with me. Wherever I go, blood will follow.'

They stood there for a moment, together against the world. Then Audun released her and walked towards the stables to fetch his possessions.

Helga turned to Ustain, the king's recruiter. His smile faltered for a moment when he saw her face and he took a reflexive step backwards. 'Tell me,' she said. 'And tell me true. Johan Aagard told you about him. Didn't he?'

'I'm afraid he did,' Ustain said.

Helga nodded slowly. 'Good. Thank you.' She dug around and produced a small spike from somewhere in the folds of her skirt. Her eyes alighted on a piece of wood lying in the yard. She picked it up and carved three runes on it in swift, sure-handed slashes. 'Give this to Audun. I will know if you don't,' she said, handing it to Ustain.

Then she walked to the house and closed the door.

She did not watch Audun leave.

They'd gone about a mile when Ustain stopped Audun. 'Here. She wanted you to have this,' he said, handing him a piece of wood.

Audun took it but made no attempt to communicate.

'Fine. Don't mind. You don't look like a storyteller, anyway. Here's what we're going to do. You'll be joining Forkbeard's army. He's heading east to beat up the Svear and he needs more spear-meat. We'll be about ten days getting there, during which time we'll pick up whatever we find. I've taken most of what there is to have around here, so there'll mostly be kids, creeps and criminals.'

Audun shrugged.

'Good.' Ustain looked at him. 'Now . . . I don't think you'll be running anywhere, will you?' Audun still didn't answer. A smile took hold in the recruiter's face and warped his features in slow-blooming delight. 'No . . . I don't think you will. In fact, I think the king will like you. Come on, let's get moving,' he said, walking along.

They'd walked another four miles when the silence was broken by loud barking. Something was coming towards them at high speed.

'Fucking country dogs,' Ustain said. 'Ought to snap their necks.' The horse snorted beside him.

The big black and white dog stopped a good thirty yards from them and growled low, but did not come any closer. Instead it sniffed the air.

When it caught Audun's scent it let out a whining, keening sound and took off away from them at a dead run.

'What—? I've never seen them do . . .' Ustain's voice trailed off. He looked at Audun, who kept walking south.

The king's recruiter pulled his cloak a little tighter and directed his horse a couple of steps away from the broad-shouldered black-smith.

Three days later there were five of them: a gap-toothed old horse thief, a sniffling youth who spoke with a slur and a nervous young man who kept asking Ustain questions.

Audun marched on in silence and tried not to think, letting the endless questions of the man he'd named Mouthpiece wash over him.

'—and is it true that the king is nearly eight feet tall?'

'Yes,' said Ustain. 'And he has three arms.'

'Really?'

'Indeed. And he speaks the language of the One God. But those who still worship the false gods see him only as a regular man, apparently. Can you imagine?'

'No,' Mouthpiece huffed. 'I cannot. One cannot doubt the king.'

'No,' Ustain said. 'One most certainly cannot.'

The old horse thief hawked and spat. 'I don't know what they want more gods for,' he muttered. 'We were fine with the ones we had. Never seen this new one.'

'Oh, you will,' said Ustain. 'You certainly will.'

They marched south with winter at their backs.

The wind snapped at their heels, buffeted their faces and slipped in between the worn-out layers of old clothes, carrying a smell of salt and cold. The plains stretched out before them. Due south, the horizon thickened a little.

Ustain pointed. 'There we are,' he said. 'Hot stew, a blanket and the word of the Lord. What more could you want?' He turned away and leaned into the wind.

Audun's gut twisted with longing for Helga and he bit down to stifle the growl. He could feel the warmth of the fury but there was something different this time. He saw his forge in Stenvik, but the fire wasn't consuming everything it touched. Instead it was banked and ready to be used. Audun snarled at Ustain's back, but he remained in control. He tried to imagine adding a little bit of wood to the fire.

His nostrils flared and he felt dizzy; blood coursed through him, pounded in his ears, made his heart beat faster. He could feel his muscles tightening, but the sensation of helplessness, of being swept away on the tide . . . was gone.

His lips pursed in a sharp smile.

SWEYN FORKBEARD'S CAMP, SOUTHEAST JUTLAND
LATE NOVEMBER, AD 996

Ustain's voice trailed off as they closed in on the camp. 'What the—? Where the fuck is everybody?'

King Forkbeard's mighty host consisted of a couple of tents and a handful of scarred fighters sitting around a campfire. Audun counted about twenty of them. A broad-faced man with ruddy cheeks rose to greet them when they came close enough. 'Ustain! Shitface!' he shouted by way of greeting. 'Back so soon? Did they not have any sheep to your liking?'

'What's this?' Ustain shouted back.

'Left last week for Svealand. We've been waiting for you lot to come back with fresh meat.' The man calmly removed mailed gloves from their resting place near the fire and put them on. He was tall, but walked with a bit of a stoop. Strands of thinning blond hair hung limply on his head.

'Well, here I fucking am, aren't I?' Ustain snapped back. 'Where are the others?'

'"Not here" would appear to be the answer,' said the man, grinning. 'But then, they don't have your charm and good looks.' This earned the man a giggle around the campfire. He proceeded to look critically at Ustain's recruits, who stood in an awkward, squinting line behind him. 'Is this it? And all dicks, too. Should have brought us something nice for our troubles,' he said. 'Something that fights back this time.'

'This is all there is,' Ustain said, sighing as he dismounted. 'There's nothing much to be had any more.'

'That's true,' the broad-faced man conceded. 'It's a shame, too.'

'And he wouldn't like it if I'd brought one in. Near had my head off with the last one,' Ustain said, mechanically grooming his horse.

'Where's the king?' Mouthpiece squealed. 'I was told there would be ceremonies!' The broad-faced man walked towards him, smiling, and punched him in the jaw. Mouthpiece dropped like a stone.

Beside him, the old horse thief made a point of studying his toes. The kid stared at Mouthpiece, lying still on the ground. Blood trickled out of the corner of his mouth.

The broad-faced man turned towards Audun. 'So what's your story, stranger? You look solid enough. Why are you here?'

Audun didn't answer.

The soldier's eyes sparkled. 'You're not very well brought-up,' he said. 'You answer when you're spoken to. Do you understand?'

'Yes,' Audun said. The mailed gloves clinked as the soldier flexed his fingers. Behind the man he could glimpse the dull gleam of anticipation in his friends' eyes.

'Good! Good. Now we're getting somewhere. You a tough guy?' the soldier sneered, limbering up.

'Jomar, I don't—'

'Shut your sick-meat mouth, Ustain,' Jomar snarled without taking his eyes off Audun. 'I was talking to our friend here. Are you tough enough to be a member of King Sweyn Forkbeard's army?'

Audun didn't answer.

'*Are you?*' Jomar screamed, a hair's breadth away from his face. '*Are you ready to kill?*'

At the edge of his vision, Audun registered more faces: men emerging from nearby tents. So he was to be tonight's entertainment, then. He had to stifle a smile. They did not know where he was coming from.

Jomar pushed him, and Audun allowed himself to go with it. Flat hand, middle of the chest. Maybe half of the man's strength. His stance had changed ever so subtly, waiting for the flailing retaliation, no doubt. Instead, Audun simply regained his balance and looked straight ahead.

Jomar was on him again, pushing hard. '*What the fuck are you – some kind of pussy?*' he screamed in Audun's face. Audun retreated and regained his balance.

'*I'm going to—*' Jomar stepped in and pushed harder. Audun

shifted to the side, grabbed the man's wrist, pulled and brought his knee up as hard as he could. The satisfying crunch of a snapped rib sent his pulse racing, but he remained in control.

Jomar sucked air back into his lungs with a pained wheeze, yanked his arm free and clambered to his feet. 'You're fucking dead, you—'

Audun slapped him and felt skin split under his hand. Jomar staggered away from the force of the blow. 'Shut up,' Audun said.

The broad-faced man howled in rage and launched himself forward, arms flailing – but he went in too quick; Audun's heel took him in the hip-bone and spun him around and he hit the ground hard.

Audun walked to Jomar where he lay on the ground and knelt by his head. A terrified man well past his prime looked back up at him, eyes watering, mouth quivering.

A heavy straight right broke Jomar's nose and drove the bone up into his brain.

A spasm – and he lay still.

Audun rose and found himself surrounded by a circle of stunned, wary faces. He scanned them all in turn, but found no one likely to mount a challenge.

'Don't just fucking stand there,' Ustain barked. 'Do what needs doing.' No one moved. 'Come on. You all knew this was coming. Just thank God the big bastard' – he gestured to Audun – 'is on our side.'

The men around the campfire shuffled into action. Within moments, Jomar had been stripped of his valuables. As an afterthought, a couple of scrawny greybeards dragged him a short distance from the camp, where they dumped him unceremoniously.

Audun turned away from the fire. The old horse thief was

looking him up and down from a safe distance. Satisfied, he shuffled a half-step closer and nodded at him. 'Nice work. Now watch your back,' he mumbled as he moved towards where Mouthpiece lay crumpled in a heap on the ground.

The other recruiters arrived over the next three days. They brought tales, furs and food, but few bodies. On the morning of the third day, Ustain gave the orders and King Forkbeard's reserves moved out. There were forty of them in all, men between the ages of eighteen and fifty, sparsely armed and barely fed. Ustain had assumed command, mostly because Audun didn't.

Every single man in the party gave him a wide berth. In fact, he suspected that if he'd turned around and left, no one would have tried to stop him.

But where would he go?

In the days since he left Helga's house, he'd been struggling to understand the world. There was something bigger at play here; a bigger purpose. When he and Ulfar had slain the woman on the boat they'd started something – something bigger than themselves. He was no longer the master of his own destiny, and in a way it felt oddly *freeing*. He didn't need to *decide* any more. He could just go where the blood was.

And following an army was as good a bet as any to do that.

Seagulls circled lazily in the distance.

'Can you smell it?' Mouthpiece mumbled. His face was still a fetching mix of purple and yellow, but the jaw was healing well. The old horse thief – Thormund, his name was – had put a brace on it and tied it in place with rags, then sat by his twitching, whimpering patient and held him down through the worst of the pain. Now Mouthpiece was slowly getting back the use of his jaw, which apparently wasn't broken.

'Of course we can,' Thormund shot back. 'We don't have a nose full of blood after the welcoming committee.' Mouthpiece glared at him, but the boy smiled. Once they'd accepted their fate, the three men very quickly started sounding like they'd always known each other.

'Never liked the sea,' the old horse thief muttered.

Ustain was busy talking to their newest recruit, a rider on a dappled horse who'd caught up with them as they neared the coast. For a moment, Audun thought the man had been staring at him, but he'd dismissed the thought quickly. He was miles and miles away from anyone he'd ever known and he wanted to keep it that way. The new man was just one of those people who was . . . *familiar*; that was the word.

'We can catch a boat,' Ustain shouted over their heads. 'Ivar here says there's an old twenty-bencher just over the hill. Only a handful of sailors waiting with it. Follow me!' he said, spurring his horse on. The new man turned and gave chase.

Thormund glanced at Mouthpiece. 'Lucky us, boat just sitting there,' he said.

'Happens,' Mouthpiece mumbled. 'Weather or something. One should always accept the gifts of God.'

'Judging by your face, that's probably more of a guess for you,' Thormund said. 'Ain't that right, Boy?'

Boy giggled. He'd warmed to the old man from the first and had stayed close ever since Jomar had clouted Mouthpiece, but he had still not said a word. They'd named him Boy – he reacted to it, so it'd do until something better came up. Sometimes Audun thought he felt Boy's eyes on him, but he never caught him looking.

So all he could do was march along next to the thief, the boy and the blabbermouth. He smirked to himself. 'Should have stayed with the Swede,' he said.

'What Swede?' Thormund said. Boy peered over his shoulder, eyes sparkling.

Audun shot them a dirty look and said, 'Nothing,' with great finality, but the old man didn't back down.

He ran Audun over with an appraising eye. 'Nothing seems to be on your mind,' he said. 'Care to tell us?'

Audun shook his head and veered away from the group, keeping pace but staying out of conversation range. They'd get absolutely nothing out of him.

The sea breeze hit them full in the face as they crested the hill. White-tipped waves crashed on the beach, where a worn-out old raiding boat had been dragged up onto the sand. The sad remains of the crew – Audun counted ten – huddled around a pathetic fire. Ustain and Ivar stood by, talking to a broad-shouldered man who was gesturing out to sea.

'That's our boat all right,' said Thormund. 'It's a good thing we haven't eaten much.'

'Mmph,' said Mouthpiece.

They side-footed their way down the steep sandbanks and by the time they reached the fire, the men from the boat had made space for them and were sharing out dried beef. Ustain ambled towards them, chewing on a reddish-brown strip.

'We'll set sail at sunrise,' he said, 'so find cover somewhere and bed down. These men have been raiding, lost a lot of their crew. They're signing on with us for the privilege of shipping us across the water,' he said, grinning. He returned to the fire, still chewing on the beef.

Around Audun, the men started talking.

'Don't like the look of this—'

'—probably bloody Swedes. Should kill 'em in their sleep . . .'

'Who's got first watch?' someone asked, and they bickered among themselves as they went about finding the right spot for their night camp. They finally settled on a hard, flat square in the lee of a big sandbank, in sight of the boat but a bit further up the beach. As the sun started its descent, tents rose and a fire-pit was dug. Mostly as a way to avoid their owners, Audun tended to the few horses they possessed.

Silent as a ghost, Boy drifted into his field of vision. He acknowledged Audun, then picked up a brush and got to work tending horses. Audun looked him up and down, nodded back and continued brushing down a dappled mare.

Behind them they heard Ustain and Ivar return to their muttered conversation. Boy's brushstrokes lost their rhythm for a moment, but then he resumed as if nothing had happened.

Audun's mare snorted and tossed her head.

'Ssh,' Audun muttered in his best soothing voice. 'You're not going on the boat. We're going to cut you open and eat you raw tomorrow morning for breakfast.' Across from him, Boy snickered. Audun smiled at him. 'If horses understood us we'd be in real trouble,' he said. Boy nodded. 'You understand me,' Audun said. Boy nodded again. 'But you can't speak.' Boy looked away and his horse whinnied in protest at his hardening strokes. 'Don't take it out on the beast,' Audun snapped. 'I asked the wrong thing. No need to get all angry,' he added. Boy's shoulders relaxed a little, but he didn't look at Audun again, even as they put away the equipment.

Darkness crept over the beach as Audun bedded down. Behind them, a cheer went up from the men as the flames took hold in the fire-pit.

Eventually, Audun drifted into a dreamless sleep, not sensing he was being watched.

EAST OF SKAER, JUTLAND.
JOHAN AAGARD'S FARM
NOVEMBER, AD 996

Every morning of his life, Johan Aagard had woken up early, so it was quite a surprise to him that when he opened his eyes, the autumn sun, such as it was, was already high in the sky. A weak light seeped in through the gap in his curtains. 'I must be ill,' he mumbled. The shift clung to him as he struggled to push off the rough-spun woollen blanket, but eventually he managed to clamber out of bed.

If he moved wrong, his arm hurt like hell. All he had to warm himself with was the thought that he'd turned Sweyn's scabby recruiter on to that bitch Helga. She could rot for all he cared, and her freak Norseman with her. Or not, as it were . . . He had only wanted to give her some kind of future, free her from scratching a living alone on that big farm. Maybe he could go again in spring, see if the old bird had thawed out some. A rattling cough set him to grimacing in pain.

'Boys!' he shouted. 'Why did no one wake me up?'

It was oddly quiet for morning.

He pulled aside the curtain that covered his sleeping alcove and froze. The bodies of three young men lay sprawled on the floor of his chamber, scattered like broken toys, with bloodied hands and torn faces. It hurt to look at them. Words gathered in his mouth, then tumbled out all at once, along with the remains of last night's dinner. The bile heaved out of him, followed by sobbing gasps for air.

Johan flailed around blindly for a moment, until he found what he was searching for – his axe. Clutching it in his left hand and wincing with every movement, he stepped out into the middle of the room. 'Boys!' he shouted, his voice breaking.

Somewhere within the house, something clattered into furniture.

'Who's there?' he shouted. 'Boys!'

The sound of breaking timber grew closer. A fine sprinkle of dust drifted down from above. 'It'll start to snow soon,' Johan Aagard thought. 'I must make sure we're stocked with firewood.'

Something huge crashed through into the next room and the light changed; as if someone had ripped a hole in the wall. A heavy, almost animal smell filled his nostrils.

Johan gripped his axe as hard as he could. 'Come on, then,' he hissed between gritted teeth.

None of the farmhands had wanted to wake Johan up in the morning. Since he fell and broke his arm at Helga's farm he'd been even more ornery than usual, and he was always first up anyway. However, when noon came and went without the old man rousing, they drew straws. The youngest of them pulled the shortest one. He inched into the bedchamber.

Johan Aagard lay where he had gone to rest, his face contorted in pain, blood soaking his bed. He had gouged out his eyes with his fingers.

After much discussion they called on the Elders at Skaer, who said Johan should be buried in a mound to fit a man of his stature, entombed in his bed so he had somewhere to rest in the afterlife. Besides, he'd clearly cared a lot for his bed, to commission such nice runework.

The farmhands didn't recognise the runes, but they all agreed that they were very new.

When the day came, all of his neighbours showed up, except one.

'Where's Helga?' Johan's foreman asked the town blacksmith.

'It's the strangest thing,' Skakki said. 'We swung by Ovregard, but she's not there. Must have been raiders or something. The whole place has been burned down – the horse has been stolen and something's dug up in the shed. It's almost as if she never existed.'

From the cover of a stand of trees half a mile away, Helga stood and watched the ceremony, idly playing with a rune-carving knife. Beside her, Streak munched contentedly on some moss.

'You weren't to know, Johan Aagard,' she said to the wind, 'but I have seen a lot worse than you, and I'm still here.' In two swift movements she mounted the protesting Streak and guided the mare north, away from Skaer, her farm and her former life.

A dull pain behind Ulfar's eyes blurred his vision. The beams in the roof above his head felt miles away. His backache told him he'd been lying on the ground. Someone had placed him on furs just thick enough to take away the cold of the earth, and blankets had been draped over him, wrapped tight enough to make him uncomfortable and sweaty. His head throbbed and his stomach hurt.

The blonde woman leaned into his field of vision.

'You . . . you're not my wife. Don't have a wife.' Claws of fear scratched at his spine. His voice was not his own. His words were slurred and all that came out was a quiet whisper.

'I know,' the woman whispered. 'Drink this.'

'No – hnnh—' Ulfar struggled, but he was as weak as a newborn child. She held his head firmly and tipped a small water-skin to his lips. Drops of a liquid of some sort tipped out. Ulfar tried to clamp his mouth shut.

'Don't,' she said. 'Please don't. You have to.' She pinched his nose shut. 'Just drink it. Everything will be fine.'

He gave up long before he wanted to, swallowing, coughing and gasping. The mixture had a bitter taste, masked with sickly-sweet honey.

She eased his head back onto the ground. 'Now rest. I am sorry about last night, but you wouldn't have come with me. I know how you loved her. Now we'll be fine, though.'

Poisoned.

He'd been poisoned.

Ulfar thrashed and tried to spit out the foul substance, but his body wouldn't move. A cold chill went through him as he felt the liquid thicken his throat, seep into his blood and cool him down, down below life. His heart beat faster, fighting against the invader, but it was no good. A rattling breath escaped him.

'What?' she asked.

'H-help . . .' Ulfar hissed.

She looked at him, confusion written all over her features. 'You'll just fall asleep. Then you'll be weak for a little bit. He told me.'

In a last act of defiance, Ulfar held her gaze until his heart stopped.

The moment he fell off the precipice into death, pain drove through him from his cold, blackened core, slicing his flesh like shards of a breaking stone. Every muscle in his body tensed, wrenched and trembled. His jaw clamped shut and the veins in his forehead throbbed. For a moment he was suspended, half a step from the blissful black . . . and then he was dragged from the abyss. His heart started beating again, weakly.

His captor stared at him in mute horror.

'. . . help . . .' he hissed. He could still feel the poison seeping through his veins.

The woman looked at him, tears running down her face. 'What . . . what can I do?'

Ulfar tossed his head feebly. '. . . drink . . .' he muttered, but it was too late; his heart had started slowing again. He gritted his teeth and waited for the pain.

The light had changed. Everything in his body ached, his eyes included. Straining them, he could just make out the edge of the roof. Night-time, then.

With a mighty effort, he rolled his head to one side.

He saw the woman, crouching by a fire-pit. A small pot was suspended above it; she was stirring with purpose. He couldn't smell anything.

The ground was packed dirt, but not covered. So: outhouse of some sort? His eyes travelled along the edge of the bubble of light around the cook-fire and shapes in the dusk slowly resolved into pens and a feeding trough.

He was in the pig house.

It would be easy enough to escape if he could only move. His heart felt a little stronger, but not much.

He turned his head to get a better look at his captor.

The woman was no longer stirring. Instead she sat still, watching him. Her eyes were puffy and her hair was unkempt. 'I . . .' Her voice trailed off.

Something sparked in the back of Ulfar's head.

She looked . . . familiar.

He tried as hard as he could to remember the Uppsala girls from all those years ago. Greta's screaming face came first, unbidden, and vague forms followed, but he could find no match in his memory, no recognition. No one from his travels, either, unless—

Another thought struck him.

'I'm so sorry,' she muttered. 'I never thought you'd—'

'Hurt so bad,' Ulfar said.

The small blonde woman cried then, silent tears. 'I don't understand. You were just supposed to . . . He told me you'd be confused, like you'd just woken up, and I could drag you with me on a horse. You'd be ill, but only pretend. Not real. Not . . . like that.' The words tumbled out of her, faster and faster. 'He gave me the powder and I poured it into your ale. He said to put just a little and I was careful. I was *careful*.' She lapsed into silence and her lips trembled.

'Inga,' Ulfar wheezed.

The woman's eyes widened and the words ground to a halt. 'How—?'

'You're her,' Ulfar said. Every word hurt. 'Stenvik.'

'Yes,' she whispered. 'You remember?'

Ulfar nodded. The light from the cook-fire faded sharply at the edge of his vision, and he fainted.

When he came to again, the air smelled of morning. He felt like a dead fish that had been struck against a stone a couple of times, but he was alive.

Inga sat and watched him. Her face was pale and drawn, her eyes ringed by exhaustion. 'I'm sorry,' she muttered again.

Ulfar spoke before he thought. 'Shhh,' he said. 'Don't be afraid. I'm all right.' He shuddered. 'Well, maybe not quite bear-wrestling-ready yet,' he said, grinning weakly. 'But I'm very tired, and I haven't seen you in a long time. How are things in Stenvik?'

Inga just looked at him, trembling with a mixture of sadness, guilt and . . . what? Everything about her appeared to slow down. 'Stenvik is – Stenvik has—' She looked around the outhouse for the missing words. 'Stenvik changed,' she said finally.

'Oh?' Ulfar did his best to sound just curious enough. 'How so?'

'When King Olav . . . *rescued* us, we learned about the word of this One God, Christ. He's very kind, and loving, and . . . and . . .'

Mustering all his strength, Ulfar placed a hand on her knee and looked at her. 'They're not here, Inga. He's useless and soft and Thor would smash his skinny little arse.'

The smile that lit up Inga's face was beautiful, radiant, guilty – and gone. She looked around, quickly, then turned a stern eye on Ulfar. 'Sssh,' she said, pursing her lips. 'As I was saying—' The ghost of a smile hovered at the corners of her mouth. 'Everything changed. Olav imprisoned Sigurd and Sven for worshipping their own gods, but the rest of the raiders were allowed to go free.'

Ulfar fought against a tide of emotion. He was still in danger, and he needed information. 'Really? But what about Harald?'

True fury flashed in Inga's eyes. She spat, and suddenly looked neither frail nor feeble. 'That bag of shit got what he deserved,' she hissed. 'Less, if you ask me. I'd happily have tied him down and cut his dick off, slice – by – slice.'

They sat together in silence for a few moments, remembering. After a while, Inga spoke up again. 'I looked for you, you know . . . after. But you'd disappeared – you and Audun. There were stories.'

'Really? Like what?'

Inga started scratching at the ground, absent-mindedly. 'Like you being someone's agent – some said King Olav's, some said King Erik's over here.'

'Hm. Well, for what it's worth, I kind of was, but not like that,' Ulfar said. 'Geiri and I were travelling on King Erik's behalf.'

'I was told that you worked for the Forkbeard. That's why he sent us to get you.'

'And who was that?' Ulfar dropped the question almost without thinking, convincing himself he didn't really want to know, that it was just curiosity, just an innocent—

Inga backed off as if she'd just seen a wolf in the room. 'I – It was . . .'

He looked her in the eyes and smiled, a reassuring smile that he immediately suspected would comfort no one, but—

'It was Valgard.'

For a moment, Ulfar forgot most of his aches. He frowned and scratched his head. 'Valgard? The healer?'

'Yes,' Inga said. Her mouth trembled. 'He said that we were to go and catch you and bring you back because he wanted to meet you, because you might know something about Forkbeard. But then, once when he'd had a little too much to drink and was running his mouth, he said he needed to have you because of something that happened on the wall when King Olav came.' She was caught up in her own world, so Ulfar had a crucial moment to pick his jaw back up off the floor. 'He said . . . he said . . .'

Finding a hidden reserve of power, Ulfar lifted himself up onto one elbow. 'What?' he muttered softly.

'He was drunk, but he said . . . I could soften you up and then, after he was done with you, he'd get rid of you like your useless cousin,' Inga said.

And just like that, everything fell into place.

Ulfar bent his knee and slowly, torturously, rose from his pallet. 'Where is he now?'

'Up north somewhere, I think,' Inga said. She looked at him, and when she saw his face, she shuffled backwards.

'He lied to you,' Ulfar said. 'He used you. He—'

There was a firm knock on the door. 'Ulfar!' Goran's voice was loud enough to be heard through the walls. 'Are you there?'

Ulfar glanced at Inga, then staggered towards the sounds. After a brief struggle with the latch, the door swung open.

'Oh,' Goran said. After a brief pause, he added, 'Are you well?'

'I've seen better-looking corpses,' Heidrek said, standing behind him. Next to Heidrek, Arnar grunted his agreement.

'What are you doing here?' Ulfar wheezed.

'Looking for you, pukeface,' Heidrek said. 'We got—'

'Ingimar left,' Goran said. 'We had a little too much fun and passed out. He picked a couple of likely lads from town and ran off the next morning. Probably got them for cheaper, too.'

Arnar harrumphed in the background.

'So we got to talking with the locals. Then Goran said we should check whether we could find someone rich, stupid and annoying who needed to leave very soon,' Heidrek added.

The sunlight and the sounds of town brought the full force of the headache smashing into Ulfar's forehead from inside. He smiled at the pain. Pain meant life. 'Did you, now? Well – it just so happens that I've got places to go and people to see.'

He caught Goran examining him, uncomfortably like one would check a lame horse. 'When were you thinking of leaving?'

Ulfar caught his eye. 'Now,' he said. 'Go to the stables.'

A moment later, Goran nodded, and the three men turned and walked away. When they'd gone, Inga emerged from the shadows. 'Take me with you,' she said.

'No.' Ulfar turned and walked towards the door.

A strong, slender hand grabbed his shoulder and twisted him around. 'Did it sound like a question?' Inga said. 'I'm coming with you.' She stared straight at him. 'I don't like being used.'

Ulfar looked down at the fire blazing in the woman's eyes and sighed.

When he showed up at the stables, no one asked any questions; they simply handed over the reins to five horses, unremarkable mares past their prime but well fit for their purpose. The stablehand brought out bags of rations.

'Thank him for me,' Ulfar said to him.

When Ulfar emerged, Heidrek whistled. 'He goes into the stables with no money and comes out with five horses and supplies. Impressive.'

'Alfgeir wants us gone,' Ulfar mumbled. 'Before there's trouble.'

Goran checked the horses in silence.

Inga sat her mare gingerly. Ulfar reached over and adjusted her reins. 'Hold like' – he wrapped the band around her hands twice – 'this. And squeeze with your legs, or your arse will hurt for days.'

Heidrek opened his mouth. The look he got from Goran nearly knocked out his teeth.

'Thank you,' Inga said.

The still, dark wave of trees rose slowly ahead of them and soon they were swallowed up. The cold shadows in the forest had a restorative effect on Ulfar's head; at last it was clearing. He gestured to Goran to take the lead and rode up alongside Inga.

'What do you think of the horse?' he asked. When she didn't answer he asked, 'You have ridden before, haven't you?'

She looked at him as if he was an idiot. 'Can you pick and clean a four-man net in half the time it takes to unload a boat?'

Ulfar's finger throbbed with the memory. 'I'd be a bleeding mess in the blink of an eye,' he said.

She smiled. 'And I'm scared out of my wits up here.'

He smiled back. 'They're terrifying beasts, aren't they?' His mare whinnied in assent.

They rode side by side in silence for a little while.

'You want me to tell you things, don't you? About . . . him,' she said, almost too softly to hear. Ulfar bit his tongue and waited. The gentle, rocking rhythm of the horses and the soft silence of the forest would do his work for him. 'He . . . went straight over,' she continued. 'I don't know why, but King Olav's men spared him – they put him in charge of converting the faithless. About a week after the assault, he started being all friendly, asking how I was, whether I missed . . .' Inga lost her words. She glanced at Ulfar, who looked back at her.

'Every day,' he said quietly. 'When I'm just about to sleep. And when I wake. Every single day.' He took a deep breath, held it for a moment, then let it out slowly. 'Please continue.'

Inga's words rushed out, eager to pull the story in another direction. 'He was very nice to me, told me I was needed, that I was important. No one had ever done that. He said I could start doing the king's work for him. And I got confused.

'Then he told me to go and get you – me and four men. He told us all kinds of tall tales about how you'd poisoned Harald, how you'd seduced Lilia with rune magic, that you were evil. They were to strong-arm you, I was to be . . . bait.'

'And he gave you the powder,' Ulfar added.

'Yes – the powder. He made it himself; he said it'd knock you out, make you look ill, make you easy to drag home. I don't understand. I always thought he was very good with herbs and that stuff.'

Ulfar thought for a while. 'He is,' he concluded. 'He really is.' Inga looked at him. 'Sometimes things just go a bit wrong.' There was no doubt – of course Valgard had meant to kill him. It would have been absolute proof of his immortality.

'The thing is,' Inga said, 'I don't think . . .'

Ulfar turned back to her. She looked worried.

'I don't think we were the only ones he sent out to get you.'

The next thing Ulfar heard was a whistling sound – and then Heidrek slammed forward, coughing up blood. The arrow was buried deep in his back. The next arrow took him in the shoulder, spinning him off the panicking horse.

With speed belied by his bulk, Arnar spurred his mount around to face the attacker. He dropped to hide most of himself behind his horse just as the third arrow took it in the neck. It whinnied in a panic, but he had a good hold on the reins and pulled for all he was worth.

Only a couple of moments had passed.

'Goran!' Ulfar called.

In between the trees, Ulfar saw a flash of white. There was a bone-crunching snap and a scream of pain and Arnar's horse went down. The bearded man leapt from the saddle just in time and ran to grab the reins of Heidrek's panicked animal.

'You fucking . . .' Ulfar muttered. To Inga he hissed, 'Stay there! Make yourself small. We're being hunted.'

He leapt off his horse and ran to cover behind the nearest tree.

'*Karle!*' he shouted. 'Fight like a man, you skinny little bitch! I'll break your arm again, if I need to!'

An arrow thudded into the tree next to him, setting it vibrating with the force of the impact. A voice rang out, some way away. 'I'd fight a man, but you're less than that, Ulfar Thormodsson. Animals get hunted. I'm going to enjoy this. Alfgeir Bjorne is not here to send you into hiding.'

Ulfar felt the air move as another arrow whistled past the trunk of the tree. 'Fine. If that's the way you want to play,' he muttered, 'then that's how we'll play.' He touched the sword at his belt and looked up, then down. Bending his knee and taking care not to reveal any part of his body, he fumbled in the undergrowth until he found what he was looking for. Then he reached up, trying to make himself as tall and narrow as possible – there. A knothole. Just big enough for two fingers. And another, just above.

Ulfar hauled himself up as fast as he could. He was soon within reach of thick branches on both sides.

Left – no. Right. He swung towards his right and sure enough, a flash of white sable in the distance, circling away from them. Having had his sport, Karle would no doubt be looking for the perfect shot, something that would start counting.

Ulfar climbed higher still. Now he was up above the height of two men. Down on the ground, Arnar was busy keeping the horses calm. Goran had made Inga crouch behind a fallen tree for cover, and now they were all scouting the perimeter nervously. Ulfar had to lever himself up half again a man's height again, until he found a thick enough branch, stretching over to the next tree.

His plan wasn't perfect – in fact, it couldn't really be called a plan at all. But it was better than cowering down on the ground, waiting to be shot. He just had to hope the bastard didn't look up.

Even wearing almost glowing white, Prince Karle still did a damn good job of hiding in the undergrowth. Ulfar scanned the ground below – there! The prince was close – too close. Well within range.

Working quickly, Ulfar leaned against the trunk and freed both hands. He pulled a piece of string off his belt and used it to lash together the three pine cones he'd found on the ground.

He'd have only one shot at this.

In his mind he charted the leap and winced. It was going to hurt like a bastard, too. However, surprise sometimes helped.

Sometimes.

With all his might, he threw the pine cones arching over Karle's position.

The prince's head whipped round and a moment later, his body stiffened. In a flash he was up out of his crouch and heading towards Uppsala at a dead run, caring nothing for who might see him.

Ulfar was left standing halfway up a tree, his mouth agape.

His eyes narrowed. He clambered down. Goran was waiting for him at the foot of the tree.

'How'd you do that?' he said, with more than a touch of admiration. 'What did you—?'

Ulfar didn't reply. Instead he walked straight over to where Prince Karle had been waiting to pick them off. Then he inched outwards in expanding half-circles, staring at the ground until he found what he'd been looking for, about forty yards away.

He knelt down, traced a pattern with his fingers and picked up his pine cones. Then he went back to their little clearing. He looked at Heidrek's body, lying there in a puddle of his own blood. Then he turned to Goran.

'It wasn't your idea, was it?' he said.

Goran looked at him. The guard's stance shifted slightly, unconsciously anticipating the fight. 'What do you mean?'

'Coming for me. It wasn't your idea, was it?'

'I can't remember,' Goran said. A cloud of confusion crept over his face. 'No – wait. I sat with Ingimar. But there—'

'There was something strange about him. He was older. Thinner,' Ulfar snapped, scouting the perimeter.

'How do you—?'

'And let me guess,' Ulfar added. 'He had real trouble seeing out of one eye.' Goran and Arnar stared at Ulfar.

'What did you find out there?' Inga asked.

Ulfar looked at her, his face dark with anger. 'Wolf tracks.'

Suddenly there was no lack of shadows in the forest. Every noise sounded louder and more significant.

Arnar broke the silence. 'Hrmph,' he snarled, grasping the reins of the four remaining horses. He reached out and pulled Inga up, helping her to mount her horse again. She moved slowly, as if she'd just woken up. Arnar looked at Heidrek's body and then at his own horse, lying on the ground and twitching in pain.

'Go,' Goran said.

As he walked off, Goran drew his belt-knife and sighed.

A while later, Goran and Ulfar were walking again, following Arnar and Inga, heavy sacks by their sides. They walked in a relaxed silence.

'. . . like that. Soft, see,' a deep voice rumbled. 'Look. Look how her head droops. She likes that.'

Goran's eyebrow rose.

Ahead, blurs of colour became shapes.

Arnar stood by Inga, guiding her hand as she brushed her horse down. A tilt of the head showed the bearded man had noticed their approach, but his eye remained trained on the young woman. 'Good, good,' he said. 'You're doing well. Last one,' and with that he moved her hand gently away from the horse's flank. 'See? She's happy now.'

The mare shook her head and nudged Inga affectionately.

Even from a distance, Ulfar and Goran could see something in the young woman's shoulders soften as the smile lit up her face.

Beside him, Goran took one step to the right and broke a twig with his foot. 'Arnar!' he called, clearing his throat. 'We're back.'

'About time, too,' the bearded man rumbled. 'Need to get going.'

Later, as the sounds of Karle's flying arrows faded into memory, Ulfar sidled up to Arnar. 'You saved our lives,' he said.

The bearded man nodded. 'Bad business.'

'Bad business,' Ulfar agreed.

There was nothing more to add, so he spurred his horse to catch up with Goran.

They rode together up front in companionable silence.

After a while, Ulfar spoke. 'Tell me about him,' he said.

'I don't know,' Goran replied. 'He was . . . old?'

Ulfar raised an eyebrow. 'Nothing gets past you, does it?'

Goran frowned. 'I can't really remember,' he said. 'Everything he said made such sense at the time. Find someone, he said, someone who's a bit of a, you know—'

'A bit of a cock.'

The old guard nodded, smiling. 'Well, yeah. So, someone like you, and then see if they would pay us to follow them.'

Ulfar struggled to keep a smile on his face. 'Let me guess. He bought you drinks?'

Goran still looked vaguely confused. 'I suppose he must have. My purse is no lighter.'

'And you passed out and missed the caravan,' Ulfar said. 'Funny, that.'

Goran's shoulders slumped and he cursed silently. 'Who . . . ? Was he—?'

'I don't know, but I think he may have been following me for a while. I also think he's watching us, but I don't know why.'

Arnar trotted up alongside them. 'Hunh,' he grunted.

'Good question,' Goran said. 'Where are we going?'

'We're going to find a friend of mine. He's somewhere to the south,' Ulfar said.

'One man? You're going to "go south" and he'll just appear, will he?' Goran said.

'Don't worry,' Ulfar said. 'I don't think we'll struggle to find him.'

They felt the setting of the sun on their skin. The heat went out of the air and around them everything dampened. Sounds died on beds of pine needles as the horizon crept closer and closer. Overhead, thick clouds drifted slowly across a darkening sky.

'Do we ride for the edge?' Goran asked.

'Hm,' Ulfar said. 'Yes. We need to get out of here before dark, I think.'

Soon enough, the party was making reasonable time through the woods. The shadows grew longer around them as the tree growth thinned; they broke out of the woods around Uppsala just as the sun dipped below the edge of the world.

'There,' Ulfar said, pointing to a pass between two small hills. 'Through there and we're on the road.'

'Might be good to stay on this side of that hill, then, just while we wait for daylight,' Goran said.

Ulfar looked back towards the woods. Somewhere in the back of his head something crackled. His tongue tasted like fresh metal and he could feel the sword in his gut.

For a fraction of the blink of an eye he knew everything again – but then it was almost all gone. The only thing that remained was a sense of danger.

'I don't know what I like worst, the forest or the road,' Ulfar muttered. 'Doesn't feel right.'

Arnar dismounted and led his horse towards a thick tree trunk. 'Here,' he said. 'As good as any.' He pulled out a brush from his pack and started methodically brushing the horse down.

Inga's mare followed, and Inga whimpered as she clambered off. 'Can't understand why anyone would choose this over sailing,' she said. 'I hurt *everywhere*.'

'Just wait,' Goran said, smiling as he pulled the reins to guide his horse to Arnar's side. 'Tomorrow you'll be crying until well past midday.'

Inga raised an eyebrow, but didn't answer. Instead she turned

to Arnar. The bearded man had produced a hand-axe from somewhere within his packs and was busy whittling branches from a
fallen tree behind the thick trunk. He stopped long enough to
hand Inga a knife with a big blade.

Ulfar watched as they fell companionably into work together.
He looked at Goran, who grinned. The guard had thrown down
his bedroll and nearly finished clearing the space for a small fire.

At Inga's feet, innocent-looking sticks were piling up. She took
what Arnar passed her, made three or four nicks in the middle of
the wood, then laid the stick down carefully.

'What are these for?' Ulfar couldn't help himself.

Inga looked at Arnar, then she placed a stick at Ulfar's feet. 'Go
on,' she said. Ulfar stepped on the stick – and it broke with a snap.
'We'll place them around the camp when darkness comes,' Inga
said. 'Any night guests might avoid them – but they might also
give us a little bit of a warning.'

Ulfar smiled his approval, then went to see to the fire.

The stars twinkled overhead. Goran gnawed on a strip of half-
burned, half-raw horsemeat, licking the blood off his lips.

'So where are we going after we find your friend?' Arnar
grunted, half-hidden in shadow.

Ulfar leaned back. His stomach was full and now he just wanted
to fall asleep and wake up three years ago, when everything had
been so much simpler. 'North, then west,' he said. 'We're going
to find another man and avenge my cousin.'

'Not a lot of money in revenge,' Arnar said.

'I have a suspicion that by the time I get to this particular
worm, he'll be lying on a pile of gold,' Ulfar said.

'Who is he?' Goran said.

'Inga . . . ?'

'His name is Valgard,' Inga whispered. Even here, she still glanced furtively into the darkness before continuing, 'He's a . . . healer. Or was. He's . . . He used to live in my town – Stenvik – only we got turned over by King Olav, and all of a sudden we were thralls in our own homes. All except Valgard, because he'd squirrelled away books and a cross so the king thought he was one of them. You know, the Mumblers.'

'We know the Mumblers,' Arnar said. 'That's one of the reasons I can't be doing with the Christ thing. All the mumbling.'

'He . . . went over to their side,' Inga continued. 'And how. He was suddenly King Olav's right hand, and then . . .' She looked at Ulfar, then whispered, 'Then he came for me. He said he needed me to find Ulfar and bring him back to Stenvik because—'

'—because he killed my cousin Geiri and he was worried that I'd find out and come and get him, so he wanted Inga to get to me first,' Ulfar finished.

'Hmpf,' Arnar said.

'So you owe him,' Goran said.

'I do,' Ulfar said. His blood felt cold. 'I certainly do. But we'll speak of that later. I'll take first watch.'

Above their heads a bloated, pockmarked moon rose and dragged the shadows of the forest with it. It shone down on a fading fire and soon, three sleeping forms.

Ulfar looked at the wall of rock-black trees. 'I know you're there,' he whispered. 'I know it. And I know you've got something to do with this. And when I'm done . . . I'll come and find *you*.'

The animals of the night stayed well clear of the travellers' camp.

FAR NORTH OF TRONDHEIM, NORTH NORWAY
NOVEMBER, AD 996

Spiked sealskin boots crashed through the frozen shell of the snowdrift and sank into the dry powder underneath. Botolf, at the head of the line, picked a careful sideways route down the hillside. Far below they could make out the outlines of Egill Jotun's longhouse. The horses snorted in protest as they picked their way along the narrow boot-trodden path. A line of muttered curses drifted towards Valgard at the rear.

Cramps wrenched his legs, jabbed at his spine and twisted his shoulders a half-inch further into a solid knot with every step. They'd found little cover on the crest of the hill overnight. The soldiers had lit fires, but they hadn't helped. The cold had been bitter, sharp and personal, and Botolf's men were even more surly than usual. The morning had been difficult.

'We should sledge down,' one of the men shouted.

'Or I could just break your neck right now,' Thora shouted back.

'Shut your hole, you fucking whore!' the man cried, 'or I'll open another one in your belly and f—' The snowball hit him square in the jaw and made him choke on his own spit as he lost his footing. His arms flailed as he fought for balance, then went rolling head-over-heels, kicking up delicate clouds of powder as he went. Thora stood still, watching the falling man with contempt.

Valgard couldn't help but smile. He looked funny, bouncing down the hill like that. Almost like a kid at play.

Ormslev shot him a dirty look. 'He's dead,' he said.

'Wha—?' He didn't have time to finish the sentence.

In the blink of an eye, the man was airborne as he bounced off something hard hidden in the snow and when he met the ground again, his head snapped to one side as the weight of his body landed on his neck. Moments later he was just lying there, a pile of rags halfway down the hill.

'Anyone else want to take the quick way?' Thora barked over the line. None of the men looked up. Even the horses stayed quiet.

They inched their way along after that, step by careful step. When they were nearly halfway down, one of Hakon's men stepped on a sheet of ice hidden by a dusting of snow. Both his feet left the ground and he twisted in the air. The dull sound of breaking bone as his skull met the jagged, ice-crusted rock cut through the heavy, cold silence.

Valgard watched the blood soak through the snow and thought of Botolf's words.

The north would take them.

'Watch your feet, you thick-faced lamb-diddlers!' Thora growled. For a moment, Valgard thought she might consider the man's death a personal affront and go and kill him some more.

The men stepped over the fallen warrior, careful not to meet the same fate.

'Try not to die of stupid!' Thora growled and turned to Botolf. 'Where did you find these idiots?'

'The waiting line outside your mother's house?' Botolf shot back. 'Give them a break. They're cold and wet, but whatever they are, they're not idiots.'

'How do you figure?' Thora said.

'For one, they didn't build their houses this far north,' Botolf muttered.

Despite the situation, Valgard spotted the odd smirk in the line.

The valley that had looked so inviting from above was nowhere near as easy to cross as Valgard had hoped. The snow was chest-deep and too loose to walk on. Treacherous rocks and roots hid underneath, but the men didn't appear to care. They might grouch and grumble, but under Bug-Eye's shouted commands they soon had a work-party going. Valgard stood to the side, hunched over. He was wet and cold and hurting like a bastard. He didn't even consider offering to help. If he did have a shovel, he'd just be getting in their way.

While the men worked to clear the snow, Botolf conferred with Thora. The chieftain looked tense; like a caged animal. He was pointing to the far end of the valley and scowling, but the woman didn't appear to care; she was all smiles, shaking her head and grinning. Botolf motioned for Bug-Eye to come over and the trek-master stood impassively at his side, like an ugly cow, and listened, nodding occasionally. When Botolf had finished giving orders, Ormslev turned smartly and strode towards the work party, pointing, shouting and gesturing. Valgard followed the chieftain's eyes. An odd-shaped shadow halfway up the hillside caught his eye. Was that . . . a cave? Something in the valley was worrying Botolf and Valgard didn't like to admit how uneasy that made him feel.

The men fell into a rhythm. Snow flew up above their heads, covering the midday sun. They dug themselves down into the sparkling white snow and soon nothing was visible but the ridges of the enclosing hills and the blue sky above. Valgard shuffled along behind them, staying as close to the warm horses as he dared. The party trudged along, inch by inch, heading straight for the centre of the valley.

'Our hosts look to have been away a while,' Botolf said as they approached the first covered house. The four men in front redoubled their efforts, and soon carved fence-posts rose from the snow. Further still, and a big plank of wood emerged.

'Look!' The first of the shovel crew pointed. ''s a door!' He banged it with his shovel.

The cloud of white rose and fell, revealing four snowmen and a bare roof.

The soldiers laughed and cheered. Even Bug-Eye stirred.

'Come on, you lazy bastards,' Botolf shouted at the fresh piles of snow. 'Stop playing around!' The snow mound in the middle trembled and a hand burst out. Clawing at the air and flailing about, all it managed to do was to draw more laughter from the men.

'So much for a cautious approach,' Thora muttered.

'Whoever's around has known we were coming for a long time,' Botolf said under his breath. 'It's been a good bit of walk. They need a laugh. You need to relax.'

Thora shot Botolf a look that said a lot of things and muttered something very quickly and quietly. Botolf didn't reply, but a smirk spread across his weathered face. Valgard observed their exchange and marvelled at the spiky-haired woman. He'd watched her glide into the fellowship of the men; one moment they were an impregnable circle of scowls, the next she was one of them. She'd won them over like he knew he never could. When the prisoners in Stenvik had told him of Skargrim's boatswoman, it had sounded like so much nonsense; he had not been able to connect that to the screaming, knife-wielding maniac who had come crashing through Stenvik's gates. Now it took effort to remember that she probably wanted him dead, and could kill him with nothing more than a flick of her wrist.

The unfortunate diggers emerged from the drift, shaking themselves and cursing their fellow travellers, who answered back in kind.

'This is just a cabin. Find the longhouse,' Botolf snapped and started wading through the snow. Silence and focus spread in waves among the men and they fell in line behind him.

Up close, Egill Jotun's snowbound longhouse was a thing of beauty. They shovelled the white powder off the steps, and Botolf moved to the fore with Thora by his side.

'You've been here before,' he said to Thora.

'Which makes you my guest. After your good self,' she answered immediately, bowing towards the door.

Botolf grinned. With one hand on his blade, he pulled open the great carved door.

Black forms exploded out of the darkness in a flurry of flapping wings. Botolf had sidestepped with terrifying quickness and crouched, his eyes trained on the dark space within. The birds were out and gone in a flash.

'Ravens?' he asked.

Thora did not reply. The men traded glances. Behind Valgard, one of the soldiers muttered, 'Two of them. Odin does not want us to—'

Someone else walloped the man and hissed, 'Shut up, you idiot.'

Without a word, Botolf disappeared inside and Thora followed him like a shadow.

The silence they left behind was suddenly impossibly vast, overwhelming, crashing through the valley like a snowslide. Valgard held his breath – and then the door flew open with a bang.

Botolf stood in the doorway, straight-backed and imposing, like a hunting dog denied its kill. 'Nothing here,' he said, looking straight at Valgard. 'Nothing – at – all.'

As night fell, the men settled in the longhouse, seating themselves comfortably around the edges. As it turned out, Botolf had been rather quick to dismiss the bounty of Egill Jotun's house – they discovered a cellar full of dried meats and cheeses, barrels of mead and a stack of well-dried firewood. The roaring flames drained some of the cold from their bones and the soggy smell of drying clothes soon wafted out through the air vent.

Botolf had claimed Egill's high seat on the dais. It was the biggest piece of furniture Valgard had ever seen, easily half again the size of a normal chair. The chieftain looked almost boyish sitting there. Thora had taken the seat to his right, leaving Valgard to scurry to the one on the left, but now that the men were settled, he had the sinking feeling he'd played himself into a bad position.

Where was it?

And *what*, exactly, was he searching for?

For the first time in many months he allowed himself to wonder. He'd thought himself so clever; he'd reasoned that all he needed to do was find out where to go and then go there and he'd find whatever had created the monster in Stenvik. He hadn't even stopped to think about what he might be looking for. He'd searched the house himself and found nothing of consequence. There were bear pelts here and there, some signs of worship and a crude drawing of a claw, but nothing that made any sense.

Botolf leaned over towards his chair. 'So, Healer. Grass Man. Thinker, planner, friend of kings.'

Against his will, Valgard swallowed.

'Now what?'

'I . . . don't know,' Valgard said. 'I don't know how . . . long it's going to take to find it. But we will,' he added quickly. 'And soon, too. I can feel it.'

'Can you?' Botolf asked. 'That would be most . . . *impressive*. Because if you don't . . . If you don't, then you've dragged me all the way out here for nothing. And then you might have an accident on the way back. I'm sure King Olav wouldn't mind an advisor with a little more . . . steel.'

Valgard swallowed and smiled weakly. 'It's here. I'm sure of it.'

'We'll see in the morning,' Botolf said. 'We'll see about a lot of things.'

Movement caught Valgard's eye. The trek-master was coming through the hall, looking less than pleased. Thora, sitting beside Botolf, was already half out of her chair.

'Botolf,' Bug-Eye said.

'What?'

'You want to come and see this,' he said, then turned around and walked away. Botolf looked to Thora, but she was on the trek-master's heels.

After the fire inside, the night air was as cold as a blade to the throat. Bug-Eye headed down the steps to the snow corridor they'd dug earlier in the day.

'What do you want me to see?' Botolf growled at Bug-Eye's back, but got no answer. as he just stormed across the tramped-down snow, a shadow in the faint moonlight. Thora followed him, chasing the scent of danger, blood and action.

A hundred yards further on, Bug-Eye stopped by a pile of black cloth.

Instinct kicked in and Botolf scanned the horizon. 'What happened?' he growled.

'Two lads, out to take a piss,' the trek-master said. 'They've had their skulls bashed in.'

'Tracks?' Thora asked before Botolf could say it.

'Snow's tramped down,' Bug-Eye replied. 'The edges are too high to climb. We can look in the morning.'

Botolf crouched by the bodies. 'They've not just been bashed; they've been torn as well,' he said. 'Big knife. Sword, maybe.'

'What the fuck?' Thora said. 'Seems a lot of trouble.'

'You know how it is,' Botolf said. 'Once we've put the armour on, we might as well get our kicks.'

'Think there's someone out there?' Thora said.

'Only possible explanation,' Botolf said.

'But—' Bug-Eye started.

'Ghost? Spirit? Monster? If that's what you're going to say, don't even open your fucking mouth,' Botolf growled. 'I've not seen any of those, and I've seen a lot. This is the work of three, maybe four men – and I'll bet it has something to do with those little shits we stopped on the way.'

'Hardly,' Thora said. 'They were just boys – and stupid boys, getting caught like that,' she added with pursed lips. 'We'll have a look for tracks in the morning.'

'Fine,' Botolf said and turned to Valgard. 'You're a lucky bastard,' he said.

A lifetime spent with Harald had taught Valgard when to shut up. He waited for the next sentence.

'You're alive, Grass Man – for now,' Botolf continued.

'Thank you,' Valgard said.

'Don't thank me. Thank whoever did this. There's obviously something here – and someone doesn't want us to find it. I look forward to pissing them off.'

The chieftain turned and walked back towards the longhouse. Valgard could have sworn there was a spring in his step.

Behind him, Ormslev had approached Thora. 'Do we tell the men?' he mumbled.

'No,' Thora said. 'They can do with a nice rest. I'll sort what needs sorting. It's been a long walk,' she added.

'That it has,' Bug-Eye said. He mumbled something else, but Valgard couldn't make it out and didn't care. The rim of light under the longhouse door was a lot more tempting.

If the north was indeed coming for him, he would prefer for it to do so when he was warm and dry.

Valgard woke up in the dark. The air was so heavy with the smell of warm, damp bodies that he might as well have come to in a barn full of wet dogs. His skin crawled. Moving carefully, he pushed off his thick woollen blanket.

The winter cold was still there, on the edges. He raised his head and looked around, allowing his eyes to adjust to the darkness. Soon the bodies of the men faded into shapes, a deeper black against the night inside the cold hall.

The ray of moonshine that slashed through the doorway as the longhouse door opened was a shimmering, pure slice of silver.

A shadow slipped through and in an instant the door was closed again, all without a sound.

Taking care to move slowly, Valgard eased his head down onto his bedroll. His heart thumped so loudly in his chest that he was sure he'd meet a blade any second. A sharp one, wielded without mercy.

The shadow form was burned into his eyes, backlit by the moon. Only one person in their party was that short and slim. Something about the way she moved . . .

With infinite care, Valgard pulled the blanket over his head and hoped Thora hadn't seen him looking.

'*Up! Get up!*'

The screams jolted Valgard awake.

The longhouse was all chaos and fear. Men were leaping to their feet, cursing, reaching for swords. Without thinking, Valgard rolled out of the way and under a table. His world was reduced to a line of stomping feet and rough, rasping voices shouting, 'They're outside!'

The walls shook as something bashed into them.

'Blades to the door!' Botolf ordered.

Thora's voice sliced through the noise. 'Stand firm, you fuckers! Don't flap about like chickens! You'll end up sticking each other, and that's for personal time only!'

Laughter and cheers.

The walls shook again. There was a roar on the other side that sounded like several men – or one really big one. Thora roared back and the men soon joined in, banging their swords on tables, shields and anything else they could find.

Whatever was outside didn't appear to like the sound of that. When the noise died down, there was nothing to be heard.

'Hjalmar, Skapti, Einar, to me,' Botolf growled from the doorway. 'Bring five bastards each. Thora!' Orders were shouted. Someone called for a torch, and flickering light heralded the smell of burning pitch. The door opened and large men filed out, armed and dangerous. Then it slammed shut.

The men inside the longhouse grew deathly quiet as they listened for the sounds of clashing blades.

There was nothing.

Valgard crawled out from underneath the table moments before the door flew open and Botolf stomped in. The men nearest to the door took two steps backwards.

'Nothing out there,' he growled. 'Nothing.' No one spoke. 'No tracks. Nothing.'

'Post eight men by the door,' Thora snapped. 'And another eight outside.' Some of the men groaned, but a dirty look silenced them. 'You fucking do as I say or I'll personally slit your throat while you sleep and save our northern friends the trouble, whoever they are. Get to it – the rest of you, back to sleep.' With that, she stalked in Botolf's wake to the dais, where they'd dropped their bedrolls.

The men started bickering among themselves about guard duties. The ever-present Ormslev appeared to be everywhere at once, poking and prodding the men into submission. One by one, surly warriors shuffled to the door.

Valgard pulled his coat on. His legs and back ached as he shuffled forward, willing himself not to think about what he was doing and hoping he'd called it right. 'I'll do a shift,' he said.

Bug-Eye turned and looked at him with poorly disguised contempt. 'Will you.'

'I'm ready and—' He didn't finish the sentence. Instead he ignored the screaming protest of his back and twisted to the left as hard as he could, shifting his body out of the way of Bug-Eye's meaty hand. The trek-master's eyes opened in surprise when Valgard wasn't where he thought he'd be. Instead, the skinny healer grabbed his wrist and pulled. Holding it in a vice-like grip, Valgard fell on Bug-Eye's elbow, bringing a forearm to the bigger man's face. Already off balance, Bug-Eye crashed to the floor. Valgard ended up lying on top of the trek-master, elbow on his throat. 'Ready and able. You have a problem with that?'

The fat, bald man coughed, spat and laughed, a coarse, braying sound. 'Fuckin' 'ell, d'ya see the fucker! Fast as a snake, this one!

D'ya see 'im?' he said, lying on his back. 'Fucking take all the shifts you fucking want.' He chortled. 'Do we need the others? Heh.' Bug-Eye laughed to himself as he clambered to his feet. 'I'm getting old. Fucker. Heh. See that?'

Their encounter over, Valgard limped away. In his head, a plan was forming, but he needed more information. When he glanced behind him, Bug-Eye was back to his usual commanding self.

'Inside or out?' A square-jawed man with a short red beard – Skapti – somehow managed to bite even the shortest words in half. Around him, the men were looking at Valgard like they had never seen him before.

'Out,' Valgard said.

'Suit yourself,' Skapti said and opened the door.

Valgard wrapped his coat tighter. The cold night air smelled of blood, steel and promise.

The landscape outside was an odd blend of ghostly greys, pitch-black and the occasional silvery strand of moonlight on frozen snow. The longhouse faced the sea, and beyond the coast the world opened out into an endless line. Closer to home, shadows danced a silent dance beneath the white dunes.

Pretty hard to hide anyone in this, Valgard thought. It had stopped snowing soon after he stepped out, and soon after that his brilliant plan deflated. He would find no tracks to show Botolf. He had no idea where the attackers had come from. He did, however, now have wet and achy feet to go with his knotted back.

When he noticed Thora standing right behind him, he very nearly added a stopped heart to the list.

'Nice night,' she said.

After a couple of attempts to catch his breath, Valgard managed to squeak an agreement. He glanced over her shoulder as casually as he could, but for some reason he couldn't see any of the other guards.

'Listen,' she said, leaning in. 'I don't have much time. I know what you seek. And I can tell you where it is, but I can't come with you to get it.'

Valgard blinked. He stared at her, searched for the telltale twitch, but there was nothing. If it was a lie, it was the best he'd ever seen. She looked older, somehow. More settled.

'Oh, really? And what am I looking for?' he said.

'You seek the powers that Loki bestowed upon Skuld,' Thora said without preamble. 'You want to find the source of her magic, the runes that made her strong. I know where they are – I sailed with the crazy bitch.' She turned to him and looked him straight in the eye. Valgard found himself wishing that she had a knife to his throat instead. 'Do you think you're strong enough, Healer?'

'I – I . . .' he stammered.

To his surprise, Thora's face softened. 'You're stronger than you know,' she said. 'You're stronger than they know. And I think you always have been.'

Valgard stared at her. His head struggled to make sense of it, but his heart flew. She understood him. She said the words he'd never spoken. She saw who he was.

'I . . . am strong enough,' he said.

'I know,' she purred. Valgard swallowed and pushed distracting thoughts away. 'You need to get to the cave.' She pointed towards the hillside, towards the black spot on the white that suddenly looked so obvious. 'I won't go with you. My survival depends on Botolf believing that I'll never leave his side. You'll have to speak your own case and I will not be able to support you or recognise you. Do you understand?'

Valgard nodded. 'I do.' He took Thora's hands. 'Thank you.'

She looked at him then, her eyes filled with wisdom and mirth. 'No, Valgard. Thank *you*. Just remember who your friends are, hm? Now go inside. Your shift is up and they'll come looking.'

He turned to face the longhouse and struggled to sharpen his thoughts. Visions of power, strength and victory swirled in his head. He staggered towards the stripe of light around the door and soon man-shapes came into view. He raised a hard; they did likewise.

When he entered the longhouse, he blinked and shook his head. Somehow Thora had made it back before him and was now deep in conversation with Botolf. Valgard tried to comprehend how fast she'd need to be to have managed that, but his mind warped at the thought.

'—your spot?' He became aware of a presence close to him. A big, thick-necked man, one of Hakon's, was talking to him. 'Where's your spot?'

'Down by the channel, between the two huts,' Valgard muttered.

The man left, muttering some less than complimentary descriptions of southerners.

A clear thought popped into Valgard's head: rest. He'd need rest. He had a big day tomorrow.

It could hardly be called a dawn. The night just became slightly less determined, slightly less oppressive. A couple of rays of light with the best of intentions could be discerned over the mountains, creeping interminably slowly across the peaks and slicing through the bleak blackness of the ocean.

Valgard tried to rub the aches out of his legs. His calves felt like ancient roots and his thighs might as well have been bone. *No wonder the raiders are always furious*, he thought. *A couple more weeks of this and I'd be very happy to split someone's skull just because he looked at me wrong.* He shifted, pushed and stretched until he was finally standing up, then tried to roll his shoulders. The result was neither pretty nor pleasant, but he was up.

He limped outside and found Botolf sniffing the air, with Thora by his side. Valgard was relieved to see that she was playing her part perfectly. She looked mildly annoyed to see him. 'Wolves,' the chieftain said without looking at him, 'two of them. Last night. Big ones, too. We found tracks down there – by your post, actually. You keep your luck, Grass Man.'

Valgard looked towards his guard spot. The red was vivid in the pale half-light, the white bones even more so. There was not much left of the thick neck. Bile rose in his throat, but he clamped his mouth shut and forced it back down. 'I think we need to check the caves. If you send Bug-Eye, I'll go with him,' he blurted out.

'Hm? Fine,' Botolf said. 'The men need something to do. Take thirty. Skapti will follow,' he added. 'Thora?'

'Send the fucker up the hill if he wants. Couldn't give a shit,' she snarled, then went back to staring at the endless expanse of snow. 'Can't see a single flake out of place,' she muttered. 'As if they flew in.'

Botolf wandered off, apparently led by his nose.

This was the moment. 'I'll be back,' Valgard said to Thora.

She turned to look at him. 'What?'

'I'll come back,' he said.

She looked at him as if he'd lost his mind. 'Bring your entire fucking family of crippled goat-babies for all I care, you reedy, dick-faced pus-bubble.' With that, she turned and went back to hunting tracks.

Valgard couldn't help but smile. And here he'd been thinking *he* was good at games. This was a proper player right here.

'Crippled goat-babies.' He chuckled and shuffled off to find Bug-Eye.

The light was the colour of lamb's wool, grey and cloudy. Skapti's handpicked bunch stood in the yard, shuffling their feet and silently hating him. A handful of Hakon's men stood to the side. Valgard swallowed and motioned to Bug-Eye. It was time.

'Let's go.'

They woke swaddled in a blanket of thick, heavy cold that the morning sun did nothing to dispel. Goran stretched, grimaced and stretched again. Behind him, Arnar rose and went about his business with slow, steady movements, buckling on his sword-belt and feeding the horse some choice straw from his bag. Inga stirred on the ground.

Without taking his eyes off the shadowy forest behind them, Ulfar shook his head. 'Let her sleep,' he said. 'She'll need the rest.'

'She gets the time it takes me in the bush,' Goran said. 'If south is where we're heading, we need to get going.' With that, he disappeared behind the trees, loosening the string around his waist as he went. Ulfar was left with Arnar, who made no more effort than usual at idle chat.

Ulfar felt for his legs, expecting them to ache after yesterday's troubles. They didn't, and that made him feel vaguely ill. He healed five times as fast now, but it felt . . . wrong, somehow. Like he'd stolen something. And try as he might, he couldn't shake the feeling that someone was watching them from the shadows.

Goran walked back into view. 'Wake the girl,' he said.

Arnar bent down and gently touched her shoulder and Inga mumbled something, voice thick with sleep. When she opened her eyes, she looked utterly confused for a moment. She rose and looked at them dully, awaiting orders. Arnar handed her the horse's reins. She accepted without question.

A few heartbeats later, they were mounted and leading the horses down the path at a slow walk. The road turned out to be just beyond the hills, as Ulfar had said. Behind them the forest around Uppsala faded out of view with the rising sun.

At midday, they met two riders flanking a medium-sized wagon.

'Hail, travellers,' Ulfar shouted.

'Hail,' the portly man in the driver's seat replied. The men on either side of him were just like all the swords for hire Ulfar had ever seen: lean, silent and observant, exactly as interested as they were paid to be. Their master was bald, with a face that looked like his favourite thing was catching people in a lie. 'May the road protect you and shield you in the dark.'

'May the road favour you and yours,' Ulfar replied. The mercenaries sized them up and appeared to decide they posed no threat. 'What news?'

'Forkbeard is in the south, stirring up shit,' the merchant said, curling his lip. 'Utterly ruins my route, the motherless goat-buggerer.'

'Sorry to hear that,' Ulfar said. 'Heading to Uppsala?'

'Aye,' the merchant said.

'They're doing well these days,' Ulfar said. 'The young king looks like he could be one to bet on. What are you carrying?'

'A whole wagon full of none of your business,' the bigger guard said. His partner on the other side shifted in his saddle.

'Well,' Ulfar said, casting a glance at the wagon. 'From what I saw, none of your business – especially in sacks like that – sells for a fair amount in Uppsala. Or it did three days ago, at least. You'll do well.'

At that, the merchant's face softened a little bit. 'Kind words, traveller. Easy, boys.' The guards relaxed, but their hands stayed near the hilts of their weapons.

'Add some news and we're even. Where's Forkbeard having his fun?'

'Down south – far south, close to the west coast down Skane way.'

Ulfar raised a hand in thanks and nudged his horse onwards. Behind him, his three companions followed.

The soggy ground slurped as Arnar's horse approached Inga's. 'How are you feeling, girl?' Arnar rumbled. Thin tendrils of cold mist floated like patches of wool around the animals' legs. Up ahead, Goran picked their path through the marshes.

'I am well, I suppose,' Inga said. 'Getting the hang of riding.' She leaned forward and patted the mare's neck. 'Old Amber here will make sure I die from a sword rather than a broken neck.' The horse snorted.

'Sssh,' the big man said. 'Calm now. You will have a long and happy life. Long and happy. And I know, because I'm old. So shut it, you twig,' Arnar said, twinkling at Inga. 'She's treating you well enough?'

Inga straightened up in the saddle. 'We know each other now,' she said. 'Thank you. My thighs are sore, but that can't be helped.'

'No, it can't. We'll stop soon. Rest will do you good.'

She smiled at him then. 'You are a kind man, you know.'

'Piss,' Arnar said. 'I just can't stand soft, squishy womenfolk crying, is all.'

'Shut up, old bear,' Inga said affectionately. 'You love me like a dog loves his master, you do.'

'Oho! You're a sight more lively than last night, you are.' Arnar grinned through his bushy beard. 'I should—'

The sound of hoofs on hard ground added to their conversation. 'Thanks be for that,' he added. 'Hate the bogs.'

'Why?' Inga said.

'The smell,' Arnar said. 'It smells like desperation.'

'No,' Inga said. 'That's not it. Desperation smells like half a bed, and salt on the air, and a horizon that's never broken by the right sail.'

Arnar glanced at the girl. 'You're older than you look,' he said.

'And you're kinder than you think,' she replied.

They rode on.

The light was fading to their left. 'Company,' Goran said under his breath, as three horsemen approached them at a leisurely walk, the sun at their back. 'Hail, travellers!' the rider on the left shouted.

'Hail,' Ulfar shouted back. 'Heading?'

'East,' the man said, closing the distance. 'But happy to share a camp.'

Ulfar glanced at Goran, who glanced towards Inga and shook his head quickly. 'We're pushing on a little further, thank you,' he said. 'Best of fortune to you.'

'And you, travellers.' The three men were only twenty yards away now. Ulfar's senses screamed at him, and he found himself struggling to keep from drawing his sword. Goran's face betrayed similar tight-lipped restraint. The distance closed and then the men were past, without giving them a second glance. The leader just nodded casually and then they were gone.

A good while later, Arnar came up to them. 'Hmph,' he said.

'You're right,' Goran said. 'I'd be worried that I'd wake up with steel in my throat.'

Behind them, a smooth blackness was spreading across the sky.

'Find a place to camp,' Ulfar said. 'We'll have two men awake tonight.'

'It'll be fine,' Goran mumbled. 'They were just bony little buggers. Ill-kempt and ill-fed. Horses weren't much better. Probably on their way to Uppsala to seek work. They weren't interested in us. It'll be fine.'

The campfire had died down to a handful of smouldering embers. The night sky was clear and a waning moon shone softly in a darkened dome dusted with white specks.

Ulfar watched over his travelling companions. Arnar slept peacefully, snoring into his big beard. Inga lay curled up close to the warmth; she tossed and twitched. Her eyes flew open and a curse died on her lips. Twirling around, she searched for Ulfar. 'On my grave,' she said. 'I knew – I knew those men.'

'Really?' Ulfar tried his best to sound uninterested.

'I did. They . . . they were from Stenvik,' she whispered, looking out into the darkness. 'I – think I saw them with Valgard. Just before I left.'

'I see,' Ulfar said. A gust of wind caught the fire and blew a handful of sparks into the air. 'And you think—'

'I don't know,' Inga said. 'I hope I'm not right. I thought I should tell you about it.'

'Good decision,' Ulfar said. 'Now get some sleep, if you can. You'll be up and on guard in a while.'

She looked on the verge of saying something, but held her tongue and lay down on her side. The dim glow from the fire caressed her curves as she drifted off to sleep. Moments after the tension left her body, the darkness near Ulfar shifted and Goran appeared at his side. The old man wouldn't be too bad for blood-work, Ulfar mused.

'She's scared,' Goran said. 'Nothing out there – is there?'

'Saw some trees earlier on,' Ulfar said. 'Oh, and a bush. Looked scary. Hold on a minute . . .' Ulfar shaded his eyes with his hand. 'Hm. Can't see anything right now. Because there is no light,' Ulfar muttered under his breath. 'And because "out there" is a big place. Those three runts are out there. Definitely. But they're not the only ones, and there's not much we can do about it apart from staying awake and making sure we're not gutted in our sleep.'

'Hmph,' Goran said. 'Fine. I just didn't like the look of them, is all.'

'Well, if you'd have trusted your sense of whose looks you liked and didn't like, you wouldn't be in this mess in the first place,' Ulfar said, grinning.

Goran appeared to accept that and slunk off to his sitting place.

Ulfar threw a handful of wrist-thick branches on the fire and turned his back to the flames as they crept around the wood. It was going to be a long night.

They hit the camp just as the first stripe of sunlight emerged in the east.

Arnar's life was saved by a carved stick. He threw himself forward off his makeshift tree-stump seat and felt the wind sweep the back of his head as the steel passed him by. '*Up!*' he bellowed.

Ulfar and Goran rolled over and sprang to their feet to find three shadowy figures among them, swinging axes.

Inga got to her knees, then screamed as one of the figures hit her with a vicious kick in the back. Goran stepped into the breach and aimed a swipe at the man's ribs, forcing him backwards to create space for Ulfar and Arnar.

Arnar growled and swung at the bigger of the two black shadows remaining. The man just managed to block the blow, staggering backwards from the force of it. Arnar followed, pushing him away from Ulfar and Inga.

The last man swung his axe wildly. Shadows and moonlight made his face look like a snarling skull.

'Who sent you?' Ulfar snapped.

'You're coming with us,' the man said. His voice sounded hoarse, as if it was struggling with the words.

'We can talk,' Ulfar said, stepping back from the wild swings.

'He said no talk,' the man said, swinging at him. Ulfar blocked the swipe and felt his teeth jangling. They traded blows in the gloom, metal clanging against metal.

A movement in the dark, a burst of sparks.

Ulfar's opponent screamed in pain and whirled around, holding his head and looking for his new attacker. Ulfar ran him through, put his boot in the man's side, kicked him to the ground and yanked his sword free.

The moonlight caught on Inga's face, fingers splayed, a wrist-thick tree branch from the fire at her feet.

A crunching sound came from their left. 'Fucker,' Arnar grunted.

Moments later, Goran emerged from the shadows, bloodied and dazed but still standing.

Ulfar knelt by the fire and blew gently on any embers he could still see. Slowly, reluctantly, the flames rose again. Arnar disappeared, only to return shortly after with three suitable sticks.

'Here,' he grunted at Ulfar.

Goran sat silently and watched as Ulfar bound kindling around the tip of each branch and held them gently over the fire until they flared into life.

The dancing tongues threw odd, shifting spheres of light on the ground. Thickening blood pooled underneath Ulfar's attacker. A lump with a misshapen head lay where Arnar had been fighting.

'Where's your man, Goran?' Ulfar asked.

'Fell in the water,' Goran said. 'Sank like a stone.'

'Was he dead?'

'He's not coming up anytime soon.'

Ulfar rubbed his left eye with his free hand. 'Inga?' He gestured with his toe at the dead man.

Inga knelt down and studied the dead body. 'I know him,' she said. 'He was in Stenvik for the market when the raiders hit. Had a farm near Moster, I think. That one . . .' She looked at Arnar's fallen opponent. 'I'm . . .' Inga made to go over to the corpse, but Arnar reached out a hand to stop her.

'Hit 'im in the face,' he said, almost apologetically. 'Won't be much use.'

'One's enough,' Ulfar said. 'We'll get going, I think. Never know if they have some friends coming.'

The group of four broke camp without more words and were on their way with the rising sun.

The morning mist lingered, drawing a faint, grey veil over the ground. Goran grunted and cursed under his breath.

'That's the third time!' Ulfar said.

'Hmph,' Arnar said. 'Thought we'd cleared 'em.'

The grey-haired guard mumbled something and pulled on the reins of his horse. With great effort, the animal dragged itself out of the knee-deep bog.

'Not a step wrong yesterday, and now you're practically ready to swim south, Goran. What's up, old man?' Ulfar said.

Goran did not reply. Instead he mounted and rode on.

Inga looked at Ulfar, who shrugged. 'Leave him to it, I guess. Maybe this morning got to him.'

The old scout rode ahead, silent and slump-shouldered.

At midday, Ulfar sat down on a roadside rock. They were mostly clear of the bogs and mires, but grey clouds bunched and roiled overhead, promising rain and misery. The mist had still not quite left them. Arnar and Inga sat by themselves, engaged in conversation. The woman appeared to be the only one of them the big, bearded man had more than four words to spare on.

Goran was suddenly there beside him, unnervingly quiet. The old man looked more spirited now. There was a glint in his eye. 'So. South, is it? Tell me again what for?'

'We're going to find a friend of mine – Norse bastard, thick as half an ox and twice as strong. Scary, too. And then he and I are going to go and find another man and take off his head.'

'Up north, then?'

'Yes.'

'And you're sure that's the best way to do it?'

Ulfar looked at Goran and frowned. 'Why? Got any other ideas?'

There was something different about Goran this morning. He looked oddly sure of himself. 'As a matter of fact, I have. I've been thinking about this.'

'Oh, go on, then. I'm listening.'

'Have you considered that Jolawer Scot might not be the best man to lead the Svear?' Goran said.

'What? Why not?'

'He's young. He's green. He'll have to rely on men who are

old and cautious because they've learned to appreciate long life and soft furs. He'll have neither the drive nor the fearlessness of someone a bit older. Someone proven in battle. A born leader.'

'I don't know – he's untested, but he's his father's son. There'll be some steel to him yet.'

'Unless there's steel in him,' Goran said.

Ulfar remembered moments later that his lower jaw belonged above his chest. 'What . . . ?'

Goran turned to Ulfar. 'Think about it! You are a man of honour. You have seen battle, unlike that squeaky pip. You are a good man and true. You are just the right man to lead the Svear, proud and powerful, against that bastard King Olav! Turn around and take what you're owed!'

'Are you drunk? Alfgeir Bjorne would have my head off before I got close. And why should I? No one owes me anything.'

The mist curled around his rock, around his legs. Ulfar glanced down. Then he turned around.

Arnar and Inga were nowhere to be seen. The landscape looked wrong somehow, like someone's *idea* of a location more than an actual place.

He turned to Goran.

'What's happening? Who . . . who are you?'

Slowly, uncomfortably, Goran changed before his eyes. The man in the saddle was young, dark-haired and handsome. A sweep of black hair sat above a thin, sharp nose. Green eyes sparkled with mischief. When he smiled, Ulfar half-expected fangs.

'Me? It is not important. I am a friend.'

'I doubt it. Where's Goran?'

The stranger's smile was tinged with sadness that looked almost genuine. 'Poor Goran was not as young and fast as he thought he was. He killed the Norseman but he took a blade in the belly. We met last night and made a deal. Don't worry about him. I am here to give you a great opportunity to join me and reap rewards you couldn't dream of.'

Ulfar looked at the man. 'Last time I got fed horseshit like that, it was by an old scrawny fucker with one bad eye.'

The stranger's skin turned a dark shade of blue as he hissed and bared a row of big, sharp teeth. The next moment he was back to normal. 'A misunderstanding. Ulfar Thormodsson, you are destined for great things. Surely you've been told this?'

A smile spread over Ulfar's face. 'Yes. Yes I have.'

'And—'

'And if you want your belly opened up so you can see what you look like inside, do tell me again.'

The stranger looked him up and down. 'You don't presume to refuse my offer, do you? I can make you rich beyond your—' The breath stopped in his throat and he looked in astonishment at the hilt of Ulfar's sword as it inched closer to his breastbone.

'I just told you this would happen.' Ulfar said. 'I've had enough of being toyed with.'

The stranger looked up at Ulfar – and smiled back at him. A thin line of blood leaked out of the corner of his mouth. Another line formed around the wound in his chest, blossoming out all too quickly. 'We're not done, you and I,' he whispered. 'Not done at all.' The stranger's face . . . withered, like a field in winter. The hair faded and turned grey at the temples, then at the top.

And suddenly it was Goran staring at Ulfar in surprise. He tried to speak, but nothing happened. Only blood, pulsing faster and faster as his life faded away. The sword stuck obscenely out of the old guard's back, caked in blackening, thickening blood. Ulfar dropped the hilt of the blade as if it was on fire and whirled around.

Arnar stood beside Inga with his sword drawn. 'Step closer, boy, and I'll gut you twice over,' he growled. 'I don't know what's got into you but you're not coming near us.' He muttered something to Inga, who shook her head without looking at him.

Ulfar opened his mouth, but nothing came out. All he could think of was that voice.

Not done, you and I.

Behind him, Goran coughed, twice. The sickly, faintly metallic smell of blood drifted past.

Ulfar blinked – and Inga was there, right in front of him, thunder in her eyes.

The slap was fast and hard enough to make him taste blood.

'Remember who you are,' she said, looking him straight in the eye. 'And get your head right. When you can be trusted, come and find me.'

She turned and walked towards Arnar; she mounted her horse with ease.

Ulfar watched them ride away without a second glance. He heard Goran's body fall to the ground, but he didn't turn.

The mist faded. The clouds disappeared. A bird even sang to him from a nearby tree, but Ulfar didn't note it. Instead he methodically drew the sword from Goran's body, ignored the smell of the dead man and set to cleaning the blade with long strokes of a rough rag.

'It's important to clean your blade, Ulfar. If you just bang it back in the scabbard, the blood will make it stick, and then you're dead,' he muttered. He wondered whether Uncle Hrothgar had sat like this, on a stone, when he'd taught him about blades for the first time. Whether he'd looked down and seen the spark of heroism in a child's eye. Ulfar tried to remember how old his big uncle had been, and couldn't. That was another life, another world.

So what was this life, then?

He looked at the sword he was stroking. It was clean, and had been for a while.

Easing the blade into the scabbard and looking down at Goran's corpse, he said, 'I'm sorry, old man. If I find him again I'll get him properly.'

The horses had shied away from the blood, but they were old enough not to stray far. Ulfar sent a bundle of silent thanks to Alfgeir Bjorne as he saddled up and headed south. He looked over his shoulder at Goran's corpse and urged his mare into a run.

'Can you smell it?'

The horse didn't reply, but Ulfar didn't mind. Two days on the road and he was starting to think he was alone in the world. Now, however, there was something in the air: something fresh and cold to replace the smothering smell of dank pine and wet earth. He'd swapped horses once a day and kept up a good pace, but he still felt as if the forest would never end. Now the trees ahead were thinning out and there was something up ahead.

The world of wood he'd been living in dropped away from his eyes and he gripped the reins so hard that the horse whinnied in protest as his vision filled with blue. The path inclined down to the sandy banks of the water and the fresh breeze made him sit up straight in the saddle. Ulfar shivered.

It was the big lake. He'd heard of it, but never seen it before. A full morning's crossing by boat, it sliced the country near in half, if the stories were true.

But there was something else as well. His stomach detected it before his brain caught up.

Somewhere close, someone was cooking fish.

Under him, the horse tossed its head and snorted, bringing

Ulfar back to his senses. 'Easy,' he muttered to the mare, 'easy. Let's . . . give you both a break.'

He dismounted and led the horses into the forest, far enough so he couldn't see the path any more. He tethered them to trees close enough to patches of brownish grass and they accepted their fate with resigned calm and set to eating what could be eaten.

Ulfar was stiff and sore, but the walk back towards the path and the lake limbered him up. The smell was stronger now, and in the distance he could see tendrils of smoke rising lazily.

A smart man would pick his way through the forest and observe from cover, he thought. A smart man would get a feel for whoever started that fire.

But there was a familiar tingling sensation somewhere in the back of his head, so disobeying all his instincts, Ulfar strode out onto the lake-front and started walking very slowly towards the source of the smell. Soon enough he saw shapes huddled around a line of smoke just past the curve of the coastline. He glanced inland and noticed the two scouts he would have run straight into if he'd gone sneaking and smiled to himself.

He inched closer, making sure his hands were visible at all times, but when he was within shouting range he wondered whether he needed to be so careful after all. The men huddled around the half-buried fire looked cold and weary. There were twelve of them. A particularly bony man sat by the fire, turning speared fish this way and that, flicking them onto the broken shields that appeared to be serving as plates.

'Greetings to the fire,' Ulfar shouted the moment he thought he could be heard.

A couple of heads turned, but no one rose to greet him.

Taking their silence as consent, Ulfar sidled closer. The smell of the roasting fish was almost too much to bear.

He was within spear-throwing distance when he saw the injuries.

Every man had them: heads wrapped in dirty, blood-caked cloth, broken forearms crudely splinted, a leg hacked off at the knee. The gaunt cook looked up at him. He flashed a quick signal to the scouts behind Ulfar's back. The reply must have set his mind at ease. 'Make way, fuckers,' he growled at his fellow men. 'Guest rights.' To Ulfar, he said, 'Welcome, traveller, to my court. I am Lord Alfrith. We're a bit short on the furniture at the moment, but we've got fish.'

'I haven't found a bench that tastes better than a well-roasted trout,' Ulfar replied. 'I am honoured, Lord Alfrith.' That raised a few smirks. The gaunt man nodded and gestured to a space that had appeared between two hunched and hairy fighters.

'Where are you coming from, then?' Alfrith said as he deftly speared another fish to go on the fire.

'Uppsala,' Ulfar said. On his left, someone hawked and spat into the fire, making a loud hiss.

'Oh? And what did King Cushion say?' Alfrith snarled. 'Is he going to meet Forkbeard the day after he learns to wipe his own arse?'

'He's scared to,' a man with a badly scarred face chimed in. 'He might hurt himself. Wiping your own arse is plenty dangerous.'

'You'd know, Uthgar!' Alfrith said.

'Besides, Alfgeir's teats give mead these days, so he's fine where he is,' another with a broken arm added. There was laughter around the fire, but it wasn't the happy kind.

Ulfar chose his words with care. 'Jolawer is young,' he said, 'and like with the wenches, you don't necessarily want to let a young man at the fighting. He'd be over and done in three strokes.' There was no laughter, but he saw the twinkle of amusement here and there. 'No, just like the fucking, you want to leave the fighting to real men.' Some of the wounded fighters were nodding now. 'I think Alfgeir Bjorne will protect the boy, but I don't believe he'll hold him back when the time comes. And when it does, they'll know that Forkbeard was held by Lord Alfrith and his men when they needed it the most. I knew King Erik, and he did not beget a fool.' He had their undivided attention now. All he needed was to time it right. 'The old goat could have fucking done it ten years earlier, though.'

The laughter that ripped around the fire was genuine now, a release of anger and pressure. Not for the first time, Ulfar thought of old Sven. *Make them like you*, he'd said. Not bad advice, that.

'And we do not need to establish the fact that Forkbeard was born from a thorny fart and a bad idea. So what is Old Shithead up to?' Ulfar continued.

'He's raiding the plains, mostly,' Splint-arm said. 'But he's being quite clever about it.'

'He's split his men up into groups of fifteen to twenty and has them spread out over the largest area possible,' Uthgar added. 'They strike, burn farms, kill, rape and run away. No battlefields, no big fights.'

'All we do is run after war bands,' Alfrith said. 'And all of my men are worried that their homes are being hit next.'

'We've nailed a couple of them, though,' Splint-arm said. There were nods and smiles of grim satisfaction around the fire. 'Nailed a couple of them right proper. And we would have got the last group, too. Except for that one fucker,' he added. 'I told you he was bad news.'

'Oh, don't you fucking start,' Half-face snapped. 'All week: *told you, told you, told you*. Well, you tell me about him again and I'll set fire to your arm.'

'Oh yeah? And I'll bang it on your good side,' Splint-arm shot back. 'And you'll thank me for it.'

Half-face made to stand up.

'Shut up, both of you!' Alfrith snapped. He swung the stick with the half-cooked fishes at them, pointing at each in turn. 'There's nothing you can do when you're up against one of those.'

Ulfar's chest felt like it was sinking into itself. He had to sit on his hands and bite his lip.

'Fucking fucker,' Half-face muttered. He looked across the fire at Splint-arm and mumbled something. The other warrior nodded back. Argument settled.

'I've never seen anything like it,' a man with a stump-leg said. 'I mean, who fights with hammers?'

Alfrith turned to Ulfar. 'Forgive me, traveller.' He grabbed a piece of shield and slapped a portion of silvery fish onto it. The blackened skin cracked open, revealing the steaming pink flesh. 'Here you go.' Ulfar nodded, still biting his tongue. 'Will you camp with us?'

'I am afraid not,' Ulfar said, fighting hard not to show his excitement. 'I think I'll need to be on my way very soon.'

SOUTHWEST COAST OF SWEDEN
LATE NOVEMBER, AD 996

It was less of a beach and more of a strip of sand spotted with yellowing tufts of dried grass. At Audun's back, the sea was a dense blue-grey, and thickening clouds signalled a storm.

'Hate ships,' Thormund muttered. 'Fuckin' hate 'em. Ain't right. I've got legs for walking, not fucking gills for swimming.'

'That's why the smart ones thought to make boats,' Mouthpiece mumbled. His jaw was still a mess, but he could speak more every day, much to everyone's misery.

'You go, then,' Thormund snapped. 'You go and roll around out there, pissing over the side, spewing every day, for some stinking fish guts. I'll stay on land, fuck your wife and steal your horse.'

'Make sure you get that the right way round, old man,' Ustain chimed in from up front, and the men chuckled. 'Although, saying that, it would explain some of the kids I saw up north.'

More laughter.

Sweyn Forkbeard's waifs and strays were massing on the beach. Ustain looked back at them and raised his voice. 'Right, you sorry lot!' he said. 'We're going east, then north. The king has a plan, and we're perfectly placed to make it happen.'

As Ustain continued to shout over the men's heads, Audun

saw Mouthpiece check furtively before sidling back towards him. Someone had learned a lesson or two, then.

'Wanna watch your back, big man,' he mumbled. 'Some of them new boys have been staring at us since we got aboard.'

'Well, your face is kind of funny,' Audun said.

'They haven't been looking at me,' Mouthpiece said.

Audun glanced around, but the men all looked the same. Still, he couldn't quite dismiss Mouthpiece's words. On the trip across the channel he'd felt . . . *uneasy*. 'Thank you,' he said.

Mouthpiece shrugged and drifted away again.

'. . . so find yourself some running mates and go and break things!' Ustain finished, to cheers from the men.

The soldiers wasted no time splitting into two groups. Audun was left with Mouthpiece, Thormund, Boy and a handful of the more feeble men from the camp. About sixty yards away, the crew from the old boat stood silently, looking at them.

'Come on, then,' Thormund shouted to them. 'You're with us.'

One by one the crewmen moved towards Audun's group, but none of them spoke up. Mouthpiece muttered something about 'wrong' and 'suspicious', but no one was listening to him.

'What's the matter? Cod got your tongue?' Thormund said.

The sailors exchanged looks. There were nine of them, ranging from a thick-necked bear of a man to two small, weasel-faced boys who could not be a day older than fourteen. In the middle was the man Audun thought looked familiar.

'Olgeir,' said the man in the middle, followed by a murmur of other names.

'Where are you from, Olgeir?' Thormund said.

'Around,' Olgeir answered.

'Hm. You sound like a Swede. Been sailing much?'

'Yes – left Sweden a long time ago.'

'Fine,' Thormund said. 'You want to lead?'

Olgeir shook his head.

'Great.' The old man pointed to Mouthpiece. 'That one can't talk but does when he shouldn't.' He glanced at Audun. 'And that one should but won't, though he can. I guess I'm in charge,' he concluded, scanning the group with hopeful eyes.

When no one protested, he rolled his eyes and spat. 'Off we go, then,' he muttered. 'East, then north.'

The sailors turned and started making their way up the bank. On either side the other war bands had already started doing the same.

'Tell you again – watch your back,' Mouthpiece mumbled under his breath as he passed Audun. 'I don't know why, but it looks like some of them boys don't care for you at all.'

Audun watched the sailors moving up ahead.

'I'm used to it,' he said as he started walking.

The sour smoke of wet, burning thatch rolled over Audun, stuck to his clothes and bound with his sweat. Screams rang out as Olgeir's men rounded up the last of the workers behind the farm.

Thormund stood in front of the barn, barring the weasel-faced boys' way. The smaller of them had his hands full trying to hold on to a skinny young girl in a soiled dress. Tears streamed down her face as she kicked and squirmed in his grasp.

Audun was vaguely aware that his knuckles hurt.

Thormund's voice came to him like in a dream. 'No, you little shits: because she has a father and a brother, and if you take her now they will not stop until they find you.'

'Come on, old man! We'll let you watch and everything,' the bigger boy said. He was of a height with Thormund.

'No,' Thormund said.

The smaller boy inched up alongside what had to be his brother, still clinging on to the girl. 'If you don't step away right now, you scratchy fart, we'll let the little bitch go and make sure you have an accident instead.'

Thormund gestured to Audun. 'Want to go up against him?'

The boys turned and stared. Audun suddenly felt numb and tired. The people in front of him didn't look real.

He shrugged and walked away from the surprise in Thormund's eyes. The boys howled in triumph and the bigger one pushed the old horse thief to the side.

The girl's shrieks died down soon enough.

Later, when they were on their way again, Thormund caught up with him. 'I don't need you to save anybody,' he hissed, 'but where I come from you do as your chieftain asks you.'

The buzz from the blood-rage, the fist-fights and the four men he'd knocked down had turned into a dull, throbbing ache. It had been an effort to control it, but he'd managed. Now he just wanted to lie down.

He looked at Thormund. 'It doesn't matter,' he said. 'It won't change them, won't change her.' He saw, or thought he saw, disgust in the old man's face, but he didn't care. 'Fate is fate,' he said.

'Well, I hope I don't need your help when I meet mine,' Thormund said.

Audun thought of the wall, of the blonde woman. 'Most of us do, sooner or later.'

The old horse thief saw the look on his face and inched away from him, carefully. 'Just saying, it's a shame about the girl.'

Audun turned and looked ahead, at the gritty road, at the

setting sun, at the back of the man in front of him. 'It always is,' he said quietly.

After a while, Audun struggled to tell the days apart. They blended, one into the other, like blood into water.

The farms were big, or they were small. The farmhands could fight, or they couldn't. Sometimes they met men who'd seen battle before, steady hands holding rusted swords that had rested for too long in an oilcloth somewhere.

They died like the rest.

He could remember one thing, though: the weasel-faced brothers had suffered a bit of bad luck. They'd dragged a girl behind a bush, but she had a knife on her and managed to stab them both. Mouthpiece wanted to ask how they'd both been stabbed in the back, but Audun stopped him.

Thormund had been in a good mood since.

The warband, now down to eighteen men, had sought refuge in the dense oak forest and now trudged along the path leading through the trees. Up ahead, voices rang out.

'. . . just fucking climb, you lard-arse,' Thormund snapped.

'I'll step to the side, if you don't mind,' came Olgeir's terse reply.

'Suit yourself,' Thormund said.

'What's going on?' Mouthpiece mumbled.

'Trees across the path,' someone said. 'Four of them. Weird that they've all fallen in the same—'

The forest came alive with war cries and up front, two men leapt out from the cover of the fallen trees, thrusting spears. Thormund disappeared from view. Metal clanged to their left where Olgeir had stepped into the thicket.

Audun whirled on Boy. 'Play dead, face down. Now,' he snapped, and Boy fell as if he'd been smacked on the head. He lay on the ground, head buried in his arms.

The moment after the first attacker had burst out from the thicket by the roadside, Audun reached for his hammers and let go of the world.

Somewhere on the edge of his senses, he felt the retreat. There was a difference in the fighters, the shift from killing rage to fighting for your life.

The hammers rose and fell; bones broke, blood gushed. The stench of voided bowels was all around him, but Audun didn't mind. He liked the feeling of life as he dealt death, the heightened senses, the pulse of the blood coursing through his veins.

Most of all he liked the control. With every fight he felt more in charge of the fire that coursed through his body: he was stronger, quicker, more powerful. He could hit harder and take more punishment than ever before.

He didn't notice the wound until much later, when the others had all been seen to. Boy came up to him, concern written on his pale face, and pointed at Audun's left leg. Puzzled, Audun looked down. A gash the width of his thumb gaped back at him, crusted over with blood, dirt and ripped cloth.

'Well, shit,' he said.

A pinpoint of pain spread and bloomed from the wound, coursing up and down. His thigh muscle cramped and he reeled from the blood loss. His knee buckled, and a fresh wave of pain shot through his leg as he pushed off it to steady himself.

'Easy there, big man,' Olgeir said. The soldier was covered in blood and gore from head to toe, but appeared unharmed. 'You come over here and get that looked at.'

Something about Olgeir's voice . . . but the pain in his leg was too bad. Audun limped along to where Mouthpiece was making himself useful patching people up. Three of the soldiers from the camp were dead, as were seven of the attackers.

'They were waiting for us,' Olgeir muttered.

'Fuckin' rat bastard Swedes,' someone shouted from the path, and Thormund's bony hand emerged from underneath a tree, shortly followed by his head. A big, blood-caked lump was prominent in the forest of stray white hairs. 'Pulled me down and knocked me on the head. Couldn't even finish the job. Farmers,' he grumbled as he clambered upright. 'We got ambushed by fucking farmers.'

'And if it hadn't been for my men they'd have farmed your bony arse,' Olgeir shouted back. 'Now keep your voice down, old man.'

'That's what your mother said,' Thormund shot back, shambling towards Mouthpiece.

Olgeir smirked. 'I think you mean my grandmother. And if it was her, your dick will have been snapped clean off.'

'Speak from experience, do you?' Thormund said.

Wounds and war were forgotten for the moment as the back-and-forth drew a couple of chuckles from the men.

'Mouthpiece! Fresh rags for my grandfather here. It's the least I can do for him after I fucked his wife!'

Thormund's grin was visible through the winces of pain. 'Fun for the whole family,' he said.

'Well, we are in Svealand,' Olgeir said to cheers from the men. 'That's how they do it in the countryside. Go and get yourself patched up. We'll see if we can fix the big man, too.'

'What's with him?' Thormund said.

Olgeir answered, but Audun couldn't make out the words. The colours drained out of the world around him, and he passed out.

*

Audun blinked. His leg stung and itched, but he was too weak to scratch it.

'. . . can't have him limping after us,' a voice whispered, five or six yards away.

'If it weren't for him we'd all be dead,' another voice replied. Older. Thormund.

'How would you know? Thought you were knocked out?' the first man said. Odd accent. Olgeir.

'Been listening to the men,' Thormund shot back.

'Fine. But he's not coming with us. He can barely move.'

Audun propped himself up on an elbow.

'Audun,' Thormund said. 'How's the leg?'

'Hurts,' Audun said.

'Can you walk?' Olgeir said.

'Don't know,' Audun said. He gritted his teeth, bent his leg, put weight on it – and hissed as the pain sparked.

Olgeir looked at Thormund and raised an eyebrow. 'We'll have to hide him until he heals and come back for him. They'll chase us, not him.'

Thormund scowled. 'Fine. Audun, we'll—'

'I know,' Audun said.

Boy emerged out of the half-light and stood by him as he lay there. He stamped and pointed at the injured man.

Olgeir turned to Thormund. 'There you go, then. The kid stays with him.'

'The hell he does,' Audun said.

'You don't have a say,' Thormund said. 'You can't stand and you won't be on your feet for any number of days. You're going to need someone to bring you water, find you something to chew – maybe even distract search parties if needed.'

Boy nodded enthusiastically.

Audun scowled and spat. 'Fucking stupid,' he muttered, but the decision had been made. Olgeir walked into the shadows to find his men. Thormund went over to where Mouthpiece sat, and Audun could hear them muttering about supplies, bandages and other practical things.

Boy sat down beside him, looked at the leg wound and raised his eyebrows.

'Yeah, I know it's not good,' Audun said. 'I fucking know.' Boy shrugged, rubbed his cheeks with the knuckles of both hands and pulled an exaggerated sad face.

Audun stared, incredulous, for a couple of moments. Then, despite the pain, the wet and the cold, he laughed. It was a sharp, rough sound. 'You're right,' he said. 'I shouldn't cry about it. I'm still alive.'

As the stars twinkled overhead, Boy smiled at him.

Morning crept over them, dull and grey. They'd made their way off the road and found a glade with some shelter. Thormund had forbidden fires and they'd posted a double watch, but the ambushers had not returned. The fire was lit the moment dawn gave them sight. Soon enough the smell of burning meat made Audun's stomach rumble.

'Have at it, big man,' Thormund said, passing him a chunk, and Audun wolfed it down, savouring the sharp tang of blood. 'We'll be away soon as the men get a bite each, and then you two are on your own.'

Audun grunted. Boy just sat there, silent and watchful.

Mouthpiece sidled up to them. 'I thought being a King's Man would be more . . . honourable,' he mumbled. 'No leaving our friends behind.'

'They have to,' Audun said. 'I'm no good off my feet.'

'Better than me on mine,' Mouthpiece said.

'Off,' Olgeir snapped, and the men all around them made ready to go, even though they were still tearing at half-cooked meat with bloodstained mouths. They checked weapons, adjusted what armour they had and shook out the night's aches.

'That's it,' Mouthpiece said. 'See you in a couple of days.' He stood up and moved over to Thormund.

Before the sun was even properly up, the men were gone. The forest was suddenly very quiet, save the odd bird singing in a tree. Boy busied himself with a small knife he'd taken off a dead man. As he started whittling at a stick Audun leaned back and allowed time to pass. Already the pain in his calf was throbbing less and the wound felt like it was starting to heal.

He closed his eyes. 'I'm going to sleep. Watch for bears and wolves,' he muttered. He felt Boy's gaze on him as he faded into dark dreams of cold iron, high walls and roaring fires.

The headache woke him some time later. The sun wasn't quite at its high point, but the birds were prattling up above. Audun shifted so that his back was against a thick tree and sat up, grimacing with pain. There was no sign of Boy anywhere. He groaned and felt for his calf. The wound was still sore, but the skin had almost healed over. He bent his knee and tried to put weight on the leg, but the pain was still too much.

A rustle in the leaves on the other side of the glade made him twitch and reach blindly for his hammers, but when they weren't where his hands landed, he looked around quickly, his heart beating faster.

He saw the pack with the hammers and his belongings just as the dark shape behind the leaves moved at the far end of the glade. There was no chance he'd get to them in time.

Boy stepped out into the clearing, holding a big mug carefully. Big-eyed, he gestured to the mug.

Audun grinned. 'Thank you.' The words had only just escaped his mouth when Boy tripped on a root, sending a big gulp of water flying. The terror on his face forced a loud, barking laugh out of Audun, and the angry scowl set off another burst of laughing. 'You are good company, Boy,' he said once he'd recovered.

Boy looked genuinely upset as he handed him the mug, and Audun said, 'Calm down. It's just water. Thank you. Did you have to go far to fetch it?' Boy didn't appear to understand the question and Audun repeated it, looking intently at his face.

Boy seemed to snap out of some kind of trance-state, shook his head and looked towards the pack. Moving quickly, he walked over to busy himself with what meagre supplies they had.

'Suit yourself,' Audun muttered and lifted the mug to his lips. Man, but he was thirsty. The water was cool and refreshing. He downed the remaining contents of the mug in one and burped loudly.

'Thank you again!' he said to Boy, but the kid didn't seem to hear. A brief spark of annoyance lit. 'I said "thank you",' Audun repeated. 'And I'm sorry I laughed at you.'

Boy turned then. 'That's okay,' he said in a bright, clear voice.

Audun felt like he'd been slapped. 'You can – talk?'

'Of course I can,' Boy said.

Suddenly Audun felt very cold. The lad's accent was unmistake-able. 'You're from—'

'Stenvik. Yes.'

Audun pushed his back against the tree and tried to use his good leg to gain height, but it was hopeless. He felt weak – weak and ill. He slumped back down. 'What have you done?'

'You're ill. You need medicine.'

'You little shit! You've poisoned me?'

Boy looked less sure of himself now. He'd taken the pack and retreated across the glade. The words tumbled out: 'No, it's not poison – the master said you were ill, that you were war-crazy and I should give you the medicine and you'd be all right once he got to see you.'

'Who?' His words slurred and he felt a growing chest pain, like he was sinking down into the black winter sea. Boy spoke, but Audun could no longer make out the words. Everything was blurry, and the ground suddenly looked warm and inviting. He tried to imagine the forge, but he couldn't see it clearly.

'Who?' he managed again.

He could only just make out Boy inching closer, looking at him like a hunter studying a dying wolf. Audun could feel his heart slowing down now as the fire within him was snuffed out. 'Who said that?' he muttered.

The last word he heard before he died was, 'Valgard.'

His nerves were on fire and his spine felt like it had been raked by a steel claw. Audun's eyes opened again, and the black, hard core behind his breastbone was a clump of ice. He drew breath again, a man twice drowned. Hot and cold shivers shook his body and cold sweat poured out of him.

When his vision returned, the first thing he saw was Boy, staring at him in horror. 'You . . . died,' he stammered.

'Fuck your medicine,' Audun snarled. He pushed off the tree again and got his one good leg under him. He was almost up when he felt his veins constricting, tightening, pulling his arms in, crushing his body into itself. 'And fuck your master,' he hissed between clenched teeth.

The world spun, twirled and twisted and he crashed to the ground, gasping for a breath that never came.

When he came to again, the thin strip of light he could see suggested morning had arrived. His body felt like it had been smashed with a hammer. Everything hurt, from his hair to his toenails. Audun closed his eyes, willing the pain to go away.

It didn't.

A wracking cough shook him and the sour taste of bile followed as he threw up the contents of his stomach.

'He's not so terrifying now, is he?'

Someone at his back.

'Tie him up, sling him on a horse and home we go,' another said. Familiar voice. Olgeir again.

Audun twisted around.

There were five of them: Olgeir, the big man off the boat, and three wiry sailors.

'Good morning,' Olgeir said. 'How are you feeling?' Audun bit back his first response – he didn't even glare. Instead, he smiled.

In his mind, he could see the forge. 'Me?' he asked. 'Why don't you ask your boy instead?' He flooded his body with fire, pushing the hurt away, and propped himself up onto his elbow. 'Why don't you ask your boy,' he continued, 'how well he kept his balance when he brought me the mug?' Audun pushed with his arms until he was sitting up. His body throbbed with pain, but he ignored it.

'Why don't you ask,' he said, taking care to move slowly, as if he were in full control of his movements, 'whether he managed to give me the full dose of whatever it was?' Audun pulled himself up to his full height and cricked his neck.

Behind the five men, Boy's face went ashen, and he slunk off into the forest, his pack in hand.

The sailors exchanged looks.

'If you want to turn around and fuck right off, we can forget about this,' Audun said. 'If not – well, we've fought together for a week and a bit now. You've seen what I can do.'

Olgeir swallowed. 'You're bluffing,' he said with a sneer.

'Am I? Come on, then,' Audun said.

No one moved.

'Bjorn,' Olgeir said. The big man looked at him, then at Audun. 'He's weak. Go on.'

The bearded man stood a head taller than Audun. He grinned. His mouth was a gaping wound of broken and rotten stumps. His callused hands formed into rock-like fists. 'Want me to smash him around?'

'Whatever you like,' Olgeir said.

Audun furtively tested his wounded leg. It supported his weight, but only just.

Bjorn squared up against him and advanced, his massive fists raised.

Audun took two steps forward and felt a wave of nausea wash over him as the poisoned water sloshed around in his gut.

'This is not right!' a familiar voice shouted. 'Shame on you, Audun Arngrimsson!' The sailors turned around as a tall man entered the glade midway between them and Audun. His face was drawn and his long, black hair hung in limp, wet strands, but he moved with ease. He wielded two blacksmith's hammers; a pack was slung off his left shoulder. He moved like a man strolling into a friend's house as he grinned and nodded at Olgeir and the three sailors.

'How so?' Audun said, a grin spreading across his own face.

'There's one of you,' the man said, throwing first one, then the other hammer towards Audun. 'But only five of them.'

The spell was broken the moment Audun plucked the hammers out of the air.

'Go! For fuck's sake, *go*!' Olgeir screamed and Bjorn launched himself towards Audun – and screamed in pain as his right fist smashed straight into a hammer. His left hand did connect, however, sending Audun spinning away.

Three long steps sent Ulfar into the middle of the glade, past the sailors, and the long, thin blade at his hip hissed as it left the scabbard; a single whip-like stroke and it was in front of him, pointing at the sailor in the middle.

To his left, the sailor's companion collapsed with a wet gurgle as his brain and his breathing caught up with his severed wind-pipe and a stream of jugular blood welled up from the man's open throat.

The smell of blood kicked the two remaining sailors into action and they moved together to advance on Ulfar, sturdy swords drawn.

'Aren't you boys annoyed that you forgot your shields?' Ulfar said conversationally. A lightning-quick swipe forced one of the sailors into a very clumsy backwards hop even as Ulfar twisted back and down to avoid a flying fist-sized rock.

Olgeir glared at him, then turned towards Bjorn, who was staring straight ahead in mute horror, his bloodied right hand forgotten.

The giant looked at his left hand, then at Audun. 'You can't do that!' he rumbled.

But Audun was standing up.

More than that, he was smiling, even as his jaw swelled grotesquely and blood dripped from his lips and gums. It did nothing to make him more attractive.

'Told you,' Ulfar shouted. 'He gets really annoyed when you hit him.'

Sparks flew as Audun bashed his hammers together and advanced on Bjorn. Olgeir's next missile smashed into his hip with an audible crack, but it didn't even slow him down.

The hammers sang and Bjorn's head was a mess of blood and bone. Without missing a beat, Audun shouldered his body out of the way and turned towards Olgeir.

'Tell me who sent you and I'll make him stop,' Ulfar shouted.

Olgeir's eyes were wide open and his mouth worked to catch up with his brain as he shuffled backwards. 'Valgard! It was Valgard! He said to bring the big guy in!'

'To where?' Ulfar shouted.

'North! North! He went north with King Olav! To Trondheim!' Olgeir screamed, but too late: he had backed into a tree and his tunic caught on a branch as Audun bore down on him.

The raw terror in their leader's voice was contagious. The two remaining sailors turned and ran away as fast as they could.

Ulfar didn't need to look to know Olgeir was dead. The crunching sounds told the tale.

Audun spun and faced Ulfar. Globs of blood dripped off him, off his jaw and his chin, off his shoulders and his chest, off the edges of his hammers. Behind him, an unsightly mass of red that had once been Olgeir slumped to the ground.

Ulfar froze.

The blond Norseman blinked, grimaced and shook his head, sending droplets flying. 'Took you long enough,' he muttered. Then his eyes rolled up into his head, his knees buckled and the big blacksmith passed out.

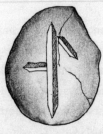

The mouth of the cave was much bigger than Valgard had thought it would be. A gust of cold wind blew a dusting of fine powder across the shadows.

Behind him, Bug-Eye hawked and spat. 'So, Chief – what now?'

Valgard bit back a sharp reply and took a deep breath before answering. 'Torches,' he said loudly. Behind him, Skapti's men started working on cloth and pitch.

He glared at the trek-master, who stared back with all the malice of a milking cow and said, 'Torches. Good idea.' Flaring flames hissed at the cold and the snowflakes in the air as tongues of shifting light reached into the darkness, only to be pushed back again.

'Come on, then,' Valgard said. 'At least we'll be out of the wind.' With little enthusiasm, his band of men inched forward.

The cave within ballooned out into a dome, three times the height of a man and about ten times as wide. Shadows grew and shrank as the men waved their torches around. The flickering light caught on some sort of markings – irregular blobs and strange stick-shapes. Once past the opening, the floor was surprisingly smooth.

'Eyes,' Skapti snapped and Valgard had to pull on all his reserves not to jump as the men, as one, drew their weapons.

'What?' he hissed.

Skapti reached out with his spear to a shadowy corner of the cave. Something dry rustled in the dark.

When he withdrew the spear, a human skull was hanging on it by the eye socket. The jaw was gone and the left side of the head was smashed in.

Gritting his teeth, Valgard turned and inched forward, deeper into the darkness.

At the far end, the cave narrowed and the ceiling lowered, turning the dome into a tunnel that sloped gently downwards. Now there was only space for five of them to walk abreast, so a line formed with Skapti and his men at the front, then Bug-Eye and Valgard a couple of steps behind them. The rustle of furs and the clink of weapons told Valgard how slowly the men were inching along.

The weight of the rock above their heads quenched the men's chatter, and soon they were shuffling further into the mountain in silence. A good bit later, the tunnel branched.

'Now what?' Skapti said. His voice was loud in the tomb-like silence.

'Send a handful of men along that branch,' Valgard said, pointing. 'Tell them to return with whatever they find. If it branches again, they are to turn back and wait for us here.'

The red-haired man issued a series of clipped commands and the seven men selected quickly disappeared down the tunnel, the light from their torches fading quickly. Within moments it was as if they'd never been there at all.

'Onwards,' Valgard said, trying hard to sound like he wasn't worried.

The silence crept in around them. It was in the stones, in the slope of the floor. They'd walked a while longer when they found the second branch. Skapti just glanced at him, then sent another handful of men down that one.

More walking, more silence. The six remaining men shuffled along, torches swinging to illuminate every shadowy corner, but the points of their blades were slowly dropping. No one stayed alert for long where there was no danger.

'So,' Bug-Eye said, 'what are we looking for?'

The roar washed over them, filling the space around them, bouncing off the cave walls and setting Valgard shaking with pure animal terror.

'*Blades!*' Skapti screamed as the shadows trembled into life and the bear burst out of the darkness, all bristling fur and bared fangs. He was easily the height of a man and more, and he filled most of the tunnel, leaving only a little space on the sides.

'*Move! Back!*' the front men screamed over each other, but the bear struck and the lead man in the middle folded, screaming as the claws opened him up and raked out his guts. The smell of sour blood in the tunnel only seemed to enrage the bear more.

Valgard froze. To his shame he found he'd wet himself.

When Bug-Eye finally moved, the fat man moved fast: a meaty arm shot across Valgard's chest, slammed into him and lifted him off his feet. The old warrior turned and strode back up the tunnel dragging the healer as the four men behind him spread out and retreated slowly, using their spears to stab at the bear to keep it at bay.

A piercing scream told them the four were down to three.

Panicked shouting drifted towards them as they approached the second junction. The erratic flickering flames came to meet them, but too fast – much too fast. Three of the second group came sprinting up the slope, wild-eyed and frothing, brandishing the torches as more screaming and wet slurping sounds chased them. They sprinted ahead along the tunnel and Bug-Eye followed, dragging Valgard.

The healer found his feet as the slope began to level.

Five men were standing in a circle, torches out. Bug-Eye and Valgard joined them, and moments later so did Skapti, unarmed and covered in blood.

Standing in front of the opening, its fur the bluish-white of frozen snow, was the biggest snowbear Valgard had ever seen. The beast swung its head from side to side, sniffing the air and baring its fangs.

'Torches,' Bug-Eye muttered. 'Not a bad idea.'

Rumbling growls heralded the arrival of the bears from the tunnel. Blood dripped from their jaws, and one of them had Skapti's sword buried in its shoulder.

The white bear at the entrance roared, and the others answered in turn. As the beast stepped into the cave, a gale swept with it and battered their feeble flames. Daylight seeped in around its figure, offering a tantalising glimpse of snow-covered freedom.

'Botolf!' Skapti shouted.

A tall man stood in the entrance, half in light and half in shadow. A dark cape billowed behind him and the faint outline of a satchel was slung over his shoulder.

'That's not . . .' Valgard's voice died in his throat.

The man walked into the cave. The bears growled at him, but none of them stepped near. 'I don't think so, *Father*,' he snarled. 'He's mine.' The steel appeared in his hands almost instantly. As one, the bears stood on their hind legs and growled together, as if warning the intruder. The noise in the cave was deafening.

With a sound like an indrawn breath the flames went out, plunging the cave into grey half-light. As one, the men screamed and pushed their backs together. A wave of animal stink surrounded them, born on a fey wind that circled the cave, carrying shadow and sand and the sound of steel slicing veins, carving flesh. Roars bounded from wall to wall.

Moments later, the only sounds in the cave were the hoarse voices of eight men screaming.

'Light,' Valgard croaked. 'Torches—'

Skapti fumbled with his fire-steel and got a torch flaring. The yellow light spread from the burning rags and illuminated drawn faces; each was as surprised as anyone at their continued existence.

Then they looked around.

The light reflected in growing pools of silky blackness. The bears lay where they'd been cut down, throats open and pulsing thick, dark blood. The stranger was wiping off his knife with a piece of cloth. His long, black hair glistened like raven's feathers in the torchlight and his eyes gleamed with malice.

'Out,' he said. 'And wait.'

Bug-Eye moved first, then Skapti and his men, then Valgard.

'Not you.' Valgard's brain had not yet caught up and as he took two more steps the man said without looking at him, 'I said, *not you*.'

His back seized up first, shortly followed by his legs and his shoulders. Pain like he'd never known exploded in his brain. The backs of his eyes hurt. His throat closed, and he tried and failed to gulp down air.

'You're staying.'

Whatever it was released its hold on him all at once and he became painfully aware of his piss-stained breeches.

'For a little while, at least.' A faint smile played on the stranger's lips. 'We're going to have some words, you and me.'

*

The men were all waiting for Valgard when he came out, but none of them dared look him in the eye. Didn't matter. He walked right past them, heading down to the longhouse.

He felt, more than heard, the men line up behind him.

The descent was much quicker than the early-morning climb up to the cave mouth. The little village looked peaceful, almost serene under the suddenly bright blue sky.

'It's quiet,' Skapti said.

'Mm,' Bug-Eye mumbled.

They saw the first bodies when they rounded the corner. The men had served Botolf and Hakon in real life. In death they were just meat in rags.

'Who's that?' Skapti said, poking his toe at a dead man on the ground. He tipped the corpse over and a weathered, leathery face with glassy eyes stared back at them.

'He wasn't with us,' Bug-Eye said. No one doubted the fat man.

'Blades,' Skapti said quietly.

The soldiers picked up what weapons they could find on the ground – spears, swords, a hand-axe – and scouted around for enemies. The trampled snow was stained with reddish-white crystals, but nothing moved. The village was as dead as when they'd first arrived.

Bug-Eye nudged Valgard and pointed silently. The door to the longhouse was slightly ajar.

Skapti signalled to two of his men and walked towards the door, blade up and pointed at the darkness within, prepared for whatever might come bursting out. His companions flanked him. The silence went on for ever as the red-haired warrior crouched by the door and listened. He shot Valgard and Bug-Eye a sharp look and nudged the door open.

Sweat, blood and fear leaked out of the room like pus from a wound. Valgard watched as those who entered first fought not to vomit.

The longhouse was full of bodies. Their marching compatriots had been slaughtered, some where they lay sleeping, others fighting. The floor was sticky with hardening blood and the smell of it was everywhere – in the air, in the walls, on their tongues.

A ray of light squeezed in through a rift in the airing flap and shone down on Egill Jotun's throne. A familiar figure lay slumped on the steps before the massive chair, clutching his belly.

Botolf.

Despite his dislike and fear, Valgard hurried towards the throne.

When he was a few feet away, he saw the chieftain's arm move as harsh wet coughs shook his body. Botolf's hand moved too slowly to catch the globs of blood he hawked up from his lungs. The pain scraped the glazed look off his eyes. As he recognised Valgard, he grinned. His teeth were coloured the sickly pink of blood mixed with saliva. He cradled something in his arms.

'. . . never saw it . . .' he wheezed.

'What?' Valgard asked.

'The bitch,' Botolf muttered, still smiling. 'She had me from day one. She just wanted to get up here to meet with them.' Skapti, Bug-Eye and the others hung back, not sure what to do with the idea of Botolf being injured.

'Who? Meet with *who*?'

'Big fucker. Two thick scars on his neck. Axe. Stay the fuck away,' Botolf said. He moved his arm and guts spilled out. Valgard could smell death on him; he could feel the heat seeping out of his stomach. The chieftain winced. 'Raiding party walked through us. Hardest bastards I've ever seen. Somehow . . . the kid . . . the kid from the path . . . was with them. She must have planned it.'

His eyes grew bigger and his face softened. 'Can you do anything? Am I gone? I don't want to meet the gods just yet.'

Valgard looked at the fearsome killer and smiled. 'You will meet the gods when the time is right.' Botolf tried to say something that drowned in a bubble of blood, but Valgard was already moving. He stepped up onto the dais, put his shoulder against the throne and pushed.

The block of wood shifted only slightly.

His thighs felt like they were on fire, but Valgard pushed harder, the wood creaked, and slowly the throne of Egill Jotun gave way and toppled over, revealing a hollow space underneath.

Within it was a knee-high chest.

His heart thundering, Valgard flipped open the lid of the chest.

A cylinder lay within, wrapped in calfskin.

He bent over and retrieved it, then unravelled the package with trembling fingers.

'What's that?' Skapti called from the middle of the longhouse, curious but unwilling to come closer.

Valgard didn't answer. His shaking fingers revealed strings of runes, charts, shapes. His trembling lips muttered words that had not been uttered for a long time.

Behind him, Botolf screamed. It was not a human scream.

When he finished the spell, he turned around to look at what he had created – and smiled.

Epilogue

The burning twigs crackled and snapped in the centre of a faint circle of light and heat. Cold mist drifted in over freezing ground and over the piles of leaves that had drifted against thick tree trunks. Above the treetops the vast black winter night stretched endlessly, dotted by white points, snowflakes that would never fall.

Audun sat on a rock, wrapped in an assortment of rags. 'Did you do that thing? Home?' he said.

'Yes,' Ulfar said. Leaning up against a big trunk, he was almost invisible in the shadows.

'How did it go?'

'I'm alive,' Ulfar said.

'So not too bad,' Audun said after a moment's pause.

'Not too bad,' Ulfar agreed.

Audun sat still for a while, looking into the fire. 'What now, then?' he said.

'Valgard killed Geiri. He's with King Olav's army. We're going up north to kill him.'

Another pause. 'Oh.' Then, after a while, 'Where, exactly? And how many men does he have? And how are we going to do it?'

Ulfar emerged from the shadows and came to sit down by the fire. 'No idea,' he said.

Audun noticed the shift in the darkness; Ulfar smelled the blood. They both jumped when the dead deer landed with a thud at the edge of the light.

A familiar voice spoke from the darkness. 'The bony bit on your arm's your elbow. The one you were sitting on is your arse.' The glade was suddenly alive with quiet, soft movement. Silent, hardened, grey-haired men emerged from the trees all around them. Five, ten, twenty, thirty. They made no move, drew no weapons.

Two men walked through the group. One of them held a big axe.

The other one grinned at Ulfar through a thick white beard and stuck a curved dagger in his belt. 'Sounds to me like you're going to need some help, son.'

THE END

Blood Will Follow

DRAMATIS PERSONAE

VALGARD'S STORY

Valgard	Deceptive herbalist.
Finn	Loyal lieutenant.
Hakon	Troublesome Trondheim tyrant.
King Olav	His Kingliness.
Jorn	Prince of the Dales, King Olav's right-hand man.
Runar	Jorn's stuttering helper.
Botolf	Tall, dark and deadly, Chieftain of the South.
Skeggi	Brawny bundle of sadism.
Sigurd	Chieftain of Stenvik, imprisoned.
Sven	Advisor to Sigurd, imprisoned.
Gunnar	Commander of Stenvik in Finn's absence.
Ormslev Bug-Eye	Botolf's stoic and lardy trek-master.
Kverulf	Botolf's man; not too sharp on judgement.
Skapti	Botolf's lieutenant.

AUDUN'S STORY

Audun	Cursed blacksmith berserker.
Fjölnir	Ageing farmer with one bad eye.

Breki	Caravan leader.
Bjorn	Breki's brother.
Ivar	Man in charge at the Sands.
Hrutur	Rugged sea captain.
Skakki	Useless blacksmith.
Johan Aagard	Bulky bothersome beau.
Helga of Ovregard	Handsome woman with a dark past.
Streak	Her horse.
Ustain	Forkbeard's recruiter.
Jomar	Forkbeard's man.
Thormund	Ageing horse thief, reluctant soldier.
Mouthpiece	Nervous, verbose, all-too-keen and would-be honourable soldier.
Boy	Mute boy.
Olgeir	Sea captain and commander of ten, suspiciously familiar accent.

Ulfar's story

Ulfar	Dashing hero, leading man and potentially cursed warrior.
Anneli	Just a small-town girl.
Torulf	Young gallant.
Jaki and Jarli	Torulf's brothers, older and less gallant.
Gestumblindi	Wandering mercenary recruiter with one bad eye.
Gisli	Turnip farmer, not overly wise.
Helgi	His idiot cousin.
Hedin	Greedy merchant and boat-owner.
Goran	Grizzled caravan guard.
Heidrek	Young, cheerful caravan guard.

Regin	Surly caravan guard.
Ingimar	Caravan owner and merchant.
Arnar	Burly man of huge beard and few words.
Prince Karle	White on the outside, black on the inside. Owes Ulfar for a broken arm. Cousin to King Jolawer.
Galti	His henchman.
Hrodgeir	Galti's servant.
Alfgeir Bjorne	King Jolawer's right-hand man, Geiri's father, Ulfar's uncle.
King Jolawer Scot	Son of Erik the Victorious, king before his time.
Greta	Former flame of Ulfar's; not happy to see him.
Ivar	Greta's brother; even less happy to see Ulfar.
Lord Alfrith	A chieftain in the field.
His Merry Men	Not merry at all.

Acknowledgements

As usual, this has not been a solitary enterprise. If it weren't for super-agent Geraldine Cooke, it wouldn't even be an 'enterprise'. This doubly counts for Editor, Publisher and all-round wonderwoman Jo Fletcher, who not only publishes my merry Vikings but also makes my writing look approximately 93% better (numbers = truth = science). My fledgling writer's soul would be crushed but for the tender ministrations of Nicola Budd, Tim Kershaw and Andrew Turner, key cogs in the lean, mean publishing machine that is Jo Fletcher Books.

I owe thanks to the good people of Southbank International School – first and foremost librarians extraordinaire Christine Joshi and Ian Herne, who have given me enough encouragement and research for a football team's worth of writers – but also every single student who has stopped me in the corridors, asked 'how the book is going', read the thing and complimented me on the horrifically inappropriate swearing. You know who you are. I sincerely hope that none of you are actually intending to read this one, because it's a fair bit worse.

To my dearest friends who read and even liked the first one – I am still stunned, frankly, by the reception. Thank you for putting up with me before, during and after. I would promise to make more sense and tell shorter stories in the future, but we all know that's not happening.

To Dagbjört at Nexus Books in Reykjavík for giving me my first-ever book launch – thank you. To kings of Viking Metal Skálmöld for the credits and the music.

To Nick Bain, who taught me to write. Technically, all of this is your fault.

To my Mother, Father and Brother – you are still the most terrifying readers I've ever met. Without you, this wolf would be a poodle.

And finally, most and always – to my wife, Morag. You are probably the most patient woman in the world, and I love you dearly.

Snorri Kristjansson
Hitchin, Hertfordshire
March 2014

PATH OF GODS
Snorri Kristjansson

Reunited, Audun and Ulfar have a new sense of purpose: to ensure that the North remains in the hands of those who hold with the old gods. To do this, they must defeat the people who seek to destroy all they have ever known with the new White Christ. But these are powerful enemies and if they have any chance of victory, they must find equally powerful allies.

In Trondheim, King Olav, self-appointed champion of the White Christ, finds that keeping the peace is a much harder test of his faith than winning the war. With his garrison halved and local chieftains at his table who wish him nothing but ill, the king must decide how and where to spread the word of his god.

And in the North, touched by the trickster god, something old, malevolent and very, very angry stirs . . .

Jo Fletcher
BOOKS

www.jofletcherbooks.co.uk

SWORDS OF GOOD MEN
Snorri Kristjansson

For Ulfar Thormodsson, the Viking town of Stenvik is the last stop on a two-year-long journey, before he goes home.

But for other, larger powers, Stenvik is about to become the meeting ground in a great war: one that will see a clash of the old gods versus the new White Christ. One that will see blood wash the land.

As Ulfar becomes ever-more involved in the politics of the town, and prepares to meet these armies in a battle for Stenvik's freedom, he is about to learn that not all his enemies stand outside the walls.

Jo Fletcher
BOOKS

www.jofletcherbooks.com